When I Should've Stayed

When I Should've Stayed

max
New York Times Bestselling Author
monroe

This book is a work of fiction. Names, characters, places, and incidents are the product of the author's imagination or are used fictitiously. Any resemblance to actual events, locales, or persons, living or dead, is coincidental.

Entangled Publishing, LLC
644 Shrewsbury Commons Ave., STE 181
Shrewsbury, PA 17361
rights@entangledpublishing.com

Amara is an imprint of Entangled Publishing, LLC.

Visit our website at www.entangledpublishing.com.

Edited by Silently Correcting Your Grammar
Cover design by LJ Anderson, Mayhem Cover Creations
Edge design by LJ Anderson, Mayhem Cover Creations
Stock art by Lucie Kasparova/GettyImages, Lera Danilova/GettyImages, Dezein/GettyImages, Nadezhda Kurbatova/GettyImages, and Marchiez/GettyImages
Interior design by Britt Marczak

Paperback ISBN 978-1-64937-904-7
Ebook ISBN 978-1-64937-926-9

Printed in China

First Edition April 2025

10 9 8 7 6 5 4 3 2 1

AMARA
an imprint of Entangled Publishing LLC

ALSO BY MAX MONROE

Meet Me at Midnight
The Girl in the Painting

Red Bridge series

What I Should've Said
When I Should've Stayed

Dickson University series

Learning Curve
Playing Games

Billionaire Bad Boy series

Tapping the Billionaire
Banking the Billionaire
Scoring the Billionaire

To the power of love.
To the dichotomy of beauty and pain.
To the hope that resides in new beginnings, and to finding the one person who puts your fears at ease.

And to the love story that sits between these pages.
You'll stay in our hearts forever.

Playlist

Sometimes Around Midnight by The Airborne Toxic Event
Silver Springs by Fleetwood Mac
Elastic Heart by Sia
Maneater by Daryl Hall & John Oates
Wuthering Heights by Kate Bush
She Wants Revenge by Tear You Apart
Lay, Lady, Lay by Bob Dylan
Make You Feel My Love by Bob Dylan
The Night We Met by Lord Huron
Formidable by Stromae
Someone Like You by Adele
Dedicated To The One I Love by The Mamas & the Papas
I Can Do It With A Broken Heart by Taylor Swift
Counting Stars by One Republic
Stick Season by Noah Kahan
Revival by Zach Bryan
So Far Away by Dire Straits
Fortnight by Taylor Swift
Don't Speak by No Doubt
Stay by Rihanna ft Mikky Ekko
Be My Baby by The Ronettes
Can't Take My Eyes Off You by Frankie Valli
Dog Days Are Over by Florence + The Machine
Baby I'm Yours by Cass Elliot
Clocks by Coldplay

Author’s Note

Dear Reader,

This is a love story that we felt so deeply, it has imprinted itself onto our bones.

Thank you for reading.

All our love,
Max & Monroe

Disclaimer: This story contains sensitive subjects such as child loss, death, and child neglect.

"In each loss there is a gain,
As in every gain there is a loss,
And with each ending comes a new beginning."
-Buddhist Proverb

The Moment I Should've Stayed: Part 1

Josie

Tuesday, December 20th

Fresh ink stains my fingers, and a sharp ache stabs my heart as I tuck the large envelope into my purse and swallow the very real and ragged pill of what I've done.

Of what I'm *about to do*.

I rush out of the library, heading straight for the streetside parking, and climb into my car as quickly as possible in the hopes that no one will see me. Gossip runs like an Olympic sprinter in Red Bridge, and right now, I need to fly under the radar more than I need my next lungful of oxygen.

I should be cold, freezing my ass off, in fact, but adrenaline is pumping so hard through my veins that it's impossible for me to notice anything but my heart galloping like a racehorse out of the gates. With a hard crank, I start my car, and the cold air makes the engine rumble with hesitancy. When it finally revs with life, I pull my seat belt across my chest to secure it in the buckle.

A year ago, I never in my wildest dreams imagined I'd be here. A year ago, I was happy. I was healthy. I was hopeful and invincible.

But more than any of those things, I was incredibly and painfully naïve.

Life isn't the version we view through rose-colored glasses, and love, sometimes, isn't even close to enough.

Love, in fact, can be the very thing that hurts us the most. It steals our breath and makes fools of our actions. It sinks its teeth into our innocence and begs for happy endings when there aren't any to be had.

It robs us over and over, and, at some point, you have to stop feeding yourself to it as a victim.

I don't want to leave, but I can't stay. I *can't*.

My legs are numb, unable to move even with the proverbial train coming right at me. I know Clay would reach out a hand—would sacrifice himself if he had to. But that's exactly why I *have* to do this.

With my hand on the stick shift, I glance over at my purse, and the large envelope sticks out poignantly. A stark reminder of why it's there in the first place, and the D word sits heavy in my mind.

There's no other option.

I back out of the spot and drive toward Grandma Rose's house, my vision a blur of routine and simple objects. I see the courthouse and The Diner. I see Earl's Grocery Store and Fran's flower shop and Melba's bakery and the Red Bridge Police Department. And, of course, I see Clay's bar, The Country Club—the brick-and-mortar that make up nearly every aspect of my life.

But the only thing that registers is heartbreak.

There are ghosts at every corner. In the stolen kisses while I waitressed at The Diner, in the town festivals in the square, in the many jokes about Betty Bagley and her pie at the Fall Farmers Market, and in countless nights spent watching Clay make drinks with that handsome smile of his plastered on his face while I sat on a stool at the bar.

It should all feel familiar and comforting, and yet, it makes it hard for the person I am now to breathe at all.

I wish I'd been stronger. I wish I'd been wiser. I wish I didn't have to do this.

I *wish.*

But wishing doesn't matter anymore, and I can't turn back time even if I want to.

I have to go. I have to get out and not turn back, and I have to do it as soon as possible.

Sorrow and guilt and grief and shame claw at my throat, and the scratches are deep enough to bleed. My heart tries to compensate, but the loss is too much.

It's *all* too much.

I turn into Grandma Rose's driveway, shut off my car, and go inside to wait.

Tonight will be a defining moment for the rest of my life.

I have to end it now…

…before it ends me.

Before the Moment: Part 1

The Start of It All

1

Clay

Saturday, May 24th

On a scale of one to ten, how bad is it to make yourself a third wheel on a date with strangers?

Generally speaking, I'd rate it at an eleven. It's tacky and borderline narcissistic—something I'd watch the wealthy pricks from my old life in New York do with sickening confidence and something I'd ride them for every time.

But this isn't New York, and this date I'm considering cutting in on isn't *just* a date.

"Oh, Drew! You're too much." Blond curls fly over her shoulder as she turns coy eyes to the schmuck in front of her, and I lean into the bar to watch her in action.

A real-life man-eater, this unbelievably beautiful woman I know through town lore as Josie Ellis, has been inside my bar every Friday night for the last four months, each time with a different man. She teases and taunts and flirts, her siren's call luring them into the calm waters of overconfidence.

They study her green eyes, tanned skin, and colorfully tattooed arm like there'll be more to see at the end of the night, and she leans into the attention to hang on their every word. They long to make her theirs, to feel the heat of her around them, and to brag to their friends about the one they managed to bag.

But her eyes dance with secrets and plans of her own—something I recognize from all the times before—and it won't be long until this guy, just like all the rest, falls flat on his face and trudges out of here with his tail between his legs.

Not once have I seen her leave with her date. Instead, their faces turn ruddy red with anger and embarrassment, arguments breaking out between them as she shakes a finger in dismay, holding her own and grinning in satisfaction.

Besides the various gossip I've picked up throughout town, I don't know much about Josie Ellis, but her constant display in my bar proves she's a strong, independent woman who does what she wants and makes no apologies for it. Though, it could be said, there's a whole other layer to her that is soft and warm and loving. She lives with her sweet grandma, Rose Ellis, and attends church with her every Sunday. She works at Harold Metcalf's diner, and oftentimes, people request to have her as their waitress.

This woman is loved and adored by the entire town. Even Sheriff Pete Peeler talks about her like she's his own flesh-and-blood.

But tonight's version of Josie Ellis isn't ooey gooey. It's calculated. *Strategic.*

I watch closely, studying the big man with a beard and muscles who's easily two times her petite size, and wait for him to break. There's a frisson of danger in the air, although she doesn't let on, and I have to wonder if this little game she likes to play is eventually going to catch up with her.

I grab my bucket, rag, and spray bottle of cleaner and head for the table behind theirs to get a closer listen. Sure, it needs to be cleaned, but I've also got a bar full of customers waiting on drinks and a twenty-two-year-old named Colby to do my bussing. This isn't what I should be doing by any stretch of the imagination, but since all of this is going down in my very busy bar, I feel I have a responsibility to finally get to the bottom of it.

"What do you say we get out of here and make this date a little more interesting?" the chump asks just as I arrive within eavesdropping distance. He leans in to get a better view of her plumped-up cleavage, and his big, meaty hand grabs ahold of her tattooed arm.

I spin around the table and clean from the other side as she flutters her eyelashes and fake laughs, expertly extricating her arm out from under his in the motion. I'm impressed but not convinced pulling her arm away from this guy is going to be enough to keep her safe when she flips the switch.

"I don't know, Drew," she hums. "I think we can make this date a lot more interesting without leaving here at all."

"We can?"

"Oh yeah," she says eagerly, leaning into the table and resting her chin on her fists.

I slow the motion of my wipe with anticipation. Four whole months of watching her show, and I've never actually had the pleasure of hearing what she says to them before now. General busyness and false decorum have kept me trapped behind the bar.

Obviously, I've let all that go.

Drew's excitement is undeniable as he suggests, "Should I meet you in the bathroom?"

I have to hold myself back from snorting. *Fuck, this guy is going to crash so hard.*

She tilts her head to the side, secret mischief narrowing her eyes. "You probably take a lot of women to the bathroom in places like this, huh?"

His eyebrows draw together, and a tingle of concern-induced anticipation shoots all the way to my toes. It's been a long time since I fought, but I'm pretty sure I still know some of my old moves.

"No way, baby," he says and reaches out to run one beefy finger down her cheek. "I just really like you."

Right.

"That's nice," Josie comments, ending the final word in a hiss of sarcasm. Her face morphs from smile to serious in a second. "Or, at least, it would be if I didn't know it was *total fucking bullshit.*"

Oh *shit. Here we go.*

The man's big head jerks back in shock. "Excuse me?"

"Drew Hadish," she rattles off his full name and doesn't stop at that. "Thirty-one years old, married, two kids under three with your high school girlfriend turned wife, Hillary Bosworth. Grew up in Rodesh but moved to Hilsborough last year for a job at the factory with a two percent pay raise and health benefits. That's you, right?"

"What the fuck is this?" he demands then, standing from his seat and leaning into the table threateningly. She leans back in her chair with a grin, somehow managing not to look scared at all.

"You're a cheater, Drew," Josie chastises, and her eyes are so expressive they basically blink out the words *fuck you.* "You have been for a while, and now, you're caught. I suggest you grant Hillary the divorce when she asks and you don't contest the child support."

"Are you a fucking PI?" Drew slams his ham hock of a fist down onto the table, and I'm shocked when Josie doesn't even flinch.

Instead, she just shakes her head and offers a nonchalant shrug. "I'm just a girl."

"You better fucking watch yourself, *girl*," he threatens, jerking forward so hard the table scoots toward her, and unable to stop myself, I jump in.

I drop the bus rag and stand up tall, putting myself in front of him so I'm the only thing he can see. "It's time for you to leave."

"Fuck you, dude," he spits and bumps his chest against mine. "Fuck your bar and fuck this cunt!"

"I said, get the fuck out of here," I demand, clenching my jaw and pushing a stiff arm into his chest when he tries to posture toward me again. "Now!"

He bends around me to point an angry finger at Josie. "You're through. I'm gonna tell every fucking dude I know about you and what you're doing."

She has the audacity to laugh in his face. "That's a good idea. I'll do the same for you."

"Don't you fucking dare!"

"Aw, what's wrong, Drew?" Josie taunts, even blowing him a sarcastic kiss in the air. "I thought you liked me? I mean, just a moment ago, you wanted to take me into the bathroom and fuck me, remember?"

He lunges at her, and I grab him by the throat to stop him, sending him backward with a shove. "Get the hell out of my bar!" I shout before turning back to Josie with a scowl. "Stop."

She holds up her hands innocently before blowing another kiss at Drew over my shoulder. I roll my eyes and turn around swiftly to stop yet another lunge, carting him all the way out the front door this time before stopping.

His boots scramble on the gravel of the parking lot as I release my hold on him with a shove. "Don't come back, understand?"

"Don't fucking worry, bro." He scoffs. "I won't set foot in this piece-of-shit town ever again."

I stand at the door as he climbs into his old black Bronco and revs the engine, flooring it out of the parking lot and spraying gravel everywhere. Tad and Randy Hanson, a couple of brothers who've just arrived for a drink, have to jump out of the way, but they laugh and shake my hand as they pass me on their way to the entrance of The Country Club.

"Night's off to a good start, I see?" Randy taunts with a smile as Tad waggles his eyebrows.

"It seems we missed the show."

I snort. *Yeah. It was some show, all right.* Honestly, I can't decide if Josie Ellis is downright crazy or the most intriguing woman I've ever met.

Randy and Tad walk inside the bar like they didn't almost get run over by the angry bastard in the Bronco, and I silently wonder if everyone in Red Bridge is off their rocker.

If I watched someone tear ass out of a place like that, I'd think twice about coming inside. Not here, though. If I've learned one thing about Red Bridge, Vermont, since I moved here a few years ago and opened The Country Club, it's that they live for the drama.

Watch it, be it—they don't care. As long as it's interesting.

Trust me, supposed small-town, simple life is *far* from boring.

They hold the door for me as I follow them inside, and I scan the place for troublemaker Josie Ellis. She's at the bar now, yakking it up with other waiting patrons, and I don't think twice before heading straight to her.

I don't know all the details of her little game with these clueless dicks, but after tonight, it's clear the woman has created her own real-life version of that show *Cheaters* in my bar. And for the past several months, I've unknowingly sat back and watched it all go down.

But now, after I just had to shove some aggressive asshole out by his damn throat, there's *no way* I can let it continue.

I tap Josie on the shoulder until she spins around, her wild blond curls fanning out behind her as she does. She's an unbelievably pretty woman—there's absolutely no question in my mind how she lands all these dates—but I'm afraid if she keeps on like this for too long, someone's going to rearrange her perfectly delicate button nose.

"Cute little stunts you've been pulling in here for the last four months, but this was the last one, got me?"

She narrows her eyes. "Fine."

"I'm serious," I push, and she purses her lips as a few ladies around her hover close, trying to listen.

"And I said *fine*," she emphasizes, holding eye contact with me in challenge. We stay that way for a long moment, and then she widens her green eyes dramatically. "I won't bring any more dirtbags in here. Promise."

Satisfied, I nod and head for the end of the bar to get back behind it and catch up on all the waiting drinks. However, her voice is just loud enough for me to hear it when she tells Sue Nagel, "I'll take them somewhere else."

Against my better judgment, I stop in my tracks, turn around, and walk right back over to her. "Did I just hear you say you'll take them somewhere else?"

"Yeah." She narrows her eyes again. "And?"

"I don't know if you noticed, honey, but that shit is dangerous. If I hadn't been there to step in, you could have gotten seriously hurt. I can appreciate what you're doing, but it's not smart."

She shrugs. "It's worth the risk."

"See, that's where we don't agree."

"Good thing we don't need to, then." Her laugh is defiant as hell, and I start to think I might be the crazy one when I find myself loving the way her green eyes shine and her full lips part with each chuckle. "You're not involved," she adds with a cheeky smile.

"I don't know, I look pretty fucking involved, if you ask me." I hold out two knowing hands, palms up. "I just threw a guy out of my bar over it."

Her pretty green eyes roll heavenward. "I told you, I'll go somewhere else."

I sigh, gesturing toward a stool at the end of the bar. "Sit down. Please. Let me catch up on all these drinks, and then we'll talk."

"Why do you care so much?"

"'Cause I've been watching you for a while now. And I kind of like your smile the way it is." *And because you've become a mystery I'd really love to solve.*

Her lips part in surprise, and Sue elbows her in the side before turning around and pulling out a stool.

I hope and pray and hold my breath. And smile so big my chest hurts when Josie finally sits down.

I'm almost sure it makes me a fool, but I think this girl might just be something special.

2

Josie

Saturday, May 24th

My heart pounds as I sit down on the stool at the bar and wait while Clay Harris serves the hordes of people waiting for drinks. I don't know him well, but I've heard plenty of talk about the handsome bar owner since he took up residence here a few years ago and opened the only watering hole around for miles.

He's originally from New York, moved here a couple years back, but has settled in well and has generally been accepted by the masses. Which is a feat in this small town. It's not that we don't like any outsiders, but there's a hazing of sorts, just like in a frat or a sorority—a test of loyalty that you must pass.

From what I hear, Clay Harris has managed to pass it in spades despite all the chatter about his wealthy parents and sordid past.

Eileen Martin, the town gossip and editor of the newspaper, has been telling people he's a member of the Gambino family—like legitimate mob boss, Sopranos-type of stuff—since he arrived in Red Bridge, and supposedly, Sheriff Pete Peeler kept him under twenty-four-hour surveillance for the first year he was here. But these days, I don't know a single townsperson who wouldn't let him babysit their kids or invite him over for some meatloaf and mashed potatoes on any given night.

The man has some kind of magical charisma, that's for damn sure. The way everyone in town loves him now is proof.

It's a typical Friday night in Red Bridge, and The Country Club is bustling with nearly half the town's population and a third of the people from one town over. Basically, the only ones not here are the poor souls working the overnight portion of their swing shift at the Phelps plant just outside of town, and as a result, Clay is hustling.

I watch as he prepares drink after drink with a smile on his face, chatting up everyone he encounters with amusement and patience. It's almost as though he didn't just have to throw someone out of his bar because of me—like the work is soothing to him.

He's muscular, and his T-shirt stretches across his chest with every bottle of beer he uncaps. His white smile stands out against his tanned skin, and his dark, nearly black hair curls freely at his hairline. I dig my teeth into my bottom lip as I consider what he must think of me and the work I've been doing for the sisterhood.

It's not, like, an official job or anything—catching cheaters. I work my regular shifts at Harold Metcalf's diner on Main Street. This is just…a hobby. A public service, maybe. A way to add value with my time. But I'm well aware it's not commonplace.

Six months ago, it would've been the very last thing I pictured myself doing in my free time.

Clay is finally getting close to me, having worked his way down the bar from the far end, and when I see him pouring a glass of Pinot Grigio—my drink of choice—I know the time for my "talking-to" is near.

Surprisingly, I find myself smiling at the thought of him chiding me. There's something charming about having a rumored mob boss give you a scolding about safety, even if the only mob he's actually in charge of is the drunken one inside this bar.

The glass hits the wooden surface of the bar top in front of me, and I grin. "It's almost like you know my drink or something."

He smirks. "I know everyone's drink, doll."

"Yeahhh. But you've been watching me for months. You said so yourself."

He nods. "Figure someone needs to look out for you since you're not looking out for yourself."

"I can handle my own shit, Clay."

"How old are you, Josie?" he asks, catching me a little off guard.

"Uh…twenty-five. Why?"

"Well, I'm twenty-eight, which means I have three more years of wisdom on you." He winks. "Not to mention, I grew up in New York. A certified rich city kid who had everything at his disposal and spent the majority of his youth and his early twenties in trouble, *lots of fucking trouble*, because of it. And that on its own adds, like, an additional ten years to my wisdom scale."

"Wisdom scale?" I question on a snort. "Is that supposed to mean something important? Because I'm lost."

"Well, if you do the math, I have thirteen years of extra life experiences—*highlighted with a hell of a lot of fuckups*—on you." He taps his hand on the bar. "Which means you should take my advice and quit all this shit with these assholes while you're ahead."

I purse my lips. "News flash, Clay, I grew up in New York too."

"Wait…" His eyebrows pull together. "You aren't a Red Bridge lifer?"

I shake my head. "I was born here, but after my father died, my mother moved us to the city so she could bag a rich man. I spent the majority of my teenage years being a city kid just like you. I didn't come back to Red Bridge until I was eighteen." I place both elbows on the bar and rest my chin on my fists. "And if you knew my mother, you'd know that dealing with her narcissistic, vapid, manipulative, cruel ass adds about twenty years of wisdom to your belt."

After the words come out of my mouth, I'm a little shocked that I even went that deep into my past. Besides my grandmother, I don't have a relationship with my family, just horrible memories, loss, grief, and loads of trauma. All of which I never talk about. Or at least, I don't usually talk about.

"Yeah, well, you haven't met my father, *the great Carl Harris*, a man who loves money more than anything. And when I say anything, I mean literally *anything*, even his one and only own child," Clay counters. "The only good thing that bastard's done is help fund this bar..." He pauses and leans forward with a secret grin. "It's minor details that he thinks The Country Club is an actual country club."

My jaw drops. "You're lying."

"No lies, Josie. *Never* lies. I'm an open-book kind of guy. So..." He smiles at me, tapping his chin thoughtfully. "If I do the math again, our parents cancel each other out." He points one finger at me. "I'll even give you some leeway on growing up in the city, but I know for a fact you didn't get into half of the fucked-up shit I did. But even then, it still leaves me with three years more than you." He smiles at me like he's won some kind of prize. "And that leaves us with you taking my advice and stopping meeting up with these dirtbags."

A sigh escapes my lungs. "You don't understand what I'm doing."

"I didn't. Not until tonight anyway. Just thought you were teasin' guys up to drop 'em on their ass. But I got enough of an earful of your conversation with your pal Drew to understand it's a hell of a lot different from what I originally thought."

"And let me guess, you think it's stupid."

"Not stupid." His eyes turn serious. "Just concerning."

"Wait... You're not going to give me some line about minding my own business? About what happens between a man and a woman being a sacred, intimate thing where they make their own choices?"

"I take it you've gotten that speech a couple times, huh?"

I nod. "From the sheriff. And the mayor. And Earl. And Harold Metcalf."

"Is that all?" Clay asks with a laugh.

My smile is wry. "Not even close."

He leans a hip into the bar. "No, I'm not going to give you the same old sad speech. And I wasn't going to, even before."

"That's good news," I answer with a little smile. "Because I'm not so sure I should take advice from a mob boss."

"Mob boss?" His laugh is hearty and happy and warms my body from my head to my toes. "Eileen Martin needs to stop spreading those shit rumors."

"So, this bar is just a bar, then? Not a cover for your racketeering operations?"

"It's just a bar. And I'm just a man with zero ties to the mob."

"Man…" I pause and feign a frown. "That's a bit of a letdown."

"Well, sorry to disappoint, Miss Cheater Catcher, but your whole operation is kind of hard to live up to," he says, his words one hundred percent amused. "But now that we're back to the topic at hand, how did you end up doing it in the first place?"

"How did I end up catching cheaters? How else?" I shrug. "The internet."

"The internet?" His laugh is incredulous, and it matches the curious quirk of his brow. "Please explain."

"It's hard to explain something that happened in the most random of ways." I lean back on my barstool and tuck some of my curls behind my ear. "I was in a few local online groups for towns nearby. Mostly for my grandmother, to keep an eye out for upcoming flea markets and garage sales. And one day, this poor woman from Molene posted about how she was suspicious that her husband was cheating on her and didn't know what to do. She was devastated, clearly, and I don't know…" I pause and fiddle with the stem of my wineglass. "I just felt awful for her. The post was flooded with comments, but none of them helped her. If anything, people's opinions probably made her more on edge. So, I sent her a private message, and, I guess the rest is history."

Truthfully, none of this was planned. It just happened. Once I helped that woman, another woman messaged me, and it spiraled into me being the woman from Red Bridge who caught cheaters.

"Look, I think what you're doing is important and courageous. Men are shit a whole hell of a lot of the time, and if you can help some lady see the light about hers, I'm down with it."

"Oh, man." A laugh bubbles up from my lungs. "Are you telling me that men are dogs in your own special bark?"

He grins. "It's hormonal. Some of us are just bred and trained, you know?"

"House-trained, huh? To do what? Not piss on your pretty coworker or neighbor or random stranger's vagina while your wife is at home with the kids?"

He grimaces and chortles at the same time. "Fuck, that's an image."

"It's also incredibly realistic." I grin as I take a sip from my wine. "I've single-handedly caught forty cheaters since I started, and I've only been working in the towns around us. The freaking population isn't that big, for crying out loud!"

"Then your service is paid."

"Ah-ah," I tsk. "No, it's not. There are more. I can do more."

"Josie. You're going to get hurt." Clay leans into the bar, his hands splayed out to the sides and his built shoulders flexing. His voice is unbelievably soft. To be honest, it's a miracle I can hear him over the crowded bar noise around us. "That man wanted to hurt you, and I can tell you from watchin', he's not the first. They get an inkling of thinking they're going to get a taste of you and then get humiliated instead. I'm not saying they don't deserve it, okay? They do. But some of them don't have a lick of sense or an ounce of manners, and if you keep it up, someone is going to do something to you I can't stand for."

For the first time tonight, a very real fear of what Drew could have done to me if Clay hadn't been there to step in washes over me. I don't want to stop, but...Clay might be right that I should.

There's a part of me that will feel guilty if I stop. It's scary how many women have asked me to help them find out if their boyfriend or husband is running around on them. Honestly, the requests have become more than I can even technically handle. And it's all been by word of mouth, which makes it feel even worse to cut it off at the knees.

I sink my head into my hands and push the mountain of my curly hair back when it falls forward. By the time I look up, Clay is pouring a shot of vodka and setting it on the bar in front of me and then doing the same in another glass right in front of himself.

The bottle hits the counter with a thud, and he jerks his chin toward the glass. "Come on. All your hard work deserves a shot to celebrate." His wink is powerful, hitting me in all the right spots as I pick up the glass, and we clink them together.

"To the cheater catcher," he announces with a big smile.

"Yeah, yeah. The *former* cheater catcher, if I listen to you." I laugh, tipping the glass to my lips and swallowing the burning liquid in one gulp.

"You can still come in here on Friday nights," he says with a heartbreaking smile as he drops his glass to the bar. "Just leave the other guys at home."

"The cheaters, you mean?"

"I don't know." He shrugs one muscular shoulder, and his smile is so addictive, I wonder if it should be considered illegal. "Feels like I might not want to see you with a good one either."

"Why not?"

His golden-brown eyes sparkle. "Thinking maybe I'd like to see you with me."

"Ah," I hum. "I see now. Maybe there's a secret agenda to getting me to stop catching cheaters, then…"

"Only in my dreams. In the real world, my agenda's fully on the up-and-up—swear."

I roll my eyes, shoving off the stool and adjusting the waistband of my jeans. He's undeniably attractive and, by all accounts, a good guy, but if I stay here any longer, I'm pretty sure I'm going to end up in a different kind of trouble. "Goodnight, Clay."

"Goodnight, Josie," he says with a smile, snapping the end of his rag out in the air and making it crack.

I turn and strut my way out of the bar, putting a little extra sway in my hips just for him. I don't look back to see if he's watching, but I feel like it's undeniable that he is.

I shove through the front door and out into the parking lot, looking up at the crisp black Vermont sky and soaking in the slight chill of late spring night air. It feels good on my overheated skin, and the stars shine bright in the inky dark.

A rush of air from inside pours out behind me, and before I know what's happening, I'm being spun around and pulled toward Clay's warm body. There's a question in his eyes as he looks down at me and a beat of pause while he waits for me to stop him.

But he feels good, and I'm too overcome by the endorphins to think better of it. His lips meet mine in a soft mesh of breath and tongues, and he sinks his hand into the wild curls of my hair.

My stomach flips at the feel, and I chase at recreating it as he swipes my tongue with his own. He tastes of vodka and fresh mint, and I'm not done exploring the combination when he pulls away.

He smiles and rubs a soft thumb over my lips before turning for the door. "That," he says. "Now *that*, Josie Ellis, is a goodbye."

Nope. I'm not done at all.

3

Clay

Sunday, May 25th

Josie bows her head in prayer in the pew to my left, her Grandma Rose at her side.

She looks beautiful as always, but this morning, the long sleeves of her baby-blue dress cover the tattoo sleeve on her right arm. Last night was the first time I found myself studying it up close, and now, they're etched in my mind. Even with them covered, I can still perfectly imagine the colorful mix of the monarch butterfly, fading sunset, Venus flytrap, and female superhero with a high red ponytail and fiery eyes that are engraved into her skin. And the thought of all of that hiding away under there, while she sits demurely in a pretty dress next to her sweet grandmother, makes me smile.

I'm not usually much of a churchgoer myself, but I've seen her coming out of here enough on my drive to Molene to pick up kegs to know this is where I'd find her on a Sunday morning.

And this Sunday morning, in particular, I *had* to find her. If I concentrate hard enough, I can still taste a hint of her on my lips from last night's kiss.

Thankfully, everyone in town is eager enough for me to join in on the worship session to let the idiosyncrasy of my presence go, and I blend in like butter into hot potatoes.

I bow my head too, but not without sneaking in a lingering look at Josie's serene face. Her features are delicate in contrast to her strong personality, and her wild curls are clipped up at the back of her head to keep them out of her eyes.

"O Lord, do not withdraw from us your Word and Spirit, but grant us a strong faith, patience, and steadfastness in all suffering and adversity. Help and sustain us, your children, and deliver us from opposition, ridicule, and tyranny. We pray this Sunday in particular for our great and loving friends, the Grift Family, as they prepare to welcome a new member of their precious family and ours, sweet baby Ginny, who we ask to come safely and prosperously in your loving hands and for a smooth and seamless delivery for Kate," Reverend Bob prays from his spot on the stage. "As always, we thank you for your gifts and opportunities and for this beautiful community we call home before we're called home to you. Amen."

"Amen," we all recite in various volumes and cadences, lifting our heads and opening our eyes as Reverend Bob dismisses the whole of the congregation with wide arms and a warm smile.

"See you here next time," he says simply as people rise and begin to file out. I scour the crowd, looking around heads and bodies and leaning from left to right to follow the head of platinum curls as Josie makes her way out of the pew with her grandma and walks toward the back of the church.

Betty Bagley pauses to talk to someone in front of me, holding me up, and I watch somewhat helplessly as Josie and her grandma get closer and closer to the exit, Melba Danser chatting at their ears.

Betty is nearly a million years old and feeble of body, and I can't shove her out of the way, so I do my best to be patient even as my heart starts to race when Josie's head disappears out the front door.

"Excuse me," I try, but without both of her hearing aids in, Betty can't hear me.

Grandma Rose waves at someone and steps outside, and a desperation builds that I can't control.

One hand to the back of the pew, I launch over it like a log in the woods and take off at a run up the aisle. Sheriff Pete laughs, and Reverend Bob hollers a chide, but I'm out the door and chasing after curly blond hair before either one truly registers.

Halfway through the parking lot is where I find her, and I slide to a stop in the gravel as the traction of my boots gives out with the immediate change in speed.

"Jesus Christ, Clay!" Josie yells, startled by my quick entrance and hand at her elbow.

"Josie, we're in the church parking lot, for crying out loud!" Grandma Rose scolds. "How about we save the crass use of Our Savior's name for another time."

"He scared me!" Josie protests, making Grandma's blue eyes roll beneath the set of her perfect silver curls.

"I'm sorry," I apologize immediately and then turn to Grandma Rose. "I'm sorry, ma'am."

Grandma Rose smirks, and a crowd of other people gathers on the steps of the church, watching and pointing in our direction.

Josie glances around, her brows drawing together and her cheeks turning pink when she sees the sheriff, the mayor, Betty Bagley, Old Lady Mouser, and the Hanson brothers all watching us avidly. Harold Metcalf is watching, too, but given that he's Josie's boss, he's at least trying to be secretive about it. His wife, however, peers around him unabashedly.

Josie bugs out her eyes, the action a demand. "Just what exactly do you need that couldn't *wait*?"

I drop down to a knee and take her hand in mine, and I hear a collective gasp behind her.

"Clay, what are you *doing*?" Her green eyes threaten to fill the entire space of her face, and Grandma Rose's tiny head spins around to face us like a crane.

"Proposing, of course."

Grandma Rose swallows a guffaw, and Josie yanks her hand out of mine like it's on fire. "Excuse me?"

"I'm proposing," I say again, doubling down, my smile only growing as she squirms. I know it's probably embarrassing, but it's also memorable. And Josie Ellis's mind is one place I'm determined to be.

"Clay, I don't even… We don't even…" She trips over her words. "I hardly even know you."

"I know, doll. That's why I'm proposing…" I pause, letting the silence linger just long enough to make her squirm a little more. "A date. A first date. Just the two of us, so we can get to know each other beyond the taste of each other's tongues."

Pink renews in her cheeks, even deeper this time, and she clenches her hands into fists as her grandma devolves into laughter beside her. At least I've managed to amuse one of the Ellis women.

Not the right one, of course, but still, a win is a win.

"Stand up. Right now," Josie grits out, grabbing me by the collar of my shirt and physically forcing the command for good measure.

"I'm not leaving until you say yes," I promise straightaway, cutting off her urge to punish me for the stunt right at the knees. "I can't eat, I can't sleep, I can't do anything else until you agree."

Josie sighs. "My God, men are so pathetic."

"We are." I nod without shame. "We're dogs and we're weak and we're desperate."

She narrows her eyes. "Clay."

"Josie. Say yes. You know you want to. You're too curious, too invested in the plot."

"Plot?" Her nose crinkles up in the most adorable fucking way. "What plot?"

"Of our story."

"We don't have a story, Clay."

"Not yet," I agree. "Not yet."

"Clay…"

"If you don't say yes to this poor fella and put him out of his misery," Grandma Rose edges in, "I will."

"Grandma!" Josie exclaims, and I just stand there, smiling like the fool I am over this woman.

"Josie, he's got the whole dang town watchin' him," Grandma Rose adds. "And all he's looked at is you. Give the poor schlep a date."

Josie clenches her teeth and lets out a deep sigh before turning to me, her eyes challenging. "Fine. One date. On Saturday. I have work, and I'll need the week to run a background check on you."

She needs to run a background check on me. Is it too soon to be in love with this woman?

I grin. "Saturday it is."

It doesn't matter that I have to wait a week or that her grandma basically peer-pressured her into it. I have an official date with Josie Ellis, and just like before…

A win is a win.

4

Josie

Saturday, May 31st

A bouquet of red roses is the first thing I see when I open the door, Clay's smiling face appearing shortly after as he pulls them down and holds them out to me on the front stoop of Grandma Rose's house.

I've lived here since I moved back to town seven years ago, when I was just a fresh-faced eighteen-year-old looking to escape from under my mother's thumb. At first, I thought I'd be eager to move out and find my own place, but I'm comfortable. Grandma Rose is nosy sometimes but, by and large, gives me all the freedom I ask for. I mean, to her credit, she's not even spying on me right now, and if I were her, after the way Clay proposed this date in the first place, I don't know that I'd have nearly that much restraint.

It also doesn't hurt that she only charges me a minuscule amount of rent and money for my share of the groceries. And I know she only burdens me at all to make me feel like I'm making a contribution and not freeloading. As a woman working as a waitress and surviving mostly on tips, I appreciate it more than I can say.

"Wow. You look beautiful," Clay greets, handing me the bouquet and leaning in to place a single, gentle kiss to my cheek and then stepping back to take me in.

Low-rise jeans, a belt with a big buckle, and a fancy off-the-shoulder top was my fifth option for the night, and tired of taking off and putting on clothes, I finally settled. Still, Clay's eyes are alight with appreciation, and my happiness with the choice is renewed.

"Thank you," I say, studying his appearance with sly eyes. He looks absolutely delicious in a formfitting, crisp white T-shirt and well-apportioned jeans and boots. His hair is neatly combed and styled, and his smile is bright and white. His features may be slightly rich Italian, but his aesthetic is full-on country.

And there's no doubt about it—Clay Harris is one fine-ass man. Seriously. He's what eighteen-year-old me would've called hot. And he's what midtwenties me secretly wants to eat with a spoon.

"What?" he asks with a smirk. "No return compliment for me?"

I shrug, feigning neutrality despite my current state of lust. "You look all right, I guess."

Clay Harris might be one of God's gifts to women, but I refuse to show my I'm-totally-into-you cards before we even start our date. I'll stick with playing hard to get and will have zero shame in that game.

He tilts his head, and his smile grows. "So, that's how it is?"

"How what is?" I ask coyly, sliding past him, pulling the door shut behind me and walking toward his souped-up dark green Ford F-150. I'm not exactly an expert on vehicles, but I know enough to realize it's not brand-new. The upkeep on it, however, is immaculate. I see no scratches or spots of rust, and the chrome door handles shine like a brand-new copper penny.

He follows after me with both pep and patience, the warmth of his breath a gentle breeze on the back of my neck I've left exposed with an updo.

"The whole tough-nut thing," he explains, hustling past me to open the passenger door to his truck and hold it for me. I climb inside, and he surprises me by following with his upper body, grabbing the seat belt, pulling it across me, and securing it in the buckle. His face is *this close* as he whispers, "I'm real good at cracking them."

"We'll see," I challenge somehow, even though I can barely breathe. His smell is entrancing, and if I'm honest with myself, I already feel a fissure in my shell.

Clay's face is bright with happiness and ease as he edges back out my door, secures it shut, and rounds the hood to jump in on the driver's side. As he climbs in and fires it up, I test out giving this thing—this date—an actual chance. He's a fun, attractive-as-hell guy, and I'm an adventurous single girl. Besides a few hours, I really have nothing to lose.

"So..." I pause and look over at him as he pulls out of Grandma Rose's driveway. "Where are we going?"

"You know Molene?" he asks.

"Of course I know Molene. It's the closest town with a Walmart."

Clay laughs and takes a right turn off the main road to lead us out of town. "Well, they're having their Spring Fling tonight in the town square."

I nod. I know that too.

"I figured you'd be more comfortable getting to know me if the whole Red Bridge phone tree wasn't looking on."

I scoff. "Didn't seem to bother you on Sunday when you physically got down on one knee to ask me out in front of all of them."

"Yeah, but that was different. I wasn't even myself." He glances at me out of his periphery. "I was a man possessed."

"Possessed?" I ask with a shocked giggle. "You should have stayed in the church, then."

"Not possessed by the devil," he corrects with a wag of one finger via the hand held loosely on the steering wheel as he weaves almost recklessly in and out of traffic. I glance between him and the road, trying not to gasp every time he switches lanes. "Possessed by *need.* The need to know you. The need to be near you. It's *totally* different and far less damning."

"You're a cheeseball," I accuse, even as a whole flock of butterflies takes flight in my chest. "And you drive like you stole this truck. Which…I'm really hoping that's not the case. Asking me to be the Bonnie to your Clyde is a little too much for the first date."

He laughs. Hard. And I love the way his Adam's apple bobs on his throat with each hearty chuckle. "Josie, if there's one thing you need to understand about me, it's that I'm honest. When I'm consumed, I say I'm consumed. Plain and simple." He winks over at me, just one perfect blink of his right eye. "And I own the truck outright, doll. I'm saving the Bonnie and Clyde shit for date two. Gotta take things slow, you know?"

It's my turn to laugh. "How about you take your own advice and ease that lead foot of yours off the pedal?"

He grins at me, but he also does as I ask, slowing down his speed as he fiddles with the stereo. He turns the knob, switching through various radio stations until he stops on one that's playing a popular song by OneRepublic. "Counting Stars," I think it's called. And there's something intoxicating about the lyrics filling the inside of Clay's truck as he drives us toward Molene.

It makes me think about the possibility of being with a man like him. The possibility of this first date going well and turning into a second date. And a third and a fourth. I don't know if anything will come of this, but damn, I agree with what the lead singer says about hope.

Tonight, it feels like the word belongs to us.

"Clay?" I ask, grabbing his attention enough for him to glance away from the road briefly and meet my eyes. "How many times, exactly, have you been consumed before?"

His brief glance morphs into him actually turning to face me. He stares at me hard in the dancing, fading light of the sunset, his view of the road completely precluded. I panic, of course, looking away to watch traffic for him, but there's none. It's a back road through the boonies, and all he has to do is keep it between the ditches.

"Never," he says. And I never thought one word could hold so much power.

But again, I refuse to show my cards so early in this game. So, instead, I shake my head with a scoff. "Watch the road, Clay."

"I'm not lying," he contests. "Though, I know why you'd think I am. But I've never, not once, been so consumed by a woman I've jumped over a pew in church to follow her. Or, you know, gone to church in the first place."

"What?" My head jerks back, bumping the base of my skull on the headrest of my passenger seat. "You jumped over the pews?"

"Betty and Old Lady Mouser were blocking the way."

I smile at that and look down to my lap, working the fingers of both hands together in a knot. From the side and seemingly out of nowhere, Clay's hand sneaks on top of my left one, weaving our fingers together.

I feel giddy and absolutely drunk with affection as he rubs the back of my hand with his thumb and drives into the old field behind the Molene Civic Center in silence.

Something about him and me feels like magic. Like, one day, probably far too soon, I could find myself falling for him. *Or maybe I already have.*

5

Clay

Saturday, May 31st

Josie's chin brushes the middle of my chest, her head tucked close as we sway to the music pouring out of the loudspeakers in a crowd of Molene residents.

She smells like heaven and hell at once, thanks to the ever-tightening fit of my pants, but I soak it in anyway, hovering over her blond hair to get an extra whiff of lavender shampoo.

She dances slow and steady, trusting me to move her in time with the soft melody of onstage music coming from a couple of local guys with guitars.

It's almost the end of a perfect night of flirting and teasing, eating corn fritters, gravy fries, and cider doughnuts out of paper dishes, and close cuddles while we went down a big plastic slide on burlap bags, and I want more than anything for it to never end.

"Bad news, doll," I whisper in her ear, tilting her head by

sinking my fingers in the soft sides of her ponytail. "First date exorcism didn't work." She laughs, just once on a startle, and I smile against the delicate skin of her neck. "How about you? How am I doing?"

With her hands at my jaw, she pulls my face from her neck and forces our eyes to meet in the sexiest of ways. "Feeling pretty brittle," she admits softly, her body melding to mine as we sway from side to side. "Might even break soon."

I lean forward and push my lips to hers, wrapping my arms around her back and pulling her in so tight she has to brace herself on my shoulders to keep her own feet. Our tongues clash, tasting and teasing in a mess of lust as we spin around in a circle, the whole world around us disappearing.

"Shit, Josie." I pull away and groan, my whole body breaking out in a sweat. "Any more of that and I'm going to be the new town flagpole," I admit, spinning her around and into a twirl as she giggles.

It's an unbelievable sound, so uninhibited and sexy it makes me wish I had the camouflage of her body against mine still.

A quicker tempo catches fire, and I put our rhythmic chemistry to the test, winding her faster and faster under the peak of my arm, twisting and turning myself, to spin us all over the floor.

A crowd starts to gather around us to watch, and her gorgeous green eyes dance even more than we do as I pull her around and behind and forward again, ending in a lift and a flip and a dramatic dip at the end. People clap and cheer as we fall into a crescendo with each other, demanding new skills and untested waters with every move we complete. She follows me flawlessly, letting me lead her in the right direction and keeping a delicate balance of putting on a show of her own at the same time.

I haven't danced with someone like this in a long time—maybe ever—and the synchronicity of our bodies makes me wonder just how in sync we'd be in a different way entirely.

As the song comes to a close, so do we, wrapping up in each

other's arms and laughing through the deafening applause of the crowd.

I'm not ready to go home, but we sure as hell can't stay here. I need Josie all to myself, and now that we've put on an exhibition, the Molene vultures are going to be circling us all night. "You wanna go somewhere else?" I ask, and she nods instantly, no coy games or denials in sight anymore.

We're both into this—into each other—and there's no sense in avoiding it.

"Come on," she says, grabbing my hand and pulling me out of the crowd and in the direction of my truck. "I know just where to go."

I wait until we're out of the bright lights of the town square, but once we're in the shadows, behind the Molene Public Works building, I pull her to a stop and put my lips to hers again. I delve even deeper this time until a buzz takes up residence in my head and sets the rest of my body on fire. "I sure hope this place is close," I whisper against her perfect mouth, and I feel her grin against my skin.

"It's just outside Red Bridge, but don't worry. I'll drive fast."

I lean my head back to meet her eyes. "*You'll* drive fast? We're in my truck."

"Yep." She quirks a defiant brow at me, her gaze teasing and playful and confident in a way that makes me want her even more. "And I'm driving, baby." Her whole face glows as she holds out a hand, palm up to the dark, clear sky, and I have no choice but to comply.

Pulling my keys from the back pocket of my jeans, I drop them into her fingers and shake my head. "I never let people drive my truck, but something about you feels like an exception." I don't know why, but the idea of *her* driving my truck is incredibly sexy and it makes me wonder if she isn't just an exception but the fucking rule.

"Something?" she asks with the cutest tilt of her head, and I don't mince my words.

"Damn near everything, really."

"Good." Her beautiful smile consumes her entire face, lifting her cheeks and lighting up her eyes in a way I hope I'll get to see a million more times. "Now, come on! Last one to the truck has to wait for the other to initiate the next kiss."

I'll be damned if I've ever put my everything into a race with a woman before, but I turn on the turbo jets and run as fast as I can until I have to stop my momentum with two hands to the bed of my truck. When I turn around to look back, she's walking.

Sashaying, really.

I throw up my hands as she's finally arriving, asking, "What the hell?"

Her smirk is cunning. "I kind of like letting you be in control, but it sure was fun watching you run."

I pull her to me then, spinning her around and pushing the back of her body up against the truck and trapping it within mine by placing two hands on the bed near her shoulders. She goes willingly, the corners of her mouth curving up even higher as I run a hand to her hip and pull her in tight. "I guess you owed me one, huh?"

"Uh-huh." She nods, and I love the way her long eyelashes flutter up at me. "Though, a hardly crowded field of strangers' cars isn't quite on par with the church parking lot in Red Bridge."

"You're right," I agree. "I've still got one coming for me."

She shakes her head. "What is that? How are you like that? Just saying whatever you feel…conceding a point so easily… I've never heard a man…be so honest."

"Nothing to lie about, I suppose. I am who I am, and right now, I'm a man who wants more than anything to be close to you." I brush my lips against hers. "*Really* close."

I know I'm pushing it, but I'll be damned if Josie Ellis isn't pushing me. I've never felt like this about anyone. Ever. I spent my early twenties being a rich prick—*who hated my father for turning me into just that.* I spent most of my days and nights partying and dating all kinds of women in New York, and not a single one of them made me feel like *this*.

Frankly, nothing has ever made me feel like this.

Thankfully, Josie is completely undeterred by my forwardness. "Get in," she says with a wink. "I know the perfect place to go."

I jump in the passenger seat of my truck and watch helplessly as she gets in on the other side. I'd never have let this happen a week ago, but facts are facts.

Josie Ellis is shaping up to be the dream girl.

And as a result, my priorities are shifting.

6

Josie

Saturday, May 31st

Out of all the places I could've taken Clay, I chose the one place that's always been a little secret of mine. A place I ran to when I was a kid, trying to escape the grief of losing my baby sister Jezzy and, later, my father. A place that's always given me peace and solace and felt like freedom when I was an eleven-year-old girl who wanted nothing to do with her horrible mother.

A place that I still go to sometimes. Just to think, just to breathe, just to be.

I don't know why I wanted to bring Clay here, but here we are. At my water tower.

"I kind of thought this *perfect place* would be at a lower elevation," Clay complains from behind me, climbing the beige rungs of Red Bridge's one-hundred-and-thirty-foot-tall water tower like a puppy clinging to its mother.

I clear the edge and go under the bar to the deck, turning back to face him as he scales the last part of the ladder. "Come on, you big baby. You're almost there."

"Fear of heights is a real thing," he says seriously, and it's a struggle not to laugh in his face. Not because being afraid of heights isn't real, but because I never imagined his cocky ass would ever look this pathetic.

Instead, I reach out a hand and help him up, and he doesn't waste any time melding his back to the surface of the sphere. He's a good five feet from the edge, but it doesn't matter; his knuckles are white with fear.

"Listen, we can go down if you want," I offer and honestly mean it. The last thing I want to do is make the man have a panic attack. "I didn't realize it would be this big of a deal—"

"No, no." He shakes his head, but his wide eyes don't match the gesture.

"Clay, it's fine. We can find somewhere else to—"

"No, now that we're up here, going down is even worse." He peers toward the edge for the briefest of moments before finding his safety net against the water tower again. "It's better to just be here."

I actually guffaw, I laugh so hard. "Like…forever? We'll have to go down eventually."

"Yeah, I guess you're right." His eyes are avoiding the edge entirely now, looking everywhere but down. "Maybe if you distract me a little bit, it won't be as bad."

I let my eyes run up and down the length of him, his big, muscular frame still towering over mine, despite the fact that his current fear-induced state has him cowering. Clay Harris wants me to distract him, and I'd be a liar if I said my ideas revolved around conversation.

"Oh yeah?" I lick my lips. "What were you thinking?" I push up close to him and onto my toes to touch my lips just barely to his. "Something like this?"

"Okay. Yeah." His eyes are closed tight, and his lungs move up and down with heavy breaths. "That's not bad."

"What about this?" I ask, placing another kiss to the side of his neck. He nods and, emboldened, I keep going. "This?" With my hand to his belt buckle, I grab the front waistband of his pants and pull him against me.

"Yeah." His words are thick on his tongue. "That works."

"And this?" I slide my hands around his back and beneath his jeans, grabbing his ass over his cotton boxer briefs.

"Uh-huh," he says gruffly.

I take his hand in mine then, guiding it up my side and across my chest until the skin of his palm rests hot on the exposed part of my breast. His eyes pop open, and I bite my lip in a smile.

"That work, too?"

"For what? Making me hard? Because yeah, it's working." Instantly, a giggle escapes my throat, and his eyes jump from his hand to my eyes. "Fuck, Josie. I love that sound."

The frankness and grit in his voice catch me off guard, and my breath freezes in my chest. Damn, this man. He's making me feel things I don't think I've ever had a man make me feel. My nipples are hard beneath my bra, and every nerve ending in my body feels like it's been lit with a match. I'm so swept up in him, so overwhelmed…I want him.

Actually, I more than want him. *I have to have him.*

"Take my clothes off, Clay."

"Up here?" he nearly squeaks.

I smile and nod. "Yeah, baby. I figure fucking me right here is a really good way to distract you. Maybe even get rid of your fear altogether. Don't you think?"

"You're serious?" His chuckle is rough and so damn sexy I feel it in the throb between my thighs.

"Never been more serious in my life."

His movement is fast and stilted, but all the hesitation and clinging to the tower are gone as he strips his shirt over his head and pulls my body against the heat of his bare skin. I run my hands down the tops of his arms and over the surface of his chest, stopping on the hard feel of his pecs and gasping when he pulls my hips in close to his own.

We both shake now, the adrenaline of what we're doing far

outweighing his fear and my calm of before.

I lick my lips, and he watches for a millisecond, his eyes turning hot and burning in an instant. Between one moment and the next, our lips are together and our tongues are clashing for supremacy, trying to be the one to get the best taste. He lowers me down to the surface of the deck, putting his discarded T-shirt behind my head to pad the surface and then pulling my shirt even farther off my shoulder to expose the lace of my bra.

My nipple is pert and completely visible, and he sucks it into his mouth through the thin material. I moan.

"Definitely feeling way better about heights right now," he says around the flesh, making me laugh and sigh at the same time. "Definitely."

I thread my hands into the strands of his hair, pulling his mouth up to mine and experimenting in yet another style of kiss. It's slower but deeper, inquisitive and open, rather than greedy. He's an expert at it, and I feel the sensation all the way to my toes.

Carefully, I wrap my legs around his hips and cross my feet at the ankles, meshing us together so tightly it's hard to breathe. He trails his hand down my side and into the top of my jeans, and after a quick fiddle with my belt and the button, he's got them open for easier access.

Fingertips skim at the delicate lace of my underwear, hypersensitizing the skin underneath and pulling my hips up in an arch of desperation for more. It's everything and not enough all at once, and I breathe deeply to try to savor the moment instead of rushing it.

He pulls moisture from my center and sweeps it up over my clit, circling lightly and sending my body into the kind of hum that vibrates.

"Clay," I whisper with all the breath I have left, and he pauses with pressure and sinks into a groan.

"God, baby. My finger on your pussy and my name on your lips might just be the best combination to ever live."

I would laugh if I weren't so eager. Instead, my words come out like a beg. "I don't know, I'm pretty sure it'd be even better with your cock."

"Fuck," he damn near groans, pulling his hand from my pants enough to free himself from his own. I glance down at how hard he is in his hand and breathe both a sigh of relief and trepidation.

He's big. Possibly the biggest I've ever seen, and it's not like I've spent the last several years with micropenises.

I need to feel him to know for sure, but I've got a sneaking suspicion he's going to make me feel fuller than I've ever felt before.

"Please," I ask as he digs around in the back pocket of his jeans and comes out with a condom. Tearing the wrapper with his teeth, he sheathes himself quickly and efficiently before covering me again and pressing himself in gently but completely.

There's nothing left outside, just the base of him against my flesh, and I have to close my eyes against the most overwhelming feeling that this moment is going to be one I look back on and dream about.

"Damn, Josie Ellis. You feel just as pretty inside as you look outside, and I can promise you, that's saying something."

"Clay," I whimper.

"I want to make you feel so good," he tells me. "I want to make you feel so fucking good you go crazy, you understand me?"

I nod, desperate for him to move, my eyes latched on to where we're connected. "Clay, *please*."

"I want to make you come so hard you see stars—and not just the ones in the sky. I want you to feel me in your throat and your toes and everywhere in between."

"*Clay*. Please, I'm begging you, *move*."

His stroke is slow but strong, and my head falls back to the soft pad of his T-shirt.

"No, doll," he says. "I don't think I'm moving fucking anywhere." He's playing with my words, making them out to be something more than they are, and yet, I can't find it in myself to stop him.

Because being up here on this water tower with Clay Harris feels like something akin to flying in the sky, and I'm not sure I ever want to be anywhere else either.

I hold on tight as he moves in and out of me, digging my fingertips into the bare skin of his shoulders as he bows his face into my neck and groans.

"Fuck, Josie, you feel unreal."

My heart pounds as my climax approaches, and I dig my teeth into the soft skin of his shoulder to control the volume of my scream. Out here, everything echoes so loud. And I'm afraid if I let out the sound I could, we'll be the front page of the Sunday paper tomorrow morning. Eileen Martin is always so hungry for a damn story.

His grunts intensify as we both sprint toward the finish line, and my whole body shakes with the pinnacle of need for release.

It washes over me in a giant wave—we're talking tsunami—and he covers my mouth with his own as he tumbles over the cliff right after me. The sound of our mingled breaths is the only thing in the slightly chilly air, and a feeling of overwhelming rightness is all I can think of.

Never in my life has it felt like this.

A hard, grated water tower deck beneath us, and it was still that good?

Never in my life.

"Oh yeah." He's still inside me, still filling me up. But his eyes are entirely locked on mine. "I think I'm going to have to convince you to be mine."

"Clay—"

"No, baby, don't even try. Water towers are my favorite place, and you're officially my favorite thing."

The feeling is surprisingly and completely mutual. After tonight, I have a strong suspicion that I'm going to be seeing a whole hell of a lot of Clay Harris.

7

Clay

Wednesday, June 19th

Josie throws her head back and cackles as Sheriff Peeler regales her with his third whiskey-inspired tale of the night, and I pop the cap off a couple of Miller Lites and pass them across the bar while I watch.

"Thanks," Harold Metcalf says, and I reward him with a two-finger salute and a nod. I could be friendlier, seeing as his patronage is what keeps me in food and shit, but all I want is a little time with my obsession, and it's like all these fuckers are expecting me to actually tend bar.

I dole out two more mixed drinks and a bucket of beers for the boys in the back, and I finally find myself in front of the dazzling blonde with the magic smile and perfect eyes just as Sheriff Peeler gets scraped away by Hal Newton and Earl Lathers, the owner of our sweet little town's one and only grocery store.

"You know what I just figured out that I'm really afraid of?" I ask by way of greeting, earning a special glare from my gal.

"Clay. Come on already." She rolls her pretty little eyes at me. "Don't you think that joke is played out?"

Ever since our night on the water tower, I've been using the power of fear to experiment in the most exciting of sexual ways. It's not my fault, though. It's the only thing that helps, you know?

I wave her off and settle my elbows into the bar, leaning toward her as she plays with the stem of her cherry with the tip of her tongue. If she wants me to think about something other than sex, she's doing a really shit job.

"Nah, Jose. I'm for real. This isn't one of those made-up fears. This is legitimate."

She narrows her eyes. "Oh really?"

"Yeah," I say, punctuating the word with an enthusiastic nod. "I'm not messing around."

"All right. Fine. I'll bite," she says, and I sink my teeth into the flesh of my bottom lip to keep from smirking and getting myself in trouble. "What's got you so scared this time, Clay?"

I lean in, my face and voice grave as I whisper, "This bar full of people. It's feeling real claustrophobic-like, you know? As if the walls are closing in on us. I think I need to find somewhere to be alone, but alone in the way that it's with my mouth on your pussy."

"Clay!" she shrieks, smacking me in the shoulder as I stand up to my full height again and wink at her.

"I don't need long," I carry on, utterly loving the way her cheeks are now flushed pink. "Just a few minutes upstairs, and I swear I'll be feeling better."

"You're too much." Her laugh is music to my ears. "I don't know what I'm going to do with you."

"Take off your pants and fall on my face?" I suggest yet again, making her stand up from her stool with a shake of her head. I reach out and grab her by the hand. If she's on her feet, I've almost got her convinced. Just a little more sweet-talking and we'll be upstairs in a heartbeat. "Come on, doll. I'm scared if I don't taste you, I'm going to—"

"Clay," a deep voice interrupts from right behind her, pulling us both up short and making Josie spin around. It's not out of the ordinary these days for the two of us to get lost in each other even in the middle of The Country Club's crowd, but it's completely out of character for someone to interrupt.

We've been going strong *and* hot and heavy ever since that night on the water tower. The sheriff and Harold and Sue and everyone else…they've all overheard too many risqué things at this point to approach without warning anymore. It doesn't matter that it's only been about a month since I convinced her to go on that first date with me—Josie Ellis and I are damn near inseparable.

I stand up straighter and squint through the dim light to focus on the face in front of me. He looks a little worse for wear, and I haven't seen him in years, but it only takes a moment or two to register who it is.

Bennett Bishop, my best friend from childhood and my brother from another mother.

The guy I've been through more with in this lifetime than I've been through with anyone else in a million lifetimes put together. We did prep school and college together. We partied and messed up and grew up together. We made poor choices and spent our parents' money and fucked around until it got us both in way too much trouble.

I haven't seen him since I decided I couldn't live that life anymore and left New York three years ago, though we've texted and talked on rare occasions.

But now, he's here, standing in the middle of my bar with a baby-filled car seat in one hand and a diaper bag in the other, and everything we've been to each other for our entire lives comes rushing back in an instant.

I round the bar and go to him, pulling him into a hug only our kind of brotherhood can foster. I don't know why he's here and I don't know why he's holding a baby, but I know I'll do anything he needs once I find out.

"It's good to fucking see you, man," I say, and when I step back from the hug and grab his shoulders with my hands, I see tears in his eyes as he gathers himself.

"Good to see you too."

Bennett Bishop is not a man who cries. Not fucking ever. If people think I'm tough, Ben's made out of steel. Whatever's going on with him—whatever brought him here—is more than a middle finger to his father like it was for me. Whatever this is is serious.

Josie comes to stand beside me, and after staring at Bennett for a long beat, she turns directly to me. Her face is gentle and considerate, but it's also teasing. "I'm open-minded, Clay, but if you tell me this is your lover and your baby, we're going to have to figure some stuff out."

Bennett's eyebrows draw together, and I guffaw, pulling Josie up and under my arm as I introduce them.

"Josie, this is my best friend, Bennett. We grew up together in New York. He's the closest thing to a brother I'll ever have, and I haven't seen him since I left."

"And the baby?" Josie asks, glancing between the two of us a few times before her eyes latch on to the little baby doll in the car seat. I'm no expert when it comes to babies, but this little lady dressed in a pink outfit is so small, I wouldn't be surprised if she was literally born yesterday.

I smile down at the baby, taking in the way her eyes are closed shut with sleep and the way her blond hair makes her look downright angelic. I move my eyes back to Bennett. "You didn't steal her, did you?"

Josie smacks me in the chest. "Clay."

"She's mine," Bennett affirms then, looking down in awe before looking back at me and Josie. "And it's a long story. But man, I could really use your help. I can't go back to New York. Summer and I…her name's Summer…we can't go back to New York."

"Say no more," I reply without hesitation, ready and willing to do whatever's necessary.

Josie rolls her eyes and pushes me again. "While that's a sweet sentiment, the whole *say no more* thing, I'm personally hoping you'll say a little more. What do you need? A place to stay? A job? Something else? The more we know, the better we'll be able to help you."

"Yeah," I agree then. "What she said."

Josie shoots me a look, and I know in an instant the best thing I can do is shut up. Bennett may be brand-new to Josie's life, but with one word about how important he is to me, she's ready to welcome him and Summer with open arms.

Family to me is family to her. Just like that.

Funny thing—when I'm not messing around, I'm not feeling afraid of much of anything anymore. Josie Ellis makes sure of that.

After The Moment: Part 1

The "It's Only Been Four Months" Pain

8

Josie

Tuesday, April 11th

Eileen Martin snaps a photo of the glass bakery case at the front, and I straighten the mason jars filled with flowers on the tables with a million watts of nervous energy.

For the last three months, I've poured my every waking moment and even more dollars into building the coffee shop I've always dreamed of. It's been both a labor of love and just plain old labor, and opening it today seems like the conclusion of a journey that was years in the making.

I spent many hours and days and weeks and months and years sketching designs and dreaming up drinks, and to say that it's actually happening now feels surreal. Grandma Rose would be so proud to see me making it come to fruition, even if it means I'm twenty grand in debt and scared to death.

But I did it. At twenty-eight years old, I'm officially a proud

Red Bridge business owner of a brand-new coffee shop named CAFFEINE.

Sheriff Peeler pokes his head in the door and smiles, and I straighten my deep green apron down my hips. "Hey, Josie. You about ready to do the ribbon ceremony? Crowd's started to crow and holler out here about needing some caffeine."

He smirks at his little pun, having used the name of my shop playfully.

I smile, take one last look around at the brick walls, wood beams, and my very first barista and close friend from the diner Todd behind the counter, and nod. "Yep. I think CAFFEINE is officially ready to open."

"Well, all right then. I'll tell 'em to get the ribbon ready," Pete replies, knocking once on the wood frame of the door before stepping back into the group of townspeople who've gathered outside.

I look around for a brief moment to find someone to share my excitement, and it's only then that I feel the ever-present pit in my stomach—there isn't anyone.

Not my dad or my grandma or either of my sisters…and not Clay either.

The last one is my fault and, nearly four months since making it so, still for the best. But it doesn't make the pain feel any better.

I put a splayed hand on the surface of my stomach and take a deep breath. "This is good, Josie," I say to myself, my voice so quiet I can hardly even hear it. "You're doing the things you always talked about and moving on with your life." I feel the dull ache of my always-present emptiness, and I hate that even now, in the midst of making one of my biggest dreams come true, memories of the bright, piercing, terrifying light when I was in *that* room all by myself threaten to take over my thoughts. I swallow hard against the painful onslaught and tell myself it doesn't get any worse than that. This is the dream. This is happy. This is *not* that. "You're—"

"Josie?" Sheriff Peeler says, startling me, his head poking through the open door again. "You ready? You're about to have a riot out here."

"Yeah," I answer, and I have to clear the discomfort from my throat. "Of course. Let's do it."

Pete smiles again and backs out the door, and this time, I follow him. I see tons of familiar faces in a sweet little crowd and a beautiful pink ribbon out in front of the store. Fran and Peggy, two of the other small business owners in town, hold each end, and Eileen bends down at the edge of the sidewalk to get the best angle for the camera shot.

I make a point to smile at faces I know—Harold and Felix and Pete and Melba and even Betty Bagley—as I make my little speech.

"I just want to thank all of you for being here for me on this really special day. Opening this coffee shop has always been a dream of mine, and putting it into action has been my whole life for the last few months. I hope you'll stop by each morning to see me, and that it'll be the kind of start to your day that puts a smile on your face."

"We love you, honey!" Melba claps, and I shrug a little self-consciously.

"So, yeah…" I look around the crowd, not sure who I'm even looking for, "I guess it's time to cut the ribbon!"

Todd taps me on the shoulder to hand me a pair of scissors, and I snip the cute little strip dramatically. Instantly, tears hit my eyes, and everyone breaks into applause this time.

Summer's toddler cheer is especially loud, almost like the shriek of a giant bird, and my gaze snaps to the back of the crowd at the sound. She waves, the tiny pink cast on her right arm sending me straight into a pool of emotion I'm not ready for at all.

I've missed her so much over the last few months and thought of her often, but it hasn't felt quite right to keep myself inserted in Bennett's life when he's so close with Clay. Losing him means losing everything.

Bennett stands behind Summer's stroller, and I don't miss Clay's presence beside him or the fact that his mouth is set in a firm but handsome line. I have to look away from the three of them before I start crying right here in front of everyone. I'm not surprised he's here—he's on the Red Bridge city council committee that does all of these small business ribbon-cutting ceremonies—but I am surprised he's hung around this long.

Instead, I focus on welcoming the first customers into the store and rounding the counter to get to work. I have drinks to make and people to serve, and living in the past isn't going to do anyone even one ounce of good.

We can't go back. The finality of the papers I handed him in Grandma Rose's kitchen four months ago made that reality.

I smile at Melba as she approaches the counter, her eyes glowing with a special sheen of tears I know is for my grandma. She clutches her chest, and I reach out to grab her wrist.

"Don't," I say softly, not wanting yet another reason to cry.

"She'd just be so proud of you, is all."

I nod. She would be. Grandma Rose was my best friend and my biggest supporter, and having to live without her for the last almost seven months is a crime I'll never forgive the universe for committing.

"All right, then. Enough of that." She waves one hand in the air. "What can I try that's not coffee? My stomach doesn't handle it too well, and I don't wanna have to make a doo-doo in the square."

Her commentary is a relief that leaves my body in the form of shocked laughter. "Melba!"

"Just wait, dear," she says with a shameless shrug of her petite shoulders. "Not even your bowel movements are reliable when you get to be my age."

"How about one of our specialty lemonades?" I suggest, moving the conversation along to something that doesn't revolve around Melba's intestines. "They're homemade and perfect for a warmer day like today."

I point up to the menu behind me, and Melba pulls her reading glasses out of her purse, sets them on the bridge of her nose, and scans through the options before settling on one. "I think I'm going to try the Pink Flamingo."

"That's a good one." I smile. "Strawberry and cherry lemonade topped with a little lemon sweet cream cold foam."

Melba knocks her knuckles on the counter. "Yep. I like the sound of it."

"Pink Flamingo!" I yell out to Todd behind me, ringing the very first purchase into my cash register. "That'll be $5.75."

Melba rummages around in her change purse, dumping four dollars' worth of quarters and two dollars' worth of nickels and dimes on the counter, and each coin clinks against the wood musically. The woman is known for her change, and I don't mind counting it all out for her. Though, when I start to hand her a quarter back, she shakes her head. "No, no, dear. You keep it as a tip."

It's so sweet, but also...so cheap. Right in line with what I know of my grandma's dear friend Melba, and the thought warms my body from my heart to my lips to my eyes. Some things, I suppose, stay the same even in the wake of a whirlwind of change.

Maybe one day, it won't feel this hard at all. Maybe one day, I'll feel whole again.

9

Clay

Tuesday, April 11th

The whole town is here, supporting Josie in her coffee shop's big debut, and I feel like a schmuck standing in the background when all I want to do is be the man at her side.

Watching Josie move on with her life so completely is indescribably difficult. It's not that I don't want good things for her…I do. I just want her to have all the good things she deserves and still be with me, too. And standing here on the fringe of CAFFEINE's opening, a useless extra in her story, feels downright sadistic.

Yet here I am, like a heartbroken fool, staring toward the only woman I want to be with but who doesn't want to be with me.

"What time is your appointment?" I ask Bennett, trying to distract myself from the absolute burning rage and anguish I feel poisoning my veins.

"In about an hour and a half. We'll probably take off here in a minute," Bennett answers, and I nod, turning back to look at the front of CAFFEINE again. My focus goes straight to Josie's warm smile through the open door. Seeing her look at Pete that way and knowing she'll never do it while she looks at me again makes me rub at the pressure in my chest. Bennett's eyes are narrowed when I turn back toward him. "You know, Clay, I think you should probably take off too."

"I'm fine," I say, my jaw locked.

Bennett laughs in my face, the bastard. "You look ready to spit bullets. Put yourself out of your misery and go home. Or anywhere else. Just leave here."

I take a deep breath and refocus my energy. Away from Josie and back to Bennett and Summer and the most important things in front of us—her hard road with Osteogenesis Imperfecta Type III and supporting my best friend and his daughter in all the ways that I can. "So, what exactly did Dr. Brock say? You're going to have to keep doing this all the time?"

"Yeah," Bennett answers, swiveling Summer around in her stroller and handing her another plushie. Most of the time now, it's safer for her delicate bones if she only plays with soft toys. She smiles a toothy grin up at us, and I fall a little more in love with her. "He said the best way to be proactive is to have Summer do monthly scans. We went ahead and booked a standing appointment for the second Tuesday of every month. We can change it if we need to, obviously, but that way, we're staying on top of any new breaks she might have gotten every month."

"And, what? That's it? You don't do any other treatments or anything?" I question, my mind still trying to understand how this beautiful, vibrant little girl has been dealt such a shit hand. The instant Bennett told me about her diagnosis when he first came to Red Bridge, I spent hours and days researching it all on Google. Most people know it as brittle bone disease, and unfortunately for sweet Summer, she has one of the most advanced cases of it.

Honestly, with the innovations in medicine and technology, it rattles my fucking skull that all her treatment plan revolves around is being proactive. Surely there should be a damn cure by now.

"I guess it'll be a take it as it comes kind of thing." Bennett shrugs, his jaw working furiously to keep himself in check.

Summer's pain is his pain. And even though she's just about the happiest little girl you'll ever meet, her daily struggles and limitations are challenging. She'll never be a normal kid. She'll never get to play at the playground or be on a sports team. Her life revolves around being as cautious as possible.

"He says we can brace and cast where appropriate, but one of our best weapons is just handling her with care to try to prevent the breaks in the first place," Bennett adds, and I clap a gentle hand to his shoulder and squeeze. There's nothing else I can say, you know? All I can do is be there for him and Summer as much as I can.

"Daddy! Go!" Summer exclaims and claps her hands. Her little pink cast knocks her plushie onto the ground, and Bennett picks it up and hands it back to her.

"We're going to go in just a minute, baby," he says and gently brushes his hand against her cheek, his eyes warming in a way they only do for his daughter.

I glance back through the open door of the coffee shop with a different perspective, found in the eyes and soul of a father's love, and everything I'll never have with Josie—*the family I'll never have*—hits me right in the face.

I just don't fucking understand how it all went so wrong.

"Uncie Clayyyy!" Summer calls from down below, grabbing my attention again and making me squat in front of her.

"What's up, pretty girl?"

She holds up her plushie in front of me and smiles. "Pink puppy."

"Yep." I grin at her and make a show of shaking her pink puppy's paw. "Nice to meet you, Mr. Pink Puppy."

"She a gurl!" Summer exclaims. "Gurl like Summer!"

"Oh, sorry," I apologize with dramatic wide eyes before smiling at her puppy. "Nice to meet you, *Mrs.* Pink Puppy. And what a cute girl puppy you are."

She giggles. "Daddyyy Clay Daddy Clay," she babbles, and I nod again before Bennett sighs heavily as he checks the time on his watch.

"All right. Yeah. We better go. I don't know what traffic will be like getting into Burlington." He turns serious eyes to me. "But, really, you should leave too."

I glance inside the store again, watching as Earl stares up at the menu with his hands in his back pockets, holding up the line behind him. A crowd full of people showed up here today, and still, I imagine she's feeling the absence of Grandma Rose pretty acutely. I wish I could be there for her—wish I could help. "Maybe I'll just go in and order a drink. Be neighborly, friendly-like, you know?"

"No, man. I *don't* know." Bennett's voice is incredulous. "Because I don't think that's a good idea at all."

"We're going to have to be civil at some point, I'd think," I say, ignoring the burning indignation I feel every time I look at her to spout some bullshit.

Unfortunately for me, Ben isn't buying it at all.

"Yeah, but I don't think we're at *some point* yet," Bennett says. "Really, Clay." I turn back to look at him, and his face is hard with warning. "This is a special day for her, and despite all the bullshit, you seem to still really care about her. Maybe you should just let her have this moment."

I sigh and slide my hands into the pockets of my jeans. I mean, Bennett is right. I don't want to ruin this for her any more than I wanted to get the stupid divorce papers from her four months ago in the first place. I love her and, at least right now, it feels like I always will.

"I'll behave, okay? You guys get going to your appointment and don't worry about me."

Bennett shakes his head but sighs again. "All right, Sum. Let's hit it."

Summer waves her chubby uncasted arm at me excitedly, and I grin at her so big my face hurts. She's a constant happy piece in a puzzle full of negative emotions. "Bye-bye, Uncie Clayyy!"

"Bye, baby girl. You and your daddy be sure to come over for dinner soon, okay?"

Summer nods, babbling, "Dindin, daddy, doooo."

"I think that's a yes." I laugh and Bennett smiles.

"We'll come over next Monday when the bar's closed."

"Sounds good."

"But seriously, behave yourself." Bennett claps me on the shoulder one last time before walking away to head to his truck, and I turn back to face CAFFEINE one last time, my hands on my hips.

Maybe I can just congratulate her? Be the bigger person for a shadow of a moment and then get the hell out of here. Surely I can do that.

Right?

Right. Of course. I've loved this woman for years. She may not want to be with me anymore, but maybe, I don't know, she just needed time?

Maybe I can show her how big of a person I can be, and she'll realize that we really are supposed to be together…

I glance back to make sure Bennett and Summer are gone—to rule out my best friend's thwarting—and then head for the door, falling in line behind Deputy Felix Rice and Sheila Higgins. Josie doesn't notice me back here; she's too busy, and that's probably a good thing. The goal is to get in and out of this unscathed, not to make a scene.

I'm just going to show my support. That's it.

To distract myself from the woman behind the counter, I strike up a conversation with Sheila Higgins, who stands directly in front of me in line. "Hey, Sheil, how's it going?"

"It's okay, I guess." She shrugs, a little frown turning down one side of her mouth. "Marty's a little down and out because he got laid off from the plant."

"Oh, no way," I say, feeling genuine sadness for them. If Phelps is laying people off, it's bound to affect a lot of folks in town. "Marty's a good guy and a good worker. I'm sure he'll get back on his feet soon."

Sheila's smile is brittle. "That's what I've been telling him, but he's having a little bit of an existential crisis over it. Says he wants to try doing something else entirely."

"A whole new career path?" I question, and she nods.

"I don't know exactly what his plan is, but I'm hoping he comes up with something soon." Her mouth forms a grimace. "Money's bound to get tight, if you know what I mean."

Instantly, an idea pops into my head. "You know, why don't you tell him to come down to the bar and talk to me? I'm slammed most nights, and being the only one making drinks is getting a little overwhelming."

"Are you serious?" Sheila asks, and for the first time since I stepped into this line, the stress lines around her eyes have lifted.

"Of course I am, Sheil. I mean, I don't know if he'd be interested in bartending, but maybe I could take him on at least part time if it sounds like something Marty would want to do."

"Oh my God, Clay!" she cries, jumping up to hug me. "That would be amazing."

I feel a little high off Sheila's joy, thrilled that I could be a bright spot in her down-and-out day. I hug her right back, but when I look over her shoulder, Josie is staring at me, hard. We lock eyes, and my mood instantly shifts from happy to bone-deep fucking sad.

And every single part of my plan when I first came in here, when I first stepped into her coffee shop line, goes right out the window.

I don't know how to be here. I don't know how to be anywhere.

Truth is, I don't know how to be without Josie at all.

10

Josie

Tuesday, April 11th

Clay steps back from Sheila, his jaw turning rigid as I'm unable to tear my eyes away from him. He's a kind human with a big heart and an even bigger personality, and while I don't know exactly what led to Sheila Higgins hugging him so tightly, I'm not surprised to see it either.

He's always been generous with the people of Red Bridge, even more so after becoming a city councilman, and community outreach is an important part of his persona.

I didn't think in my wildest dreams, though, that he'd take his sense of duty this far. Seeing him, like this, standing in line in my brand-new business to patronize it on its maiden voyage just under four months after I forced him out of my life…it's got me feeling some kind of way.

Ooey, gooey, *dangerous* feelings. Ones that are a stark reminder of the four-letter-word I still hold in my heart for him.

And in an attempt to smother each and every vestige of the notion, I lock my heart in the attic of my chest and throw away the key, hardening my every emotion with ice until I'm cold all the way through. I don't need Elsa to work her magic—I'm already an ice queen.

Sheila turns around as she realizes that Felix is done and gone, and she runs up to the counter, a huge smile on her face and tears of gratitude in her eyes. It's all I can do not to ask her why—not to invite more conversation that I know will make me melt—and my whole body shakes as I take her order for one of my specialty coffees made with brown sugar and cinnamon and try to carry on like I'm not dying inside.

My body is on autopilot, calling the order to Todd and writing Sheila's name on the cup before taking her cash, the heavy heat of Clay's eyes burning right through me the whole time. I know I'm currently making small talk with her and thanking her for stopping by, but truthfully, I wouldn't be able to recall what I'm even saying if Sheriff Peeler had to interrogate me about it.

I take a deep breath and steel myself against the sting of tears in my nose, licking my lips and smoothing my apron down my body with almost untenable anxiety when I turn away to grab her drink from Todd.

And I have to swallow hard as I hand it over the counter with a smile that feels as if it could crack like an eggshell. "Thanks again for stopping by, Sheila."

"Of course! Congratulations, Josie!" she exclaims before turning on her heel to leave me out in the open to my next customer. I feel like I'm living a real-life nightmare, the one where you're naked in public and everyone is staring at you. But my heart is the only thing that's bared, and Clay's eyes might as well be the optical version of a hawk.

Just breathe, Josie. Just breathe.

His face is a mask of unknowns as he steps up to the counter, and I discreetly inhale much-needed oxygen, even though the room feels like someone has sucked out all of the air.

"Hi," I say simply, hoping it doesn't sound like I feel. "What can I get you?"

I know it's distant. I know it's cold. I know it must sting. But it feels incredibly reasonable right now, given it's the only viable way for me to survive.

His jaw clenches hard, pinching the skin of his tanned cheek into a dimple I know he doesn't have. "Is that really how it's going to be?" he asks bluntly, and it's not that I don't expect it—Clay's never been one to beat around the bush. But, still, it feels akin to a nuclear bomb...absolutely impossible to withstand.

My hackles rise as a method of self-defense. It's the only option left before crumbling right here. "You didn't have to come in here, you know."

My lashing lands just as I'd expect, breaking open more than just the skin, and Clay has to take a step back to keep himself in check. The less he recognizes the woman he fell in love with, the better off we'll be. To be fair, at least, I don't recognize her either.

"I was trying to do the right thing," he says, but there's nothing gentle about his delivery.

"The right thing at this point would be to leave me alone." Every word burns, but I force them out all the same, watching as they turn the most loving man I've ever known into someone else entirely.

There are some wounds you can't heal, and I hate with every fiber of my being that that's what I'm hoping for.

"You know what, Jose? If you want to be left alone, I'll leave you alone," he spits. "Not just now either. I'll do you one better and never fucking set foot in CAFFEINE again. How's that?"

His voice is much louder now, and the dull roar of other chatter in the café slows to a stop. I don't dare look around to see who's watching—I already know it'll be everyone.

"That's perfect," I say instead, not feeling a single truth in my words. "I don't want to see you, Clay, and the sooner you get that through your head, the better. You stay out of here and I'll stay out of The Country Club, and both of us can move on with our lives."

He stares at me for a long moment, time ticking slower than it's ever ticked before.

And when he finally opens his mouth, he says two words that should bring me relief, but all they do is slice my chest open and make me bleed.

"We're done," he replies, his voice choked with so much pain.

"Yeah, Clay," I agree, forcing myself to ignore the clawing ache of emotion that wants to migrate up my throat. "We are *so* done."

Spinning on his heel, he shoves through the two people behind him without any care or regard, and I hold my breath so completely I don't know if it'll ever start again.

Just like that, he's gone, out of my coffee shop and out of my life.

I can't wait for the day this won't hurt so fucking much.

Before The Moment: Part 2

The Love

11

Clay

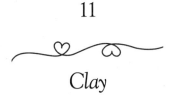

Monday, September 22nd

"Here you go, man," I say as I hand off a freshly made bottle to Bennett.

He takes it gratefully and walks over to where Summer sits in her little swinging chair. She's starting to fuss a little, having just woken up from a nap, and I head back into the kitchen, choosing to make myself useful at the sink while he feeds her.

It's been three months since Bennett showed up in my bar with a baby. Three months of getting reacquainted with my old friend and falling in love with his extremely special little girl, and three months of learning I'm not nearly as good at shit as I once thought.

Summer has a coo and a baby grin that can light up any room, and more patience than I've ever known an infant to have—a very important trait for dealing with her father and me. Ben's effort score is high, but execution, as it were, still leaves a little something to be desired.

Our past lives in no way prepared us for taking care of a baby—and in this case, a special needs baby—at all. Summer was diagnosed at birth with Osteogenesis Imperfecta Type III, and because of that, all the normal care that comes with a delicate newborn is even more tenuous.

Ben and I were wild. We partied and drank and spent our parents' money recklessly while they lived their lives like they didn't have kids. We had nannies to do our bidding and assistants when we got older. Both of us were tailspinning in our parents' footsteps of wealthy neglect and disdain.

It wasn't something we chose, but it wasn't something we understood either. After moving here and opening The Country Club as a final *stick-it* moment to my father, my entire outlook on life and how it should be lived changed. It's not about money or things or even me. It's about time spent with good people and finding the ways to make a difference in their lives.

Bennett and Summer stayed with me for the first few nights, but a cramped apartment above a bar isn't exactly the ideal location for a newborn baby. Ben, fortunately, thanks to a lucrative art career, isn't destitute by any means. But it took some time with Hillary Howard, Red Bridge's resident real estate agent, and a load of patience to find the right place to call his own.

This farmhouse is old and in need of some reno, but it's the perfect setup to create the kind of accommodations Summer is expected to need as she gets older.

Bennett pops his head in the kitchen. His scruffy beard and haggard eyes are two of many signs that he's not getting a whole lot of sleep these days. "How many scoops of formula did you put in this?"

"Um..." I freeze in my scrubbing of Summer's previous bottle. "Two...I think?"

"You think, or you know?" Bennett grumbles, stepping up to the sink and dumping the obviously wrong liquid down the drain in front of me. "They put instructions on the can of formula for a reason."

Shit. I wince. "I never was much of a reader, you know that. That's why I had to get Gina Rapuano to do my English homework every night."

He sighs. "You got Gina Rapuano to do your English homework every night because you liked to make out with her and feel her up."

"I mean..." I laugh and offer a wry smile. "There were multiple benefits."

"Just remake the bottle, please?" he asks, and a singular, soft chuckle is the only sign of his amusement as he sets it down next to the sink. And just as he turns to head out of the room, Summer's cries pierce the air. "A speedy remake of the bottle would be nice, too," he calls over his shoulder.

Quickly, I grab the bottle and go back to the can of formula, reading the directions this time. *"Use one level scoop of unpacked powder per two ounces of water. Your baby's health depends on carefully following these directions."* The castigation is quick and deserved, and I feel my face warm with embarrassment at being called out by a fucking can of formula.

Carefully, I add six ounces of water and three scoops before capping the thing and shaking it up vigorously. Ben is still busy, I can tell from the sounds of crying and his desperate pleas to calm Summer down in the living room, so I walk the bottle in to him.

He's doing his best to secure a fresh diaper, but there's a glob of yellowish-brown baby shit on the couch underneath and another streak on the back of his hand. I jump back, but he waves me forward, eager for some backup. "Clay, come here. I need you to take her while I clean all this up."

"Oh no. No, no." I shake my head and hold up both hands. "I really don't think I should hold your baby."

"Clay."

"Ben, no."

"Clay, take her right now." Holding a baby is intimidating enough, but holding Summer is even more so. Because of her condition, her bones are extremely apt to break if handled with even the slightest roughness. I don't know what I'd do with myself if I somehow—

Ben gently forces Summer into my arms and steps away, waving his hand with poop in my face as he does, and I bob and weave while trying to float on fucking air. I don't want to jostle her. My heart pounds as she looks up at me with her sweet little doe eyes, and her mouth works restlessly, searching for something to eat. The bottle sits on the side table at the end of the couch, but I've never fed a baby before and doing it now feels like I need a special license or something.

"Ben, I think she's hungry. Maybe you should—"

"Handle it!" he yells back ruthlessly.

Fuck. "There, there," I try to comfort, swaying my hips with my arms locked to my chest. I'm hoping it'll create some motion without actually moving her.

As Summer's agitation grows, so does my desperation, and I pick up the bottle on the table and try to figure out how to hold it. It seems like it should be simple, but she struggles to drink at first, and I have to adjust the bottle a little higher for her to get a good suction on it.

As she starts to drink, a wave of overwhelming satisfaction and affection settles over me. "Yeah, that's it, sweet girl. Drink all you want."

I stare down into her little baby face and bright eyes, wondering how in the world her mother could say the kinds of things Bennett told me she did—how she could think Summer was anything but perfect. How she could just…give her up.

It doesn't make a lick of fucking sense, and if I think about it too hard, I'm liable to get angry enough to hunt down Jessica Folger and have it out with her.

Just then, Summer starts to cough a little, sputtering out the nipple and spitting up, formula coming back out and shooting all over her chin and hands and up the sleeve of my shirt.

"Oh, oh shit! Ben, you better get in here. She's throwing up or something!"

Bennett comes down the hall at a run and swoops her gently away from me, and I put a hand to my forehead and pace as he tries to figure out the problem.

"What's wrong?"

"I don't know," Ben says, fussed. "She's never had an issue with this formula before."

Not liking this at all, I get on the phone and call someone I feel like might be able to help us clueless fuckers.

My girl. Josie Ellis.

12

Josie

Monday, September 22nd

Bennett and Clay hover over me as I put the thermometer to Summer's forehead gently and wait for a reading. It beeps pretty quickly and comes back normal.

"Well?" Bennett asks, frantic to make whatever's wrong with his little girl right, and I have to smother a smile not to laugh at Clay when he bugs out his eyes dramatically.

"Is she okay, Jose? Do we need to take her to the hospital?"

They're a walking sideshow of worry, and Bennett's farmhouse is their stage. And this isn't the first house call I've had to make for them. Ever since Bennett and Summer arrived in Red Bridge, I've handled my fair share of panicked moments related to the care of this special little girl.

"She's fever-free and doesn't need to go to the hospital," I tell them. "Honestly, she might have just choked on it a little when it was going down—"

"Choked?" Bennett cries, aghast.

I stand and busy myself with closing a curtain to block the piercing ray of dwindling sunlight that was shooting right in Summer's face, and she coos and squeaks in my arms. Pulling the curtain *and* moving is a little counterproductive, but I'd rather be doing anything than looking at this panicked version of Bennett directly in the eye.

"Orrrr she just has a little bit of an upset tummy," I offer, keeping my voice as calm and soft as I can. Ben is the sleeping bear that's already been woken, and Clay looks like he's one baby cough away from curling up in the fetal position. "A little bit of spit-up is completely normal in babies her age. Now, if it's regular in frequency or projectile or something, then it's more of a cause for concern."

"How projectile?" Clay asks. "I mean, it definitely shot onto my arm." He holds out his sleeve as proof, and I finally let myself smile.

"Your whole body would be coated."

He frowns. "They can do that?"

I laugh. "Oh yeah."

"How do you know so much about babies?" Bennett asks, taking Summer back from me and tucking her carefully into the special straps of her braced swing.

"I babysat. I had a younger sister." Truth is, I had *two* younger sisters. One died when I was young, and my mom makes sure the other one is dead to me. But I'm not exactly ready to get into all that right now. "Plus, they do a pretty good job of explaining this on a place called the internet."

Bennett makes a face, and Clay chuckles, shoving Ben in the shoulder and nodding his head toward me. "I told you she's funny, Ben. A real cutup good time."

Bennett glares before leaving the room with the discarded bottle, and Clay waggles his eyebrows at me as soon as he's gone, strolling over and wrapping me up in the kind of hug that envelops me completely. I can smell and feel him, and it's pretty much become the place I'm happiest on this earth in the last few months. "Don't worry about him," he assures, jerking his chin toward Bennett in the other room. "He's grumbly with everybody."

"Not with Summer," I hedge. Honestly, if it weren't for his daughter, I'd probably think Bennett Bishop was a total a-hole. But the way he softens for her, the way he spends every waking moment of his days prioritizing her needs, tells me he might be a real grouch, but his heart is made of gold.

"No, not with Summer." Clay agrees. "He'd fight the whole damn world off for her, I'm pretty sure."

Knowing what we now know about the diagnosis she got at birth, and what a tough road it is for her and for her loved ones, makes the sentiment all the more bittersweet. I did some research as soon as Bennett gave us the whole story, and it's a guaranteed long and hard journey. I don't blame him for being the way he is—he's carrying the impossible on his shoulders. Type III is the most severe and progressive form of OI that can be survived past birth and has an almost invoiceable prognosis. The chances that Summer will live to teenagerdom are extremely low.

"You know, he should consider hiring a nurse or an aide or something," I say. "Not, like, full time or as a replacement for doing stuff himself, but it would probably put his mind at ease a lot when it comes to some of the more nuanced things about her diagnosis."

Clay's face is warm and loving as he touches his lips to mine and pulls back to whisper, "That's a good idea, baby. I'll tell him." He considers me for a moment before moving us around to hold me close, my back to his chest. His breath is a comfort as he whispers into the skin beside my ear. "You tired?"

"Yeah. I think I'm going to go home and put my feet up for a while. I never should have worn my new shoes to an entire shift at The Diner without breaking them in first."

"Why don't you come home with me? Bar's closed tonight, and we need to take advantage," Clay whispers, curling the corners of my lips up in a smile. I turn to peek at Summer, who's now sleeping peacefully in her swing, and then look back to Clay. His eyes look like hot honey in the now-dim room.

"I maybe could. Grandma Rose *is* at bingo tonight with Melba."

"See that?" He presses a kiss to my nose. "I love when a plan shapes up so nicely."

I giggle. "But what about Ben? Does he need your help?"

"I'm pretty sure at this point Ben would be happier to be without my help tonight."

"Why?" I snort. "What'd you mess up this time?"

He shrugs, spinning me to face him. "The bottle. A little. Maybe. But I remade it really carefully the second time."

"I swear, watching the two of you is like watching baby ducks trying to learn to swim. Or…like Tom Selleck and Steve Guttenberg try to take care of Mary."

His chin jerks back, confusion about my reference rife in his features, and my mouth drops open, appalled.

"If you tell me you haven't seen *Three Men and a Baby*, we might have to break up," I threaten.

He should be scared, but instead, he smiles. "Break up, huh? Are we official?"

"Don't change the subject, Clay. Have you seen the movie or not?"

His eyes narrow. "We can watch it tonight."

I pull away in a tease, grabbing my purse from Ben's taupey-tan living room couch and slinging it over my shoulder. "Well, that was a close call. To think I almost ended up with a man who hasn't seen—"

Clay scoops me up and over his shoulder, and I shriek as he carries me right past Ben in the kitchen and out the back door. "Sorry, Ben, we gotta go! I have to get Josie out of here before she loses her mind and says something she'll regret!"

I pound at his back, but Bennett cracks a smile and waves, and I devolve into giggles at the sight. Seeing Bennett lean toward cheerful is like spotting a baby at the top of Mt. Everest. It doesn't happen, and maybe even deserves a call to the cops.

I'm beginning to think Clay Harris and his boldly beautiful personality can brighten even the gloomiest of rooms.

It's a superpower not held by many, and even though we've only been dating for a few months, it makes a future life without him look pretty damn bleak.

13

Clay

Monday, September 22nd

I kiss Josie's chin and her neck and her collarbone and run a hand along the line of her perfect thigh as she straddles my hips. She's laughing—my favorite sound in the world—and I'd do almost anything to keep it going.

"Okay, you were right," I whisper between kisses. "Seeing *Three Men and a Baby* is definitely a relationship deal-breaker."

She shoves me in the chest, and I grab her hand and pull her in to seal my lips to hers again. Our tongues tangle in a fight for kiss dominance, but when I put my hand to her ass and pull her up to meet me, she relents and lets me win.

I reward her selflessness, deepening the kiss until it starts to tingle, and we have to come up for air before we're depleted of oxygen.

Watching her with Summer today…everything I've thought

about how special she might be and how hard I need to fight to keep her in my life was affirmed tenfold. Her confidence and gentle nature and even her ability not to laugh too hard in Ben's and my faces at our ineptitude—it's exceptional and speaks volumes about what a life truly shared with her would be like.

Growing up, I never thought I'd be a one-woman kind of guy. I lived hard and fast, and I chewed my way through Manhattan with all the gluttony my parents instilled in me. I figured I'd end up dead or arrested at some point, but at least I'd enjoy the journey to get there.

But since distancing myself from mommy dearest and my nothing-but-money-is-ever-good-enough dad, I've found that living that way wasn't living at all.

I still had my doubts that I'd end up with one woman—but I guess I hadn't met her yet. Josie Ellis is the kind of woman who changes the way you think about a lot of things.

I lay her down on my couch, her back pressing into the cushions, and open her legs. I sink myself inside her, bare for just a wonder of a moment to feel all of her. She lets me, and I imagine what it would be like to come inside her and make little babies of our own.

Surprisingly, it's the opposite of scary.

I stroke once, twice, and then a third time, and her head falls back on the sexiest moan I've ever heard in my life. It'd be so easy to keep going, to let myself go inside her—but we've got a little bit to prioritize before we get there.

I know it, and I respect it. I haven't even asked her to be mine. I haven't even told her I love her—and I do. With my whole heart and soul. Nothing has ever felt so right.

"You feel so fucking good, doll, but I have to put on a condom."

Her eyes pop open in surprise, almost as though she forgot I wasn't wearing one, and I kiss the tip of her nose as I slip out of her. Her face fades at the loss, and I can't wait another second to tell her how I feel.

"I love you, Josie."

Her eyes are even wider now, rife with surprise and overwhelm, and I take the pressure off by pressing my lips to hers again. This isn't a situation with pressure. This is a moment of open honesty and heartfelt affection.

I scoot back and slide on a condom before pressing into her again, and I go about showing her I love her with more than just words.

Because, the thing is, she tells me she loves me every day in the way she talks to me, the altruism she gives, the way she holds space for me to be myself even when it's over the top or annoying. She's the yin to my yang, and I don't need to hear her say it to know it.

Josie loves me too.

She's a woman of action and affection—a strength and depth of character I can only dream of having. She breathes life into me in ways I never dreamed were possible, and I want to be the same for her.

"Clay," she says softly, a tiny fleck of a tear shimmering in just the corner of her eye as I love her with my body over and over again. I pull her leg higher on my hip to press deeper, to feel her more, and she gasps at the change before her eyes soften with warmth and pleasure.

I run a finger gently along the line of her chin and lift her mouth to mine, pressing the kind of kiss to her lips I imagine would happen between the angels way up in the clouds. It's light and airy and somehow just as deep as all the aggressive ones we've shared before.

Her lips are gentle and so are mine, and a buzz takes shape in the bottom of my spine as we climb toward our climax together. I press myself deeper, my strokes growing harder and faster, but my eyes never leave hers.

"You're so beautiful," I tell her, studying the green intensity of her eyes like it'll tell me everything I need to know about life and then some. Her irises are beautiful nets and webs, an intricate mess of tiny green fibers of all different shades, with a golden fleck just beside the pupil in only the left eye. A literal twinkle in her eye.

Right there. This. This is heaven.

"Come with me, baby," I encourage softly. "Together. In sync. You and me."

"Clay," she exhales, a desperation in the sound of my name that makes me speed up—just a little.

In and out, in and out, the cadence just right, she builds and builds, and I stare into her eyes, our breaths mingling in the most impeccable combination. I have to fight against the intense pleasure that's growing inside me, every nerve ending in my body ready for release.

But I won't go without her. I *refuse* to go anywhere without her.

"I love you," I say again, confirming it wasn't an accidental slip of my tongue or a plea for confirmation. It's a feeling, a need, a truth. I need it in the air, out between us, in the stroke of our bodies, and I need it out there over and over. "I love you so much, Josie Ellis."

She moans then, and her body shakes and trembles as pleasure washes over her. Her head falls back and her eyes close, and I allow myself the release, too, cascading over the cliff and landing firmly in a whole new world.

A world where the only thing I need is her. A world where if everything is good and right, we're together.

A world where Josie knows I love her and doesn't doubt it for a single second.

A world where she's mine.

14

Josie

Tuesday, September 23rd

"Sixty-five," I mutter to myself, unfolding various bills from my apron and setting them in a neat stack on the counter. "Seventy-five, eighty-five, ninety-five."

I reach back into my apron to grab the leftover wad of dollar bills, Red Bridge's favorite currency at The Diner, and finish counting out my tips until I reach one hundred and fourteen dollars.

Tonight was a pretty good night, but we were also so busy I barely had time to pee, much less sit down during my seven-hour shift.

Now, the sky is dark, and the moon has made itself known between the stars, and I am more than ready to go home. I check my phone, finding a missed text from Clay, and when I open the screen to read it, I can't wipe the smile off my face if I want to.

Clay: *You almost done at The Diner? I miss you. I need to see you.*

Me: *Just finishing up now. And you saw me last night.*

Goose bumps appear on my arms as my mind recalls all the things that happened last night at Clay's. We watched *Three Men and a Baby* together. And we ended the night with the kind of amazing, unforgettable sex that I'll probably think about when I'm one hundred years old on my deathbed.

It was magic. Perfect. *Everything.*

He told me he loved me. *Clay Harris loves me.* But I didn't respond. I don't know why I didn't respond, but it's like the words got stuck in my throat or something.

But do I love him back? Yes, one hundred percent, I do.

Clay: *And I need to see you tonight. And tomorrow night. And the next one thousand nights after that.*

Me: *That's a lot of nights.*

Clay: *What can I say? I'm a greedy bastard when it comes to you. Sleep at my place tonight?*

Me: *Give me, like, ten minutes and I'll call you.*

Clay: *As in, you'll call me while you're on your way to my place?*

It's tempting as hell to spend another night at Clay's, but there's a part of me that feels guilty for not heading back to Grandma Rose's. Lately, I've been sleeping at Clay's a lot. And yes, I know I'm an almost-twenty-six-year-old woman and my grandmother can certainly do just fine without me, but she's important to me.

Honestly, I wouldn't be where I am today if it weren't for her.

Me: *As in, I'll call you. LOL.*

I grab my purse and slide my tip money into my wallet. I double-check that I've completed all of my after-hours tasks, and when I note that all of the tables have been refilled with napkins and ketchup bottles and salt and pepper shakers, I glance toward the hostess stand and make sure the menus are in their rightful place and there's enough freshly rolled silverware to last the morning shift.

Time to go home.

"I'll see you tomorrow, Harold," I say, hanging my apron on the hook by the back door of the kitchen and pulling my purse up onto my shoulder.

Harold gives me a nod and a groan while he cleans the last of the grill, and I step out into the alley and close the door behind me. It's a short walk up the sidewalk to the square where my relic of Ford Focus is parked, but now that we're into fall, it's getting dark earlier and earlier, and I have to rely on the light pole at the corner to see where I'm going.

I feel safe, though, just like I always do here in our little hamlet of a town, and the crowd across the street at the local movie theater—that features only one screen—is an assurance as well. I see the sheriff and the mayor and half of the staff of city hall all in just one glance. If anything were going to happen tonight, it wouldn't be here.

It's a stupid thought—one that starts all the murder vibe shows I've ever seen—and I instantly regret it when a tall, dark, intimidating shadow steps out of a little nook in the wall and comes to a stop right in front of me. I scream, of course, and turn to run, but a strong hand stops me and pulls me back.

"Get away from me!" With both fists swinging wildly, I start fighting with everything I have.

It's a struggle, and the man tries to subdue me with shushes, but I just scream louder. Clay was right. I had no business doing all that cheater shit. It's coming back to bite me in spades, and now I'm going to be in a real-life episode of *Law and Order: SVU*.

Sheriff Peeler is yelling as he comes toward us at a run, and it's not surprising, given his penchant for both keeping order in his town and me—having taken up an almost fatherly role for me when I came back to town at the age of eighteen—but still, I feel desperate. My ears are humming and my heart is racing, and I swear I feel like I'm in a deep pool of water.

"Josie," I think I hear, but it's muffled and hard to understand. "Josie, stop. It's me," I think I hear again, but I push harder on my assailant's windpipe to try to get him to let go.

"Josie!" Sheriff Pete Peeler yells finally, making me breathe a sigh of undeniable relief as my attacker releases me and stumbles toward Pete.

"Oh God, Pete, I'm so glad you're here." My breathing is stilted and shallow, but the relief of knowing I'm safe is enough to keep me on my feet. I grab at my chest and suck in as much air as I can.

"Uh, Jose," Pete remarks, for some reason patting the back of the guy who was just trying to kidnap me. "Is there a reason you're attacking Clay Harris tonight?"

My head jerks up and I take a closer look, and the startling realization of who was holding on to me hits me square in the chest. Clay makes it all the worse by waving a hand like I didn't just go psycho Hulk on his ass. "Hey, babe."

"Oh my God, Clay!" I rush over to him. "I'm so sorry. I thought you were a stranger or one of those guys I messed with during my cheater-catching phase!"

"S'all right, babe," he says again, still struggling to breathe. "Really. I'll probably barely even bruise."

"I was caught off guard!" I exclaim, my chest tight from the remnants of adrenaline that are still rolling around in my veins. "And I thought I was supposed to call you! What are you even doing here?"

"Because I needed to see you. It's safe to say I've been catching you off guard a lot lately, huh?" Clay manages, his voice still a little gruff. "Like when I told you I loved you last night. Caught you off guard," he says then, right in front of Sheriff Peeler.

My eyes widen, and Pete whistles, turning away on his heel but not leaving. His ass is just as nosy as the rest of this town. A normal person would dismiss themselves from the conversation now that there's no need for the law anymore, but not Pete. He's got to get the whole scoop so he can get the story right for all of his gossip cronies.

"Clay, I..." I pause, completely out of my depth and unsure of what to say. Being vulnerable with my words isn't my strong suit. Has never been my strong suit. I blame my mother for that.

"Don't worry, Jose," Clay says, a warm smile on his lips as he moves closer to me. "I know you love me."

"You do?" I look into Clay's sweet eyes and fall head over feet into his smile.

"Oh yeah, babe. I'm afraid of a lot of things, but you not loving me back isn't one of them." He reaches out for my hand and holds it in his, rubbing at the skin with the pad of his thumb. It's a simple touch, but the effect is electric. "I want to be official, Josie. Me and you. A real live couple. Two people in it together with the goal of staying together."

"I…I want that too," I admit. Everything is better with Clay.

"Well, all right, then," Pete finally says, tipping his hat. "You all let me know if you have any real needs for police assistance."

I shake my head as he leaves, and Clay pulls me into a hug so tight I can hardly breathe. "I'm sorry I scared you. And that I'm always embarrassing you. And that I haven't convinced you it's safe to tell me you love me yet."

I roll my eyes.

"But I want to be official, and I want to do it in a way where we have a toothbrush at each other's places."

I snort. "You want a toothbrush at Grandma Rose's house?"

He nods.

"She's my *grandma*, Clay."

"Yeah, doll. How do you think she got that moniker? It wasn't by following in the Virgin Mary's footsteps."

I cover my eyes in mortification. "Good grief."

"Don't blush, baby. It's true. Your grandma is no fool. She knows what goes on between a man and a woman, and she knows you're no kid anymore. I want a toothbrush there. And I want you to have one at my place too. Fair's fair."

"What's with the urgency? You had to accost me as I was leaving work to tell me this?"

"Uh, yeah. Because time's always ticking, and every second I spend not telling you what you mean to me is a second I don't want to spend."

My throat feels thick, but I force the truth through it anyway. He deserves to know, and I deserve to let myself feel it.

"I…I do love you, Clay. I love you so much it scares me."

"That's an oxymoron, baby," he says with the kind of smile I feel all the way to my toes. "I promise, if you let me love you the way I want to love you, you don't have anything to be afraid of."

I nod, just once. It's all I manage before he swoops in and scoops me up into his arms, swinging me around and sealing his lips to mine.

It's everything I've dreamed of and beyond, and I don't know if I even saw it coming. I love Clay Harris all the way into my bones. I love Clay Harris in a way that doesn't stop. Ever.

His excitement is contagious as he sets me down and pulls out two plastic-wrapped toothbrushes.

"You already have the damn toothbrushes?" I ask, laughter vibrating my chest.

"Damn straight, babe." The handsome bastard winks. "Now, let's go get set up."

Clay Harris is mine. Officially. And I don't know if I've ever felt so lucky in my life.

After The Moment: Part 2

The "How Has It Already Been Five Years?" Reality

15

Clay

Saturday, July 31st

I pace the alley behind The Country Club and check my watch again, only getting more pissed off when I see what time it is.

I've been waiting for an hour for Bennett to show up here with the beer kegs I need to be ready for the afternoon rush, and if he doesn't get here soon, before I open, the guys who come here when they get off at Phelps are going to riot. In their world, a hard day's labor ends with a beer, a ball game, and a home-cooked meal at home, in that order.

It sounds barbarian and a little sexist, but I assure you, these guys are the salt of the earth and the best humans you'll ever meet. If their wives are cooking for them, it's because they want to.

Still, they have a routine, and I'm a carefully crafted part of it. If it weren't for my damn father's quarterly check-in call, I would have gotten them myself. Instead, I spent two hours making up facts about green pitch and fairway length and ended the call with a false promise for a future tour of the pro shop. Yeah, my dad still thinks The Country Club is, in fact, a country club.

We're going on a decade of this charade, and it's honestly just become comical at this point. I mean, I don't need his money. Hell, I don't even need my trust fund. Red Bridge keeps my watering hole in steady enough cash flow to live comfortably. I could quite literally tell my father to eat shit and be fine.

It also helps that my view of money and how much you actually need to enjoy your life is vastly different from the way I was raised. I have Red Bridge to thank for that.

Which begs the question, why do I even keep up with the lies to my father? I guess there's a masochistic side of me that wants to see how long he'll continue to be the surface-level dad he's been since the day I was born. His follow-through when it comes to me is statistically zero-in-a-million. He's never put in more effort than a phone call in the ten years I've been here, and I can pretty much guarantee he never will.

A glint of sun catches my attention as Bennett's truck finally rounds the corner into the alley, and I let out a huge, relieved breath at the sight.

"Hi, honey," Bennett greets, climbing out of his truck with an annoying smirk and slamming the door behind him. "I'm home."

"What the hell, man?" I ask, still annoyed that he's had me out here pacing my ass off without even so much as a phone call. "What took you so long?"

"Relax." He opens the tailgate, and I help him roll the first keg to the back of the bed and out. "I had to make a few pit stops."

"Pit stops?" I scoff. "You said you'd be here over an hour ago." We each grab one handled end of the keg and carry it toward the bar, waddling funny, thanks to the weird distribution of weight.

"You do realize I'm here because I'm doing *you* a favor, right?" he says in a tone I know is supposed to be snide. But I've done this fucker enough favors to last a lifetime, so he can suck my dick.

"Where were you?"

"I had to make sure Josie Ellis's sister made it to her house and get gas."

"What did you just say?" I ask, freezing completely and yanking Bennett to a stop as my heart kicks up to a fucking gallop at the mention of her name. It doesn't matter that it's been almost five fucking years since we split up at this point. You never get over the love of your life. Period. "You were at Josie's?"

"Not really."

"Then why did you just say *Josie's house*?"

"Her sister is in town and a complete fucking toddler. I was just making sure she didn't get herself killed."

"Her sister is in town, and she's a toddler?" I drop the keg as it slips from my hand, distant memories of Josie and her sister Norah and her horrible mother at Grandma Rose's funeral swimming in my mind. Bennett grunts at the weight, but he's got enough muscles. He'll survive. "How the hell do you know that? *Why* do you know that?"

"Well, technically, she's not a toddler," Bennett corrects, grunting to pick up the keg on his own. "She's a grown-ass woman with a penchant for terrible life choices."

I'm fully aware that Norah, Josie's only surviving sister, isn't a toddler. But I'm also aware that her baby sister Jezzy, who is no longer alive, was just a toddler when she died. Ben doesn't know that, but I do. I know everything there is to know about Josie Ellis. So much so, that I sometimes wish I could forget she exists.

But I can't. My heart refuses to forget a single conversation, memory, or moment that includes her.

I stare at Ben, waiting for him give me something, fucking anything, more, but I swear this asshole must have lost his mind or bashed his head in or something because he's not getting to the point. I know he knows I'm not over Josie. He *knows.*

Having known each other our whole lives and all, he *should* know me better than anyone.

"You can take a breath," he says so teasingly my head nearly explodes. "I didn't even see your ex."

He adjusts the keg in his arms and rolls his eyes, walking toward the back door while I follow him.

"But her sister…what happened with her, Ben?"

It's a big fucking deal, Norah being in town, and Bennett is painfully failing to realize that. With all the shit Josie and her sister have been through and the basically no contact they've had since Eleanor dragged Norah away from Grandma Rose's funeral that day, her sister wouldn't just show up here for a fun time. And I know with certainty Josie wouldn't be ready for it to happen at all.

Bennett sets the keg down on the bar with a thud, explaining simply, "On my way back into town, after picking up *your* kegs, she waved me down for a ride."

It's a basic fucking answer, and instantly, I'm even more annoyed. Why is he being the absolute dictionary definition of taciturn today?

"And what did Josie say about her sister being in town? Was she surprised? Angry?" I offer, thinking maybe, just maybe, if I make the question multiple choice, it'll entice him to answer. "She doesn't have the best relationship with her family."

"I don't know."

"What do you mean, *you don't know*?"

"I didn't hang around for the family reunion," he says on a sigh, seemingly just as aggravated with me as I am with him. I know he's got important shit of his own—our sweet, now seven-year-old Summer is the most important girl in the whole wide world—but I still don't appreciate the attitude. "Now, are you going to help me move your last two kegs out of my truck, or should I just do it myself?"

"You're such a dick sometimes, Ben."

"Me?" he snaps with a laugh. "The guy who drove forty minutes to pick up *your* kegs and is currently helping you move them into your bar?"

"The guy who doesn't know shit about anything, even though he was all up in the shit today."

He puts his hands to his hips and stares hard at me. "I take it we're still talking about Josie right now?"

I groan and grind my teeth, busying myself with changing out the old empty keg for the new, and try to talk myself down from strangling my very dear best friend.

My bar will be full soon, and as much as I hate it, Josie Ellis will still want nothing to do with me.

I have to let it go before it eats me alive. *I have to let her go.* At least, that's what I've been telling myself for the last five fucking years.

16

Josie

Saturday, July 31st

I take another sip of tea and scroll through the article in the Red Bridge Newsleader one more time. LOCAL BAR, THE COUNTRY CLUB, TAKES ON EXTENDED HOURS

You'd think, after almost five years have passed by, I wouldn't feel anything from reading it. Wouldn't have a twinge of pain inside my chest at the mere sight of his bar's name. But as always, it's a special form of torture to read about Clay and imagine all the things we could have been.

Eileen spotlights how well he's doing and what led him to make the decision to open a few hours earlier in the afternoons. And for as much as it stings, I still love to see him succeed.

I've barely had time to sit and relax lately, but just like always, that's for the best. The more I sit still, the more I think, and I'd rather be busying my hands than trapped in the messy web of thoughts in my mind. I closed CAFFEINE down for the day about an hour ago, and now it's time to get moving on other things.

I rinse out my mug and set it in the sink and then head down the hallway to my bedroom to put on a pair of cutoff shorts and a tank top so I can do a little work in the garden beds outside. It's ungodly hot out, but Grandma Rose would chew me a new one if she saw the slightly unkempt state I've let them get to. She called her flower beds the *windows to another universe* and bordered them with fairy statues and gnomes and frogs to drive the point home.

I tie up my curls in a loose and messy bun and grab my gardening gloves from the top of my stonewashed oak dresser before heading back down the hall toward the front of the house. I snag a bottle of water from the fridge, my AirPods from the counter, and am just about to force myself to get to work when three harsh knocks sound off through the pink front door.

I roll my eyes to myself as I think of just about the only possibility of who it could be. Randy Hanson, no doubt, trying to get me to sell Grandma Rose's house *yet again* for way too little money.

I swear, I spend half my time off telling him to blow a goat these days.

Setting my water bottle and earbuds back down on the counter, I charge through the living room and yank open the door, ready to rumble with Randy. But the person standing there isn't Randy at all.

No. It's my sister.

"Norah?" I ask, my heart in my throat at the sight of her. I haven't laid eyes on her light brown curls or sweet brown eyes in half a decade. I haven't laid eyes on her since the day we put Grandma Rose in the ground.

She's nervous. That much is obvious in the way her voice shakes as she says, "Hi, sis."

But she'd be stupid not to be after the way we left things five years ago. The way she sided with our mother, even after Eleanor had said downright vile things to me, is hard to get over. It's not an easy pill to swallow when your own mother wants to think the worst of you. And it's even harder having your sister stand there and not have your back at all.

I was Norah's everything when we were kids. *We* were everything to *each other.*

"Uh…" She pauses, her eyes flitting from her shoes to my still-shocked gaze several times. "I was in the neighborhood and thought I'd drop by and see how you're doing."

"In the neighborhood?" I scoff, narrowing my eyes. "Red Bridge is nine hours away from New York."

She's fancy personified, down to her black boots, designer jeans, swanky shirt, and Louis Vuitton suitcase, though there's a coating of dust on it all nearly a quarter of an inch thick. She looks like a city princess who took one hell of a wrong turn.

"Okay, so I wasn't exactly in the neighborhood, but I…wanted to see you."

"You came all the way to Red Bridge because, suddenly, after five years of no contact, you wanted to see me?" I ask, my skepticism at an all-time high. "You really expect me to believe that?"

"I did. I *do* want to see you. Five years is too long for anyone, and it's definitely too long for us," she says, clearly romanticizing our past for dramatic effect. I appreciate the effort, but the suitcase in her hand and the sweat covering her face tell a completely different story. "And…I kind of…sort of…need a place to stay for a little while."

Consider me absolutely gobsmacked at the level of her audacity.

"You want to stay here? With me?" I question, and I don't hide the outright indignation in my voice. A year ago, she probably wouldn't have likened me to anything better than a piece of gum stuck to the bottom of her designer shoe. But now that she needs something, we're the best of friends? I don't buy it for a second. "And you didn't think it was a good idea to give me a heads-up?"

"I tried to call you," she lies, pissing me off even more. I have no missed calls on my phone, and she doesn't even have my number. Eleanor made damn sure after I left New York that the two of us never had direct contact without her in the middle.

"Bullshit."

"Okay, so I didn't try to call you because I had a feeling you'd strongly discourage my presence."

I can't help but laugh at her. The rift in our relationship wasn't some one-sided mystery. She was there at Grandma Rose's funeral. She knows exactly why things are the way they are and all the reasons why I wouldn't want her here in the first place. Though, I can't deny I'm definitely wondering what happened to make her think it was worth coming anyway. "Very perceptive of you."

"So…can I come in, or…?"

Can she come in? *Ha.* At this stage in our relationship, we may as well be strangers. I know zip about her fancy life in New York, and she doesn't know shit about mine either.

I quirk a defiant eyebrow at her. "How about you tell me why you're here first, and then I'll decide."

"It's a long story."

"I've got time," I challenge, crossing my arms and leaning into the doorjamb. I level her with a look and study the very real fear in her eyes as a million thoughts flit through her mind.

"I just needed a break."

"You left New York because you needed a break?" I ask, pressing her to be bold enough to lie to me a little more. She clearly thinks I was born yesterday, and I don't know if that's all Eleanor's influence or if she's truly just that naïve. "And why do you need a break, exactly? Life getting a little hard in the penthouse?" I laugh. "Or maybe you're low on maids and overwhelmed at doing your own laundry? Or, *I know*, maybe you're distraught because Hermès won't let you buy the latest bag?"

Her cheeks pinken, and her face turns stony as anger stirs her backbone. "I know it's probably bringing you great enjoyment to find me on your front porch like a stray cat, but I just took a nine-hour Greyhound bus ride and got dropped off in the middle of nowhere and had to hitchhike another ride from a complete stranger who also happened to be the world's grouchiest man, which ended in me walking here from the center of town, and I'd really like to just sit down," she rattles off with her head held high and her mouth moving a mile a minute. "And maybe…you know…drink some water to stave off a hospital stay for dehydration."

There's a glimmer of the sister I used to know somewhere inside there, and I take a little bit of pride in watching her stand up for herself.

"Could you find it somewhere in your apparently cold, dead heart to let me come inside first before we get into all the tragic details of the current state of my life?"

I consider her closely, wondering if she's had enough of Eleanor Ellis and the phony, money-driven life she wants for Norah back in New York to truly listen to me when I talk or if she's still puppetting all the things our mother has spent years teaching her. I consider, if I let her stay, whether it'll end in a truly healed sisterhood or if it'll be just another mistake I've made.

I don't need to add another to the list.

"Please?" she begs then, a single tear finally freeing itself from her eye and falling slowly down her cheek. "Show your sister some mercy?"

"It's not bringing me enjoyment to see you cry," I assure her, trying to maintain the strength I need to protect myself without being unfairly cruel to her. "Not at all, but it's been *five* years, Norah, and it's not like you were the nicest person to me the last time I saw you. Actually, you were a total bitch." She stood there and watched our mother destroy me. And she didn't say a word.

"Josie, you have to admit that you weren't being nice either. You told Mom to 'get the fuck out' in the middle of a funeral. Actually, you *screamed* it. In front of everyone. It was quite the scene, if I recall."

All the pain I was feeling that day crawls into my chest and reminds me it'll never be gone completely. Norah doesn't know… she has no fucking clue, and it's ridiculous that she'd pretend that she does. "It's not my fault that Eleanor decided to show up somewhere she was definitely not welcome."

"Josie." Her eyes are wide and her voice pleading. "It was

Grandma Rose's funeral. Pretty sure that wasn't the time or place to go off on our mother."

"I think it was the perfect time," I refute, holding my ground. "After Dad died, Mom treated Grandma Rose like shit. For *years*. The last person she would've wanted at her funeral was Eleanor. You and I both know that. Not to mention all the other evil shit she's done."

After our father passed away from a brain tumor that took his life within six months of diagnosis, our mother didn't even shed a single fucking tear. If anything, she started planning her exit from Red Bridge the instant he took his last breath. It was so sick and calculated and emotionless that I often wonder if she's a true sociopath.

Grandma Rose tried to convince her to stay in Red Bridge; she even tried to fight for custody of Norah and me, but Eleanor was determined to take us with her. Only a few weeks after my dad passed away, we left Red Bridge and headed to New York like thieves in the night.

Norah finally breaks down, multiple tears falling and her whole body starting to shake.

"Josie, I know we have a lot to talk through. I know there are a lot of unsaid things that need to be said and apologies to be made. But I've just had the worst week of my life, and I have nowhere else to go. Do you think you could find it in you to show me some temporary compassion and let me come inside?"

My whole body locks on what it might mean to let her in—all the ways that it'll turn my carefully crafted life upside down.

"You know if Grandma Rose were still alive, she'd let me come in."

"You play dirty," I admit on a sigh, even knowing that Grandma Rose would have fucking loved Norah's ruthless, self-serving move. "Fine."

Relief floods her face. "Thank you."

"Yeah, yeah," I mutter, rolling my eyes and stepping back from the door. And I thought Randy was going to be a pain in my ass. He would've been a hell of a lot easier than this. "You can stay here, but don't think I'm agreeing to this being some kind of permanent roommate situation," I say, heading down the hall and back toward the kitchen.

She drags her dusty suitcase up over the threshold and follows me inside, and I get down to protecting myself again.

She may be here, but that doesn't mean I can't ignore her.

Ignoring the people I love is what I do best.

17

Josie

Sunday, August 1st

Norah is still asleep when I leave the house on Sunday morning, destination not entirely known. I'm a ten-pound lump of feelings in a five-pound bag in that tiny house with her, and for the good of both of us, I figure I should take some space when I can.

When I left New York fourteen years ago, at the legal adult age of eighteen, I did so knowing it would be at least a little at the expense of my sister. My mom is cunning and conniving enough to control the narrative how she wants, and Norah was still young enough that it would have been hard to fight amid all the glitz and glam of the uberwealthy life my mother was hell-bent on getting the day she moved us out of Red Bridge shortly after our father passed away.

I dreamed Norah would find a way out—that she would use all the knowledge I'd given her and the fight Grandma Rose and our dad put into our DNA—and break free, but I have to admit, I never saw her showing up on my doorstep yesterday coming.

I pull into one of the spaces in Earl's Grocery's parking lot and cut the engine, climbing out of my SUV with extra care as my bare legs stick to the hot leather and rip away in a painful peel. I grab my purse off the front seat and slam my door shut, hustling across the already steaming black pavement and gliding through the automatic front doors.

It's pretty quiet in here, thankfully, since most of the town is still at church, and I have a clear line to the produce section to find what I'm looking for. Normally, I'd go for something a little fancier than grocery store flowers, but since Fran's is closed on Sundays, I'm willing to take what I can get.

I look carefully through the bucket of carnations and then the roses, and I finally settle on a nice bouquet of Gerbera daisies in varying sizes and colors.

I turn to leave and then go back again, looking for another two bouquets. I wish more than anything I didn't need so many.

Holding them close to my chest and moving through the store, I step up to the only register that's open. It's being staffed by lanky teenager Lance, which is pretty much the worst-case scenario, but I'm not surprised since Earl is an every-Sunday churchgoer.

"Hey, Lance," I greet, smiling slightly as I set the three bouquets on the conveyor belt and step up to the credit card machine. He jerks up his chin in hello but doesn't make any move to start scanning.

I clear my throat, and he raises his eyebrows at me. A silent, "What the hell do you want?" gesture.

The sigh that leaves my lungs is audible. "You have to scan them in for me to be able to pay."

"Oh," he says matter-of-factly. "Solid."

I stand there for another fifteen seconds without him moving, and my patience completely evaporates. "Lance!"

He startles and nods then, grabbing a bouquet by the top of the flowers like a complete heathen and slides it across the scanner.

I grit my teeth. "You have to scan the actual barcode."

"Ohh," he hums, finally spinning the bouquet around and turning it over to run the plastic wrapping across the scanner.

It's going to be a miracle if I don't walk out of here with three bouquets that are just petal-less stems. I suck my lips into my mouth and clench my fists as he continues to struggle with the other two, petals falling onto the conveyor belt as he does, before finally getting it and granting me a total on the screen.

I pull out my card to pay, and he questions me immediately. "No cash?"

"No," I say, incredibly suspicious. Lance is…interesting. He's young and a little—okay, a lot—lazy, and if there's a scheme to be had, I'm pretty sure he'll figure it out. Without Earl on the premises, I can only imagine he's hoping to pocket some cash sales for himself. "I don't have cash on me, and I'm well above the limit for using a card."

"Whoa, lady, relax." Lance's hands both go up defensively. "I'm just asking. No need to call the cops."

I roll my eyes and finish the transaction, and I then snatch up the bouquets and head out the door without another word. I'm so beyond being in the mood to be given crap right now, I don't have the energy to do anything else but get the hell out of the grocery store.

I climb back into my SUV and set the flowers and my purse on the passenger seat, pulling my phone out of my bag and dropping it into my cupholder.

When I glance at the screen, I'm surprised to see two messages stacked on each other. I didn't feel it vibrate, but I'm notorious for forgetting to turn on the ringer and not feeling the buzz at all.

It's an unknown number, and I click open the first message to see what it says.

I guess your toxic influence finally sank into your sister. If I find out you were behind all this, I'll make sure you pay.

Well, then. I guess the sender isn't unknown anymore.

No one, and I mean no one, does vapid nastiness like my mother. The second message, I know, will be more of the same, and I don't even bother reading it before hitting delete.

But one thing is certain—Norah is going to have to start talking soon before things get completely out of control.

Because there's one thing I've always known about Eleanor Ellis—no matter who gets hurt or who she has to kill to get them out of the way, she won't stop until she gets whatever she wants.

18

Clay

Sunday, August 1st

One minute, I'm just minding my own business, heading toward the back parking lot of Earl's to grab some essentials, and the next, I'm watching Josie walk out of the automatic doors, her eyes fixated on her feet and a bunch of bouquets of flowers in her hands.

She climbs into her SUV, and I don't know what possesses me to forgo my grocery shopping plans entirely, but I find myself pulling out after her and following her from a distance.

I'm hoping if I'm asked in a formal—*you know, police-like*—setting, I'll be able to spin it as something other than stalking.

"I swear, Sheriff Peeler, I pulled into the back of the parking lot while she was pulling out of the front, and next thing I knew, I wasn't pulling into a spot and parking, but instead, I was still moving, and I was doing it in the same direction as her."

Completely reasonable. Completely innocent.

Right?

God almighty, I have lost my freaking mind. And not only that, I show absolutely no signs of finding it anytime soon.

I put the truck in park just behind a cropping of trees on the far end of the cemetery as Josie drives into the parking lot and pulls into a spot. It's a tense minute or two before she gets out, and I spend the time calling myself every name in the book and even a few that didn't make the traditional insult cut.

Festering knob.

Desperate prick.

Sneaking snake.

Much more of this and I'm going to have to break down and have myself committed—

Every part of me freezes, my breath catching in my chest. She climbs out of her red Chevy Acadia, and I can't pull my eyes away from her.

She looks beautiful as always, her wild hair down around her shoulders, and her soft yellow sundress hugs her petite body just right. Her Jezebelle of the Fiery Eyes, the tattoo she broke down and told me one night when we were still together that she'd gotten for her late sister, and the Venus flytrap etched beside it stand out in the bright sunlight, and her cowboy boots are well-appointed for stomping all over my ragged heart.

She's perfect. Just like she's always been.

And if I look close enough, I can even spot the necklace she always wears. The sun glimmers off the gold letter J that sits at the base of her neck, another poignant reminder she keeps of her sister Jezzy. One that I know she never takes off, not even to shower.

It's mind-blowing how I can know someone so well—*so fucking well*—yet feel so far away from them.

Josie stops at Grandma Rose's grave first, laying a bouquet of flowers on the headstone and sitting down in the grass in front of it for a spell. I can see her mouth moving, and I know she's talking to Rose. And I imagine Rose is listening, even if her bodily presence isn't with us anymore.

I rest my chin on the steering wheel as memories of nights with the two of them assault me.

Spaghetti noodle fights and warm cake fresh out of the oven. Firefly nights on the back porch with a good book read aloud by Rose while Josie and I got wine tipsy from the cheap stuff in a box. Movie madness bingeathons anytime either one of them was feeling under the weather and hot soup cooking on the stove for hours and hours anytime I was.

It was the best time of my life, so I guess it's not a surprise I can't stop wishing I were still in it.

Josie kisses the tips of her fingers and touches them to Rose's headstone before climbing to her feet again, and I watch her like a love-sick creep as she walks two spots over to her dad. Again, she places the flowers and sits down in the grass, and I imagine her telling him how Norah's just shown up in her life again and the million mixed ways she feels about it.

I can practically hear the words in my head as I imagine her telling him, *I need a breather*, the coping skill he was smart enough to give his girls from a very young age. I didn't know her dad, Danny Ellis, personally, but with the way this town talks about him, I sure wish I had.

What Josie's going through now is way more complicated than long-lost sisters, and I wish more than anything I could be a sounding board for her to talk through it. Instead, I watch patiently—and helplessly—as she uses the silent presence of her dad, and I pray it helps her. Because as painful as it is, I know damn well my showing up uninvited won't.

My phone rings in my cupholder and startles me so badly I nearly jump through the roof. I try to grab it quickly and end up bobbling it, smacking it between my hands until I can finally catch it and put it to my ear.

"Hello?" I answer on a nervous whisper, despite the fact that Josie is completely occupied as she moves to her sister Jezzy's grave now, more than a hundred yards away.

"Why are you whispering?" Bennett asks, his voice already annoyed with me.

There's no way I'm telling him the truth, so instead, I find a way to gain my composure and raise my voice to a normal volume and cadence. "No reason. What's up?"

"Summer was asking if you could come have dinner tonight. I told her I was vehemently opposed, but she insisted."

I laugh. "You really are such a dick sometimes."

"Yeah," Bennett affirms, owning the title without shame. "I know."

"Of course I'll come." These days, even with it being as hard as it is to see Bennett's sweet girl in pain and her chronic condition progressing at an alarming rate, Summer is the highlight of my life. I love her so much. It's only been seven years since Bennett showed up at my bar with her in a car seat, but the love I have in my heart for that little girl feels like it's been growing for a lifetime.

"Figured," he grunts out. "I told her you wouldn't have any other plans."

"What is this?" I scoff. "Shit on Clay Harris Day?"

Josie gets up from her spot in front of Jezzy's grave and heads back in the direction of her car, and I duck down lower in my seat on instinct. I don't think she can see me, but now that she's actively facing this direction, I'm not so sure.

"I'm just trying to figure out if we're both going to be a couple of single fucks for the rest of our lives or if it's just me," Ben says, and his responding sigh is both grumpy and amused. A dichotomy only Bennett Bishop can pull off at the same time.

Josie climbs into her car and backs out of the spot seemingly without noticing me, and I relax enough to scoot back up in my seat, rubbing at my face as I do.

"I think you know where I stand," I answer honestly, hating the words and myself for being so fucking impossibly attached to a woman who doesn't want me anymore. *Who hasn't wanted me for years.* It's a pathetic stance to take, but evidently, it's a hill I'm willing to rot and die on.

Bennett chuffs. "At least we'll have each other, I guess. See you tonight at six."

Yeah. At least we'll have each other. *Great.*

"Six," I agree.

I hang up the phone and consider driving away, but before I can stop myself, I'm out of the truck and walking toward Grandma Rose's grave myself.

I take a seat in the grass Josie occupied not long ago and stretch out my legs, picturing Rose's sweet but mischievous smile in my mind.

I have a lot of regrets in this life, but knowing and loving Rose will never be one of them.

"Hey, Grandma," I whisper, looking up at the clouds as they float across the sky. "Sorry it's been a while since I visited."

She doesn't answer, of course, but I imagine she's not nearly as mad at me as I am at myself.

"I've been thinking about you a lot. Josie told you, I'm sure, but there's a whole lot of stuff coming up for her now, with Norah and Jezzy and their mom, and I'd really appreciate it if you'd send her some strength from wherever you are. I know Josie has to be… terrified. Guilty. Fucking torn up, in plain English, though I'm sorry for cursing. She still blames herself for not watching Jezzy in that tub even though she was just a kid herself, and I know she's probably blaming herself for cutting Norah out of her life all those years ago when she came to Red Bridge."

I pick a blade of grass from the ground, twist it between my fingers, and then toss it in the air to float in the wind. Sadness sticks in my throat, and I have to swallow around the emotion several times before I can speak again. "I'm…sorry I didn't let her call you when she wanted to on our wedding day. So unbelievably sorry."

A tear falls from the corner of my eye, and I brush it away, trying to suck myself back inside to the hollow place where I survive. "I regret it every day, and I'm sure Josie regrets it even more. I know she blames me. I blame me too."

I pull my lips into my mouth, chuckling lightly. "Still, if I had another chance, I'd do it all right. I promise you that. I don't know if this is your specialty or if you've got a line to the Big Guy up there, but if you can find it in your heart to guide her back to me, I'd appreciate it."

I reach out to touch her stone just like Josie did and imagine our fingers touching each other. "I miss you, Grandma. And I really miss her too."

Before The Moment: Part 3

The Pure Bliss

19

Josie

Saturday, September 17th

After two years of Red Bridge Fall Farmers Markets selling my grandma's candles, you'd think I'd be used to getting up at the crack of dawn to load them, but I'm not. Especially on nights like last night when I stayed way too late at Clay's and drove home in the wee hours of the morning.

I yawn and cover my mouth with a palm, fighting for my life.

"Come on, Josie," Grandma Rose calls from the front door. "You'd better pick up the pace, or that hag Betty is gonna get the table I like again."

It's on the tip of my tongue to say, *at least Betty Bagley actually home-bakes her pies instead of scamming people with ones from Amazon*, but it's not a good idea to get on Grandma Rose's bad side this early in the morning.

Grandma's candle scheme is a secret from the whole town, and until the end of the market last year, it was a secret from me too. As it turns out, my surprisingly internet-savvy grandma has been ordering candles from Amazon in bulk, de-labeling them, and then slapping on her own sticker of lies.

"*Made with Love by Rose Ellis,*" my asshole. These things are mass-produced in a factory somewhere by people making way less than they should be and then upcharged for small-town consumption in the con of the century.

"I'm coming," I say as I lift the final box of candles with a heave, balancing it on my knee until I can get both hands under it in a good grip.

"Be careful, Josie," Grandma chastises as I toddle out the front door. "You know those candles are one of Red Bridge's hottest commodities. Certainly better than those inedible things Betty tries to pass off as pies."

If I had to describe my grandma and Betty Bagley's ongoing rivalry, I'd compare it to Angelina Jolie and Jennifer Aniston circa 2005. Only, instead of fighting over Brad Pitt, they're fighting over table space and farmers market customers.

It's straight fact that Betty's putting a hell of a lot more effort into the game. The woman bakes her pies from scratch. Grandma one-clicks candles in bulk. Though I'd never say that to my grandma. She'd ream my ass. Hell, I've yet to try one of Betty's pies—even though they smell like heaven—because the risk of being on Grandma Rose's bad side isn't worth the reward.

Ignoring my grandmother's badgering about being gentle with her precious candles, I walk down the steps to the trunk of her Buick, setting the box inside with the others before she hurries behind me and slams the trunk down with a slap.

"Put your seat belt on, dear," she says as I climb into the passenger's seat. "I'm gonna have to gun it the whole way there."

She fires up the engine, and driving thirty in a twenty-five, we "gun" our way down the street and head for town.

The sun is bright through the window and feels warm on my face while I let memories of how good it felt to sleep in Clay's arms last night run through my mind. I'm half tempted to text him, even pulling my phone out of my purse to look at the screen, but I decide at least one of us deserves to get some sleep this morning.

Almost two years together, and I still feel like I'm floating on a cloud—even if he did stupidly run for a city council position last year and win it. His phone rings constantly, and there's never not someone trying to bend his ear at the bar, but he listens with the patience of a saint and genuinely tries to fix everyone's problems. He's a good fit for the role; I just wish it didn't come at the expense of spending some of our date nights hearing Eileen Martin bitch about Mayor Wallace proposing to use city funds to paint Red Bridge's red bridge a different color or Peggy wanting to find a way to get an additional two parking spots in front of her pawn shop.

It should be noted that the bridge is still red, and if they added more parking spots in front of Peggy's shop, the only people who could park in her small lot would have to be driving one of those tiny smart cars.

Small towns are great in the fact that they create a community where everyone in town feels like they have a say. And small towns are also bad for that very reason, too. Especially when your boyfriend is on the city council. Last week alone, he must've received a hundred text messages about the graffiti that appeared on one of the stop signs near the center of town. A teeny-tiny sketch of a penis and balls really threw everyone into a tizzy.

Truthfully, you'd just about need a magnifying glass to see it from your car, but that's neither here nor there.

"I saw your sketchbook last night, you know," Grandma Rose says, startling my attention away from the window. "While you were still at Clay's."

I chew at my lip. "Yeah?"

My sketchbook is something I've had for years, and every time I get a new idea that revolves around my big dream of opening my own coffee shop, I keep tabs on it in there.

"One day, you're gonna have to grab yourself by the cojones, tell Harold Metcalf you're done workin' for him, and open the coffee shop you want to."

I look back out the window. "I'm not ready yet. I don't have the savings."

Grandma laughs. "You think I was ever ready for any of the stuff I did? For your dad? For him to get diagnosed with that horrible brain tumor and pass less than a year later? For losing Jezzy so tragically? For your witch of a mother taking you and Norah away from me? For you to be so grown on me?" She shakes her head. "Biggest lesson in this world is that you're never ready. Now, a bad feeling, that's different—you listen when you have those because that's your intuition speaking. But not ready? That's just the fear of the unknown talking."

I wish it were as easy as she says. I wish I could just follow my heart to start my own coffee shop in the same way I followed my heart to Clay. But I don't know. The dream feels almost too big to achieve.

Grandma pulls into the parking lot behind the market pavilion and turns off the car without another word. I follow her lead and climb out too, stacking our boxes onto one of the carts they keep for vendors and wheeling the load into our booth.

Grandma puts out her signature purple tablecloth, and I start unloading candles into their normal display.

"Hold down the fort, hun," she says, stepping around the table and tapping the surface with her fingers. "I gotta go talk to Melba before Betty gets here. Tell her about bingo last week while she was out of town."

I chortle. "You think you and Betty Bagley will ever bury the hatchet and get along?"

Grandma's face is disgusted. "Not even when I'm dead, hun. That little schemer can rot."

"Grandma!"

She shrugs. "There's a whole history there with me and her and your grandpa, all right?"

"Was she his mistress?" I ask, instantly intrigued.

"She wishes." She scoffs. "Let's just say she tried her best to be his mistress, but he wasn't taking the bait." She nods knowingly toward the candles. A silent, *You just focus on that, dear.* "Be back in a jiffy."

"Okay." I laugh and make a show of taking another candle out of the box. "I'll keep unloading candles."

Grandma winks and scoots off at a near jog to find Melba. I look around at the booths and people around us inconspicuously, but I'm not much in the mood to talk to anyone for real. I don't want to have to answer questions about the candle-making process or if Rose has a special batch today.

And trust me, *everyone* in this damn town wants to know how Rose makes her amazing candles.

I still can't believe the con she's managed to run without anyone ever finding out. Most of the time, she leaves the manufacturer stickers on half the damn things, and I have to find them and peel them off when I go through them.

I guess no one suspects a sweet old lady like her to be running such an elaborate scheme.

I bend over to grab more candles from a box, and a warm hand glides across my ass in a deliciously familiar way. Thankfully, I've gotten a lot less gun-shy and a lot more familiar with Clay's touch in the last couple of years, and I have exactly zero doubt it's him from the first sensation.

I stand up and back into his arms, and he wraps me in a hug that makes everything in the world feel right. "You know, baby, I'm really starting to hate how you sneak out of my bed in the mornings without saying a proper hello or goodbye."

I smile and turn to face him, placing a gentle kiss on his lips to make the frown go away. "I know. But I didn't want to wake you when you didn't even get done closing everything down downstairs until three."

"Don't matter to me. Wake me up." He gets quiet and waggles his eyebrows. "Wake me up in a *special* way, and it really won't matter. Come to think of it, that's how I want to wake up every morning, no matter the time."

I roll my eyes. "I'm not an alarm clock, Clay."

"You should be. You work ten times better and sound a whole lot sweeter."

"That's nice."

"That's nice?" He narrows his eyes, even though he's still smiling at me. "Babe, it's a whole lot better than that. Have you had a chance to think more about what we talked about last week?"

"Last week?" I question innocently, even though I know damn well what he means. Clay wants me to move in with him, and while there's nothing more I would love, I also feel incredibly torn. I like living with Grandma Rose. We have a routine and a dynamic that works. Plus, she's not exactly a spring chicken anymore, and I like the thought of being close to help if she needs me.

"You know what I'm talking about, Jose."

I nod and admit, "I do."

"Sooo...what do you say?" He squeezes my hips affectionately. "I want to go to sleep with you every night and wake up with you every morning. I'm tired of missing you."

At that, I melt a little, relenting enough to agree. "I'm tired of missing you too. I just... It's more complicated than that."

I kiss him on the lips again, hoping to put an end to the conversation as Grandma Rose comes back to the table and opens up her cash drawer to get ready. The market officially opens in five minutes, and if the past is anything to go by, we'll be flooded in no time.

"Hi, Grandma," Clay greets, still holding on to me but leaning around to give her one of his biggest smiles. The two of them are chummy, a bond built between them immediately when he came out into the kitchen in his underwear to her in her nightgown one night about a year and a half ago. I guess sharing space in your skivvies is a level of personal you can't come back from.

"Hi, Clay sweetheart," Grandma says, her voice kind and loving in the way it always is with him. "Are you here to help or just loiter?"

My grandma, ladies and gentlemen, the sweet little ballbuster.

A chuckle escapes Clay's throat. "I'm completely ready and willing to help." He sets me aside and walks around me, but when he looks back with a twinkle in his eye, I start to get worried. He turns back to Grandma and keeps talking. "And there's something I could use your help on, too."

"Clay, what are you doing?" I ask, but he ignores me.

"Is that right?" Grandma replies.

"Yep. See, I've been trying to convince your beautiful granddaughter to move out of your house and in with me, but she's concerned—"

"Clay!" I snap.

He keeps going, even repeating the words I interrupted more slowly. "She's *concerned* that it's not good timing for you. That what you have going is too good to give up, you know?"

Grandma glances at me and then back at Clay, narrowing her eyes. "And what makes you think she actually wants to live with you in the first place, dear?"

Clay smiles, and I swear the little flicker of confidence from him is enough to fall in love with him all over again. I'm annoyed with his tactics, but this is *him*. Loud and unbothered and blunt. Unabashedly, *this* is the guy I love—even when he's a pain in my ass—and his doing this shouldn't come as a surprise. "Because she loves me."

Grandma scoffs. "She loves me too."

I have to bite my lips to keep myself from spewing humor-filled spit all over Clay's face, but when the curve of his mouth softens without malice or offense, so does mine.

The way he looks at her.

The way he looks at me.

It's not very funny at all.

Grandma leans forward, around Clay, to talk directly to me, even as customers start to consume the entire front of the table.

Hilga Hofmyer tries to ask her a question, one candle in each hand, while a burgeoning crowd pushes at her back, but Grandma Rose holds out a hand, palm out. A silent order to shut up.

Her wise eyes study my face closely. "Josie, do you want to live with this young man?"

"Well, yes. I mean, of course. But I also want to live with—"

Grandma swings her silencing hand from Hilga to me, and I stop talking immediately. When Rose Ellis gives you the hand, you obey it. "You'll move in with him at the end of the month, then."

"Grandma!"

"That gives us enough time to have some girl time, but it's like I was telling you in the car, Jose."

Not ready? That's just the fear of the unknown talking.

"So, what? This is you giving me a shove across the metaphorical street? What if there's a car coming?" I ask with a laugh.

She smiles back. "Don't trip."

20

Clay

Monday, September 19th

"I just want you to know that if this isn't a true emergency, I'm going to kill you," Bennett says as he walks through The Country Club's door, immediately voicing his displeasure with the call I made to him before dawn this morning.

The front door falls closed behind him, and he steps inside with Summer in her stroller. The braces on her legs don't distract from the cute outfit featuring a tutu she's wearing or the brilliant smile on her adorable toddler face.

Her dad, though, is glaring at me. "You better start talking soon."

Even now, with the sun barely up, I realize what an inconvenience my early morning wake-up call was for a single father with a two-year-old daughter, but I couldn't help myself. I needed reinforcements, and I needed them now.

"Josie is moving in with me at the end of the month." I get straight to the point. "And I want to propose to her before she does. I need you to go ring shopping with me today."

"I'd say congratulations," Bennett says, pushing the stroller toward me at the counter. "But it's going to be hard to propose, walk down the aisle, and move in with Josie Ellis if you're dead, and I'm still going to have to kill you, sooo..."

I chuckle. "Oh, come on, Ben. Love *is* an emergency. I can't wait another day or another week or another month. I have to make her mine."

"La-la-ka-la," Summer sings from her seat, and Bennett finally breaks into a smile. It's small, but it's there, and I choose to believe it's because his beautiful daughter just reminded him of the power of all-encompassing love. Celine Dion is probably singing in his head at this very moment.

"At least tell me why you got us all trussed up so early. None of the stores are even open right now."

"Ah, yeah. That's 'cause I don't like any of the local stores' inventories," I explain with two hands bracing the bar. "And since I don't want anybody with a big mouth seeing me and spilling the beans before I actually get to propose to the woman of my dreams, I want to drive over to Burlington. Plus, I want to take you to breakfast first, as a friendly gesture of compensation for spending the day helping me find the perfect ring."

Bennett frowns, back to his natural state. "Pretty sure I need to agree to go first."

I look down at Summer, who is currently smiling at me with her big blue eyes. "Sum, would you like to eat? Are you hungry, sweet girl?"

Bennett groans, but my sweet little partner in crime grins up at me with a big, toothy smile.

"Sum-mer eat! Hungee!"

I look at her dad, my eyebrows doing all the talking for me as I raise them knowingly at him.

"Bacon, eggs, hash browns, toast, *and* pancakes," he answers, his voice the definition of annoyed.

I smile. "Whatever you want."

Summer clamors in her stroller seat, and Bennett walks around in front of her to get down on her level. "You sure you want to go to breakfast with Uncle Clay, Summblebee?"

"Clayyy!" she says excitedly, clapping her little hands, and my smile grows by a mile.

I point right at her. "That's my girl."

"Why don't you stick to one woman at a time?" Ben teases with a smirk over his shoulder.

"There's always room for a Summer in a relationship," I hedge back. Summer laughs and smiles at me, and I make a funny face and wave.

"Come on," I say, grabbing my keys off the counter and rounding the bar to go over to them. "I'll drive."

Bennett rolls his eyes. "You'd better since this is your mission anyway."

We head outside and get Summer secured in the middle of the bench seat—compared to two years ago, it's amazing how much better we are at taking care of her now—and then climb in our respective sides. The town is still sleepy as we drive out of it, and I rest an arm around the back of the bench seat, the corners of my lips curving up.

It's not long before we're out of Red Bridge city limits, and Summer is sleeping softly between us. Ben reaches out to fiddle with the radio, not stopping until he settles on a station that's playing classical music. It's his go-to when it comes to painting in his studio and helping his little girl fall asleep.

"So, you're really gone for this one, huh?" Bennett asks, stretching out in his seat too, but focusing the bulk of his body toward the window.

"Might as well be in space, bro. She's the real deal. Everything is better when I'm with her. Hell, I don't even feel a hint of the stink of our old life on me anymore."

"Damn," he comments, glancing over at me for a long moment. "Never thought I'd see the day that Clay Harris would actually want to get married. Or, fuck, find himself loving the idea of committing himself to one woman at all."

"When you find the right woman, shit changes." I shrug. "And who knows, maybe one day, *I'll* be sitting in the passenger seat while *you're* driving us to go ring shopping."

"Good one." He snorts. "I don't think I'll ever fuck with a woman again."

"Oh, Ben. That's not... You gotta fuck women," I tease. "The alternative just doesn't work for us."

He rolls his eyes, but he chuckles too. "I didn't say I'm not going to fuck them. I'm just not going to fuck *with* them."

"In my experience, the two of them kind of go together."

Bennett shrugs, unfazed. He's been burned by so much and fallen down so many slippery slopes in his life, I imagine the thought of chancing any of that now that Summer is around is crippling. She needs stability and someone who's reliable. Bennett is that man now, and I like to think I am too. But we didn't used to be.

When you think of breaking generational cycles, wealthy families don't necessarily come to mind. But bad people are everywhere, in every station of life. Our families—and Josie's family, for that matter—are proof of that.

"You have any idea what kind of ring you're looking for?" Ben asks, and my answer is instant.

"Something that reminds me of a water tower."

"Excuse me?" He nearly chokes on his tongue, and I laugh.

"If anyone should understand that sometimes ideas are more metaphorical and abstract than black-and-white concrete, it's you, Mr. *Artiste*."

"I don't paint anymore," Ben admits, and it doesn't take a genius to understand why. Being a single father to a special needs child is no easy feat, but I also think some of it stems from giving his family and the rich people within the art world a giant fuck-you.

Doesn't matter, though. Ben's an artist—a painter, to be exact—to his core. I don't know a lot about art, but I know he has more talent in the tips of his fingers than everyone I've ever met combined. And a lot of his most famous paintings come in the form of abstract. Hell, when he was, like, eighteen or nineteen, I'm pretty sure one of his abstract pieces sold for millions.

One day, I'm sure, he'll be back to painting. It's in his blood. It's a part of his fucking soul. He can't avoid that forever. But the day that I got him out of bed at the butt-crack of dawn isn't the day I push that conversation on him.

"Just trust me," I add, changing the topic back to the task at hand. "I'll know the perfect ring when I see it."

"Don't get off at the first exit," Ben suggests. "Go to the second. It's easier."

I know he and Summer come up here for her treatments and meetings with her team of doctors fairly often, so I do as he advises, taking the second exit into Burlington and rounding the bypass back to the Starsky Diner for breakfast. It's a pretty neat place with a sparkling ceiling meant to mimic the stars, and I figure Summer will get a kick out of it, at least for a little while.

And every little bit helps while you're trying to entertain a toddler with mobility limitations during a meal.

We make quick work of unloading her after I park, and Bennett straps her into her specialized stroller again to take her inside. We take a table in the corner, and the waitress gives Summer a kids menu and some crayons to color. She starts scribbling wildly, and I settle in to figure out my order.

Bennett surprises me by asking, "Do you think she'll say yes?"

I laugh, shoving back in my seat and tossing my menu on the table. "I mean…I'm hoping. Though, I'm just chump enough to ask anyway, even if it might go bad."

His eyes widen and his brows lift. "Why?"

"Because…" I pause and shrug. "I can't imagine my life without her in it. I can't imagine going through anything—good or bad—and not going through it with her. Because when I look at her, I know I don't need to see anyone else. I see the future. I see the best version of myself reflected in every smile she gives. And I think I give those things to her, too."

He nods and goes back to looking at his menu, but his jaw works in a way that I know he's not being dismissive. He's overcome by the possibility of what I'm describing. He's like a kid with Santa—he hasn't seen it for himself, but he truly wants to believe.

"She's been through some shit, Ben. A whole lotta shit, to be honest. But she's still the most genuine, loving person I've ever known. I try to live by her example because, fuck knows, neither of our parents were good."

He jerks his chin up, just once.

"If you ever find it, don't let it go, you know?"

Bennett scoffs. "Doubtful."

"Well, whatever. Just don't count it out, is all I'm saying. And if you get it, keep it. I'm going to try like hell to."

"All right, all right. Enough with this shit already," Bennett says through a groan, dropping his menu to the table. "I forgive you for waking us up so fucking early, so you can stop laying it on so thick."

"That's the thing, Ben," I admit with a laugh. "This isn't thick at all. It isn't even sticky like syrup. I'm so in fucking love, I could go on and on and on, and it would never be enough."

He shuts his eyes and sighs. "Can you let me eat first? I can't handle all this sappy shit on an empty stomach."

I grin at him. "What can I say? I'm a man deranged."

"All right, deranged man. Let's eat, and then we'll go get your ring that looks like a water tower." He blows out a breath. "You truly are ridiculous. I hope you know that."

"Oh, I know, dude. But I promise, if you knew the story...you'd be looking for a water tower ring too."

There are not a lot of certainties in life, but right now, I'm certain. And Josie Ellis should get ready because I'm hell-bent on making her mine. Forever.

21

Josie

Thursday, September 22nd

"Ow!" I shriek, doing a hop and a turn on one leg and stretching my neck like an ostrich to distract from the pain. My toe throbs, and I reach down to grab it while tears sting the corners of my eyes.

Grandma left an hour ago to join her morning yoga group in the park, and I fell asleep on the living room couch after she was already gone, despite needing to get ready for work. Now, I'm running behind for my Thursday lunch shift, and my poor toe is paying the price.

I realize, as a grown woman, I shouldn't need my grandma to be home to keep me on schedule, but it's one of the perks of Rose's penchant for meddling. She stresses so I don't have to.

To be fair, I did get home from Clay's at an unfashionably late hour, and the lack of shut-eye becomes a very real physical limitation at some point. I wouldn't trade the time together, though. Our moments after he gets off work at the bar are always so freaking hot.

Fingers crossed, Harold's not too mad that I'm late and that my toenail doesn't fall off from trauma.

I grab my purse and lock the door behind me, hustling through a minor limp. The side of the stoop is wet from Grandma's garden sprinklers, so I look at the concrete carefully when I'm turning around to make sure I don't slip. The vintage black-and-white loafers Harold has us wear are a fall hazard on wet concrete. Trust me, my tailbone knows from experience.

When I finally look up, all the air in my lungs leaves in a rush with surprise. Clay is standing at the bottom of the stairs holding a big bouquet of red and pink flowers. His hair is combed just so, and his eyes are shining bright in the sunshine as he looks up at me. "Hey, beautiful."

It's so sweet it makes me want to cry.

And not having the time to stop and appreciate it makes me want to cry even more.

"This is so sweet, Clay. Literally the *sweetest*." He drops down into the grass as I'm talking, my eyebrows pulling together more and more with every inch he sinks. "But I'm running late for work, and I just know Harold is going to be on my ass—"

When he finally settles on one knee, I stop talking completely.

"Josie."

"Clay, what are you doing?" I whisper, a pang of the greatest joy I've ever felt stirring deep inside.

He lays the flowers in the grass and pulls his other hand out from behind him, revealing a red velvet box that makes my heart start to lope. Faster and faster, it feels like it'll flutter outside my chest if I can't rein it in.

"Clay...?"

"I love you, Josie Ellis. Whole heart, body, and soul. You're the one for me. I want to spend all my moments with you. Good, bad, hard, easy...I want to do it together." he says, and I can't tell if his voice is a little shaky from nerves or emotions.

Or, hell's bells, maybe it's me who's shaky?

"I know I just convinced you to move in with me a few days ago," he says, his brown eyes staring deeply into mine. "And you're probably still getting over that—maybe even a little mad about the way I went about it—but I can't wait to make you mine forever. Not anymore. Waiting feels like not breathing. It feels like... Jose, it feels like if I can't have more of you...have all of you, I'll expire right here. So, today, on the anniversary of the day I told you I love you two years ago, please...be my wife."

"Clay...you...you make it sound like... Are you asking to get engaged, or are you asking to get *married*?"

His lips curve up in the brightest of genuine smiles. His heart is in his eyes, and the depths of brown look like smooth honey. "I want the whole shebang, baby. And I want it now. You know me, I'm all in, and I don't like to wait. I will, of course, just like I did when you took the extra day to tell me you loved me," he points out in jest, winking when I roll my eyes. "But I want you to get in my truck right now, go to the courthouse with me, and make it official. I want to call you mine today."

My pulse thrums in my fingertips, and my stomach rides a looped roller coaster. "I'm supposed to be at work."

"Call Harold and tell him you're sick."

"I'm supposed to help Grandma label candles tonight."

"Call Grandma and tell her you're sick."

I giggle-snort. "Clay!"

"Josie, put this ring on your finger, and let's go get married. We'll deal with the rest of it tomorrow."

"You haven't even shown me the ring!" I cry, tears starting to fall from the corners of my eyes. I'm so happy. So much happier than I ever dreamed I'd be. I feel whole, and I know, even if it feels scary, marrying Clay is the best thing I'll ever do.

Clay fumbles with the velvet box but eventually gets it open, presenting it again when he's done. The large stone is in a high setting with a ring of smaller diamonds around the edge. The prongs are almost reversed from what you'd expect, wider at the base and skinnier at the top like they're little legs.

I swear it almost looks like—

"I wanted one that looked like a water tower."

Everything dancing inside me settles, a warmth spreading in its wake and filling me with visions of special dates with Clay Harris for the rest of my life.

I want it so badly, my whole body burns.

"Clay, I love it. I love *you*. I don't know how I'm going to explain it to everyone that we just went and got married without them, but—"

"You're saying yes?" he asks excitedly, jumping to his feet in front of me so quickly, he almost trips on the toe of his boot.

I nod through the tears. "I'm saying yes."

He sweeps me into his arms and around in a circle, and I relish the feel and smell of him as he groans into my hair. "Oh God, Jose. You won't regret this, I promise. And we'll have another wedding, okay? A big, official thing with the whole damn town if you want. I just want you to be my wife right now. I can't wait another day."

I nod enthusiastically, and Clay rains kisses across my face, one by one until he's covered the whole surface. I giggle the whole time and push him away after one final deep kiss to the lips.

He's the embodiment of everything I'm feeling. He's so much more comfortable in being over the top, but internally, we are twin flames.

"I just need to go change, okay?" I tell him, pushing away lightly to run for the porch.

"What? No!" Clay grabs at my elbow to stop me, but I pull him back toward the door with me, even as he fights.

"Listen, I may be okay with doing a quickie courthouse wedding, but I am not doing it in my diner uniform! It's a poodle skirt, for Pete's sake!"

"All right, all right," he concedes, releasing me. "You can change, but do it quick. The sooner I can call you my wife, the better."

Overwhelmed with happiness, I charge forward, running into his arms again and wrapping my own around him. He smiles up at me as he lifts me high, and I stare down into his sweet eyes with love and longing.

"In case I didn't make it clear…I can't wait either." My voice is a gentle whisper, but the message is strong. Clay and I are made for each other.

"I love you, Josie."

"I love you too, Clay."

His face is a beam of light. "The next time we say that, we'll be husband and wife."

22

Clay

Thursday, September 22nd

"Molene?" Josie asks as I pull into the city limits and drive up their version of Main Street to the courthouse at the center of town. I smile and reach over to take her hand, pulling it up and over with my own to kiss the back of it. "Felt like a good fit. Plus, you know we couldn't get married in Red Bridge, or we'd never get to tell anyone ourselves."

Josie smiles and giggles, and I have to fight the urge to drive my truck right into the curb so I can kiss her. She's wearing the blue dress she wore to church the first day I asked her out—ironically maudlin of her since she seems so surprised by my own sappiness—and her curls are half up and half down, cascading down her back. Her eyes sparkle with both moisture and excitement, and she's never looked more beautiful.

I swear I'd marry her twice if I thought it'd do anything legally to tie her to me a little more.

I settle for reaching over and running my hand up her bare leg instead, and she smiles so big, I almost wreck. Thankfully, we're here and pulling into a parking spot because it's clear we should not be on the road when I'm this fucking over-the-top excited to marry the woman of my dreams. Honestly, I don't think I'll be able to concentrate or think until she's officially mine.

After putting the truck in park and shutting it off, I jump out and run around to help her out.

Our eyes meet as she climbs down with her hands in mine, and I have to lean down to kiss her again.

"I can't believe we're doing this," she says, and I touch my forehead to hers.

"And I can't believe it took me this long to think of it."

I grab Josie's hand, and we practically run up the steps of the courthouse and into the main hall, where we go through a brief bout with security. I smile and joke about getting a pat-down to get married, but no one laughs.

I have a feeling their days aren't going quite as well as mine.

I follow the signs to the district judge, which a little research told me is what we needed to get married officially in this county, and pull Josie along with me at a jog. She doesn't complain, but I do try to slow myself down when it feels like I'm making her trip behind me.

"Sorry, baby," I apologize, stopping briefly to put my lips on hers. "I'm just excited."

She nods and smiles, her face alight. "I know. I'm not upset. I think I'd let you drag me like a log at this point."

I shake my head. "No, baby. As much as I'm ready, this isn't a race. I'm not going to be careless with you, I promise."

It's a small vow in this context, but I mean it in a way that is so much more. I don't just want a wife. I want a relationship with the woman of my dreams that I foster and curate and care for for the rest of our lives.

Her voice is soft as she leans up to kiss me again, pushing onto her toes. I hold the sides of her face and savor the moment as she whispers against my lips. "I love you."

My smile invades the space of her face. "I thought we weren't going to say it again until we were married."

"I think the point is to say it as much as you can."

I rest my forehead on hers. "You're right, baby. I love you."

A few kisses later, we're on the way again, this time elbow in elbow. She smiles up at me with every slow step we take, and I cherish the time as something we'll always have for just ourselves.

I hold the door to the judge's offices open for her, and she steps through first, the receptionist with copper-red hair and a frilly blouse smiling at us as we do. The wood and gold nameplate on the counter in front of her reads "Debra Katchken."

"Can I help you?"

I don't bother with sounding controlled on Debra's behalf. "Yes, ma'am. I need you to help me with the most important moment of my life and make this lady my wife."

Josie rolls her eyes at me—forever the cheeseball—but nods in agreement too. Debra smiles, our happiness contagious as she opens the judge's books and scrolls through them, her pointer finger skimming the page. Something I hadn't considered is that he might not have the time in his schedule to actually marry us today.

But that's okay. I'll drive to town after town through the whole damn state of Vermont if I have to. I can't sleep until I make her mine.

"You're in luck. He's actually finishing up his last meeting now, so he can take you in just one moment," Debra updates. "Write down your names here for me, and I'll take them back to him." She sets the paper between us and sets two pens at its sides.

Both of us scribble quickly, and we step back as she snatches the paper off the counter and retreats through the door behind her.

"We're getting married," Josie says, turning to me with eagerness. Her face is open with expression, and her eyes are clear. I'm a crazy, spontaneous asshole, but she wants this just as badly as I do. I lean forward to kiss her, and she giggles when Debra returns and talks over us. "I'll call you back in just a minute."

I smash Josie to me in a hug so tight she starts to squeal. Her supple body and her intoxicating smell—there's nothing that feels better to me. We stay like that until Debra returns.

"He's ready for you."

Pulling apart quickly, we hold hands and run into the judge's chambers like a couple of kids at an amusement park. It's not demure or composed or courthouse-appropriate in any shape or form. Luckily, the honorable Miller Faulks smiles as we approach the desk. "So, I hear you two want to get married?"

Josie and I glance at each other before turning back to the judge, two beaming faces full of teeth. "Yes, sir."

He smiles. "Well, let's do it, then. Shall we?"

I nod enthusiastically, and he dives right into the ceremony I'm sure he's performed a hundred times in his tenure.

It might not be special to him anymore, but it's sure as hell special to me. He bows his head to read from the paper on the desk in front of him, but I turn to Josie and take both her hands in mine.

"We're here today to witness the union of Josie Ellis and Clay Harris in marriage. Today, you begin a new life together, founded in love, laughter, honesty, respect, and friendship."

"And water towers," I add, making the judge and Josie both laugh. He's confused. She's smitten. Pink colors her perfect cheeks, and I give her fingers a meaningful squeeze.

"And water towers. Why not?" The judge shrugs and continues. "The promises you make to each other today should not be taken lightly. A marriage is more than a ceremony. It is a lasting and lifelong commitment."

Strangely, lifelong doesn't even seem like enough.

"Do you, Josie, take Clay to be your spouse and to live together as partners, to treat them with love and respect, and to build a marriage that grows stronger and more loving as time passes?"

Her heart is in her eyes as she stares up at me. "I do."

"And do you, Clay, take Josie to be your spouse and to live together as partners, to treat them with love and respect, and to build a marriage that grows stronger and more loving as time passes?"

"Yes, I do," I vow. "I really, really do."

The judge smiles. "If you have rings, take them out now."

Josie's eyes widen in panic as she realizes our oversight. "I don't have a ring for you. I have my engagement ring, but Clay, we don't have a ring for you."

I shake my head. "Doesn't matter, baby. We'll get one later. For now, all I need is you."

She nods, even if, in a perfect world, she'd have both.

"All right, then. By the virtue of the authority vested in me by the state of Vermont, I pronounce you married."

I pull Josie forward by her elbows and wait for the magic words, and the judge doesn't disappoint by making me wait. "You may kiss now! Congratulations!"

It's the kiss to end all kisses, and I could swim in it forever if the judge weren't staring at us expectantly. As it is, he extends his arm for us to leave, and I take my win where I can get it and get the hell out of there…with my wife.

My wife.

We damn near skip our way through the whole courthouse and out the door, down the steps, and over to my truck, and after a few more shared kisses, Josie goes to take out her phone. I know she's eager to share the news, and I am too. I'm just eager not to share her first.

"Don't call anyone yet."

"Clay, I just want to call Grandma Rose. Everyone else can wait."

I shake my head. "She can wait too, baby." When her eyebrows draw together, I kiss the wrinkle away. "Not forever. Just for a couple hours. Just long enough for us to have a little honeymoon first."

"You planned something?"

"Oh, baby, I've planned a lot of things."

And I can't wait to show them to her. My Josie. My wife. My forever.

After The Moment: Part 3

The History That Can't Repeat Itself

23

Josie

Tuesday, August 3rd

I drive in silence, tears welling in my eyes despite my refusal to let them fall. In my periphery, I glance over at my sister, who sits quietly in the passenger seat, her dazed eyes toward the window.

Three days ago, Norah showed up at my door. I didn't know why, but now I do. She was trying to seek a safe space away from her life in New York, but in less than seventy-two hours, a shitstorm of epic proportions has managed to follow her all the way to Red Bridge.

She was engaged, and a week prior to her landing on my doorstep, she left her fiancé at the altar.

It's a fucking tragedy that we know as much about each other's lives as complete strangers.

I glimpse over at her again, and she anxiously digs her teeth into her bottom lip.

She's a mess. Distraught. Confused. Scared. And all of it's valid.

This morning, her ex-fiancé, Thomas Conrad Michael King III, boldly showed up at my coffee shop while Norah was the only one there, to accost her. He threatened her both mentally and physically, and it makes my soul shudder at the thought of what she went through during her relationship with that man. It's always worse behind closed doors. Always. And I can't believe my very own baby sister found herself trapped inside.

Hell, it took Bennett Bishop stepping in to stop her violent ex from dragging her to his car. And even his intervention didn't end it. Eventually, Sheriff Pete had to get involved too.

The streetlights down Main Street glimmer, but all I can see is the vision of her scared face when I got back to the CAFFEINE this morning—and the gush of white milk mixing with blood all over the floor. Of her shaky, ashen face as they put Thomas in the back of the police car. Of her uncertainty as Pete explained her options for pressing charges when we were at the police station this afternoon. Of how scared that motherfucker made her.

God, what has become of us?

The history between Norah and me is...rocky at best. It's been five years without speaking, and I convinced myself I was doing what was right.

Five years of telling myself things to make myself feel better and to excuse away the duty I had as an older sister to get in the middle of a situation that was largely bad for me. *I can't save her. She's happy. Our mother favors her enough to keep her safe. She doesn't want my help and doesn't value me as a sister either.*

Five years of poison from our mother, seeping into Norah's every innocent crevice, uninhibited by any other family who cared.

I convinced myself I was doing the right thing with hollow arguments out of my own necessity, and now, because of my selfishness, my twenty-six-year-old sister has been through more in a quarter of her life than any woman should ever have to go through. I want to reach out and take her hand—to provide some sort of solace—but the fact is, there's not much comfort to be had when the man you were supposed to marry puts his hands on you in anger, threatens your very existence, and does it with the support of your own mother.

That's right. *Our* mother is the one who told Norah's ex where she was.

The neon sign on The Country Club shines through the windshield as I make the final turn on our way out of downtown, and I swallow thickly around memories of Clay and me that never seem to go away. Of gentle touches and genuine affection—of a life of mostly perfect moments outside of tragedy.

A complete dichotomy to Norah's relationship with her ex, and still, it wasn't meant to be.

"Pull over," Norah says suddenly, startling me. "I want to go inside."

I grip the wheel tighter and keep my foot steady on the pedal, just like I always do when I'm driving by Clay's bar to keep myself from stopping. I don't hesitate. I don't consider. I just drive.

"Josie. Please pull over," Norah pleads, turning in her seat to face me and reaching out to grab the elbow of my right arm. "I need to talk to Bennett. Apologize. Thank him. Something."

"I don't think that's a good idea." My voice sounds brittle even to my own ears.

"What? Why not?" Her questions are desperate and confused, and I can't blame her. She doesn't know all the details of Clay and me—hell, I don't even know if she ever knew we were together. According to what she told me the other day, Eleanor had her believing I opened the coffee shop before Grandma died and that I was living on my own in some apartment above the shop. I was loose and of poor character and might even be doing drugs. Evidently, keeping me out of the picture was most easily done with lies.

My grip tightens on the steering wheel as I try to keep my eyes on the road and off visions of the past, but Norah is insistent. "Josie, I got that man arrested today. I really need to go in there and talk to him. It's the right thing to do."

Thomas King wasn't the only one who got put in cuffs today. Ben did too. All in the name of standing up for my sister.

I sigh, asking myself how many more mistakes I'm willing to make before I do what's right. I'm sure I'll have more moments of weakness, but right now, sitting next to my sister with a mark on her arm from a man I can't help but think I could have prevented her from getting involved with if I'd just reached out after Grandma Rose's funeral, I have no choice but to stop being selfish.

I execute a U-turn easily in the wide-open street and swing into the packed parking lot. I move quickly to shut off the car and hop out before I have a chance to back out.

"Come on," I snip through the open window on my door when Norah doesn't follow my lead to hustle the fuck up. "Let's make this quick."

I don't have the bandwidth to be gentler—though I wish desperately that I did—and I turn and head for the bar with nothing more than a hope and a wish that she's not far behind me.

The Hill Country Hot Wings, a local bluegrass band from just outside of Molene, are playing on the small stage in the corner, and the room is teeming with bodies. People dance and chat and play pool in the far corner, and my heart feels like it'll explode if I don't manage a breath soon.

It's been five years since I set foot in this damn bar, and still, it feels like no time has passed at all. The brick walls, the hardwood floors, and the mahogany bar—they're all the same.

And that's the problem.

Norah pushes through the door and stops beside me, and I cross my arms over my chest to stop myself from exploding all over the place. I don't look around or focus on the faces I know I'll recognize. I can't.

The pain deep inside me is a ticking time bomb just waiting to detonate.

"I found him," Norah says, grabbing my elbow and pulling at me to go with her. "He's at the bar."

My feet are rooted to the spot. "I'll wait here for you."

"You don't want to—"

"Just go, Norah. I'll wait here."

Norah pushes through the crowd, and I scoot back to lean against the wall. This section has a bit of a shadow, and I'm hoping desperately it'll absorb me right into a black hole.

If I'm honest, I thought I'd be past all this by now. Sure, I thought it'd be a part of me, that I'd think of Clay and me from time to time and get a hit of happy memories, but I didn't dare dream that I would still mourn what I lost and wish for what we never had.

But every day, I do.

Five years and it all still consumes me.

I wish so fucking badly he would move on to someone else, but I also know it would quite literally kill me if I had to see him happy with another woman…

I barely have time to finish the thought before I spot the very reason for my pain. Clay heads toward me, a mask of determination on his handsome face. It's amazing how much it reminds me of the way he used to charge the door anytime I arrived, for entirely different reasons.

"Hey, Jose."

I lock myself down immediately, spinning away and trying to look beyond him to watch my sister's interaction with Bennett. "I'm only here for Norah."

"Yeah, Ben told me what happened," he says, and I hate the way his voice reminds me of cozy blankets and warm embraces. "I guess your mom is still up to all her old bullshit and building an army to help her."

The last thing I want to do is have a heart-to-heart about old times with my ex-husband. I don't even want to be civil—it hurts too much. "Clay, stop."

"What, Josie? I can't even express sympathy for your sister getting yanked around by a scumbag? You really hate me that much?"

"Clay, I said stop," I urge. "We don't need to get into any of this. As soon as Norah's done talking to Bennett, I'm leaving."

"Maybe you don't need to get into *this*, sweetheart, but I really, really do. It's been five fucking years, and I still don't know what happened," he counters, and the determination is still there inside the warm depths of his brown eyes that are directed right at me. "I want to know why you gave up on us. I deserve to know, Josie. I fucking deserve to know."

My skin crawls with memories of the accident and the bleeding and the pain. *God, there was so much pain.* I feel sick to my stomach, and I swear, if I don't get out of here soon, I'm going to coat the floor with my vomit.

Clay is in my face, not aggressively, but just *there*. Right there, his brown eyes staring into the depths of my soul. I can smell his familiar scent, the one I would practically get high off when we were together. I can feel the warmth of his skin, and I hate how my heart wants to remind me of what it feels like to have that warmth wrapped around my body.

It's all too much. *Way* too much.

I shove around him and trudge frantically through the crowd toward the bar. I know people recognize me enough to be surprised to see me in here, but I can't think of anything but getting to Norah and dragging her out of here as quickly as humanly possible.

She's still mid-conversation when I get to her, but I grab her shoulder anyway and grip tight.

"Norah, we need to go," I order impatiently. "Now."

I know Clay won't be far behind, but I take a deep breath and try to steady myself against my panic. I still consider Ben a dear friend, even if the rift between Clay and me has forced us apart for a lot of recent years. "By the way, Bennett, I really appreciate what you did for my sister today. Thank you." Hurried, I don't wait for an acknowledgment or an answer, instead turning to Norah and demanding some urgency once again. "Let's get out of here."

"C'mon, Josie," Clay pleads again, reaching out to touch my arm as he arrives, but I pull it away. "Just talk to me for a minute."

"No," I refute.

"You're in my bar, babe," he comments with a little smile. "And you never come into my bar."

"I'm only here because of my sister. Not you."

"Are you sure about that?" Clay challenges, putting his hands on his hips and throwing history in my face once again. "If I recall, you said you'd never step foot in this bar again. Not for any fucking reason."

"Sometimes we have to make exceptions and do things we absolutely don't want to do because it's for the people we love," I say, willing myself to keep it together, even though the feeling of being so brutal is nearly debilitating. Avoidance is so much easier. The last thing I want to inspire is hope. I did what I did all those years ago for him, and I'm doing what I'm doing now for Norah. That has to be the end of it.

The scrutiny of Clay's beautiful eyes is almost too much to bear.

"Let's go, Norah," I say again, but this time, I don't wait for acquiescence before pulling her along with me. My legs churn as I charge to the exit door, the humid evening air of summer a beacon of solace.

I run from everything I don't want to face, and I run knowing I need to.

When it comes to Clay Harris and me, history *cannot* repeat itself.

24

Josie

Tuesday, August 10th

For the past week, I've done my best to put the encounter with Clay at the bar behind me and focus on being the best support system I can be for my sister.

I want her to know she's loved and protected, and that as much as we butt heads, I'll do everything in my power to help her separate herself from her life with our mother and her ex-fiancé in New York.

She's trying hard too. At CAFFEINE, she does her best, though, I will admit, she is almost comically bad at barista-ing. And at home, she's conscious of her actions and considerate with my time and energy.

But I think what she's trying hardest of all to do is pretend none of her problems are actually happening, and man, can I relate to that one.

I've asked her about Thomas and Eleanor and all the things that really happened in New York, and she's asked me about Clay—after that night in his bar, the fact that there's *something* between us is undeniable. We've both declined to answer.

Some traits, it would seem, truly are hereditary.

I pull into a spot in front of my old haunt of employment, Harold's diner on Main, and turn the key to shut off the engine on my SUV. Norah's doing an interview to find something she's slightly better at than barista-ing, and even though I hesitated at first, I'm letting her use the old Civic.

It's not doing anyone any good sitting there, and maybe if I start to think of it as hers, I won't think about everything it used to be anymore and I won't think about what happened one of the last times I drove it.

I grab my purse from the front passenger seat and climb out, hustling inside and heading straight to the table I saw Eileen Martin sitting at through the window. She's been pursuing this meeting for months, and even though there's a history with her I'd rather not tap into, running some coupons for CAFFEINE in the paper really would be a good thing.

"Hey, Eileen. Sorry I'm a little late."

"Oh, no trouble at all, hun," she hums. "Not like I have things to do or places to be."

I don't bother hiding it as I roll my eyes. "Oh, don't worry, Eileen. I know how busy you are."

Everyone does. She's the textbook definition of a busybody.

She smiles, and the crow's-feet wrinkles around her eyes crinkle deeper. "I guess you saw the article about your sister and that Bennett Bishop, then? Good, wasn't it?"

"A little overdramatized if you ask me."

Eileen scoffs, sipping from her coffee cup. "Drama sells, girl."

I scowl. "You said there was a gang of vagabonds led by a dark, cloaked leader, and that Bennett single-handedly stopped their criminal ways with his hands. And that Norah was their former muse and captive. I appreciate your not using their full names, but c'mon,

Eileen, you have to admit you were pushing it."

"I like a stacked deck." She shrugs and runs her fingers over the pearl necklace she always pairs with a cardigan. "Plus, Sheriff Peeler buys me dinner sometimes if I make him look like he's got superpowers or somethin'."

I laugh despite her bullshit. That definitely sounds like something the old goat Pete would do.

"All right, well. Let's talk coupons so you can get back to... making shit up, I guess."

Eileen's mouth curves up, unashamed. "I can run them in the Sunday paper twice, but I don't recommend it."

My eyebrows draw together. "I'm confused. I...thought this meeting was about putting coupons in the paper? And the paper runs on Sunday? Why wouldn't you recommend running them twice?"

She waves a hand in front of her face. "Yeah, but the advertising section is crap. No one even reads it anyway."

"Eileen." I glare at her. "You begged me for this meeting."

"I want an exclusive," she announces and meets my current stare head on. "Heard lots of talk about you and Clay last Tuesday in the bar. Lots of *tension*."

Instantly annoyed, I grab my purse from the booth and scoot out. Eileen's voice is far more smug and far less pleading than it should be as she tries to stop me. "Oh, relax, Josie. Whatever went down between the two of you happened years ago. The least you can do is settle it all in everyone's minds. Even the government declassifies information after so many years."

"Leave me alone," I order, turning back only to point in her face. She's chastened a little, but if I know Eileen, when she's driven to get the story, nothing will stop her.

A silence falls over the diner as I storm out and run to my Acadia, jumping in and slamming the door behind me. I pause briefly and then grab on to the steering wheel, letting out a scream of frustration.

What the fuck! What the fuck! What. The. Fuck.

When I notice half the town and Eileen herself are still watching me through the window, I gather myself enough to turn the key, shift to reverse, and back out of the spot. I pull the shifter into drive and take off, my emotions running away from me like they're attached to a freight train.

I round the square and turn right and then left and then back again without a clue where I'm going. I don't stop for anything, instead holding my foot to the gas like it's linked to the pace of my heart.

I've lapped town ten times when I finally rock to a stop and shift into park. I sink my head into my hands and cry for a minute, letting the tears flow and the memories overwhelm me. I hate it here so much, in this purgatory. I can't move on, but I *can't* go back.

Sliding my face from my hands, I look up and through the windshield, and I am horrified to find that the culmination is in a place I should have avoided at all costs. The Red Bridge water tower that sits just outside of town.

I worry my lip with my teeth, considering for a minute, and then shut off the ignition and climb out before I can think too much of it.

I'm older than I was the last time I climbed this massive ladder, but as soon as I start, my mind and body go numb, and I move through the motions without trouble.

When I get to the top, I sit down and stick my legs through the railing at the edge, staring down at the town I love. It's amazing how it can feel like my greatest freedom and my biggest prison all at once.

I'm not made for the fast-paced, crowded feel of New York; I'm made for the sweet, tight-knit community of Red Bridge. Unfortunately, I'm not the only one. Clay belongs here too. Years ago, I suppose, that used to be a good thing.

And this water tower used to be *my* place until I shared it with him.

It used to be a place I'd come to breathe. To find peace. To find space. But now, it's just a place that holds all the memories I want so badly to flee.

I look down toward the town, wondering how in the hell I got here. Wondering how, at one point in my life, I felt like everything was perfect. How did it all go so wrong?

My breath catches as I see Clay's truck crossing the stupid, now-yellow bridge that Mayor Wallace painted last year, despite no one in the town wanting it. Clay's heading out of Red Bridge, probably on some errand for the bar, and I continue holding my breath until he's past the gravel road that leads to this water tower.

And I'm just about to exhale when I see his brake lights flash red, rocking the truck to a stop, and then the white lights on his tailgate brighten as he starts to reverse.

Shit.

His truck doesn't start driving forward until it reaches the very gravel road I drove down to get here. I briefly consider if I'd be able to climb down quick enough to leave, but it's only a millisecond before I rule out the notion as ridiculous. Even if I climb down, he'll be at the bottom. I'm better off staying up here, where he's afraid to come.

He hops out of his truck as I watch and comes to a stop right beside his hood, his hands on his hips and his gaze pointed up…at me.

I say nothing, instead leaning into the elevated breeze from being up this high and wait for him to make a move. He stays put for long moments—so long it feels like we'll both be here until we die—but eventually, he moves, heading straight for the ladder and starting to climb.

I fill my lungs with intention, willing my heart to maintain its pace. It's several minutes before he gets to the top, but when he does, I can't help but glance over at him. His face is ashen, and his knuckles are positively white from intense pressure. His fear of heights is still a very real thing.

He clears the landing and puts his back to the surface of the sphere, sliding down to sitting, just slightly to the left and behind me.

"You come up here a lot?" he asks, his voice disarming in a way I don't expect. It's pressure-less.

"No." I shake my head, but I don't turn around. "Haven't been up here in years. Truth be told, I don't even know what possessed me today."

"How's Norah?" he asks, and I look down at my feet that dangle off the ledge.

"She's okay. In denial, but okay. Eleanor had her so fucking snowed it's not even funny. Finding out everything's been a lie has been a shock, I think."

"I bet," he says simply, but we can both feel the weight behind his words. It's an ache he feels very personally. A longing to know why things went so wrong with us.

I'll never be able to explain how much I appreciate that he doesn't ask that right now.

"She's settling in, though," I add, desperate to make sure I don't give him enough time to reconsider his approach. "I think once all the dust settles, it'll all be good."

"And you?" he asks, such genuine care in his voice, I have to fight the urge to cry.

"I'll..." I swallow hard. "I'll be all right."

I can't see him nod, but I can feel it in my soul. "You always are."

I so, so desperately wish that were true.

"Well..." he says. "I guess I'll leave you to it."

I sit still, so still it feels like the wind might shatter me, as he climbs back down the ladder, gets into his truck, and drives away. I sit there and let the minutes tick by, so much so, I don't even know how much time has passed, only clueing in when the sun starts to fade.

I'd wait forever if I thought it would work—if waiting could make the feeling of utter devastation fade.

The thing is...it never does.

25

Clay

Wednesday, August 11th

Tad Hanson clings to the rocks glass, his knuckles tightening around it as I pull it from his grip and dump the rest of the vodka down the drain just like we agreed I would a long time ago.

His brother Randy stands at his back, ready to help him to his feet and drive him home to sleep it off, and I dig his keys out of the drawer at the back of the bar and hand them over to him.

"Thanks again, man," Randy says, and I nod.

"Yesh," Tad slurs, but he can barely hold his head up. "Thank dudes. Clays good."

When it comes to Tad, it's been this way for as long as I can remember, and to be quite honest, I don't know if it'll ever change. There's a story there, in the falsely jovial eyes of a man who spends all his time with sheep, one that isn't mine to tell.

I've heard pieces, of course, in the dim darkness of lonely

afternoons in my bar spent numbing the intensity of his emotions. It doesn't happen often, but it happens enough, and for Tad's sake, I hope with all my chest that it stops at some point.

Randy loops Tad's arm around his shoulder and gently walks him out, Tad hanging on him with brotherly affection and false jokes. He's quick with wit and unbearably light sometimes, but I know the truth.

He uses it as a tool to hide the darkness.

The door slams shut behind them, and the piercing rays of the sun disappear, once again plunging the bar into its usual darkness. I wipe down the counters and bus a couple of tables, readying myself for the evening crowd. It won't be bad tonight, given that it's a Wednesday, but I'll have a horde of regulars all the same.

After I'm done, I head back to the bar and grab the sandwich I got earlier from the sub shop the guy from Florida opened up a few months ago and pull up a stool to eat it.

I'm a man of the town and a friend to many, but since Josie left me, I'm also a man of solitude. I eat most of my meals alone when Bennett and Summer aren't inviting me to join them, and I don't pursue dating. I tried for a little bit a couple years ago, but I never made it past a first date.

None of them, no matter what they had to offer, were Josie.

I sing along to the station on the radio and flip the channel to catch some of the highlights for sports, but by and large, I'm just ticking time away until the crowd gets here tonight.

When I'm done, I toss out my garbage and run to the restroom for a quick piss and then get back to business as customers start to trickle in for the night.

It's a steady flow without being overwhelming, and I'm glad I told Marty he could have the night off tonight to celebrate his anniversary with Sheila. It would have been pointless for him to be here anyway.

I pop the top off a bottle of beer and pass it across the counter to Nick Schmitt, the local lawn guy, and then head back to the other side of the bar to bus some empties. I pull them off the counter and look up just as the main door from the parking lot slams shut.

I'm shocked to see Bennett, so much so, I don't stop myself from voicing it. "My God. What in the world's going on? Bennett Bishop in my bar on a Wednesday evening? Must be the apocalypse."

After all his past issues with alcohol, substance abuse, and debauchery in general, he makes a point not to loiter in bars—even if it's mine. Too many bad things have happened from it. Plus, he normally reserves his nights for Summer, and now that she's leaving the house less and less in an effort to keep her as healthy as possible, he's mostly become a homebody.

He sits on a stool at the end of the bar I'm at, where no one else has set up camp, and I don't waste time before settling up in front of him. The bastard looks tired, and I know there're a lot of reasons for that. Everything that's going on with Summer, being the main one, and the scuffle with Norah's asshole ex-fiancé last week that landed him in cuffs. Thankfully, the cuffs didn't end in charges, just a few hours at the station.

"Well, howdy there, good buddy." I smile at him. "What brings you in this time? Get in another shootout with some out-of-towner and spend the day in holding?" I tease. I know he's still butthurting over the article Eileen ran in the paper, and nothing makes me happier than getting his goat.

"Give me a glass of bourbon, Clay," he replies, already tired of me.

"Wowee, okay, then. Not in the mood for teasing, I see."

Bennett sighs, and I waggle my eyebrows in front of him, waiting for him to break. If he's here on a Wednesday night—his second time coming in here in about a week—it's got to be good. And as I've mentioned previously, I'm a little desperate for entertainment.

"Clay. Bourbon, please. Then I'll consider talking."

I figure that's fair enough, so I grab a glass from down below, flip it up, and set it in front of him. After one scoop of ice, I grab the bottle of bourbon to my left and pour until it's nearly touching the rim. Bennett picks it up and takes one sip, and then another, and drinking it down to half the glass while I watch.

Intrigue builds as I consider how much he seems to be teetering on the edge of control. I wait patiently, wiping at the counter and grabbing drinks when people approach, and after several minutes and an end to foot traffic, he finally starts to talk.

"Breezy's been on my ass about finding an assistant again. Says the bills are piling up, and I need to start selling shit so I can keep Summer at home and give her the care she needs." His words are bitter and a necessity all at once.

I nod, just once. I know the last thing Ben wants to do is sell his paintings to rich pricks who only see his art as a money investment, but I know without even having to ask, he'll do whatever it takes—whatever his sister Breezy says he needs to—to take care of his little girl.

"So, I put that old interview ad up at Earl's again, and someone actually found the damn thing and came to paint the barn yesterday. Summer and I took a ride down there to see it, and for once, someone actually did something worthwhile."

"Great." I love when a solution to a problem comes together.

"Yeah," he scoffs, his eyes alight with the cruelty of fate. "Except the someone is Norah fucking Ellis."

Damn, talk about ironic. He's been annoyed with Norah Ellis ever since she arrived in Red Bridge, something about her basically throwing herself in front of his truck to get a ride into town.

I consider him carefully, noting the line of his tense shoulders and the absolute grind of his jaw. This is more complicated than a woman he hates, and his problems are way too big to focus on that anyway. There's more to this, as there so often is when it comes to the dynamics of men and women, but I don't know if he even fully realizes it yet.

"And?" I eventually question.

"*And?* We've had a lot of shit between us in the short time she's been here, Clay, and not one piece of it is good. You think it's a good idea I hire her, make her a permanent fixture in my life? In Summer's?" He shakes his head, completely aggravated with what

I understand now is an overwhelming wave of emotion he doesn't want to have.

He doesn't hate Norah Ellis. Deep down, he likes her. *A lot.* And liking someone, wanting someone, when he knows his time with Summer is limited, is an inconvenience for which he's not spent any time preparing.

For Summer's illness to weaken her slowly and for his heart to break into a million pieces while he watches? Yes.

Having to share not only her but his affection with someone else? Not at all.

He stares down at his glass while I stare at him, working through all the ways I could tell him what I'm thinking. There are a million and one ways, sure, but very few of which he would find himself receptive to.

I settle for the root of the issue, the one I think he feels the deepest in the sharp stab of his nerves. Bennett is a grump and a prick and a hundred other things, but what he isn't is selfish when it comes to anything surrounding his daughter.

He can handle it if *his* heart breaks. But he can't handle the same for his daughter.

"You're afraid Summer is going to like her, aren't you?" I ask gently, leaning a hand into the counter and waiting.

He rolls his eyes, his mood sour, but his words bely his look. He knows it as well as I do...Summer Bishop is an unconditional lover. She spreads joy and compassion, and even being seven young years old, she'll be unable to stop herself from being the little angel that fixes the sadness in Norah's eyes. "Are you kidding? All that fanciness? She'll fall in love."

"Maybe...I don't know, Ben," I say as softly as I can in the din of the bar. "Maybe that's not a bad thing, you know? Maybe a little Norah Ellis in your lives is exactly what you need."

I know Josie Ellis is exactly what I've always needed in mine.

Because for as much as love can break us...it fixes us even more.

Bennett considers me closely before sucking back the rest of the glass and leaning into his hands. I knock gently on the bar directly in front of him and leave him to his thoughts to serve the crowd on the other side.

I think mindlessly about Josie on the water tower yesterday and of the unhappy ending we had nearly five years ago.

I think of the paths of our lives and how it appears they're about to intersect a whole hell of a lot more.

I sure hope we don't crash and burn again.

Lord knows, we're still trying to survive the first time.

Before The Moment: Part 4

The Honeymoon

26

Josie

Thursday, September 22nd

Flickering candles line the cobblestone sidewalk through the woods, a tiny, cozy cabin just ahead in the dimming light of day. We're a couple hours outside of Red Bridge, close to the Canadian border, and Clay carries the bag of toiletries and essentials he packed for both of us behind me.

My heart is in my throat, its normal delicate positioning only disturbed by the overwhelming feeling of joy. Clay cared for the details of today like a man who's been planning for years, though the execution was done in mere days.

On the drive up here, he shared stories about ring shopping with Summer and Bennett, and that Summer had decreed my ring as "pitty," thus finalizing it as the one.

I took Clay's suggestion and didn't call Grandma, but it'll be a few hours before she worries about me missing—she's used to me disappearing with Clay and ending up at his place at this point. But I did manage to text Harold about missing my shift, and he was surprisingly understanding.

I've resolved to let go now and enjoy my wedding night with my new husband.

My *husband*. Holy hell.

"Clay, this is stunning," I whisper, climbing the stone steps and turning back to look at his handsome face in the soft light.

He's as modest as I've ever seen him, his smile collected in a way that's peaceful. He's normally so vibrant, so big and over the top and exploding all over the place.

"What are you thinking?" I ask as he stares at me rather than answering.

The corners of his mouth curl up serenely. "I'm thinking I'm the luckiest guy on the whole of this amazing planet. I'm thinking my wife is beautiful. I'm thinking that if I'd known it would feel this amazing to marry you, I would have done it the first night we talked and I chased you into my parking lot and kissed you. I'm thinking I'm going to spend the next several hours showing you how much I love you. I'm thinking it can't possibly go up from here."

His words make my heart beat faster, and I can't decide if I want to sob tears of joy right here on the porch of this cabin he rented for us or jump into his arms.

"You're my forever, Josie," he says. "Thank you for choosing me back."

I choose the latter, rushing forward and launching myself into his arms, and he has to step back on a foot to stay upright. I wrap my arms around his strong shoulders and put my lips to his, and we disappear into an otherworldly place. A place where our kiss is the air and our connection is the water. A place where we only breathe life when we breathe into each other. A place where we can't get enough, but it doesn't make us gluttons.

A place I want to stay forever.

Clay lifts me higher, and I wrap my legs around his waist as he carries me the rest of the way inside. Small birds sing and chirp, and the buzz of falling night surrounds us in the forest. We kiss and touch and caress our hands over each other's skin, taking our time as Clay walks slowly through the little house to the bed in the back.

He lays me down gently in the middle of the fluffy white comforter, and I pull him down along with me. He sets the bag with our essentials to the side and holds my eyes, and I revel in the intensity of opening myself to him without looking away.

It's a connection unlike any other, a vulnerability I didn't know could feel so good. I don't hide or mask, and I don't expect it from him. "Clay Harris, I think you might just be the most beautiful man to ever live."

He frames my face with his large hand and dusts back an escaping curl, sweeping the pad of his thumb first over my cheek and then my lips.

A tingle spreads in my abdomen and up into my chest, and I arch up into his body in an attempt to be closer. All our clothes are in the way, but this time, it's not for a chase of pleasure. It's for a feeling, a connection, an intimacy that can't be replicated.

A thought pops into my head, and I can't stop my cheek from lifting as my mouth curves upward. "Clay, I'm actually really scared…"

His eyebrows knit together in concern, and I tilt my head to the side as I finish. "I'm scared if you don't make love to me right now, a werewolf or a vampire may appear in this forest and steal me away to be his lifelong mate right out from under your nose."

Clay chuckles then, grabbing my hips and pulling me down the bed so suddenly I gasp. "No Pattinson or Lautner kid is stealing my girl."

"Wait…*what?"* I giggle. "You know *Twilight*?"

"It was part of the husband training course I took."

I outright cackle. "Oh my God!"

He winks. "It was on TV in a marathon one day. What can I say? I got *sucked* in."

A snort escapes my nose. "You're so punny."

"I get it, you know, the whole plot. Some say it's unbelievable, but I'd totally fight a war over you."

I smile and shake my head. "Take off our pants and get up here already."

"That might be my favorite thing you've ever said to me."

I can't hide my enthusiastic grin as he undoes his belt and shoves his pants down his legs, taking the black boxer briefs I know he wears with them, and then comes back to me to roll my blue dress up from the bottom, past my belly and boobs, and up and over my head.

I hold him over me as he tosses my dress to the side, and I force him to stay. He chuckles, pushing the hair back from my face and leaning in to kiss both of my eyelids and then my lips. It's so soft, so intentional, I swear I can feel him opening up his entire soul to me.

His hips settle to mine, and as the tip of him finds my center, he pushes in with one smooth stroke. My head falls back, and a moan slips from my lips. My eyelashes flutter, and Clay's hands run across my skin from top to bottom.

Slow but firm, he pulls out and strokes back in, his hips grinding to mine as I lock my feet behind him and pull him as close as I can. This is lovemaking at its most pure. It's storytelling with our bodies, promise-giving for our future.

It's special in ways I can't even begin to describe and boundlessly fulfilling. "You're the love of my life," Clay whispers, his voice just raspier than normal.

Ditto. I nod, soaking him in and willing our bodies to become one. I need to be closer, to have more, and he gives me everything he has from his hips to his hands and all the way to his lips.

My gasp is loud in the otherwise quiet space, and the sound of his thrusts builds a rhythm in my mind. I let it climb, chasing and chasing as pleasure spikes at our connection and spreads through the rest of my body.

Clay grunts, sinking a gentle bite into the skin of my shoulder. It's not enough to hurt; it's claiming and primal and so right I can't explain it. I come in a blaze of glory and bright light and mind-pausing indulgence. I am only this moment and nothing more, and it's everything I need and then some.

Clay finds his release too, just milliseconds after me, toppling together into the most perfect union.

We're married.

Happiness from now on is synonymous with the word "us."

Serenity is this.

And I never want to know a world without it.

27

Clay

Thursday, September 22nd

Josie looks so peaceful as I slide out of the bed and run a hand along her bare hip. She's sleeping soundly, fully purged of energy from our three rounds of marriage-celebration sex, and I've finally worked up the courage to leave her long enough to get a glass of water.

My dry tongue and fatigued body thank me.

I pad gently to the kitchen of the small cabin, pulling a glass from the cabinet beside the fridge and turning on the tap to fill it halfway. A gentle lull of night sings from outside through an open window, and I take in the perfect moment with laser focus.

The crickets, the gentle breeze. They're only background for what we are—who we are—together.

I want to remember this in the times of suffering or the fights we'll have. I want to reference this when we're not sure how to carry on, and I want to hold space to get back to it.

I want the perfectness of what we are to be a constant in my mind that I never take for granted because Josie is the woman I would have created in a dream if I could've.

I want to be her steadiness in a life of chaos. She deserves that and so much more.

Josie's phone buzzes on the island counter from the spot I put it a couple of hours ago, and I lean forward to read the name on the screen.

Grandma Rose

Waking her feels criminal, but with everything I know about my wife, so does the thought of depriving her of the chance to share the most special moment of our lives with the woman she loves most in this world.

Josie's family life has been rough and lonely in some of the most horrible ways, but Rose is the light in all of it. The two of them are as close as two people can be, and I'm thankful every day Josie has her.

Scooping up her phone and rushing to the bed, I gently rub at Josie's hip until she starts to stir and then whisper in a firm enough voice that she can hear, but not so loud it'll scare her.

"Rose is calling, baby. I'm sure you can call her back, but I didn't want you to miss it if you want to talk to her."

She sits up and rubs her eyes, trying to wake herself quickly and smiling sweetly as she does. I slide the little bar on the screen to answer for her and put it to her ear before she takes over with her hand and holds it herself.

"Hey, Grandma," she says, the brightest smile in her voice.

My lip kicks up but stops abruptly when her eyebrows draw together, and she sits up straighter in bed. "Melba? What's going on? Is everything okay?"

Josie's hand flies to her mouth as she listens, and tears hit her eyes instantly. I scoot closer and grab on to her hand, willing my ears to hear and my strength to flood her. I don't know what it is, but I can tell by the devastation on her face that it isn't good.

"How bad is it? Where is she?" she asks then, jumping up from the bed and running around the room so desperately my heart shatters.

She doesn't know which way to go or what to gather because she can't gather herself.

I run to her and push her back to the bed, grabbing her dress from the floor and handing it to her and then finding her discarded underwear and giving her that too. She clutches the dress to her chest and the phone to her ear, and she listens to Melba again.

"But, like, the doctors can do something, right? I mean, people recover from strokes. Hank Basset's wife had one last year, remember?"

A *stroke*? Fuck.

I hustle to my pants and pull them up, grabbing my T-shirt and pulling it over my head just after. All I want to do right now is hold Josie to me and never let go. To seep strength into her body with my own until this feels a little more all right.

But I know that's not what she needs from me. I know she needs me to get us to Grandma Rose as quickly and safely as I can.

"I'm coming, okay?" she says almost desperately into the phone as she finally jumps up and starts dressing. "Please tell her I'm coming. I'm not at home, though, so it's going to take me a little while to get there, but I'm coming. Please, tell her I'm coming."

I grab everything we brought and follow Josie through the front door, helping her into the truck as she hangs up the phone and devolves into a deluge of tears so strong, it would flood the highest of elevation towns.

There are no words to placate, no ways to make this better, and I know it. She wasn't with Rose because she was with me, secretly eloping. And she didn't call Rose to tell her the good news because I told her to wait.

And the realization of all of that fucking sucks.

"I'm going to get us there as fast as I can, baby, I promise. Where is she?"

"Burlington."

I nod and fire up the truck, throwing it in reverse and flooring it out of the small driveway to the road. Burlington is between here and home, but we're still a good hour or more away, even if I hurry.

I reach out for her hand and hold it in mine, squeezing as tight as she'll let me, and allow the rest of the ride pass in silence.

It's the hardest thing I've ever done—leaving her to the quiet. But I know there's absolutely nothing I can say to make her feel better or change what she's feeling.

Her world just turned upside down. But I'll do everything I can to keep it from falling down and crumbling completely.

28

Josie

Friday, September 23rd

Frail, delicate skin and a loose grip are a tortured memory I'll carry forever.

Grandma Rose lies in the bed in front of me, her mind essentially gone, and her body carried only by the machines sustaining it.

She can't hear me talking, and she can't give me quips back. She doesn't even know I'm here, let alone that I got married yesterday.

I rub at the soft skin on the back of her hand and let the tears flow down my cheeks unchecked. My face is swollen and my heart is weak and an incredible pain feels like an acid burn in my stomach.

It took over an hour to get here in the middle of the night, and it was the hardest drive of my entire life. I wasn't there to help her when the stroke happened; I wasn't there to race her to the hospital. I wasn't there at all.

Instead, I was tucked away in a cabin in the woods after secretly running off and getting married. I didn't even call to tell her the good news, stupidly thinking I'd have plenty of time tomorrow.

"God, I'm so sorry, Grandma." My voice is choked as I squeeze her hand. "I'm so, so sorry."

I flinch when a hand lands gently on my shoulder, and I look up to find my grandmother's best friend standing beside me.

"Thank you so much for being such a good friend, Melba," I say softly. If they didn't have a nightly ritual of talking on the phone to gossip about the day, I don't know how long Grandma would have been there all alone. But when she didn't answer, Melba drove straight to her house to check.

"If I'd been there, maybe I could've—"

Melba squeezes my shoulder. "Don't do that, honey. The doctors said this thing was a ticking time bomb that none of us could have prevented. They said it would have been fast and that she wouldn't have even known it was happening."

My voice is brittle. "And you believe that?"

"I have to."

I nod. I understand completely. Because thinking the alternative will destroy you.

It's sure as fuck destroying me.

Clay comes into the room quietly and sets a coffee on the table beside me. I look back and try to smile gratefully, but I know that my expression is hollow. Neither one of us can change how these events transpired, and it's a helpless feeling.

One that can't be fixed or made right or explained away.

I know there's no blame to be placed—but I wouldn't wish the hell of this hindsight on anyone.

He places a gentle and fleeting kiss to the top of my head and then steps away again, giving me the space to hold Grandma's hand and work through my feelings myself.

I can't imagine if he were smothering me with affection or words of encouragement right now, and I'm eternally grateful that he seems to have figured that out.

Melba squeezes my shoulder once more before stepping out of

the room too, and I lean forward to touch my cheek to Grandma's hand.

It's warm still, thanks to the machines, but all the life it gave before is starkly gone. I can't believe it's never coming back.

"I'm sorry I wasn't there," I whisper again, a fresh wave of tears cascading down to wet the linens at her side. "I'm sorry I went off and got married without telling you. You should've been there. And I should've been with you. You mean everything to me. You always have. And the thought of doing life without you—"

My voice cuts out, my whole body breaking on a sob.

"I don't know if I can do it."

I'm not ready.

But I guess, just like Grandma Rose always told me, I won't be.

And this time, she was right. When it comes to losing her, I never, ever will be.

29

Clay

Saturday, October 1st

I hold Josie's hand in mine in the back of the last town car that follows Grandma Rose's hearse from the church to the cemetery. Our pace over the pavement gently shakes the car back and forth as Josie stares ahead, her face a mask of nothingness despite the screams I know she's feeling inside.

My heart feels raw from my own mourning, but I smooth on a balm of ignoring it as I care for my wife. She doesn't talk much, but she cries. In the morning and in the afternoon and at night, her body drains itself through tears shed, and I shove any form of fluid she'll drink in front of her.

Her face is swollen, all the light of her beautiful green eyes dimmed and fading. I hold strong to her hand and never hesitate to stand tall at her back, waiting for the day she'll use me and accepting the fate that she might not.

The car rocks to a stop, and Gerry from the funeral home holds the door open to greet us on arrival. Josie doesn't move, though, her stare so hard I'm almost sure she's using it to will reality to break.

"Josie," I whisper to get her attention. She sucks in a breath, almost like she's had moving air into her lungs on hold for the entire drive, her eyes fluttering to mine. "We're here."

She scoots to the edge of her seat, and I put my hands to her hips to help her climb out.

The sun is bright and highlights the trees beautifully, a cacophony of colors raining down their leaves all around us. It's a stark background for the black of all the funeral-goers, and the walk to the grave site feels painful and tortured.

Josie walks ahead, her eyes to her feet as she traverses the dying grass in heels, and I stay close to be there if she needs me.

My tie swings in the space between us and highlights the significance of the occasion. I'm a jeans and boots guy every day. But not today. Grandma Rose deserves my very finest.

A crowd of townspeople follow us, a wave of despair so profound none of them have even tried to get me to talk about city council issues.

Sheriff Pete catches up to me and holds out a hand, and I take it to shake as we enter the shaded space of the pop-up tent that covers the gravesite and Grandma's casket. It's a huge change in light, so it takes my eyes a moment to adjust, but when they do, I see an older woman and an early twenties girl with remarkably familiar curls sitting in the front row.

Josie sees them at the very same time.

"You've got to be fucking kidding me." They're the first words out of my wife's mouth the whole day, and her voice is raw from disuse, adding even more of an edge.

She marches straight over to them and pulls the older woman out of her seat with rough hands. "Mother, you've got some fucking nerve coming here," Josie grinds out, her whole body strung so tight, I'm worried she'll break.

I'm also quick to deduce why both women look so familiar. It's

Eleanor and Norah Ellis, Josie's mother and sister. I've never met them, but I've heard enough about them through town gossip and from what little Josie has revealed to me to know this isn't an ideal situation at all.

City meeting small town head on, they're dressed in luxury-brand clothes I know from my former life as a rich prick. Her mom's face is callous and careless, and her younger sister Norah cowers behind her imposing figure like a lost puppy.

"She was my mother-in-law," Eleanor spits. "I have every right to be here."

"Over my dead body," Josie threatens, her hand shaking with the load of adrenaline dumping into her veins. I step forward to help, but Sheriff Peeler pushes me back, his eyes begging me not to get involved. Instead, he does, placing himself between Josie and Eleanor.

"I think you need to leave, Ellie."

"I'm not fucking leaving, and you can't make me." Eleanor is stubborn, digging her heels into the grass and pitching her nose high in the air as if she's better than everyone here. "I'm mourning just as much as anyone else, my daughter has a right to say goodbye to her grandmother, and we have a right to be here to discuss Rose's will."

"*Discuss her will?* Are you that much of a psychopath that you came here to see if there was money for you to get? You're the last fucking person she'd put in her will!" Josie yells, pushing into Pete's body so forcefully, he has to hold her back. "Grandma Rose is turning over in her casket at the sight of you. And Norah isn't your only daughter, *Mom*. News flash, but you had *three*."

I've heard lore of Josie and Norah's third sister, Jezzy, who died as a toddler, through whispers in town. I've seen her tattoo and her necklace she wears to honor her. But watching her confront her mother about the truth head on and hearing the pain in her voice is like a kick to the fucking stomach.

I step forward and stand behind my wife, but Norah already has her by the elbow. "Josie, stop. Now isn't the time for this."

Josie guffaws. "Ha! You can tell you don't know a damn thing about your grandma either, Nore. Rose hated her!" she yells, pointing at Eleanor, "And she'd be absolutely disgusted to see you drinking the Kool-Aid."

"Jose," I whisper, grabbing her by the arms and pulling her back slightly. But she fights out of my hold, and I let her. Stifling her need to let all this out is about the last thing I can imagine will help.

Bennett's truck pulls to a stop at the curb with the rest of the cars, and when he sees the mayhem, he gets out and starts moving this way on a jog.

"Ellie, you can leave now, or I'm going to have to help you leave," Pete finally says, nodding at Deputy Felix Rice to come help if he needs.

"Fine," Eleanor decrees, pushing through Pete and grabbing Norah by the elbow aggressively. "We'll leave, but it's not because you're telling us to. It's because I'm disgusted and ashamed of what my eldest daughter has become," she says directly to Josie, and an anger lights in my chest and threatens to burn the whole place down.

Norah's cheeks are pink as Eleanor drags her away, but she doesn't say a word in Josie's defense either. I can't imagine how betrayed Josie must feel.

Bennett arrives just as they're climbing in their car to go, and I steer Josie around to sit in one of the chairs in the front row, squatting in front of her. "You okay, baby?" I ask, putting my hands to her knees.

"You guys okay?" Bennett asks, trying to get a look at the offending assholes but missing them entirely as they drive away.

Josie shakes her head and mutters angrily to herself. "That woman is cancer. She eats you alive until you're nothing of yourself anymore."

"Who the fuck was that?" I hear Bennett ask Sheriff Pete, but Pete's voice is low enough that I don't quite hear what he says in response. It doesn't matter anyway. My priority is my wife.

No one knows yet that that's what she is to me, of course, but there's time. When all the dust settles and Josie feels more like herself, we'll let people know.

But right now, there are important things to handle.

"I hate her so much, Clay," Josie whispers, tears streaming down her cheeks.

"I know." I gently squeeze her thighs. "But for as much gall as she had showing up here, today *isn't* about her." Her eyes flick up to meet mine, a sheen of tears still coating them. "Let's lay Rose to rest," I suggest softly, and with a racking shake in her chest, her cry welling, she nods.

I climb out of my squat and into the chair next to her, offering my hand in her lap so she can hold it. Her grip is tight, and the tips of her nails dig into the skin of my palm.

I welcome the sting of it, hoping it'll give me some of her pain.

Reverend Bob steps forward to take a spot at the casket, and the rest of the crowd files in around us to fill the rest of the seats and all of the standing space within a twenty-foot radius. A gorgeous spray of white flowers sits atop the deep-colored wood casket, a piece I know Josie picked out with care while she was making the arrangements this week.

"Thank you, everyone, for coming out today to commune in the joy that Rose Ellis brought to our lives. Our earthly world is cruel in its timing, but our Father, our God, bestows it as divine. As Rose is enveloped in heaven's arms, we must seek solace in the arms of one another and find camaraderie in the love Rose made us feel."

Josie licks her lips and clenches my hand even tighter, and her knee shakes as she bounces it, desperate to channel her grief somewhere.

"It's our time to mourn, but we must remember that Rose is not. Her earthly body is retired, but her spirit lives on in all of us and Christ himself. Rose was a pinnacle in our town, a beacon for community and friendship I know personally we'll all treasure for a long time to come. She was also a child of the Lord and a woman of repentance. I know she'll find a welcome and most perfect home on the other side, and I hope you'll join me in my confidence. God has called his daughter home, and I know he'll provide her with the tenderness and care we so wish we could."

I bring Josie's hand to my mouth to kiss the back of it, and as a sob racks her body, I pull her in close with an arm over her shoulders.

Reverend Bob places his Bible on the casket and bows his head to pray. Everyone around us does the same, but I look directly at Josie, my priority to give her any level of comfort she'll accept.

"Our dearest God, please grant your grace to us living with pain—and to our dearly departed Rose, a most peaceful rest. Please guide us through this time, and light the way to You, your courage, support, and wisdom. Let Rose continue to bestow her knowledge and encouragement on us and allow us the insight to know she's with You. Blessed we are to have known you, Rose. In Jesus's name, Amen."

"Amen."

I'll take it from here, Rose, I vow with my heart and soul, tears carving down my cheeks and ending in a salted pool at the corners of my lips. *I promise I've got our girl.*

30

Josie

Thursday, October 20th

My throat burns as I swallow hard around two ibuprofen, and I force a swig of cold water from my glass to usher them down. My whole body hurts and my skin tugs at itself and I curl up on the couch and will the thoughts in my head to stop racing.

I don't sleep much anymore, and I can't remember the last time I went an hour or two without crying. Grandma Rose's house sits frozen in time as I fail to make progress every day in going through it. Empty boxes lean against the wall, just waiting to be assembled and filled, but I can't bring myself to put away the memories.

The infancy of Clay's and my marriage is a barrage of emotions I never dreamed of, and, I'm absolutely sure, neither did he.

He's ready to live together, but he's also been patient, and

I imagine for a man with a personality as large as his, it's been undeniably hard.

I know I need to pull it together. I know I need to find a place of solace and a way forward, and I know I need to stop putting us to bed by crying every night.

And yet, I can't stop. I don't know, at this point, if I'll ever stop.

The front door closes as Clay comes inside and scooches in to take a seat next to me. Our legs brush and his hand finds mine, but I cannot mine up the compassion or consciousness to give anything more. I'm a shell of myself.

"I know it's hard, but I can help you go through things if you want, baby."

I shake my head. "I don't think I can."

There's a beat of silence as he formulates a response designed to do anything but set me off, and tears creep into my eyes yet again.

He pulls me into a hug, and I bury my face in his throat as everything overcomes me. The wedding. Not telling Rose where I was going and missing the chance to tell her after. Not being there for the stroke or for all the moments when they brought her to the hospital. Not getting to say goodbye in any way that she'd actually know and not being able to make the new start to my life feel official by sharing it with her.

I *know* she'd want me to get off my ass and get over it. I just… can't.

I pull back from Clay and wipe at my inflamed face, and he finishes the job with the pad of his thumb. "Maybe you should go to the doctor, Jose."

"For what?"

He tilts his head gently. "You're not sleeping. You cry every day."

"I'm grieving!" I snap, even though I know he doesn't deserve it. "For fuck's sake, Clay, it's only been three weeks since I had to bury her!"

"I know, baby. I know you are." His voice is almost infuriatingly calm. "You have every right to grieve. But you're not sleeping at all.

And maybe they can help, you know? Give you something so you can get some rest, at least."

My pride feels bruised and my heart overrun. I don't know how to explain to him that I want to be left in my misery, and the stunted nature of my inability to communicate makes everything feel even worse.

"Just let me be!" I lash out, pushing him away and curling up on the couch. "I need the space to feel everything, and I don't need you hovering over me while I do it!"

"Jose," he says gently. So much more gently than I deserve. "I just want to help."

"If you want to help, you'll drop it!" I yell harshly.

Clay stands to his feet and walks away, and I curl into a ball on the couch. I tuck into myself just as the front door of the house slams, and I close my eyes as tight as I can get them.

Tears pinch through the clenched seams, and I let them come, giving my body over to the emotion until it finally puts me out cold.

• • •

I sit up with a start, looking around the fading light of my grandma's living room and wondering if it's all been a dream.

If she's still with us, and Clay and I are only visiting to have some cake and gab about how magical it was to elope. I imagine she would be over the moon, despite not being there, and she'd be helping me plan a big wedding celebration to have in the center of town.

She'd help me pick flowers and have me try on my veil, and she'd kiss Clay on the cheek and squeeze him tight just like she always did.

I rub my hands over my face and look around the empty room. The house is silent, and Grandma isn't washing her hands down the hall to get ready to bake the cake.

I suck my lips into my mouth and shove back into the couch,

pulling my knees to my chest. I startle when Clay appears at the end of the hall, a measuring tape in one hand and a pencil in the other.

"What are you doing?" I ask, no tact or care or greeting at all.

I regret it immediately—I regret a lot of things about the way I've been treating him since Grandma died—but if he takes offense, he doesn't show it.

"One of the hinges on the bathroom cabinet is loose. I was just measuring to drill some new holes."

He's not renovating to get me out of here, which I'm ashamed to admit was my first assumption. He's fixing. Upkeeping. Helping. *Goodness, I don't deserve him.*

"I'm sorry about before," I apologize, my voice just barely over a whisper. "I feel a little bit better now that I slept."

He nods, his eyes softening as he drops the tape measure and pencil on the counter and comes straight to me. He wraps me up in a hug full of warmth and love.

"Don't worry about it, baby. I understand completely."

I lick my lips and pull away from his embrace slowly, crossing my arms at the rush of cool air that envelops me now that he's gone.

I hate it, and at the same time, I crave it. It's a self-serving, completely destructive punishment of some sort, I'm pretty sure, but I don't have the capacity I would need to figure out why. "You're right about the doctor, I think. I should make an appointment to see if they can at least give me something to help me sleep."

His eyes are rich with compassion. "Do you want me to call for you?"

I shake my head. "I can do it."

"I want to be what and where you need me to be, Josie," he says, his voice tender as he grips my hand for a brief moment. "I love you, and I know you love me too. Let me know when you're ready to let me help you."

He's doing everything he can to be there for me, and all I do is push him away.

I *have* to stop pushing him away.

Right then, I make a promise to myself and to Clay and to Grandma Rose, too. I'm not ready, but she'd want me to do it anyway.

"I'm going to try to let you now. I *want* to let you help me now."

Clay pulls me into a hug, and I let myself savor the bittersweet of how good he feels. Things will never be the same, but they're not supposed to be.

A world without someone you love will always be a little dimmer. The only way to survive is to hang out as close as you can to the light.

And for me, the light is Clay.

31

Josie

Friday, November 11th

The ground is even cooler than the air, but I lie on it anyway. It clings to the cold of overnight, and I cling to the memory of my sister Jezebelle.

Today marks another anniversary of the day she passed, and I clutch at the J necklace of hers I've worn around my neck ever since and try to reconcile my emotions.

It's been so long and yet feels like no time at all since she passed, and the events of Grandma Rose's funeral only emphasize the contradiction.

Jezzy died because of my mother's negligence before she reached her third birthday.

The guilt in my heart for that tragic day is still there, lining my veins with a parasitic plaque. I know I was just a kid myself, but I still wish I could go back in time and change it all.

I wish I could've been wise enough to know that my mother sending me out on an errand to Earl's while she "entertained" Ralph Rigo—an old friend of my father's and a rich businessman from two towns over—would mean that she wouldn't have been paying attention to Jezzy at all.

My mother was always trying to climb the social ladder. She was always trying to find a way to live a life that revolved around money and greed, even if that meant having an affair while my father was out of town.

I don't know all of the details of what went down that day, but I know when I walked back to the house, Norah was outside playing in the yard. "We not allowed inside, Josie. Mom said we has to play outside," she'd said.

But I went inside anyway.

The door to our parents' bedroom was locked—my mother and Hank inside.

And I found Jezzy facedown in the bathtub.

At the time, Sheriff Pete was only a deputy and Mitchell Moreland was the Sheriff. When I tried to tell Sheriff Moreland what happened, tried to speak the truth about how Jezzy was left alone and my mother was locked in her bedroom with a man who wasn't my father, Eleanor Ellis made me the villain. The problem child. The *liar.*

The cycle continued from there. I was made out to be the troubled child she couldn't control, and the treatment only got worse after my father died.

When we were kids, my sister Norah and I were close. I watched out for her much like a mother would and cared for her in all the ways I wished our mother would've cared for me. I was the voice of reason in a clog of mis-influence by Eleanor, and I thought I was doing right by leaving Norah to come back to Red Bridge when I did. She was young, but I still thought she'd see through our mother's bullshit enough to come find me when she came of age.

But I couldn't have been more wrong.

Seeing her at the funeral, clinging to our mother's back, was like a sharp knife to how I thought everything would be. I talked Clay's ear off about it all last night, including all the sordid details of Jezzy's death and the truth about how tragic it really was.

I burdened him with all my heartache and all the pain, and I let him comfort me when it all became too much. He asked if he could come with me this morning to visit with Jezzy and to the doctor after, but there's still a selfish part of me that feels like all of this is mine to work through and mine alone.

It's shortsighted and not quite fair—I know—but I'm still working on getting past it.

The alarm on my phone goes off, and I lift my head carefully, my neck stiff from how long I've been lying here in the cold.

I sit up and touch my hand to Jezzy's headstone and pray that wherever she is, Grandma Rose has found her.

"Love you, Jezz," I whisper one last time before climbing to my feet and dusting leaves and dead grass from my leggings.

My lungs sting and my breath puffs in front of me as I walk back through the cemetery to my Civic, passing straight by Grandma Rose's gravestone without stopping. It's not that I wouldn't like to visit her—I want it more than almost anything else in this world. It's that if I do, I'll never be able to make myself leave in time to get to my doctor's appointment. And it's taken me nearly three weeks to get in as it is. The last thing I need is to miss this thing.

I climb in the car and start it, heading straight for our tiny health clinic on the outskirts of town. Dr. Klenny is my regular doctor here in Red Bridge, but something about going to someone I've known my whole life and asking for drugs to help me survive didn't sit right.

I'd rather see someone I don't know, someone with a fresh perspective on me as a patient, rather than knowing my whole life story the second I set foot in the door.

Dr. Masterson is new to town and moved here from Indianapolis, so she's got more of a big-city, none-of-my-business attitude.

My phone rings from the passenger seat just as I'm pulling into the parking lot, and upon seeing Clay's name on the screen, I pick it up and answer it.

"Hello?"

"Hey, babe. Just checking in. You doing okay?"

I know it's probably killing him not to be here, but with just the sound of his voice, I'm glad he isn't. Not because I don't love him or he wouldn't be supportive. But because I'm tired of him seeing me so incredibly weak. I want to be the woman he so desperately wanted to marry, and I need to find a way to be her on my own.

"I just pulled in. I stopped to see Jezz first."

"That's good. She was talkative, I bet." I can hear the smile in his voice.

I surprise myself by laughing. It's not something I do a lot anymore. It figures it'd be something seriously twisted and morose that would actually do it for me.

"Oh yeah," I reply. "Chatty Cathy, that one."

I can hear the relief in his voice as he says, "Okay, babe. Call me after? Or come see me. Whatever you want."

"Okay."

"I love you, Jose."

"Love you too," I say simply. Because for as much of a mess as I am and as hard as it's been to rationalize how the timing of our union intersected with Grandma Rose's death, I do love him. So much it hurts sometimes.

Running late now, I click out of the call and gather my purse quickly to jump out into the parking lot. I wrap my scarf around my neck a little tighter and jog to the front door, pausing only briefly when the sickening wave of furnace heat hits me in the face.

Almost as quickly as I wound it, I unfurl my scarf and pull it off and into my hand as I approach the front desk. There's a sign-in sheet on the little window ledge, and I fill out my name and information while the receptionist smiles at me. I don't recognize her, and that feels like a good thing.

"Here," she says, handing me a clipboard through the opening. "If you'll just fill out some of these forms with your info, I'll let the doctor know you're here, and she'll get to you shortly."

I take a pen from the cup and then sit down in the corner to fill out all my information. It's pretty quick and easy since I don't have medical insurance, and as soon as I turn the clipboard in again, they go ahead and wave me back.

It's a tiny office with just one doctor, so it makes sense that I'd be the only one here for my appointment since it's a scheduled time.

"Hi," a brunette nurse in blue scrubs and stylish white sneakers greets as I step through the door. "Josie Ellis, right?"

I nod. "That's me."

"I'm Lindsey, Dr. Masterson's nurse." Her smile is friendly as she waves me forward to follow her. "Come on back. We'll do your height and weight first, and then I'll give you a cup to give me a quick urine sample, okay? It said in your appointment notes that you've been having some trouble sleeping?"

I lick my lips, moving my head up and down. "Y...yes. My grandmother passed recently, and I...I've been struggling a bit."

Her eyes melt in compassion, and she reaches out to touch my elbow softly. "I'm so sorry for your loss."

My voice sounds raw as I reply, "Thank you."

"Well, don't worry, okay? Dr. Masterson is going to do a full checkup today just to make sure we're not dealing with anything underlying, and then we'll go over all the ways we might be able to help."

"That sounds good."

She smiles softly. "Go ahead and step on the scale for me."

I do, and she writes down my weight on the clipboard in her hand. For the first time in my life, I don't even pay attention to how much it is. It's a funny thing, being a woman, but evidently, if you're dealing with enough other stuff, being skinny actually stops mattering.

She moves a spindle above my head and writes down my height too, and I step off the scale and pick my purse up off the chair I set it on.

"Here," she says, handing me a clear plastic cup with a blue lid and a Sharpie marker. "I know you're the only one here right now, but go ahead and write your name on the label and then give me a sample in the cup. You don't have to fill it. Just about halfway is good enough."

"Okay."

"Then just bring it out with you and set it on the sink in this room right here." She gestures to the exam room behind her.

I give her a thumbs-up. Seems simple enough.

It doesn't take me long in the bathroom to pee in the cup and seal it up, wash my hands, and gather myself enough in the mirror to come back out, and when I do, Nurse Lindsey is waiting.

I put the cup on the sink and my purse on the chair in the corner and climb up onto the crinkly white paper of the exam table.

She dips test strips inside the cup and lays them out on the counter on top of a medical-grade sheet, and then she smiles as she walks to the door. "Dr. Masterson will be right in, okay?"

"Thanks."

Hands in my lap, I scour the signs in the room, looking for something of interest to occupy my time. I read one about HPV and another about school physicals and then finish up on a poster of the human body with arrows pointing to each and every major muscle.

I turn my head to read one of the weird names for something in the groin area, and the door swings open with the doctor's arrival.

She's blond and petite, and her hair is pulled halfway back in a long silver barrette. "Hi, Josie. I'm Dr. Masterson." She holds out a hand, and I take it, shaking firmly before she steps over to the sink to wash her hands.

As she washes, she glances at the now-developed test strips Lindsey took in my pee. Fascinatingly, her hands screech to a stop, pausing completely mid-wash.

A couple seconds later, she starts back up again until she finishes, shutting off the water and drying her hands with a paper towel before turning to me. "Lindsey said you're here to talk about some options to help with sleeping and general stress levels from a loved one's passing."

I nod. "Yes. My grandma passed away about a month and a half ago."

There's a careful look on her face I can't quite decipher, and she pulls up a stool to sit in front of me, her clasped hands pursed in front of her chest. "I'm sorry for your loss, and I think there are definitely some things we can do to help. But, Josie…I'd like to talk first about one of your urine tests."

"Is there something wrong?"

"You've got a positive pregnancy test, Josie, and it's not a faint positive either."

"What?" My head jerks back in surprise. "I'm pregnant?"

"We can run a blood test to be sure, but yes, I'd say there's a good chance you are. Which, honey, would explain a lot of your exhaustion and hormonal imbalance, too. The early stages of pregnancy are a tough time both mentally and physically, and combining that with grief would be a lot for anyone."

"I'm really pregnant?" I ask, a million and one happinesses and heartbreaks running through my mind at once.

Dr. Masterson nods, her smile gentle. "I feel confident saying yes. False positives are a rarity with the tests these days, but we'll definitely take some blood to confirm before you leave."

"Will it take a long time to get the results?"

She shakes her head. "We have a rapid test we can do if you'd prefer. That way, we get the results while you're here. If it's positive, I'll just refer you for a follow-up with an OB."

"Yes." I bob my chin up and down several times. "Please." I can't leave here without knowing for sure.

"Of course," Dr. Masterson agrees. Getting up from the stool, she peeks her head out the door and calls for Lindsey. "Hey, Linds. Grab a rapid HCG blood panel for me, would you?"

"Sure!" I hear Lindsey chirp, and in what seems like no time at all, she's knocking on the door with it in her hand. She takes a couple of gloves from the box by the sink and dons them before stepping over to me with a small, sharp device.

"This just takes a finger prick," she assures, taking my hand and flipping it over to poke it into the pad of my index finger. It stings a little, but with the way I've been feeling emotionally lately, it's almost a welcome release. She pools the blood and feeds it onto the test, and then sets it on the counter with the rest of the strips from my urine. "Should be ready shortly."

As time ticks, so do I through my catalog of memories. Of childhood with Jezzy and Norah, of arriving back to Red Bridge as a young and naïve woman, of cherished dinners and heartfelt conversations with Grandma Rose, and catching cheaters in my spare time. Of Clay's larger-than-life love and of water towers and stolen kisses. Of late nights at the bar teasing and laughing while he works and of community in a town I love more than I ever thought it was possible to love a place. Of days and nights with Bennett and Summer and of the amazing feeling I know comes from loving something so much you'll literally give up your whole life for it.

Bennett knows the feeling. My grandma and my dad. And if this really is happening, soon, so will Clay and I.

Dr. Masterson's voice is soft and confident and matches the smile I know is already on my face. "Congratulations, Josie. It looks like you're going to be a mama."

My mind races and zooms and turns over on itself with elation and consideration and fear and joy.

I'm *pregnant.*

Now, I just have to figure out how to tell Clay.

After The Moment: Part 4

The Last Day of Summer

32

Josie

Tuesday, August 31st

My legs churn as Norah carries forward at a jog ahead of me, my mind racing with a million and one thoughts about parallel universes and the possibility that I'm a part of one.

The life I almost had versus the one I'm living now, and if today would look the same either way, hangs in every corner of the town square decorations while memories of Clay and me dance front and center in my mind.

When Norah woke me up this morning, demanding my help with final touches on the big—but fake—wedding she's planned for Summer to witness as a part of her *wish-granting mission*, an overwhelming feeling of coincidence and coordination entered my mind and took root.

During Bennett's first year here, I fell in love with Summer in a way that still haunts me despite the rift between us. During Norah's first months here, Bennett and Summer fell in love with her, bringing them sweeping back into my life at a time that will no doubt trouble me forever. It feels like kismet, even if it's torture.

Over the past several days, as Summer's body has grown weaker and the doctor's prognosis has her time here on earth calculated in weeks and days instead of months and years, Norah is doing everything in her power to make the special little girl's final days the *best* days.

And this wedding, fake or not, is something Summer told Norah that she really wanted to see. Norah set out to make it happen.

But Norah's always been like that. The type of person who never meets a stranger. The type of person whose heart is pure, and her intentions are always good. She's so much like our father it's not even funny, and sometimes I wish she would've been old enough when he was alive to really remember him.

Clearly, I said yes to helping make the day special for Summer without question, and in large part, my entire role so far today has been chasing Norah around at full speed.

"Okay, what else do we need to get done?" I ask as we step inside the tent that's been erected near the town square. For the past few hours, Norah has been running around like a madwoman, working to get all of the chairs set up and the floral arrangements in place, and I've been doing my best to keep up with her.

Honestly, a pair of roller skates would've been useful today.

"All we need to do now is get ready," Norah says in a rush, pulling a dress out of her duffel bag and tossing it at me so hard it whips me in the face.

"Dang, Nore." I snort. "How about you take a breath? It's all going to be okay."

"I'm sorry," she squeaks out as she pulls another dress out of her bag and hangs it across a metal folding chair near a mirror that has a sticker that reads *Earl's Grocery Store* on it. Somehow, in a matter of days, my sister has managed to get help from the whole town in making one of Summer's last wishes come true.

I stare across the tent at my sister as she hurriedly changes out of her jeans and T-shirt and into the bubble-gum-pink dress. When she flashes me a "get your ass moving" look, I huff out a sigh and unfold the dress she threw at me from my arms. It's a white silk A-line number with bright pink flowers embroidered in the delicate material.

"Where did you manage to get this?" I shrug off my tank top and slide down my jean shorts. "It's gorgeous."

"I found it in one of the many boxes and bags of clothes I haven't really had a chance to unpack."

"Oh, you mean, the bags and boxes that are still cluttering my entire house?" I question, sarcasm in my voice, and for a brief moment, Norah looks sheepish.

"Maybe?"

I roll my eyes on a laugh as I finish sliding the dress on, and when Norah shoves a bag of makeup and a hairbrush into my chest, I get to work on making myself look presentable. I don't have any drive to pander to the male gaze—though, Clay *always* notices me—but with a dress this beautiful, I'd like my face to live up to it.

"Okay, so what else do you need my help with before I go find my seat in the audience?" I question as I apply a final coat of mascara to my lashes. I peek out of the tent quickly to see that the other guests are taking their seats. "Everything looks beautiful, Norah."

When I turn around to face her, an expectant smile on my face, the lipstick and blush are pointedly out of her hands. Her lips are sucked in on themselves, and she looks frighteningly guilty.

"What's going on?" I ask straightaway. "I don't like that look."

"Well...you're not going to be sitting in the audience."

"Huh?" When she doesn't offer an explanation, I add, "Where am I supposed to sit?"

"I need you somewhere else." She pauses and puts a little hairspray in her curls, fluffing them up with both hands. "A very important role in making this as special for Summer as possible."

I don't miss the way she's using the sweet, sick girl against me. She's cunning when she needs to be, just like she was with the memory of Grandma Rose when she needed a place to live.

"Bridesmaid?"

She shakes her head and digs her top teeth into her bottom lip.

I scrunch up my nose, my face a mask of annoyed confusion. "Pretty sure I'm too old to be a flower girl, Nore."

"Oh, I know," she says through a stilted laugh as she shoves her makeup into the bag and walks to the other side of the tent where a bunch of bouquets of pink flowers sit. "But you're not too old to be the bride." She quickly spins on her heel, and she fidgets with one of the bouquets. "Pretty much the perfect age, if you ask me."

"I'm the *bride*?" I shout loud enough for everyone outside the tent to probably hear. *"Norah!* Are you freaking kidding me?"

"I'm sorry," she says in a rush as she turns to face me again with her mouth set in a frown. "But I didn't know who else to ask. I mean, a wedding needs a bride and groom, and I briefly considered having Bennett and me pretend to be the ones getting married, but that felt instantly wrong, you know? Like it would be pushing the moral envelope a little too far."

I can't disagree with her there. The implications of a dying girl's father getting married to a woman he just met isn't something that falls in the gray. That's something that falls in the hell-no-don't-ever-do-that red zone. "Okay, it can't be you. Hypothetically, I get it…but if I'm the bride, who's the groom?"

"Actually, Bennett was in charge of that. We kind of tag-teamed the bride and groom task."

"And who did Bennett pick?" I ask carefully, my hackles rising with a sense of dread. I already know what she's going to say, and still, the nostalgic pit in my churning stomach doesn't want to believe it.

Norah mumbles something, but her back is to me again, so I press harder. "*Who*, Norah?"

"Um…Clay Harris." Her voice is a whisper, but I hear the expected words loud and clear. Clay is Bennett's best friend. He's single, so there's no girlfriend or wife to get needlessly jealous, and Summer is attached to him, so it'll make the whole thing all the more special.

It makes sense. And yet, it's the cruelest thing the universe has thrown at me in a long time.

"I must be losing it. Because I could've sworn you just said Clay Harris, and I know there's *no way* my sister would put me in that situation," I answer on an incredulous laugh. She doesn't know the whole story—she doesn't even know half of it—but she does know we're divorced, and she's a smart enough girl to figure there's a reason. "Who is my fake groom?"

Slowly, *so slowly* it feels like a mode on a camera, she turns tenuously and meets my eyes. Apology and guilt and even a little bit of shame reside in the depths of her baby blues, and my jaw makes a bid for my knees.

She doesn't say anything, but she doesn't need to. We both know what's happening with crystal-clear clarity.

"Norah, I mean this with the most love I can muster...but what in the *fuck* were you thinking?" I blurt out on a shout, and my hands shake with anger. One glance in the mirror and I see a mess of red splotches have found a place on my chest. I look down at the dress that she convinced me to put on—it's *white*, of course—and then back over at her. My gaze is so intense, my eyeballs might as well be shooting laser beams at her head.

"I was thinking that there's a sad, scared, sick little girl who wants with all of her heart to see a wedding take place today, even if it's fake, and I hardly know anyone here, so I figured you could play the bride."

She figured I could play the bride, and with Bennett's help, they've managed to drag me into a situation I thought would only happen in my nightmares. Or if I ended up in hell.

Marrying Clay Harris? *Again?* Fake or not, it feels like the most fucked-up thing I've ever been forced to be a part of.

"Oh. I see. You just thought I could *play* the bride. To *Clay*'s groom. Are you insane?"

My sister winces. "Well, technically, Bennett and I did not confer on our choices for bride and groom, but now that it's happening, I suppose it makes sense, given their friendship and all."

I can't believe this is happening right now!

"I already married that man once, and it didn't end well," I snap, still glaring at my now-shamefaced sister. "I'd have to be 'round the actual bend to do it again!"

"It's not real, Jose," she tries to reassure me. "Breezy found some fake officiant on the internet. It's not like you're actually marrying him. This is no more serious than a young girl playing dress-up in her closet."

Playing dress-up? Is she for real? Playing dress-up is supposed to be fun. A good time. This is the equivalent of getting a root canal and major abdominal surgery at the same time without anesthesia. Though, I think in order for that to *really* equal how messed up this is, there'd need to be an actual train wreck occurring while we're saying our fake vows.

I huff and sigh and pace the small space of the tent, occasionally eyeing my sister with the kind of disdain that has her mouth spreading out into a cringe.

Fake-marry Clay Harris? Besides the first time I real-married him, this is the worst idea anyone has ever had. I growl and stomp my foot, and Norah just stands there, her tight body language showcasing her fear and hesitation.

Fuck. This is horrible.

I pace and turn and wring my hands together, desperate to find a way out of this clusterfuck. My eyes flit and wander and scour, trying to find something that'll free me from the obligation, but instead, they find the opposite.

In Norah's hands, she holds a pink bouquet I know is the bride's by the size, and a wave of emotion for a little girl I helped care for right after she was born floods over me.

Summer Beatrice Bishop.

Soft giggles, pink sunglasses, endless smiles, sweet cuddles, and unbelievable happiness. She's the embodiment of special, and now, she's someone important not only to me and the town and Bennett and Clay...but my sister.

This isn't about me. This is about Summer. And even if it's torture, I have to do everything I can to help grant this wish.

I make my way toward Norah and snag the bouquet of pink

flowers from her hands. "You owe me so big. So, so big, I can't even think of the size right now. But it's going to be huge. Bigger than this whole damn continent, do you hear me?"

Silently, Norah nods.

"Let's get this over with," I grumble and turn to face the section of the tent that opens to the aisle I'm now supposed to walk down. A second later, I shoo Norah out of the way, all but pushing her through the curtain that leads to where this shitshow of a ceremony is supposed to take place and making my fake bridesmaid kick it all off with a bang.

I can't see anything past the curtain, but soft music starts to play, and everything inside my body wants to run for the damn hills. I imagine Clay—who is probably already standing on the makeshift altar—looking toward the curtain in front of me, and I have to close my eyes to steady my breathing. Our ceremony didn't look like this, and we never got to have our celebration with the town, but none of that matters. It feels so frighteningly real I could scream.

As the Bridal Chorus starts up, my heart rate feels like it peaks at one thousand beats per minute.

Holy hell.

I might pass out.

My feet don't want to move, and I'm just about to say fuck it and run out of the tent and away from the ceremony when a familiar head pops in through the curtain. "Mind if I escort you down, darlin'?"

Sheriff Pete. He knows enough about the past between Clay and me to know this is a royally messed-up situation, though he doesn't know everything. No one does. Except for me, I guess.

He locks his arm with mine, a soft but sympathetic smile on his face as he looks down at me. "How about I help you get to the end of that aisle?"

All I can do is nod. If this fake wedding weren't for Summer, I would've already hightailed it out of here. That little girl is literally the only thing keeping me from booking a one-way plane ticket to Mexico and never looking back.

Sheriff Peeler gives my hand one gentle squeeze before he starts to move. And I follow his lead,

through the curtain and out into the open, with the Bridal Chorus announcing my big entrance.

I hear everyone rise from their chairs, but I don't actually see them do it. My gaze is fixated on the ground, my mind busying itself with counting each step I take down the aisle. I can't look up and into the eyes of the man I thought I'd spend the rest of my life with. I just can't.

"Maybe just give them a little smile, yeah?" Sheriff Peeler whispers toward me. "Will help make Summer feel like it's real."

It's a touching reminder and wholly grating all at once. I do my best to force a smile to my lips and lift my eyes enough to spot Summer sitting in her chair at the end of the aisle. She looks so cute in her pink bridesmaid dress, and a memory of her with a pink crayon in Clay's bar tries to find its way to the front of my mind.

I squash that memory like a bug. The last thing I want to do is start bawling my eyes out and ruin this for her.

Norah stands beside Summer, and Bennett stands beside Clay, and in a perfect world, this is how it would have been all those years ago.

The most important people in our lives, watching us pledge to love each other forever. I try to fight it, but without my permission, my gaze finds its way to the silky brown of Clay's eyes and holds. They're moist and, most devastatingly, hopeful.

He stands on the altar, a tuxedo adorning his muscular frame, and he looks so good, I'd give away everything I know to be able not to notice.

He rocks back and forth on his feet, and a smile that feels way too big for the pretend occasion sits on his lips. He looks larger-than-life—just like always.

It takes a monumental effort on my part to keep this smile plastered on my lips, but I do. Because I have to.

Sheriff Pete and I reach the altar just as the Bridal Chorus ends, and I get passed off to my fake groom with agonizingly jovial flare.

Clay holds out his hand toward me, that big smile so prominent on his lips it makes me ache. I take his hand, nearly flinching at the feel of his skin on mine after all these years.

He helps me step up onto the altar, and a man with a gray beard and green eyes begins to speak. He's obviously the fake officiant that Norah said Breezy hired, and he starts his speech by welcoming everyone to the wedding and thanking them for being here.

Clay's eyes are on me the entire time. I can feel them. And I look everywhere else but at his face as a matter of self-preservation.

"Now, it's time for each of you to recite your vows," the officiant says, moving this fake ceremony right along. "Josie, you'll be first."

God help me. I force a deep breath in and out of my lungs and make myself look at my ex-husband. And man, I hate how easily he can hold my eye contact. Hate how my mind can still think about how good he looks. Hate that my heart still aches at the mere sight of him.

So many memories are wrapped up in me and him and this town and even Summer, and this isn't helping them fade away. This isn't helping at all.

"Josie, do you take Clay to be your husband, to have and to hold, to love, honor, and cherish, in sickness and in health, for as long as you both shall live?" the officiant asks, and my flight-or-fight instincts kick in so hard that I feel my entire body vibrate.

I said yes once. Look at how that turned out.

33

Clay

Tuesday, August 31st

Josie swings her head away from the officiant, bypassing me entirely, to look toward the crowd. Her spine is stiff, her mouth set into a firm line, but she is still the most beautiful woman I've ever seen in my life.

This wedding, fake or not, comes so fucking close to the real Red Bridge wedding I once imagined we'd have all those years ago, I can practically taste it.

I miss her and us, and I ache to make her see that she misses us too.

I glance from Josie to Summer, her smile so bright from her chair as she looks on. Memories of her as a toddler and the time I drew a little bridal Josie and a little groom Clay in her coloring book and told her that Clay wants to marry Josie because he loves her while we hung out in the bar hold steady in my mind.

I meant it, and today, the picture I painted is coming to life right in front of sweet Summer's eyes as one of her greatest final wishes. A burn starts inside me that I'm increasingly afraid I won't be able to extinguish.

There's a purpose today. A point that's hard to miss in her specialized chair right in the front. And yet, all I see is Josie. Josie in my bar trying to catch cheaters. Josie distracting me on the water tower in the sexiest fucking way. Josie laughing like a lunatic in Grandma Rose's kitchen when I was trying to learn how to make her famous fried chicken. Josie in my T-shirt, dancing around my apartment to her favorite eighties music. Josie helping Bennett and me take care of Summer when they first arrived in Red Bridge. Josie and me eloping at the courthouse.

And now, she stands before me, dressed in a white dress, and I'm holding my breath for her to say "I do." And fuck, even though it's fake, even though we're here to grant one of Summer's wishes, *my heart* wishes it were all real.

The officiant clears his throat, probably hoping a little encouragement will get Josie to say the words. And when that doesn't happen, Bennett clears his throat, though it's to no avail.

Silence has now consumed the entire ceremony, and I discreetly squeeze Josie's hands. I clear my throat, and her eyes snap away from the crowd and back to me.

C'mon, Josie. Just say it.

She narrows her eyes. Her mouth is still set in the firmest line I've ever seen. But the words, "Fine. Yes. I do. Whatever," roll off her tongue.

A cackle comes from the crowd, and I know everyone in this town well enough to know that it came straight from Eileen Martin's lips. I grit my teeth, hoping like hell that Josie doesn't jump off this altar and throttle her, and I'm relieved when the only thing that follows is the officiant's next line.

"And do you, Clay, take Josie to be your wife, to have and to hold, to love, honor, and cherish, in sickness and in health, for as long as you both shall live?"

He doesn't have to ask me twice. He's barely finishing the question before I'm proudly saying, "I do," everything in my voice a determined declaration and loud enough for everyone in the crowd to hear. "I've done it before, and I'd do it again every damn day of my life."

Josie's eyes narrow further, her gaze directly on my currently smiling face. She's pissed, but I don't care. I've been dreaming of this day for what feels like my entire life, and now that it's here, I'm going to enjoy this moment that I get to stand in front of my closest friends and declare my love for this woman.

Because I still love her. Even after everything that's happened, I love her so much.

"Great," the officiant is quick to respond. "Then how about the rings? Do we have rings?"

Bennett pulls two rings out of his pockets, ones I know he and Norah managed to get from Peggy Samuel's pawn shop, and hands them to me.

"Fantastic," the officiant remarks. "We'll do the rings with the exchanging of vows. Clay, why don't you go first this time?"

I grab Josie's hand and squeeze it. She tugs her arm a little, trying to pull away, but I ignore her efforts and keep her perfect hand locked tight within my grasp. The burn in my chest glowing even brighter, I take a breath before reciting vows I've thought about so much that I know them by heart. "Josie Ellis, my heart, my soul, my life. I'll always love you. I know we've been through a mountain range of ups and downs, and that I've made a mess of mistakes at every turn, but you are, unequivocally, the only woman for me." I smile at her. "I always knew we'd renew our vows one day, but I also imagined you'd like me a little more than you do now while we were doing it."

"Renew our vows?" Josie questions, and her eyebrows rise in outright shock. "Clay, we're divorced! There's nothing to *renew*."

The burn is a full-blown fire, raging inside me until my secret up and jumps right out the window.

"Actually, Josie, we're not divorced," I say, admitting a truth I thought I'd carry at least until Josie decided to take me back. "Not officially."

A resounding gasp from the crowd sounds jagged even to my ears, and I know it can't compare to what Josie is feeling by even a mile. But there's no taking it back now. It's out there, and I have no choice but to go with it.

"What?" Josie shouts, anger and outrage vibrating from every cell of her body. "What do you mean, we're not officially divorced?"

I've been in love with Josie Ellis since the moment I met her, and public stunts like these are the way I trapped her into feeling it back.

Fuck it. Considering she already hates me, it can't get worse.

It's time to lay it all out there. Once and for all.

34

Josie

Tuesday, August 31st

"I never signed the final paperwork," Clay says, and my knees threaten to give out at his words. "You and I are still married, and you know what? I don't regret it."

A hazy film clouds my vision, and my body sways just enough to threaten my entire equilibrium.

"You…you didn't sign the paperwork?" I ask, my hands trembling with so much anger that I can hardly control them. I don't have to see myself to know my wide eyes take up practically my entire face.

"No, woman," Clay says, and he keeps his eyes locked with mine. "Because despite your constant yellin', I still love you. So, I'd do it again!"

Blind panic takes over, and I lunge for Clay before I can even think about what I'm doing. My hands go straight for his throat, but my fingers are only able to wrap around it for mere seconds before

I'm being yanked back by my sister.

"Josie!" Norah cries out, but I'm too far gone to have any decorum. This man just told me something he's kept from me for years.

We're not divorced.

We. Are. Not. Divorced!

My hands are fists, moving toward him in succinct waves, each pumping movement trying to hit Clay anywhere I can. But more people run to the altar, and before I know it, Norah and Breezy and Sheriff Pete are holding me back, and Bennett has Clay within his grasp.

I swear I can hear laughs and shouts from the crowd, but my heart is pounding so hard inside my chest that I can hardly hear anything else over it.

"It's okay, Josie," Norah whispers into my ear, comforting me with the same soothing tone I've been using on her for weeks. Her words—her permission to make this moment about me—are my undoing. Tears are already forming a sheen over my eyes, and sobs threaten to rob my lungs of air. With all the strength I have left, I yank my body away from my sister and Breezy and Sheriff Pete and run away from Clay and the all-too-real sham ceremony as fast as I can.

As soon as I'm away from the crowd, the tears let go. They cover my cheeks and my nose and my lips and my chin, and deep, uncontrollable sobs accompany them with a horrifying sound.

By the time I reach CAFFEINE, my hands are shaking so badly and my vision is so blurred with emotion that I can hardly unlock the door.

"Josie! Wait up!" a voice calls after me just as I'm finally getting it open.

I glance over my shoulder to see Bennett's sister Breezy jogging toward me, and the raw vulnerability of everything I'm leaking from my pores right now seizes my chest. "I'm fine!" I call out quickly, averting my tearstained face from hers as she closes the distance between us.

I try to get into my shop before she reaches me, but just before I can shut the door, she shoves her high-heel-covered foot over the threshold and stops it.

"Breezy, I'm fine."

She raises an eyebrow, her knowing eyes just as telling as the mascara stains I know mar my cheeks.

"I know I don't look fine, but I'll be fine," I insist, wanting nothing more than to curl up into a solitary ball and purge myself of years of pent-up pain.

"Yeah, I know. I'm fine too. We're all fine. But how about you let me inside for a drink?" she requests, holding up two bottles of white wine and wiggling them in the air. "Just one drink together. We don't have to talk. We don't have to do anything but put a dent in these. And after one glass, if you're ready for me to leave, you can tell me to fuck right off, okay?"

The pressure of everything I've been carrying on my shoulders for the last five years and the changes that have come since Norah got to town suddenly feel like they weigh a million pounds. I'm not strong enough to stay standing and fend Breezy off. I'm just not.

"Okay," I say on a sigh, opening the door enough to make room for her, scooting in, and then closing it and locking it behind us.

Breezy heads behind the empty counter and snags two to-go cups from beside the register. She unscrews the cap on one of the bottles of cheap wine and gives two hefty pours into each empty cup. "Here," she says, handing one to me.

I take a sip and then another and then another five, and before I know it, I don't feel like standing anymore. Literally or figuratively. I plop down in a chair at one of the tables in the eat-in area, and Breezy sits down across from me.

She drinks her wine in silence, and I do the same. Unexpectedly, it starts to feel good that she's here. As an acquaintance I've spent relatively little time with through the years, she feels removed enough from the problem to stay neutral but familiar enough to put me at ease.

"By the way, I did manage to snag your purse." They're the first words out of her mouth as she slides it across the table toward me.

"Thank you."

Breezy nods and goes back to drinking her wine.

I drink my wine too, tears that I can't hold back still occasionally streaming down my cheeks as I do.

Everything Clay and I have been through. Everything that *I've* been through. Everything that I've lost. Everything that we should've been.

It's too much.

To find out that we're not even divorced is the final blow to my composure.

My nerves are shot to shit, every cell inside my body feels like it's hanging on by a thread, and the only thing that's keeping me together is this stupid glass of wine. I've never been a drinker, but damn, alcohol certainly helps to numb the pain.

I don't know how much time passes, but I do know that Breezy hands me a second glass of wine when my phone pings from inside my purse, and I pull it out to find a text from Norah.

Norah: *Are you okay? I know I'm the last person on earth you want to talk to right now...well, besides the idiot whom I won't name. But I just wanted to say I'm sorry, Josie. I'm so, so sorry for what happened out there. I swear to you, I had NO IDEA that Clay was the chosen groom until this afternoon or that he was going to be a total asshat. Please don't hate me. I love you.*

A few more tears slip down my cheeks, and I type out a quick response.

Me: *I don't hate you.*

I've never hated my sister, even when I thought I did after Grandma Rose's funeral. Norah is pure of heart, with intentions to match. I know her big plan wasn't to have me find out my ex-husband is still my husband on an altar in a white dress in front of the entire town. Still, it fucking sucked.

Norah: *You promise? Because I feel like a real asshole for putting you in that situation.*

Me: *Promise.*

Norah: *Breezy still with you?*

I glance up to find Breezy typing out an email on her phone.

Breezy has always been a bit of a boss bitch from way back. She runs Bennett's and her family's art galleries—which have several notable locations across the world. The woman's life is a busy, city-girl whirlwind, and the fact that she's sitting here with me, being a silent source of support while I'm drinking my tears away, shows that beneath that tough-as-nails surface is someone with a heart of gold.

Me: *Yeah. She brought some wine to distract me from killing Clay.*

Norah: *Just so you know, you made Summer's day. I don't know if I've ever seen that little girl so excited. She said, and I quote, "It was the best thing I've ever seen!"*

Making Summer happy is well worth my own torment for the very worst of reasons. Without meaning to, I cry a little harder.

Me: *I'm glad at least something good came out of it. Give her a kiss for me.*

Norah: *I will.*

I don't know how much time Summer has left, but I know it's not long. And that's so much bigger than everything with Clay.

Don't get me wrong, spending five years thinking a chapter was closed, only to find out it's been open the whole damn time, isn't insignificant. In fact, if I didn't love Clay Harris so much, I'd definitely hate him.

I chug the rest of my second cup of wine, and when Breezy hands me a third glass, I take it gratefully.

When tragic thoughts of the past threaten to spill into my subconscious, I force them out of my head with sips of wine that turn into gulps that turn into chugs.

I don't know if it's possible to drink yourself out of love with someone, but tonight, I'm sure as hell going to try.

35

Josie

Tuesday, August 31st

My brain feels like it's swimming in my skull, swirling 'round and 'round in a pool of water, and it takes me a hot minute to grab my cup of yummo wine. *Good job, Josie Posie. Good job.* It's a mental party in my head when I get the cup into my hands and lift it to my lips.

And the wines go down smoooooooth. *Delicious.*

I don't know how long I've been drinking, but Breezy is still here and there's still wine. For me, right now, that's all I need to know.

"What glass is this, Breezes?" I ask, and she looks up from her phone.

"That's your fifth, honey."

"I've had fives glasses? Holy shits!" I cackle, and Breezes looks at me weird. "I don't d-rink a lot." I scrub a hand down my face after a little burp pops out. "But damn, I prolly should drink more."

Breezy goes back to looking at her phone. I dunno what she's doing over there, but I know I like her. She brought me this wine. How couldn't I like her? Wine is so good. So, so good. I take it upon myself to get up from my chair and pour another. Breezy was doing this for me before, but she's doing boss bitches shit on her phone and I don't want to bother her.

"Whoops a daisies," I mutter when some of the wine spills on the counter. I lift the material of my dress to wipe it off. *Good as new.* I smile down at the clean counter and do a little celebratory dance on my bare feet. I don't know where my heels are, but who cares. Heels suck big balls. And the men who love women in heels should shut up. They should wear the heels. Not us women.

I lift my trusty cup of wine to my lips and drink it. And when the drinking isn't enough drinking because I want more wine, *I want a lot of wine*, I chug the fucker.

But when I lift the cup again and put it to my lips, nothing comes out. "Shit," I mutter, staring into the cup to figure out where the wine is at. It's empty. "Guess I need another." I grab one of the bottles and try to pour it, but when nothing comes out, I grab the other bottle and just drink from it instead.

Though, the damn thing runs out so quickly. It's like the wine is disappearing. Where's Jesus when you need him, you know? Pretty sure he could figure out a way to get me a refill.

"Hey…" I pause when I look at my new bestie, but for the life of me, I can't think of her name. Shit. What's her name? *I think it's, like, weathery. Like, something with the weather. Rain? No. Tornado? No. Though, that would be pretty funny if her name was Tornado. Oh!* I snap my fingers. *It's the wind!*

"Windy," I call toward her, but she doesn't look up. "Hey, Windy!" I say louder this time, and she looks up at me with a tilt of her head. "We gots any more wine?"

She shakes her head.

"Shit."

"I know, it's a bummer," she says and pats a chair next to her. "But since we're out and all, how about you come sit down for a minute?" My face a pouty frown, I head back over to the table and sit down beside her. "How are you feeling?" she questions, putting her phone facedown on the table. I guess she's done boss bitching. I can't remember what Windy does, but I know she, like, runs shit. Like real boss bitch shit.

"You're a boss bitch, aren't you?"

She laughs at that. "I am. And so are you."

"I am?"

"You own this coffee shop. That's definitely boss bitch shit."

"That's right!" I exclaim and hold out my arms, looking around CAFFEINE with a smile. "I run this bitch because I'm a boss bitch."

"Damn straight."

"Windy, my grandma woulda loved to see this place. She would be so happies I started it. She was always pushing me and pushing me! Get outta that comfort zone!"

"She would definitely be proud." Her smile is soft like butter, and after staring at her pretty eyes and her perfect skin for a minute or so, I realize her name isn't Windy at all.

"Your name isn't Windy, is it?"

She shakes her head, and a little laugh leaves her lips. "Breezy."

"Breeeezy!" I clap my hands. "I was so close."

"Not really, but that's okay."

"Did you know my grandma?"

She smiles. "I wish I'd known her better—that I'd taken the time to be here more before now. But from what I know *of* her, she was awesome."

"She *was* awesome. Pretty much the best." God, I miss her. I miss her so much some days I still find it hard to breathe.

Breezy smiles. "And I know she thought the same of you. Rose loved you, Josie."

"She loved Clay too," I tell her. "Wanted me to marry him. I did. But it was the same day she had her stroke." I lean my head back to look at the ceiling. "She was all alone when she had her stroke because I was on my mooning in the woods with Clay. I hope she wasn't scared."

"I don't think she was scared, Josie." A hand covers mine, and I look down to find that it's Breezy's. "And I definitely don't think she was mad at you for not being there, you know? Women like her want to see their granddaughters live their lives. They want them happy and fulfilled."

I was definitely happy and fulfilled with Clay. Until I wasn't.

I keep staring at Breezy's hand. "I didn't get to tell her that Clay and I eloped. She didn't know he was my husband. I mean, I said it to her when she was in the hospital, but she wasn't aware of anything then."

"She knew," Breezy assures me. "She might not have been able to tell you she knew, but she knew."

"You think so?"

She nods. "When someone is dying, their hearing is the last to go. So, whatever you told her in those final moments, she heard you."

"How do you know that?"

"I've had a number of conversations with Charlie, Summer's nurse, recently," she says, and she looks so sad that I want to hug her. "Charlie has worked with a lot of hospice patients, and she says even if it doesn't seem like the patient can hear you, they can."

My lip quivers as I think of the sweet little girl I fell in love with the day Bennett showed up with her in the bar. "I'm gonna miss her so much." I think of all the time I've lost out on with her because of the rift between Clay and me, and my voice softens. "I've already missed so much."

Breezy's lips turn down in the saddest frown. "Me too."

"I remember when Ben brought her to Red Bridge. She was just a tiny baby. So cute. So sweet." I squeeze Breezy's hand. "I helped Clay and Ben take care of her. They were so damn clueless."

She laughs at that, a few tears falling down her face in great opposition. "Ben loves that girl more than anything in this world."

I nod. "He does."

"I hope he's going to be okay," she says. "He has a history of going a little off the rails."

"We're gonna make sure he's okay. Me and you and Norah and

Clay. We're gonna make sure."

"We will, won't we?"

"We will." I tap her hand.

"Norah loves Ben. So much. She loves Summer too. She'll be there. And if there's one thing that Clay is, it's a good man. Prolly the best man. He'll make sure his best dude is okay. He'll be there. He's good that way." I lift my hand to scrub it down my face. "It's prolly why I'm still in loves with him, you know?"

Breezy tilts her head to the side a little. "I didn't realize you still loved him."

"Never stopped." I blow out a breath, and it makes my lips tickle from the vibrations. "It sucks."

"Why did you divorce him?" she asks, but then adds, "Or, at least, try to divorce him?"

"We're still married," I blurt out. "How fucked is that? We're supposed to be not married, but we're married. He's still my husband. I'm still Clay's wife!"

"I can imagine that was a shock today, finding that out."

"Just about passed out from it."

"You tried to strangle him too," she teases, and I cringe.

"Not a good look, huhs?"

She shrugs. "I don't know that anyone would have a good look when they found out the man they thought they divorced had managed to keep them married."

"Bingo bongo, girl." I point one index finger at her face.

"How long ago did you divorce?"

"Um..." I try to count the years in my head, and when that feels impossible, I lift a hand and start to use my fingers. "One...two... three... Like...five years, I think?"

Her eyes are wide. "Five years ago?"

"Yeah. I've been married to that fucker for five years and didn't even know it."

She shakes her head on a laugh. "Now I see why you almost strangled him on the altar this afternoon."

I burst into laughter, but as it goes on, it transforms, turning into a sob of sorts. Tears stream down my face, and I have to clutch at my chest it feels so tight. All the stupid emotions and feelings and memories, *so many memories*, feel like they're stuck inside me, and if I don't let some of them free, I'll explode.

"I didn't *want* to divorce him, but I *had* to. Too much shit had happened. So many sad and terrible things. And the accident! I almost lost him in a car wreck, did you know that?"

Breezy shakes her head…or maybe she doesn't; I don't know. All I can do is keep talking as my vision turns a little hazy.

"I was driving and we were fighting, and next thing I knew, everything was chaos. Screeching and, God, the sound of the metal crunching. It was so terrible."

"God, Josie." Breezy's voice is near my ear, but I'm too busy staring at the table. "I'm so sorry, honey. But thank goodness you all survived."

My words are a haunted whisper. "Not all of us."

I don't even realize tears are streaming down my cheeks until she reaches out to swipe a few away. "*Josie.*" My name on her lips is the embodiment of all my pain.

"He never even knew about the baby," I admit shamefully. "I never got to tell him. I wish I'd told him."

"Oh, honey," she whispers and slides her chair closer to mine to wrap her arms around me. "I'm so sorry. So, so sorry."

"It's all my fault. The wreck. The baby. Grandma Rose being alone."

"No, Josie," She squeezes me tighter. "None of those things were your fault."

Yeah, they were. And so was the rest of it.

I find myself wrapping my arms around her and hugging her right back. Some things, no matter how much I wish they would be, will never be the same.

36

Clay

Tuesday, August 31st

Josie clings to Breezy as she cries, the two of them highlighted by the soft light of only a single lamp. The town is quiet, the wedding decorations are stowed, Bennett and Norah have Summer resting at home, and all that's left is the damage I've created.

I stand there in the street for a long moment, watching the two of them embrace and wishing things were different. Wishing I could be the one to comfort her—wishing she wouldn't rather anyone else on the planet but me.

If I were a better man, I'd say I regret keeping us married, even though I don't. That tomorrow, I'm going to call my lawyer and tell him to file the papers. I'd give her what she wants and do it without consternation or guilt trips.

But I'm not a better man.

I'm a desperate man. A man who still loves his wife more than he loves anything in this world and knows we should be together.

I can't make myself give up because it's not an option.

It doesn't matter that my best friend got in my face and read me the riot act or that we nearly came to blows after Josie ran off, and it doesn't matter that half the town gave me reproachful looks as I knuckled down to help clean up.

Josie Ellis is the love of my life. And I'm the love of hers, too. After seeing the way she looked at me during those damn vows I've been sitting on for all these years, I know it.

I want to rap my knuckles against the glass window of her coffee shop and beg her to talk to me. I want to tell her the truth—that I love her, that I've never stopped loving her, and that I'm sorry for all the ways I went wrong.

I want her to tell me why she had to leave—to tell me where the hell I went wrong so I can fix it.

There are so many things I want to say, but as I stand here, peering in her store's window like a fucking creep and watching tears stream down her face while Breezy rubs a comforting hand on her back, I know now isn't the time.

I may be impulsive and fucked up and self-serving sometimes, but none of those things are going to help heal my wife. She needs space and support, and she needs patience.

That virtue has never been my strong suit, but tonight, come hell or high water, I'm going to exercise it. After one last look at her perfect face, I turn and head for my truck.

It's a short drive home, but it feels long, spinning thoughts racing through my mind at a million miles per hour. There are a hell of a lot of us here in Red Bridge hurting today, and for the most part, it's not even because I'm an asshole.

My truck rocks to a stop in my parking spot in front of the bar, and I pull out my phone.

Me: *I'm sorry for losing the plot today, dude. I know that shit was for Summer, not for me, and I hope you can forgive me for how I handled it. How is she?*

Ben: *She's tired. So fucking tired. But I'm not ready. I'll never be ready.*

Fuck, fuck, fuck!

I slam my palm into the steering wheel and let out a scream. My sweet Summer girl doesn't have much time left here on earth, and it's so unbelievably unfair. It feels impossible, but I compose myself anyway. What Bennett must be feeling is a thousand times worse, and I have to be strong for him.

Me: *You want me to come over?*

Ben: *Not yet. But soon.*

Me: *Just say the word and I'll be there.*

I'd do anything for that little girl. *Anything.* Sadly, though, there's absolutely nothing I can do. There's nothing anyone can do. Time, now, is our number one enemy.

37

Clay

Wednesday September 1st

I don't know how long I've been asleep, but when I'm startled awake by the ring of my phone, I blindly reach out toward my nightstand to snag it into my hands. I have to blink several times before I can see the name on the screen, but when I see ***Incoming Call Josie***, adrenaline surges into my veins and I'm more awake than I've ever been in my life.

With the way she was when I left the coffee shop last night, I thought I'd have to run ten marathons before she'd ever pick up the phone and call me, even to curse me out. When it comes to me, Josie Ellis doesn't confront—she avoids.

"Josie?" I answer, my voice the kind of desperation most men would try to hide. Not me. I want her to know how much I love her every single fucking second, even if it makes me sound pathetic. "I was hoping you—"

"Bennett got arrested!" she interrupts.

"What?" I jump off my bed without even thinking, the words a shock to my system. I wasn't expecting her to tell me she loved me or anything, but I sure as fuck didn't think she'd say this either. "What the fuck do you mean, he got arrested?" I pace the hardwood floor of my bedroom and run a hand through my hair.

"Sheriff Pete took him into custody a little while ago. Apparently, Norah's ex is back in Red Bridge, ready to stir up trouble. Breezy called me first, but Norah just got a call from Sheriff Pete to come down to the station too. We're all on our way."

"Fuck!" I shout at the top of my lungs as I shove a pair of jeans on over my boxer briefs. This is the last thing Ben needs right now. Summer is in her final moments, and he's down at the police station dealing with that slimy fuckwit Thomas Kingston or whatever the fuck that rich prick's name is? "I'm gonna be honest, Jose, I want to kill that motherfucker."

"Get in line," she says, not the least bit shocked by my admission. I snag a T-shirt and toss it over my head, maneuvering it around my phone and grab my keys off the kitchen counter after I shove on my boots. "We're about five minutes out. You're coming?"

"I'm already on my way," I tell her and head out the front door. "Meet you guys there."

"Thanks, Clay," she says, and the call ends after that.

I jump into my old truck and start it up with a roar of my engine, not waiting at all before shifting into gear and flooring it. A spray of gravel flies behind me, and I squeal out of The Country Club's parking lot on two tires.

The drive is quicker than it should be—probably because I'm going exactly forty miles over the speed limit, and I see Breezy's rental fly into the parking lot from the other direction right ahead of me. I turn in and hit my brakes on a hard skid as I pull my truck to a stop in a parking spot right beside them. Norah and Josie get out of Breezy's car at the same time as I hop out of my driver's side door. I kick it shut with a slam and meet the three women on the sidewalk that leads to the front doors of the station.

Norah and Breezy are ahead of me on a jog, but I hang back to fall in beside Josie. Her body is tense, just like mine, and the stress permeating the air might as well be a warning on the weather station about dense fog.

"I'm worried," Josie whispers. They're the first words she's spoken to me without prompting in years. I place a gentle hand on the small of her back for a brief moment—seconds, at most—but old feelings of being her protector flow through me like hot lava.

To everyone else, Josie's a fireball, a go-getter, and a confident, secure woman who can handle her shit. But behind closed doors, she's soft and vulnerable and affectionate.

Her giving me a touch of that hidden side now is a gift I don't take for granted.

"It's going to be okay," I assure her confidently. Whatever it takes to make it that way, I'll do it.

"You promise?"

"I promise."

I love her. I'll never stop.

I grab the door and keep it open for all three women to walk inside the station, Breezy leading the charge toward the viper den that's brought Bennett down here in the first place.

Pete, Bennett, Josie's cunt of a mother Eleanor Ellis, and Norah's piece-of-shit ex are all squared up in the middle of the pit, right next to Deputy Rice's desk, and Bennett's face is a mask of feelings I haven't seen on him in a long time. It's not anger; it's rage.

And I can't fucking blame him.

"What the hell is going on here?" Breezy shouts, her voice a harsh demand and her face a steel-toed boot that's ready to kick ass.

"Thomas...Mom?" Norah cries as soon as she sees Eleanor Ellis and her asshole ex. "This is *your* doing?"

I immediately walk over to Ben's side, positioning myself to get involved physically if I need to. "You okay, man?"

He nods, his jaw grinding. "Just want to get home."

His words stab like a knife, knowing what he's missing—precious moments with his little girl that can't be replaced or made up for. I clap a hand to his shoulder. "I know."

"You've truly lost your mind, Eleanor," Josie spits unchecked. "Siding with an *abuser*?"

Her mother scoffs, her face a pinched-up expression that reeks of her usual self-entitled demeanor. "Thomas is hardly an abuser, Josie. Be serious."

"I am serious," Josie snaps back. "He put his hands on Norah and left a mark. Nearly dragged her out of my shop and would have if Bennett here hadn't stopped him. He's a piece of shit, and everyone here knows it."

"Folks, folks," Pete tries to interject, but the train has already left the station.

"He's a lot more than that," Norah cuts in, pulling a manila envelope from under her arm. Her voice is shaky and nervous, and her eyes keep flitting over to Ben, whose body is strung like a cocked bow. I move just barely in front of him, readying myself even more. "I have evidence here of blackmail and coercion and a pretty good feeling that there have been multiple girls the two of you have forced into abortions and other things."

"Where the hell did you get that?" Norah's hoity-toity ex asks on a shout, his voice a slithering snake of disdain.

Norah shakes her head. "It doesn't matter where I got it. What matters is that I have it. And I'm going to pursue it to the fullest extent of the law, even if that means a long, drawn-out trial against you."

Josie wraps an arm around Norah's shoulders in both comfort and pride. As it turns out, both Ellis sisters have one hell of a backbone.

"What the hell is she doing here?" Breezy snaps, pulling my attention away from Josie and Norah and over to Pete's office door. Recognition is immediate, and the hair stands up on the back of my neck.

Jessica fucking Folger. This fucking *bitch*. A goon in a sloppy suit trails behind her, but I don't pay him much mind.

"I'm here for my daughter," Jessica says, making the air leave my lungs in a rush. Josie's gasp sounds close to the same.

We were there in the beginning, with Bennett, as he navigated his new role in fatherhood. We were there for the stories about Jessica turning her baby away. We were there, and this bitch was nowhere to be found. The fucking audacity of her to come here and say that shit is mind-blowing.

"Don't give me that bullshit, Jessica Folger," Breezy spits, evidently feeling a lot like me. She points an accusing finger at the woman. "That girl is not your daughter. Your role was giving birth, and that was the extent of it."

"Because he paid me to leave!" Jessica shouts.

"He paid you a generous sum of money, yes, but you didn't need any convincing to leave, Jess. You and I both know you didn't want anything to do with that baby."

"She's saying I'm not the biological father," Bennett chokes out somehow, causing another round of gasps that suck almost all the air out of the station and set me on my toes. I've never hit a woman, but if I thought I could get away with it right now without making the situation worse, I sure as hell would.

"Is that right?" Breezy challenges, unfazed by Jessica's poison. "Well, I guess it's a good thing we did a DNA test before Bennett ever left the state with her, then."

"You have DNA?" the goofy goon behind her bumbles.

"Yes," Breezy declares. "We have DNA, a signed affidavit swearing the money was not a bribe, and a signed transfer of full rights to Bennett for Summer. I don't know what you think you have, but you don't have jack shit."

"You signed an affidavit?" the lawyer questions Jessica, his eyes widening in incredulity.

"I signed a lot of things, but I was coerced!" Jessica wails at the top of her lungs.

"Exactly!" Thomas shouts, and Breezy turns on him like a mama bear.

"You stay out of this!"

Bennett's laugh is humorless. "He's having a hard time staying out of it because he's the one who convinced Jess to come. Right?"

Norah's slimy ex and Summer's shitty bio mom are both silent for a long moment, and Eleanor Ellis puts a defiant hand to her hip, anger vibrating off her body. "This is preposterous. Sheriff! This is all lies, every bit of it!"

Josie guffaws. "Don't act like you're innocent, Mother. You've had your hand in all of it."

"Listen, folks, from what I'm hearing, Bennett is free to go," Sheriff Pete interjects. He doesn't hesitate to walk over to Bennett and remove his cuffs. "If there's anything else to be settled, I suggest you file suit with the appropriate court."

"This is bullshit," Jessica cries, pointing at Thomas. "You said I could get more money! That's the whole damn reason I even came!"

Her lawyer doesn't give two shits. He already has his briefcase in hand and is heading for the door.

"The money's gone, Jess," Bennet says. "All that's left is the daughter you never wanted. The daughter I would give *anything* to keep. So, I suggest you go back to wherever you've been because the only place you're going in the company of this guy is prison."

Eleanor and Thomas are still spouting bullshit, Jessica occasionally joining in with words that can't hold water. But Bennett ignores the shitty crowd of people who came down here to try to make his and Norah's lives hell.

"Pete, I'm leaving," he says.

Sheriff Pete nods. "Okay, Ben."

"I'll drive you," I offer, already pulling my keys out of my pocket and heading toward the exit.

But Bennett pauses midway to the door, and I turn to watch him as he stops in front of Norah. She looks so sad, so fucking sad. He whispers something in her ear, and her eyes shoot up to his. He says something else to her.

But all I can hear is her response. "I know."

Bennett heads toward me, and I steal one final look at Josie. She stands there beside Norah, her arm now wrapped around her sister's shoulder but her eyes on me.

Our people need taking care of, and today, we're a team.

38

Josie

Wednesday September 1st

Norah's breathing is shallow but sound, her eyes fluttering slightly with the restlessness of her sleep. I rub a hand over her back and pull the comforter higher, hoping to settle her some.

It's a little after eleven, and with everything she's been through in the last twenty-four hours, I'm not surprised she's already passed out.

The guilt she carries over bringing the mess of Thomas and our mother to Bennett's doorstep, while unnecessary, is at an all-time peak after this morning. Bennett having been pulled away from Summer's bedside during some of her final moments, and whatever Bennett said to her while he was leaving the police station, hasn't helped. I thought she'd still be at his house—with him and Summer—but instead, she's been here for hours, the broken mess of her story eating her alive.

She's more than the letter she got from a girl named Alexis on her would-be wedding day detailing the illegal and heinous acts our mother and Thomas have been involved in, and she's more than a woman who begrudgingly brought it to the station like Bennett asked.

She's powerful and strong and bighearted, and I know she'd sacrifice herself ten times over if Bennett and Summer needed her to.

She loves them both…fiercely. And her final goodbye to that sweet little girl this afternoon, on top of everything else, has been too much to bear.

When she got home this afternoon, I held her while she cried and buried my own feelings deep in the well of my stomach where I've been storing them for years. I wanted to be strong. To be steadfast. To help my sister in all the ways I haven't been able to for years.

But now that she's asleep, my own feelings are stirring, and by God, do they hurt.

My chest feels tight and my heart physically sick. Summer Bishop should not be dying, and I don't care about some greater plan. I want her to stay here, with us, forever.

I snag my phone from the coffee table and send a text to someone I know is hurting just like me.

Me: *How is she?*

Breezy's response comes a minute later.

Breezy: *It's not much longer. Do you want to come say goodbye?*

Instantly, tears prick my eyes, but I'm up and moving without a second thought. As hard as this will be for me, I don't want Summer to question for even a second if I loved her enough to be there when she needed me.

Me: *On my way.*

• • •

Bennett's house is quiet, the lights are dim, and a pall of sadness hangs in every vestige of the air as I step inside. Breezy sits at the kitchen table, her eyes red-rimmed and swollen, and I pull the door closed behind me as gently as I can manage.

"Where's Ben?" I ask, my voice soft. "Is he okay?" It's a stupid question. I know it. None of us are fucking okay here. But it's the desperate need to make him that way that has me asking anyway.

She shakes her head. "He's in there with her."

I dig my teeth into my bottom lip to fight back the emotion that wants to break open like a dam from my chest. Losing a child is the worst thing anyone can experience. I know this to be true, and I only had weeks to fall in love. Bennett has had years.

Breezy reaches for my hand and stands from the table, leading me toward Summer's bedroom. I hesitate just before we get to the cracked door, pulling on Breezy's arm. She stops and turns back, her brows drawn together.

"I don't want to intrude on Bennett's time."

Breezy's face is soft in a way that suggests she sees right through me. I came to say goodbye, but now that I'm here, it feels impossible.

"He's expecting you," she says simply. I swallow hard, nodding slightly, and she pushes through the door gently. Charlie is on the far bedside, adjusting the oxygen mask on Summer's face, and her chest moves up and down, painfully labored. Bennett sits on this side, his head bowed with her hand in his.

She looks so small, I have to suck my lips into my mouth to keep them from quivering. Her skin is so pale it almost looks translucent, her eyes are closed, and her lips have a bluish tint that makes a deep, nagging ache claw at my stomach.

Bennett glances over his shoulder and meets my eyes. All I can do is nod toward him. He looks back at his daughter, lifts her hand to press kisses to her fingers, and gently sets it back on the bed before rising to his feet.

He doesn't say anything to me, but I can't stop myself from meeting him halfway to the door and wrapping him up in a hug. I hug him hard and tight, and it only takes a few seconds before he's hugging me back. I can feel his chest vibrate with each sob, and I silently tell him how sorry I am through my embrace.

When I release him, his devastated gaze meets mine for just a moment before he gives my shoulder one gentle squeeze and walks out the door with Breezy.

I take a deep breath and head over to the empty chair beside Summer's bed and sit down. The closer I get to her, the more I know how bad it really is. Her last days have now become hours, and her little body can't go on much longer.

Tears stream down my cheeks as I reach out to gently place my hand over hers, feeling her soft skin for the first time in years. Between the rift and her fragility, I can't remember the last time we made contact. I weave my fingers with hers, rubbing my thumb over the pink-glitter-polished nail on her pinkie. "I love you, sweet girl. More than the moon and the stars and all the time and space in between. You showed people how to love, me included. You showed me what's right and important, and you lit up this whole town's world."

I bow my head and rest it on her hand, trying like hell to keep the sobs that want to escape my lungs under control. I've known this little girl since she was a baby. For the first few years of her life, I was her Auntie Josie. I saw her all the time. I cuddled her and played with her and fed her bottles and changed her diapers.

She's not supposed to die, and she's certainly not supposed to do it before me.

A hand grips my shoulder, and I look up, fully expecting it to be Charlie or Breezy, but I'm shocked to find Clay standing there, his mouth set in a firm line and tears already shining within his eyes.

Instantly, relief fills my chest at his presence. For as many wrongs as we've made, being here together with Summer in these final moments couldn't be more right.

We look at each other for a long moment, silence stretching between us, but it's not awkward or uncomfortable. It's a wordless exchange of the past. Of how much this little girl has meant to us. Of how she was a happy part of our early journey as a couple.

"I'm glad you're both here together." Charlie's voice grabs my attention, and I look across the room to find her walking toward us. "A few weeks ago, Summer and I were going through some of her old books and photos and coloring books and toys, and she came across this." She holds out a folded piece of paper, and Clay takes it from her outstretched hand. "She wanted me to give it to you."

Clay squats down beside my chair and carefully unfolds the paper. It's a page from a coloring book, Snow White the focus. Pink crayon scribbles are all over the page, and in the corner of it sits a drawing of a bride and groom that takes me back five years in time.

Clay loves Josie is written above the happy figures, and tears stream down my cheeks in thick waves as memories of that day in his bar fill my mind.

"I'll give you two a moment with her, okay?" Charlie says, and seconds later, she quietly leaves the room.

Summer was so little then, only a toddler, but she was just this happy, giggly, adorable little thing who loved to color with her pink crayon and ask a million questions. She had her struggles, but back then, she was vibrant with life, and anyone in her in her presence couldn't stop themselves from smiling.

She was light and love and joy, and she was so special to both Clay and me.

Clay's gaze meets mine, and I see that he, too, has tears streaming down his face.

"It's not fair," I whisper through a sob, and he doesn't hesitate to rise to his feet and pull me out of my chair and into his arms.

"I know," he whispers back. "I know."

His tight embrace is the only thing that keeps me from crumpling to the floor. I cry into his shoulder, my tears turning his T-shirt wet, as all the memories of the past roll through my mind.

This little girl is tied up in all our stuff, and it feels like I'm grieving losing her and losing Clay and losing our baby and losing Grandma Rose all at the same time.

I don't know how long I stand there in Clay's embrace, but I don't pull away until I feel like I have enough control of my emotions to tell her goodbye. He shoves the paper from Charlie into my back pocket without saying a word, and I finally work up the courage to let go.

I sit back down in the chair, and Clay stands behind me with his hands gripping my shoulders. And I reach out to take Summer's hand into mine again. Tears are a constant presence on my face, but I ignore them.

"I love you so much, sweet girl. So, so much. Getting to be your Auntie Josie is one of the greatest honors of my life." I lean forward to kiss her forehead, but I let my lips linger for a long moment before I pull away. "Goodbye, Summer."

On a shaky breath, I stand up from the chair, hug Clay one last time, and walk out of Summer's bedroom forever.

I know by the look of her and the throbbing in my heart that there won't be another time.

I drive home in a blur, drunk on sadness and devastation, unblinking until I pull into my driveway and shut off the engine. With wooden legs, I walk inside, pull out the Clay loves Josie paper that Clay shoved into my jeans pocket as I was leaving and set it on the nightstand, and climb into bed behind Norah, hugging her tight.

She's still sleeping, but I reach out and grasp her hand in mine while I cry silently into the pillow.

If only I could go back in time and do things differently. I'd take back so many things. I'd change so many things. *If I could go back in time, I'd find a way to stay.*

When the phone rings two hours later, the world is changed forever.

39

Clay

Friday, September 10th

Summer died in the early hours of September 2nd, and a day that used to be a random date on the calendar became the worst date we've ever known.

I walk into Bennett's house, unbuttoning the three buttons on my black suit jacket as I do, and I find Breezy in the kitchen. Her hip rests against the counter, a half-empty cup of coffee in her hands. A black dress covers her figure, and her dark bob is perfectly in place. Her lips are turned down at the corners, and her eyes are so far off in the distance it takes a moment for her to notice my presence.

She sighs. "I wish this day would've never come."

My nod is solemn.

She glances at the shiny gold watch on her wrist and sighs again. "I guess it's time, huh?"

I nod again. "Where is he?"

"In her room."

Ninety percent of Bennett's last eight days have been spent sitting in Summer's room.

My best friend isn't the type of person who wants you hovering over him on a good day, and in his grief, that hasn't changed.

He doesn't want words of comfort and sorrys for the injustice of it all. He wants silence. He wants space. He wants to navigate his grief in his own way.

I've done my best to channel my efforts to be there for him into other avenues, like stocking his fridge and getting takeout and hanging around on the periphery with a beer in hand, ready to listen. But today, he needs something else.

Today, he needs me to do the heavy lifting where he can't, to guide him through the motions and hold him upright while we lay his daughter to rest.

I walk down the hallway and stop at the open door of Summer's room. It's still filled with all her belongings, organized down to a T. Her favorite pink clothes hang in the closet. Her iPad sits on the nightstand. Her little trinkets and books and bracelets are spread along her dresser. Photos of her and Bennett hang on the walls, and a few pictures she drew are taped above her bed.

If I didn't know any better, I'd think she'd be wheeling through the door any second, and it's that thought that lodges emotion the size of a boulder in my throat.

Bennett sits in the chair beside her now-empty bed, and I walk over to him to place my hand on his shoulder. It's a difficult reminder of being in here with Josie, when we were both saying our goodbyes, and I have to shut my eyes tight for a long moment to keep the tears at bay.

So many memories of Josie and me are tied up in Summer. So many beautiful moments we shared because of that sweet girl. And now, she's gone. She's gone, and we'll never get to hear her laugh or see her smile. We'll never get to giggle over her excitement or witness her many pink outfits.

We'll never get her back. And if that isn't fucking cruelty personified, I don't know what is.

I squeeze Bennett's shoulder, and he lifts his head to glance up at me. I don't say anything because I don't need to. He knows what today is. He knows what we have to do.

He swipes his hand across his cheeks, removing remnants of tears, and gets to his feet. And I step back to give him space, but I stay there, with him, until he makes the first move to walk out of Summer's bedroom.

Only then, when he's ready, do I follow his lead.

Breezy grabs her purse and keys for her rental when she sees Bennett step into the living room, and she walks over to lock her arm with his. Bennett's eyes stay forward as they head out the front door, and I make sure his door is locked before I jog down the front porch steps.

Though, before Breezy can get in the front seat, I gently take the keys from her hands. "How about you ride in the back with him?" I whisper toward her, and she nods.

Once we're all in the car and Breezy is sitting in the back seat with Bennett, her hand grasping his, I start the engine and head down his gravel driveway. Toward the main road. Toward the cemetery. Toward the place we'll say goodbye to Summer forever.

• • •

Everyone in town has gathered for Summer's funeral. So many people have shown up to offer their condolences, to say goodbye to Summer, to silently give Bennett the support he probably doesn't even realize he needs.

I don't miss the fact that his parents or his brother Logan aren't here, but I don't bother asking Breezy any questions. Ben and Logan aren't on speaking terms, and his parents are too wrapped up in their own lives to do anything but focus on themselves.

Sadly, they've never had a relationship with their granddaughter, but I know Ben doesn't give a fuck about any of it. His only focus for the past seven years has been his daughter. His whole purpose has been her.

My eyes seek out Josie in the crowd, and I find her standing beside Norah. Both of them are dressed in black, both of their faces a solemn reminder of why we're all gathered here. Josie wraps her arm around Norah's shoulder and whispers something to her, and I can't stop myself from wondering how she's doing. What she's thinking. How she's feeling.

I'm grateful for her that she and Norah have managed to rebuild their relationship. I know Grandma Rose would be so happy about that, but I also know how Josie tends to distract herself with everyone else's feelings and emotions so she doesn't have to feel. To grieve.

Every muscle inside my body wants to walk straight over to her and pull her into my arms. To hug her just as tight as I hugged her when we were in Summer's bedroom, but I know now isn't the time.

Now is the time for me to be there for Bennett. Just like Josie probably feels like now is the time for her to be there for Norah.

Reverend Bob nods toward us, his head bowed in reverence as he clutches the Bible to his chest. "It's time," he says, and Bennett inhales a shaky breath before squatting down to grasp the edge of Summer's casket.

Sheriff Pete and I do the same, standing behind Bennett as we lift the casket and carry Summer over to her final resting place. Once we place it gently in the metal device that will lower it into the ground, both Pete and I stay beside the casket until Bennett finds the strength to let it go and head toward his seat.

His pain, his devastation, it's visible in every deep line of his face. It's evident in the way his shoulders sag forward as he walks over to take a seat beside Breezy in the front row and the feeble nature of his strong body.

Reverend Bob heads to the front, standing beside Summer's casket, and I don't hesitate to slide past Norah and Josie into an open space to stand in the front row across from Bennett and Breezy.

Sheriff Pete comes to a stop on my right, and Josie stands beside me on my left, her arm still wrapped around Norah's shoulders.

I know Norah wants nothing more than to be holding Bennett's hand—to be there to comfort him—but emotion has made him both stubborn and stupid, and there's nothing any of us can do about it but wait.

I hope they'll find their way back to each other. I hope that he doesn't end up in the same place as I am—standing beside the woman I love without being able to be with her. It's a fate so much worse than hell, and Bennett's already there.

Reverend Bob clears his throat as he opens his Bible and begins to address the crowd. "Welcome, everyone. I'll start by thanking you all for being here on this momentously difficult day. We're here to pay our respects to sweet Summer Bishop, taken from our earthly world far too soon."

My gaze settles on Bennett, and I swallow hard against the sadness in my throat when I see his head sink forward and his eyes move to the ground. *Fuck, man, I'm so sorry. So fucking sorry.*

"We are all suffering, but we must take solace in the fact that Summer is not," Reverend Bob says. "Her impact will be felt by all of us for the rest of our lives. And for our time with her, we are thankful. Because in that time, we were privileged to learn the value of seeking and living in joy. Summer took her misfortune and turned it around, finding pleasure in the simplest of gestures. A cookout at the church, a wedding in the square, a day with friends at the town festival," he continues, and his words are a beautiful but painful reminder of how much Summer meant to all of us.

How much she meant to Bennett and Breezy.

How much she meant to Josie and me.

How much she meant to Norah.

How much she meant to this whole damn town.

I can't stop myself from reaching out to brush my fingers against Josie's. I expect her to push my hand away. Ignore me. But I'm surprised when she does the opposite.

Her fingers brush mine until they wrap around my index finger with a tight squeeze. And we stay like that through the rest of Reverend Bob's speech.

"Over the years, I've personally had the occasion to laugh with Summer more than a dozen times—even, I'll admit, when my own mood was sour," he says. "She was a vibrant embodiment of our most innocent happiness, and I will miss her most dearly. But I know heaven will welcome her with an open gate and even warmer arms, and I know that God—my compassionate, loving God—will give her an afterlife free of pain and full of happiness. An existence she more than earned."

I wish Summer didn't have to die and that her short life hadn't been tarnished by an illness full of pain and suffering, and I wish the world wasn't cruel enough to take away people's chances to watch their daughters grow up.

I know the world isn't fair, but this isn't that. This is fucking bullshit.

Josie's fingers squeeze mine, and my hands itch to pull her into my arms, but when she releases her hold so that she can comfort Norah, I understand. I want my wife back, but on a day like today, you realize that a lot of people want a lot of things they don't get.

Reverend Bob places his Bible on the casket and his hand on top of that as he bows his head and prays directly for Summer. "Your life, we honor, your departure, we accept, your memory, we cherish. Although we are filled with grief today, tomorrow, and the rest of our days, we will be grateful for your life and the privilege of having shared it with you. Rest now, sweet Summer, and live on in both God and the hearts of those who love you. Blessed we are to have known you. In Jesus's name, Amen."

"Amen," I say with the rest of the congregation, broken by the finality of a single word.

"I invite you now to say your goodbyes to Summer's corporeal body and to facilitate the passing of her spirit to heaven by placing a pink rose on the top of her casket," Reverend Bob announces. "We'll start with the back row and work our way forward, and Hank here will be passing out flowers as you approach."

Pete and I approach first, taking flowers from Hank and saying our goodbyes. Tears stream down my cheeks unchecked as I take my turn. "Goodbye, sweet girl," I whisper. "Uncie Cay's gonna miss you."

And the pink rose serves as a painful reminder of everything I've lost, of what could've been, and of what's so desperately missing every single day.

It makes me think about the coloring book page, the one with the Josie bride and Clay groom, and I seal my goodbye with a promise.

"Clay loves Josie." *And he'll never fucking stop.*

Before The Moment: Part 6

The Thanksgiving

40

Josie

Thursday, November 24th

I shut off the shower water, wrap a towel around my body, and start the process of putting on lotion and drying my hair. All thanks to a little bout of pregnancy-induced nausea, I've been up since seven this morning. Thankfully, the hot shower I just took has definitely perked me up.

For the past two weeks, Clay and I have been like ships passing in the night. He works late at the bar, and I'm too tired to stay awake past ten.

I still haven't officially moved myself into his apartment, even though that's the plan, and Clay has by and large stopped pressuring me to pack up Grandma's stuff. I know he's ready, though, and every day I go without committing to moving builds our tension a little higher. Neither of us wants it to, but it is.

Not to mention, I haven't actually told him I'm pregnant yet, and

I'm sure that's turning me into a bit of a pressure cooker of emotion.

Once my hair is dry, I add a little texture spray to my blond curls and head out of the bathroom to wake up Clay. His big, muscular body is sprawled across the bed, his eyes are shut, and his mind is still in dreamland. He worked especially late last night, thanks to all the little birds who flew the Red Bridge coop to other towns but always manage to come back to spend the holiday with their families who still live here.

We haven't even had a chance to talk yet, but I know from the town phone tree that Fran the florist's daughter got up on the bar and took off her shirt while her husband looked on helplessly. Clay had to kick both of them out before they started a brawl.

"Clay, you're going to have to start waking up," I whisper into his ear, and he blinks his eyes open.

"What time is it?"

"A little after noon."

"Shit," he mutters. "What time do we have to be at Bennett's?"

"One."

"Fuck me," he groans and rubs at his eyes, and I smile down at him.

"You know, complaining isn't going to help you get out of bed any faster."

Clay eyes me with feigned annoyance, but then he surprises the hell out of me by bear-hugging my only-towel-clad body with both of his big arms and pulling me toward him.

"Don't you dare, Clay Matthew Harris!" I squeal. "I just fixed my hair and makeup. I am not above kicking you in the dick if you mess it up."

My words mean jack shit to him, and he just adjusts my body over his so that his big arms are still wrapped around me, but my thighs are now straddling his hips. The only barrier between me and his already hard cock is the thin sheet between our bodies.

He nips at my shoulder and grins at me. "But *Mrs. Harris*, don't you think we could fit in a little morning sex session before we head off to witness Bennett grumble like an old man about hosting

Thanksgiving dinner at his house."

"Technically, it would be afternoon sex since you slept so late. And no, we don't have time."

He makes a show of sliding his hands up my bare thighs and under my towel. His pesky fingers don't stop until they are fully gripping my ass. "Please?" He flashes puppy dog eyes at me and leans forward to bury his face into the crook of my neck, taking a deep inhale of air. "You smell so good. You feel so good." He squeezes my ass. "I think I'm just going to start closing the bar down at, like, eight every night so I can come home to you."

"The whole town of Red Bridge would riot. Not just Janie and Holden Berns." I laugh, and he lets out a deep groan.

"You heard?"

"Oh, I *heard*." My eyes go wide with amusement. "From Melba and Pete and Angie Hoffer. *Everyone* was talking about it."

Clay shakes his head. "See? Even more reason to close at eight."

"You talk a big, bad-ass game, but I know better." I tap his nose with my index finger. "You'd last one night closing at eight."

Clay smirks and squeezes my ass again. "But does my big, bad-ass game work on my wife?"

I shake my head and press a kiss to his nose. Right here, right now, it's almost as if everything is the way it was before Grandma Rose passed away. We're smiling and laughing, and my chest feels warm and gooey like a chocolate chip cookie that just came out of the oven.

We're the Clay and Josie who ran off to the courthouse to elope because they were so excited to spend the rest of forever together.

And the Mr. and Mrs. who are about to be Mom and Dad, too.

I've spent the last two weeks trying to come up with the most special way to let him in on my secret, on our we're-having-a-baby news, but it's moments like these that make me want to just blurt it out right now.

"Clay...I have something to tell you."

He kisses my forehead and heads for the bathroom, calling over his shoulder as he does. "Oh yeah? What's that?"

I trail after him, watching the bounce in his step and imagining what he'll be like after I tell him. Clay isn't a quiet kind of a guy. He's loud and impulsive and wears all his emotions on his sleeves. It's not hard to picture him buying a megaphone and announcing it to the whole town like an old-school town crier.

Immediately, memories of Carly Stamper and her husband Dan having to tell the whole town about her baby not having a heartbeat at the first ultrasound a few years ago pull me up short. They announced their news practically the instant she got a positive pregnancy test, and when it ended in a miscarriage, the pain in her eyes whenever she had to explain what happened to people who hadn't heard the sad follow-up news was downright heartbreaking.

I can only handle so much heartbreak. Hell, Carly and Dan's traumatic situation is what made me wait to tell Clay in the first place. I wanted to make sure our baby had a heartbeat. And when I went to my follow-up appointment with an OB in Burlington last week, the vaginal ultrasound she did confirmed a little beating heart inside my tiny baby's chest.

"Babe?" Clay calls. "What did you want to tell me?"

I think about the fact that we're getting ready to head to Thanksgiving dinner at Bennett's and decide to stick with my original plan.

"Never mind," I tell him with a forced smile. I really do have a plan. After leaving the office in Burlington last week, I ordered one of those cute, "You're going to be a daddy" onesies off Etsy. Of course, when it came, it said grandpa instead of daddy, so a new one's on the way, but with the holiday, it's probably not going to get here until tomorrow.

I'm going to tell him soon. And it'll be perfect.

Clay flips off the light in the bathroom and comes straight to me, pressing a soft kiss to my lips. "I love you, Josie."

"Love you too," I whisper back, and God, do I mean it. We've been through a lot—and I've been off—but Clay is the man of my dreams.

"C'mon, sleepyhead," he teases as he stares down at me and

stretches his arms out wide. "Unless you want us to be late to Thanksgiving dinner, you better get moving." He glances down at his now raging erection. "And I guess we'll have to deal with this later, huh?" He winks, and I giggle.

"Yeah. We will." I head for the closet, shrug off my towel, and start the process of getting dressed with a renewed sense of happiness. I know I'm antsy, but it's all going to work out. Tomorrow, I'll get the onesie and do the whole balloons and flower and cake thing I've envisioned in my mind, and then, we can both be in on the baby secret.

We can both be excited for the little life growing inside me. The little baby that's ours.

I'm just sliding on my bra and underwear when Clay starts talking to me over the running shower water.

"Did I tell you that Breezy is having our Thanksgiving dinner catered by some renowned chef from New York?" he calls out.

"She's not cooking?"

"Breezy is a full-on city girl, Jose. There's no way she's cooking."

"How did you find all this out?"

"I ran into her at Melba's bakery yesterday. She was picking up her ginormous dessert order because she's invited half the damn town."

"For real?" I respond as I slide my pants on. "Does Bennett know that?"

"No." Clay laughs his ass off. "But man, I can't wait to see his face when everyone shows up."

"Everyone?" I question, looking toward the shower. "Who all did she invite?"

"Earl, Pete, Marty Higgins and his wife Sheila, Reverend Bob, Harold Metcalf and his wife Carol, Todd, Melba…pretty much everyone besides that busybody Betty Bagley."

"Oh my God, Clay!" My eyes go wide as I slip on my brown boots. "Ben is going to lose his shit."

"Yeah." Clay laughs again, and the water shuts off. "It's going to be fantastic."

If there is one thing that Bennett Bishop is known for, it's being the world's biggest sourpuss. The only person who plays the exception to that rule is his daughter Summer. That big man melts like fucking chocolate for his little girl.

Once I'm fully dressed, I stand in front of the floor-length mirror in Clay's bedroom and give my outfit—cream wool pants, warm chocolate-brown sweater, and my favorite nude ankle boots—another once-over. My Grandma Rose would be adorably annoyed that I'm breaking the "no white after Labor Day" rule, and that makes me feel like giggling and crying at the same time.

God, I miss her. It's only been two months since she passed away, but it feels like much longer. I guess when so many monumental things happen, it compounds the feeling of time.

I lift up my sweater to look at my barely there belly. *There's a baby in there.* A whole-ass baby is inside me. Grandma Rose would be absolutely beside herself with excitement.

Last night, I Googled what a baby looks like at twelve weeks. He or she is the size of a lime, has little fingers and toes, has fully formed organs, and is starting to make spontaneous movements. Movements that in a few months I'll actually be able to feel.

Reading the description made it all feel real.

When Clay strides out of the bathroom with a towel wrapped around his waist, I quickly shrug my sweater back down and pretend to be fluffing my hair in the mirror.

"You look beautiful," he says, and he wraps his arms around my waist.

"Yeah?"

"Yeah." He presses a kiss to the crook of my neck.

"Is it just me or did your tits get bigger?" His pesky fingers move up my belly and find my boobs, giving them a gentle squeeze. "And your ass..." He wolf-whistles and leans back to look at my butt. "Damn, my wife is the sexiest, prettiest, most fucking perfect thing on the planet." He grinds his now hard cock into my butt. "God, Josie. Stop making me hard," he teases. "I don't have time to fuck you before we head to dinner."

I laugh and swat him away. "Stop being so horny."

"Blame my hot, sexy wife. I can't help it."

I roll my eyes. "How about you get dressed so we can get this show on the road?"

Clay grabs me by the waist again, spins me around, and dips my body down as he presses a passionate kiss to my lips. It's so deep and all-consuming that my head spins.

I'm half tempted to suggest we can be late to dinner, but he sets me back to my feet and heads for his closet to grab some clothes.

"Give me two minutes, and I'll be ready to go!" he calls over his shoulder. "And we're going to have to take your car. I need to get my truck looked at. The damn thing almost didn't start up for me last night."

"Fine, but I'm driving."

"You don't want me to drive your Civic?"

"Hell no," I retort without hesitation. It's not that Clay is a reckless driver, but more the fact that he's *hard* on cars. Honestly, I'm not surprised his truck doesn't want to start. He drives that fucker like he's trying to break it. Also, that Civic was purchased at Grandma Rose's urgence in her will that I didn't even know she had. I was the only person named, and not only did she leave me her house, but she left me some money too. A good portion of which was set aside for the very purpose of me buying myself a more reliable car.

"C'mon, babe," Clay comments, but his words are filled with humor. "I'll be gentle on your baby."

"Don't make fun of my new car, Clay. It's newer than your truck."

"I know it is. And I wouldn't dream of bursting your bubble about it like that. She's used, but she's perfect."

I snort. "Is that what you say about me, too?"

His smile is smug. "Yep."

And I don't hesitate to walk straight over to him and playfully slap him on his bare chest. "Excuse me?"

Clay chuckles, but he also leans forward to press another soft kiss to my lips. "Don't worry, Josie. That'll change when you finally let me tell people you're my wife."

41

Clay

Thursday, November 24th

"Breezy, remind me to get a restraining order on you after this dinner is through," Bennett grumbles as he stands in the kitchen, taking in the view that is half of the whole town in his living room. "You're never allowed in my house again."

Breezy laughs, her black hair swishing back and forth with each tickled chuckle. "Get over yourself, Ben. I did this because I knew Summer would love it. Our girl is a social butterfly, and what better way to let her spread her wings than to have a house full of people who love and adore her on Thanksgiving."

A barely there smile crests my buddy's lips when he witnesses Summer giggling over funny faces that Pete Peeler and Reverend Bob are making at her. She waddles toward them, her determined strides only slowed down by the two metal braces keeping her knees and ankles stable. A peal of giggles leaves her lips when the sheriff and reverend hide their faces from her.

"More silly!" she squeals through her chubby toddler cheeks. "More silly!"

Pete sticks out his tongue. Reverend Bob turns his face into a blowfish. Summer cracks up even more. Charlie, a nurse Bennett recently hired to help out during the day, encourages Summer to sit down in a chair beside the two men.

It's an intentional move, one born from knowing Summer's condition and the fact that too much movement puts her at risk for fractures. But the calm demeanor with which Charlie handles it all makes it clear why Bennett hired her. It took him months to find the right person. Lots of grumpy Bennett meltdowns and lots of nurses getting fired for not taking care of his girl the way he wanted.

But the day Charlie came into their life, she was an instant fit, and even I noticed a slight change in my buddy's mood. He's still a grouch, still a grumbling pain in the ass, but some weight has been lifted off his shoulders.

It's known that toddlers are…difficult. But a toddler who wants to move and run and play but has to be told to sit down and rest because her body depends on it? That's a whole other level of challenging.

"Here, honey," Charlie says. "Sit down."

"No sit!" Summer squeals, but it's not out of anger or frustration. Her tiny voice is only filled with fun and joy. "More silly!" She points at Pete. "More silly!"

Charlie finds a way to get Summer to sit in her lap. A discreet move that avoids a temper tantrum, keeps Summer smiling, and proves Charlie's worth her weight in gold.

Pete and Reverend Bob keep entertaining Summer, and Ben watches on with nothing but love in his eyes. I've known this guy my whole life, but I've never seen him look at another person the way he looks at his daughter. It's an unconditional love. A love that turns my asshole buddy into a big-ass teddy bear.

I look across the room to where Josie chats with Camille, a fellow waitress at the diner. They're both laughing about something, their eyes fixated on their boss Harold Metcalf. He's a goofy fucker and is currently dressed in his Sunday best—suit and tie—but his pants might as well be belted to his neck with how damn high he's wearing them.

Camille whispers something toward Josie, and my wife's head whips back in hilarity. I have no idea what she said or what Josie finds so funny, but I know, with every ounce of my being, I have never loved another human being the way I love her.

She's everything to me.

And fuck, things have been rough since we got married. Since Rose died. The first month and a half, Josie's grief was palpable. She was a shell of herself. Barely eating. Barely sleeping. Just surviving.

But the last two weeks, something has changed. There's a light in her eyes. Her smiles come more often. She actually lets herself laugh. She's still grieving, yes, but it feels like she's starting to live again.

I'm ready for her to officially move in with me so we can start the rest of our lives, but I have to remind myself to be patient. Life is a cycle of seasons, and soon enough, another will come.

"Everyone!" Breezy calls toward the living room. "Dinner is served! Grab a plate, help yourself to the delicious food that Chef Julian made for us today, and head into the dining room to enjoy!"

Pete and Reverend Bob are the first hungry bastards in line, followed by Harold and his high-waist trousers. Charlie starts to carry a chatty Summer into the dining room to sit her in her high chair, but Josie stops her halfway there.

"Let me take this little cutie," Josie says and pulls Summer into her arms.

Summer smiles and giggles, and Josie presses soft kisses to her cheek. "You ready to eat, sweet girl?"

"Cookie!" Summer exclaims. "Wanna cookie!"

Josie just grins. "Turkey first, then cookie, okay?"

"No cookie?" Summer asks, her eyes fixated on Josie's face as she tries to understand why in the hell anyone would refuse her a cookie at any point of the day.

Josie shakes her head. "Turkey first."

"But cookie? I wanna cookie." A pout forms on her little pink mouth, and her big blue eyes turn wide and doe-like. It's a look we've all experienced, and it's a look that I'm not sure anyone can deny when it comes to Summer.

Josie looks around the room, no doubt looking to see if Bennett is paying attention. He's too busy grumbling to Breezy about there being too much food and Breezy telling him there's so much food because there are so many people and then Bennett telling her there are too many fucking people too, to notice Josie's dilemma.

I, on the other hand, *have* noticed.

Josie whispers something in Summer's ear, and Summer nods. She even lifts one tiny finger up to her lips and makes a shushing sound.

And Josie, the little turncoat, discreetly walks behind Bennett and Breezy and sneaks two cookies from a tray that sits on a table by the other desserts Breezy picked up from Melba's bakery yesterday.

And when the two sneaks head toward the dining room while everyone else is getting their food, I don't hesitate to follow their lead.

"Whatcha doing?" I ask when I close the distance. Both Josie's and Summer's backs are toward me, and a few giggles escape both of their lips.

Eventually, Josie slowly turns them around. "Just looking out the window."

"You want me to pull the blinds up so you can actually see out the window?" I ask, raising my eyebrows in a challenge.

"Nah." Josie shakes her head. "We like to use our imaginations about what could be out the window. It's a whole fun game we do."

"Oh yeah?" I look at Summer. "And what are you imagining right now, sweetie?"

"Cookie."

"You want a cookie?" I ask and Josie tries to make a shushing sound toward Summer, but the little sweetheart is too honest for my wife's own good.

"Ate cookie. Secret. *Shoooooosh.*"

"Did Josie eat a cookie too?"

"Uh-huh." Summer nods. "*Shoooooosh.* Secret."

I look at my wife, who is now smiling and rolling her eyes at me. "And what do you have to say about this big revelation?"

"That you should stop being such a killjoy and let us girls have some secret fun."

I grin at that. And lean forward to press a kiss to Josie's lips. "Your secret is safe with me."

"Kisses!" Summer squeals. "I wanna kisses!"

Both Josie and I playfully kiss the air over Summer's cute cherub cheeks, and Summer giggles and snorts the whole time. Now that her bones are breaking more often, we have to be especially careful with our affection.

And when Josie puts Summer in her high chair, the only thing I can think about is how I can't wait for the day when I get to see Josie be a mother to our babies. Mine and hers. The thought surprises the hell out of me. And honestly, it makes me realize that we've never actually talked about if we want kids or not.

One step at a time, Clay, I remind myself silently. *For now, just enjoy your wife.*

42

Josie

Thursday, November 24th

Breezy taps her knife on her wineglass and stands up. "If you don't mind, I'd like to make a little speech."

"I mind," Bennett grumbles.

But when Summer starts to clap her hands and shout, "Bees! Bees! Love you, Bees!" his annoyed frown turns into an instant smile.

"I think the crowd has spoken," Breezy comments, flashing a knowing smile at her brother, and Bennett just laughs.

"Looks like I'm the odd man out, huh, Summblebee?"

"Lovoo, Daddy!" Summer claps her hands again.

"Love you too, baby," he says and reaches out to wipe some mashed potatoes off her face. Summer proceeds to dive back into her dinner while Breezy commands the attention of the room.

The dining room is filled with everyone we know and love from Red Bridge. Sheriff Pete, Earl, Reverend Bob and his wife Darlene, sweet little Melba Danser, who was one of my Grandma Rose's favorite people in the whole world. Marty and Sheila Higgins and their new baby, Ella, who is currently sleeping in her car seat on the floor beside their chairs. My boss Harold Metcalf and his wife Carol. My two coworkers and good friends Camille and Todd.

Breezy even managed to invite the town gossip Eileen Martin and the annoyingly chatty sheep farmer Tad Hanson and his brother Randy.

No one knows a whole lot about Tad and Randy Hanson other than the fact that they're sheep farmers who bought land near Bennett's property a couple of months ago, and that they're not very good at it. Last week, fifty sheep caused a traffic jam on Main Street during the morning rush. Sheriff Pete nearly froze his lips to his whistle trying to herd them back home.

It's a full house at Bennett's, and I wish Grandma Rose could've been here to enjoy it. Even though Eileen Martin is the town gossip, my grandmother was always the one woman who could get people to spill the tea. I don't know what it was about her, but she was the kind of person that you found yourself telling everything. Her aura just drew you in and made you feel like you'd been old friends for a lifetime. She might've been ornery and dry and stubborn, but she was also warm and comforting and understanding.

She was the best of us.

A sheen of tears forms in my eyes, and I swallow hard against the emotion that feels like a golf ball has lodged itself in my throat. This is my first Thanksgiving without her. This is the first year that she didn't make me help her bake a hundred pies to pass out to everyone in town just to get under Betty Bagley's skin. This is the first year that I didn't get to witness her wrestle her turkey into the oven. A turkey that she always managed to buy two sizes too big and had us eating leftovers for weeks.

The first Thanksgiving that I didn't get to sit across from her at the table and have her make me list off everything I was grateful for. Last year, our Thanksgiving dinner was a quiet one with just me, Clay, Grandma Rose, and Melba. Clay had said he was grateful for me. And Grandma Rose had said, "What about me, Clay? Am I just chopped liver?"

She loved to razz his ass. Loved to tease him. And I know he loved it too.

She wanted me to marry him; she told me that at least a hundred times. Told me I needed to marry that man and have his babies or else she'd do it herself. And here I am, married to him, carrying his baby, and she's not here.

Clay reaches out his hand to cover mine, and I realize Breezy is already halfway into her speech, while I've been a million miles away thinking about the good old days with Grandma Rose.

Clay's smile is soft when I meet his eyes, but my emotions are too raw right now to offer anything but a quick smile before I redirect my attention to Breezy, who still stands at the head of the table.

"Bennett and Summer and I are so happy you're here to celebrate Thanksgiving with us," Breezy announces, and Ben doesn't even roll his eyes or grumble. But how could he? His little Summer's face is bright with an adorable smile as she claps her hands after every sentence that his sister says.

"Yay, Bees! Yay, Bees!"

"I know this is a little clichéd, but I think it's a tradition worth doing. It is Thanksgiving, you know? And this room full of amazing people is proof we have a lot to be thankful for. So, I'd like to go around the table and have everyone just name one thing they're grateful for today." Breezy grins down at Bennett. "And when I say everyone, I mean *everyone*."

Ben just laughs. "You know what, Breeze? I'll even go first."

"Yeah?" Breezy questions, surprise in her eyes.

Bennett responds by starting us off. "Today, I'm thankful for everyone in this room. But mostly, I'm thankful for this sweet little girl." He reaches out to gently rub his fingers over Summer's cheek. "You're the greatest gift I've ever been given, sweet girl. Love you forever, Summblebee."

"Lovoo, Daddy!" Summer exclaims and claps her chubby toddler hands together. "Much much much much!"

Ben smiles and leans forward to press a gentle kiss to her lips.

Breezy goes next, her voice soft with emotion when she says she's grateful for her brother and Summer. "I don't know what it is about you, little lady. But you make everything better."

"Lovoo, Bees!" Summer exclaims, and Breezy has to swipe a tear from her cheek when she walks over to kiss Summer on the forehead. "Love you too, baby girl."

"I think we're all thankful for Summer," Melba announces with a soft smile toward the happy toddler in the high chair. "And I'm thankful for my best friend Rose. She would've loved being here for this dinner." Melba meets my eyes. "Missing her is hell, but I know she's watching over us all. And I know that she's proud, so proud, Josie, of the woman you've become. She loved you fiercely. And I loved her like a sister. And even though decades of time being best friends didn't feel like enough, I'm thankful I got them. Love you, Rose."

A few tears slip from my lids, and Clay reaches out to squeeze my thigh.

Everyone at the table continues the tradition. Pete. Reverend Bob and his wife. My boss Harold Metcalf. Camille and Todd. They state what they're grateful for, and every single person includes Summer in their list.

I can't blame them. That little girl lights up the room like no one else.

"I guess it's my turn, huh?" Clay asks with a smile and stands up from his chair. "I'm definitely thankful for our little Summer."

"Uncie Cay! Lovoo!"

"Love you too, sweetheart." Clay grins. "But the one person I'm most thankful for is this woman right here." He reaches out to grab my hand. "Josie, I love you more than anything. And I'm ready for everyone to know just how much."

I quirk a brow, but he continues.

"Right here, right now, on this Thanksgiving filled with our dearest friends, I'd like to share our good news with you," he announces, and it feels like his words are coming out faster than my brain can comprehend them. “This beautiful woman right here is my wife. And I’m the lucky son of a bitch who gets to be her husband.”

A collective confusion washes over the room, but I’m reading things loud and clear. Patient Clay has officially left the building, whether I was ready or not.

“What?” Melba is the first one to exclaim. “You got married?”

“We did.” Clay nods proudly, but my ears feel hot and heavy on the sides of my head.

All the guests shout and croon with congratulations, but I feel like I’m drowning in quickly rising water. The questions are coming—I can feel them—and the truth will be unavoidable.

On the day Grandma Rose died, I was off saying I do.

Nothing will ever be the same again.

43

Josie

Thursday, November 24th

"That was really great," Clay says as I head down Bennett's gravel driveway.

I grip the steering wheel so tightly that my knuckles are white as I turn onto the now snow-covered main road. At some point while we were inside Bennett's house, it must've started snowing.

"And we definitely need to let Melba make our wedding cake. Otherwise, Grandma Rose might start haunting us, you know?" He continues happily chatting, even releasing a little chuckle from his lungs. "It's only right that our cake comes from Melba's bakery. That's the way Rose would want it."

His head is in the fucking clouds, a smile permanently etched on his lips, but I'm still locked in a tailspin of monster proportions. The poignant, brain-altering silence that followed the news of the *specific day* we wed festers like a parasite in my mind.

Everyone at that dinner knew in an instant the selfish reason why I wasn't there when it happened. Everyone at that dinner knew she was alone. Everyone at that dinner now knows about something that'll haunt me for life.

Clay's currently one-sided conversation about cakes and DJs and whether we should have our reception at The Country Club or set up something temporary in the square carries on without me, and I swallow the vomit-filled saliva back down.

I feel absolutely torn to shreds all over again, and I can't even find all the pieces. I blink rapidly against tears, tightening my grip on the wheel again, and try to focus on the road. Big, fat flakes of snow come down and coat the windshield, and my Civic's wipers work furiously to keep up.

"So…what do you think?" Clay asks, trying once again to include me in the conversation. "I think a spring wedding would be nice. I mean, I'd sure as shit love to have our wedding sooner than that, but I guess I can find it in me to be patient to marry you again since you're already my wife technically."

I can feel his eyes on me as silence stretches between us, and I can even sense the moment that the big smile on his face disappears.

"You okay, Jose?"

At any other time, it would be a simple, thoughtful question. But right now, it feels tone-deaf and patronizing. It feels like more of a suggestion than a question—a further push to *get the hell over it already*. "I can't believe you told everyone that we're married."

My nerves are shot, and my tone is grating, and for once, I'm thankful for the excuse to keep my eyes on the road. I don't like fighting with Clay—I love him. But his lack of consideration for me in this instance stings too much to ignore.

"Wait…you're mad at me?"

"You didn't ask me before blurting it out. I didn't even have time to prepare."

This is not the vibe I wanted to have on our way home from Thanksgiving dinner, not the vibe I want between us at all, but getting everything out in the open feels too important. If I don't, I know it'll grow into the kind of resentment that breaks people apart.

Melba telling me how happy Grandma Rose would be and Pete Peeler joking that he can't wait to see little Josies and Clays running around Red Bridge while I'm still dealing with the internal crisis of the timing of it all was too much all at once. I know I'm processing slowly, but I'm processing. I don't need to be rushed.

"You're mad that I didn't give you time to *prepare*?" he questions, and shock is evident in his voice. "Jose, I'll be honest, I'm not understanding how you could possibly be mad that I told some of our closest friends that we're married. Because we *are* married. Call me fucking crazy, but in my mind, that's something to celebrate."

He's not wrong. But I don't think he's right either. His viewpoint is a narrow tunnel, completely lacking in consideration for how much more complicated this is than *married equals good*. I wish more than anything I had the emotional tether to explain that rationally and at a stable volume, but my raw nerves and pregnancy hormones assure I don't.

"It's not so black-and-white and simple as you make it sound, Clay! Eileen Martin is going to have that in tomorrow's paper. And what's the headline going to be? *Clay and Josie got married the day Rose had a stroke?* How dense are you that you can't see why something like this has me feeling a certain way?"

By the time I finish, I'm nearly shouting.

"I get that you're sad, Jose," Clay challenges back, his voice escalating too. "I get that you miss Rose. Fuck, I miss Rose. I loved that woman like she was my own grandmother. But at some point, we are going to have to start living our lives. At some point, we are going to have to move the fuck on."

Move the fuck on? It's so cavalier. So fucking selfish. He's got to be kidding me.

"Move on and live our lives? You say that like I got a paper cut, Clay. I lost one of the most important people in my entire life, and I wasn't there! I wasn't there when she needed me most! In her final conscious moments, she was all alone because I wasn't there!" I shout at the top of my lungs. "You want me to just act like none of it happened? Act like I'm happy and perfectly *fine*?"

"That's not what I meant, Jo—"

"You know, maybe I can just paint a permanent smile on my face so that no one has to see how sad I am. That would probably be easier, huh? Easier if I just hide my grief because it's such an inconvenience for everyone."

"Jose, I—"

"Don't worry, Clay," I continue, my voice still far too loud for the small confines of the car. "I'll find a way to just shove it all down. We can go pick out wedding cakes and flowers and—"

"Josie!" Clay screams just as my gaze catches sight of headlights from the other side of the road, crossing the yellow line. "Watch out!"

I hit the brakes, but it's too late. I don't react in time. The car is going too fast, and the roads are too slick to stop. My scream echoes in the tight corners, and the headlights collide with us, head on.

44

Clay

Thursday, November 24th

Time is in slow motion. Everything is black around me. Tires squealing and the sounds of glass shattering and metal crushing blare inside my ears. The car spins. Josie screams, and the airbags pop from the dashboard with the kind of force that shoves me back into my seat.

The sounds of Josie's screams fade as I feel a sharp stabbing pain in my stomach, and by the time the car comes to a stop, my ears are ringing loudly and my mind swirls with shock.

I stare straight through the place where the windshield used to be to the dark, snow-covered field in front of us. Cold, wet flakes land on my skin, and frigid wind howls past my face.

Adrenaline laces my blood, and my heart pounds so hard that it's all I can hear inside my ears. Time doesn't exist, and my cognition is definitely impaired.

Everything hurts, and any movement at all takes Herculean effort.

Josie.

I force myself up to sitting and crane my neck to the side, my breath coming in short pants. "Josie?" I ask, my voice sounding stilted through gritted teeth. She's still in the driver's seat, and her whole body is covered in glass, her eyes wide and scared. "Josie?"

"Clay?" she whispers, not looking in my direction. I think she's in shock. "Clay?"

"I'm here," I tell her and squeeze her hand. "I'm here. Look at me, Jose."

She turns to meet my eyes slowly, and I get a look at the blood that's trickling down her forehead on the other side. It's in her hairline, muddying the bright blond, too. "Fuck, Jose. Are you okay?"

Her whole body shakes as she takes me in, and I reach for the wound on her head. But a stabbing pain shoots through my stomach, pulling me up short.

"Clay!" she cries out, fear etching every line of her face. "You're bleeding!"

I look down and see that a large piece of glass has lodged itself in my stomach, just below my ribs on the left side. Every time I move, it pulls, so I reach down and pull the fucker right out.

Blood gushes from the wound, and my head spins immediately with the loss. I groan as the foggy realization that I really shouldn't have done that sets in.

Pain radiates from my abdomen, shoots like a rocket on its way to the moon, and lands on every single nerve ending in my body.

"Oh my God, Clay!" Josie screams. "There's so much blood!"

I feel like I should pass out, but I don't. Instead, I feel like I'm floating above my own body, watching Josie as she reaches out to apply pressure to my stomach with two shaky hands.

"Clay, can you hear me?" she questions, and emotion makes her voice quaver and shake. "Clay, stay with me! Stay with me. Open your eyes. Please, open your eyes!"

Her desperation crushes my fucking soul, and I try with everything I have to keep my eyes open. To tell her I'm okay. To make sure she's okay. Her head was bleeding.

Her head was bleeding.

Josie, are you okay? Tell me you're okay. I love you. I love you so fucking much. You have to be okay. I don't know what I'd do without you.

The words cycle in my mind, over and over, but they never find their way to my lips.

Everything around me grows blurry and, eventually, black, until conscious Clay Harris has officially left the building.

45

Josie

Thursday, November 24th

My bloodstained hands look foreign to my own eyes as I clutch Clay's severed flannel shirt within them and look over at the two paramedics working feverishly over his body.

His eyes are still closed, his normal exuberance completely dimmed, and my stomach cramps with anxiety and worry.

"I love you," I whisper into the air, praying he can hear me. "Please wake up. I need you. I need you so much."

His skin is pale and ashen in a way I've never seen, and with the extent of his injuries, the paramedics are too busy for me to even hold his hand.

My breath gets tangled up in my lungs. Clay is a big, strong guy, but he looks so small on the stretcher as a paramedic shoves an IV into his veins and lets a bag of fluids run into his body as fast as it can.

Another paramedic puts an oxygen mask on his face and slaps a heart monitor to his chest.

"What kind of rhythm do we have?" the one who put in Clay's IV asks.

"We're still sinus, but it's brady. In the forties."

"What does that mean?" I ask, raising my voice so they can hear me. It sounds gritty and jarring to my own ears. "Is he going to be okay? He *has to* be okay."

"He's lost a lot of blood, but we're only a few minutes from the hospital, okay? We're going to do everything we can, Josie. I promise you. I'm not going to let anything happen to Clay."

It's only then that I realize I know both paramedics. Tommy Martin and Doug Stone are Friday night regulars at Clay's bar. Tommy is Eileen Martin's nephew, and Doug Stone's mom teaches at Red Bridge Elementary. She stops in the diner every Friday after school for a slice of pie.

I still have no idea what happened on the road or how we ended up in a wreck, but I know that I should've been paying closer attention. I shouldn't have been arguing with Clay about planning our wedding or telling everyone at dinner tonight that we're married.

I shouldn't have been mad at him. I love him and he loves me, and he was right to tell all the people we love, because when you least expect it, you get in car accidents and don't get another chance! A sob racks my ailing body, but I smother it down, choking on the taste of my tears.

I can't believe he doesn't even know I'm pregnant.

Nothing can happen to him. I can't lose another person in my life. I can't lose *him*.

Doug stays with Clay while Tommy shifts to the side of the ambulance with me. The sound of the siren blares on repeat as we cross the railroad tracks on the east side of town. "Josie, I see you've got a bit of a gash on your forehead. Let me clean it up and take a look."

I nod woodenly, staring at Clay and Doug.

He pokes and prods at the top of my head, using an antiseptic and gauze and tweezers to pull at a piece of glass. We're nearing the entrance of the hospital when he finishes taping a bandage over it and squeezes me on the forearm. "It's a superficial wound. You won't need stitches. Just make sure you keep an eye out for infection."

The ambulance comes to a stop, lights and sirens still blaring, and Tommy and Doug dive into action, opening the doors and quickly wheeling Clay out of the back. I follow their lead, inside the emergency room doors of Addison County Medical Center, and have to run to keep up with their pace as they charge down the hall.

A doctor and three nurses don't hesitate to join them and assist Tommy and Doug as they wheel Clay through automatic doors and into an area that has Trauma Bay 1 written on a sign on the wall.

A nurse with red hair tosses on gloves and takes over holding pressure to Clay's wound while Tommy rattles off an update. "Clay Harris. Thirty-year-old male in an MVA. Large shard of glass went into the upper left side of his abdomen. Per the female with him, he pulled it out and immediately started losing a lot of blood. He's bradycardic."

"Were you with him?" the doctor asks me as he puts a stethoscope to Clay's chest.

"Yes."

"How bad was the accident?"

"I don't know...I don't know... The airbags went off, and the windshield is gone. But I don't know anything else. I'm sorry. I—"

"It's okay, honey," a nurse with brown hair and a soft expression on her face says as she comes over to me and encourages me to sit down. She grabs a blanket and wraps it around my shoulders. "Your boyfriend is in good hands."

"He's my husband."

"We're going to take good care of your husband, okay?" She offers a sympathetic smile. "How are you feeling?" she asks, but I can't focus on her because I swear I hear the doctor talk about surgery.

"Get us additional IV access and start blood transfusions stat. Don't bother with type and screen, just give him O neg," the doctor instructs the nurse with red hair as he carefully inspects Clay's wound. "And go ahead and call the OR and anesthesia now. We need to get him back as soon as possible."

The nurse makes quick work of sticking Clay and sliding a new IV into his other arm. And I'm just standing in the room, watching everyone hustle around, shock and fear and every horrible emotion rolling through my body while my mind tries to understand what is happening.

"He needs surgery?" I ask, but when his heart rate monitor starts beeping wildly and the number twenty-eight flashes on the screen, the room turns into complete chaos.

"Give a dose of atropine now!" the doctor shouts. "And let them know we're coming back!"

A nurse hangs a bag of what looks like blood into Clay's new IV and the doctor, two nurses, Doug, and Tommy start to wheel Clay's bed out of the trauma bay area. Immediately, I jump to my feet.

"Where are you taking him? What's going on?"

"I'll stay with his wife," the nurse who gave me the blanket says and places two strong hands on my shoulders. "Honey, they are taking your husband back for emergency surgery so they can stop the bleeding."

"Is he going to be okay?" My knees buckle, and I have to reach out to use the wall to hold myself up. "Tell me he's going to be okay."

She tries to get me to sit down again, but my body outright refuses as I watch the medical team wheel Clay through doors that have the letters OR written above them.

"I know this is scary, but they are going to do everything they can, honey. They are giving him blood transfusions, and Dr. Sarens is going to fix his wound."

"I don't want him to be alone." *I can't let him be alone like Grandma Rose.* "I need to be with him!" I try to run toward them, but the nurse wraps me up in a bear hug.

"I know you want to be there for him, but I need you to be strong. I need you to stay here and let me take a look at you and make sure you're okay. That's what I need, and that's what your husband needs, okay?"

Deep sobs escape my lungs, and I just kind of bury my face into her shoulder. *I don't want him to be alone. He shouldn't be alone. Grandma Rose was alone.*

"It's going to be okay," the nurse says and rubs a gentle hand down my back. I sob and hug her as tightly as I can. It feels like she's the only reason I'm still standing.

"How about we sit down on this bed right here?" she coaxes as she gently guides us toward an available bed in the trauma bay area. "That way, I can see how you're doing."

But when I step back from her, her concerned gaze latches on to something on my legs. "Oh, honey," she whispers, and I follow her eyes' lead to the crimson-red blood staining my cream wool pants.

I'm pregnant and *I'm bleeding*. Two things that I know are never supposed to happen at the same time.

I can hardly get out the words I haven't managed to tell Clay. "I… I… I'm…preg…preg… Pregnant."

Before I know it, the nurse has me lying on the bed and she's carefully removing my clothes to place a hospital gown on me. I sob through the whole process. When another doctor tells me she needs to do an ultrasound, I can only manage a nod.

There's a flurry of activity before the cool gel and wand are on my stomach, and a stark silence follows.

There is no whoosh. No flutter of a tiny heartbeat. No sign of movement from my little bean at all.

I know before the doctor tells me. I know with a sharp, white-hot pain.

I lost the baby.

46

Josie

Friday, November 25th

Machines beep and buzz, and a nurse hangs a bag of fresh fluids on the little metal hanger thingie that connects to Clay's IV.

The clock reads 1:02 a.m., and even though we were just at Bennett's house for Thanksgiving dinner this afternoon, I feel like I've lived ten lifetimes since then.

Clay's monitors hum around us, and I sit on the edge of my chair in a pair of maroon scrubs the nurse gave me, his big hand clamped in between both of mine. He's still out, and I find myself praying yet again that he'll wake up soon.

Please God. Please. I need him now more than ever.

Two hours ago, Dr. Sarens came into the emergency room that I was still sitting in while the doctor who did my ultrasound finished her assessment. He told me Clay was out of surgery and in the PACU recovering and that the surgery went well. Apparently, the glass had nicked his spleen and that was the culprit for all the blood, but he was able to repair the damage and stop the bleeding immediately.

Clay will have to be monitored in the ICU closely because of the overt risk associated with that much blood loss and emergency surgery, but overall, he's doing well. Or so the doctor says.

Until he wakes up himself and tells me he's okay, I'm having a hard time believing it.

His handsome face showcases bruises and scrapes—most likely from the airbags and all the glass—but his beautiful brown eyes are still hidden behind his lids.

Please wake up. Please, please wake up.

Tears stream down my cheeks, a flow unchecked by time or supply, and I squeeze his hand. "I love you. Please come back to me."

He doesn't respond. Doesn't do anything but lie there while fluid runs into his IV and machines monitor his heart and lungs. Beneath his gown, a large bandage covers his abdomen where the glass pierced his skin and Dr. Sarens had to perform surgery. His feet are bare, and when I notice they are just barely peeking out from the stark white sheet covering his body, I stand up and adjust them.

I feel helpless, and that feeling only gets worse when I feel a gush of blood leave my body. *Right now, I'm losing the baby I haven't even told Clay about.* More tears stream down my face as I think about what could've been.

And I think about the little baby that I didn't get to meet. The baby I had started to feel like was a little boy. A baby I had started to wonder if would have Clay's warm brown eyes or my green ones. Would they have had my blond curls or his dark, thick locks?

Would they have been as outgoing and lovable as Clay?

What would it have been like watching Clay hold our baby for the first time?

So many questions that will never be answered. So much love already felt for the tiny baby I never got to meet. So much sadness inside my heart for not telling Clay the instant I found out.

I can't even fathom how I'll be able to tell him now. It seems cruel and vindictive—like I'd be breaking his heart for no reason other than to feel less alone.

I can't stop the flow of tears as my mind swirls with grief and guilt and fear. All I want is for him to wake up, and I don't know if he will.

Another gush of blood leaves my body, and I know I'm going to have to get up from this chair soon to change the pad one of the nurses gave me. But I don't want to leave Clay, and I don't want to face the blood of the precious little one I'll never get to hold in my arms.

I shake my head to stave off a scream.

Everything I thought was a big deal feels so stupid now—so painfully insignificant.

When I really think about it, I have to face that it's *me* always letting people down.

I should've been with my baby sister Jezzy that day my mother's neglect ended with her drowning in the bathtub. I should've never left Norah for Red Bridge. And I should've been with Grandma Rose when she had her stroke. And I should've found a way to embrace my happiness and time with Clay.

"Jose?" a raspy voice whispers, startling me from my self-beratement.

Wide-eyed and hopeful, I lift my head to find Clay looking right at me. Warm honey and a soft smile, the man I love is back.

"Clay?"

"Baby, what happened?" His voice is dry and raspy and is the most gorgeous fucking sound I've ever heard in my life.

"Oh, thank God!" I cry out and lean forward to wrap my arms gingerly around his shoulders. "We were in an accident. We—"

"The glass," he says, his clarity coming back quickly. "It was in my stomach, wasn't it?"

I nod. "And you yanked it out. There was so much blood."

"Dumb fucking move." He laughs and then immediately stops on a groan. "Shit, that hurts. Are you okay?"

"I was so scared. I thought I lost you," I tell him instead of answering his question. And I press kisses to his cheeks and lips and eyes and forehead. "I thought I lost you forever."

"You'll never lose me, Josie. You couldn't get rid of me even if you tried."

After The Moment: Part 6

The What I Wish I Would've Done

47

Clay

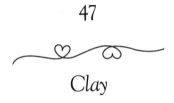

Tuesday, September 14th

"Fill her up!" Bennett shouts and slams his hand down on the top of my bar. The rocks glass that used to be filled with Pappy's bourbon is so dry, I wonder if he licked the fucking cup to get every last drop.

It's a little after midnight, and besides a few regulars, he's the only customer I've been serving drinks to for what feels like the whole night. I tried to keep a mental count when he started up this drinking session, but after five glasses and when he started to just steal the bottle from behind the bar and pour his own refills, I couldn't keep track.

The wheels have completely fallen off.

I know it's a normal phase of grief and that, with our support, it'll pass. But seeing my best friend like this—suffering so completely—and not being able to stop it is a vulnerable feeling I can't explain.

I try to ignore him, try to pretend I'm busy with something at the cash register, but the drunk bastard starts shouting, "Anotha one! And anotha one! And anotha one!" Every fifth "Anotha one!" he adds, "DJ Khalid!"

It'd be funny if it weren't so fucking sad.

When a few of my regulars start giving me annoyed looks because Bennett's voice is drowning out the music, I head over to him on a sigh. I rest my elbows on the bar in front of him and lean forward to meet his eyes.

His face is a mask of bloodshot eyes and a lazy smile. He's so numbed by the bourbon that he's lucky if he knows his name at this point.

"How ya feelin', Ben?"

"Like somebody kick-ed me in the dick and yank-ed my heart out of my chest. But that Poppy does reallll good with pain." He smiles then and tries to pick up his glass, but he ends up shoving it off the bar instead. It hits the floor with a shattering bang. "Whoopsies. Anotha one! Ha! DJs Khalids!"

Four days have passed since we laid Summer to rest, and while this is the first night he's shown up at my bar to use alcohol as a solution, I have a feeling it won't be the last. Bennett has an unfortunate history of using shit like alcohol to numb pain, and with his sister Breezy gone back to New York this morning, there's no one in his house to ride his ass about staying away from it anymore.

I understand she had shit to get back to, but it'd do Bennett and everyone else a whole hell of a lot of good if she'd just move here.

"I'll pour you another one, but only under one condition."

His head lolls to the side. "What?"

"Give me your keys."

"What, you 'fraid I'm gonna get killed in a wreck or somethin'?" he questions on a laugh. Sober Ben would know that question's not funny at all, but drunk Ben doesn't give a shit. "Might be nice, dude. I already feel like dyin' anyway."

"Don't be an asshole," I tell him, my voice hardened by my own shitty baggage. For a fraction of a second, his face sobers.

Not only is his teasing bluntly inconsiderate to me—having nearly died in an accident myself—but it's the kind of bullshit his daughter would be disgusted and disappointed to hear him saying.

Chastened, he wrestles his keys from his pocket and drops them on the bar with a clank. I grab them, slip them into my pocket, and then, begrudgingly, follow through with my end of the deal. Though, this time, I discreetly fill three-fourths of his cup with water and top it off with a little bourbon instead.

He chugs it immediately, pushing it back to me and falling right back into his original stand-up routine. "Anotha one!"

I let my head fall back, and I stare up at the ceiling, silently wondering how in the hell I'm going to get him the fuck out of here before he ends up needing an ambulance ride to the hospital for a stomach pump. The bar doesn't close for another two hours, and I don't think he'll last that long.

I could shut down and take him myself—or I could call someone who might actually get through to the fucker.

Since I don't have Norah's number, I call the one I know.

I don't know if she'll answer. I don't know if she'll tell me to fuck off. But Norah deserves to know Ben's in full self-destruct mode because she loves him, and Josie is the only way to make that happen.

I pour Ben another glass of water, adding an even smaller dash of bourbon, slide it over to him, and head toward the other end of the bar to make the call.

It rings three times before her voice is in my ear.

"Clay?"

I hate how much my heart races at the sound of my name sliding off her tongue. After all these years, she still says it best.

"Sorry to bother you, Josie, but I need your help. Bennett's here, and he's a bit of a mess."

I want to tell her I love her and miss her and explain that I couldn't file the divorce papers because I couldn't fathom living a life without her as my wife, but I know now is not the time.

"Shit," she mutters sleepily. I listen closely enough I hear the sheets rustle with her movement as she sits up.

"Yeah… I figured Norah would want to know, and I was wondering if you could maybe help him get home."

"Give us, like, fifteen minutes, okay?" she says in a rush. "We'll be there."

"Thanks, Josie."

"Of course, Clay. Of course."

The call ends, and when I glance down toward the end of the bar, I see that Bennett has decided to take a nap. His head rests on his forearm, and his back moves up and down in smooth and steady waves with each breath.

Clearly, he needs to sleep, but it'd be a hell of a lot easier on everyone if he didn't pass out until he got home. So, I head over toward him and try to wake him up.

"Yo, Ben," I say, but he doesn't budge. "Ben," I say again, shoving his shoulders this time.

The only response I get is him snoring loudly into his arm.

Without any choice, I do the absolute most assholish thing anyone could do in this situation.

"Hey, everyone!" I shout to the other customers in the bar. "Cover your ears!"

They all do as they're told, and I grab the bullhorn I keep stored underneath the bar to scare the fuck out of people who decide it's a good idea to start fighting and hold it directly in front of Bennett's face.

It only takes two blaring blows for him to jerk his head up in surprise.

"What the fuck?" he shouts, and I smile toward him.

"Mornin', sweetheart. Have a nice nap?"

He blinks several times, his mind swirling with too much alcohol to comprehend anything around him. Thankfully, he doesn't put his head back down. Doesn't do anything but shove his empty glass toward me, a sloppy request for another drink.

I shrug and do as requested, but this time, I don't even add the bourbon. He chugs the glass of water down, too drunk to realize my trick, and shoves the glass toward me again.

We complete that cycle three more times before Josie walks through the door, Norah following right behind her. Concern etches the lines of both of their faces as they quickly close the distance between us.

Norah places a gentle hand on my buddy's back, her mouth turning down in a deep frown. "Bennett?"

He moves his head toward her, but he's too blitzed to have any clue who is talking to him.

"God, he's a mess," Josie says, meeting my eyes. "How much has he had?"

"Well, he doesn't know I've only been serving him water for the past ten or so drinks, so I'd say a lot." I round the bar to meet them on the other side. "Tried to keep count, but the bastard stole the bottle of bourbon from behind the bar and started giving himself his own refills before I realized what happened. Pretty sure he managed half the bottle."

Norah sighs. Josie's eyes go wide.

"Anotha one!" Bennett slurs.

Norah places a gentle hand on Bennett's face, her eyes searching his with a sadness I can feel to my own bones. "Bennett? I'm here, okay? I'm right here." Her voice shakes with pain. She loves this man, it's written all over her face, and yet, he's not letting her be there for him.

Ever since that day in the police station, right before Summer passed away, he's been avoiding her completely. It's breaking her heart.

"Hey, Norah," Josie says softly. "How about we try to get him in the car, okay?"

Norah nods, her lip trembling.

Josie meets my eyes as I help Bennett off the barstool and wrap his limp arm around my shoulder, lifting him to his feet. He's heavy and off-balance, and as I carry him toward the door, his feet are basically dragging on the floor.

Josie does her best to keep Norah calm while still helping me get Ben to the car by holding open the doors, and we manage to get him in the back seat without too much of a fight. Josie is gentle as she adjusts his legs so they're not smashed against the door, encouraging Norah at the same time.

I feel a pang of longing in my chest.

Josie has always been a caretaker. Always calm and reassuring and supportive. *Always the best woman I've ever known.*

Once Norah is supporting Bennett in the back seat, Josie hops in the driver's seat and offers a little wave goodbye in my direction. Just like always, it hurts like a son of a bitch to watch her drive away.

48

Josie

Wednesday, September 29th

I scrub a hand down my face and squint to make out the time on the clock on my nightstand, but the numbers are too blurred for me to confirm. All I know is that it's still dark outside and way too early to have Norah standing over my bed looking at me with wide, alert eyes and rambling a mile a minute about things that sound absolutely bonkers to someone who just got woken up from a dead sleep.

Mind you, this morning visit is coming four days after she handed me a pregnancy stick with her pee on it to reveal the explosive news—she's pregnant with Bennett Bishop's baby—and after nearly two weeks of interrupted sleep from helping get his sloppy, drunk ass home safely every night while he grieves his daughter.

Norah and Ben are barely on speaking terms outside of his late-night, inebriated chats, and he shows no signs of stopping his binges anytime soon.

It's a fucking mess. So much so, it actually makes all my own bullshit feel a little less wild.

"I need to do this, Josie." She's still rambling. "But I don't want to do it by myself, and I want you—"

"Let me get this straight," I cut her off completely because my mind is having a hell of time understanding the crazy things she's saying right now. "You called a doctor two towns over and made an appointment before normal business hours—before dawn—because you're worried about someone seeing you going to the doctor and blabbing to Bennett about the impending bundle of joy before you get the chance?"

She nods along with each word I say while keeping count of I don't even know what on her fingers. And she stays silent for only a few seconds before saying, "Yes. Exactly."

Good grief. I swear, one day we're all going to have to stop playing this *no one in town can know* game. It's exhausting.

"Norah—"

"No, no, Josie." She shakes her head manically and holds up one hand. "You don't get to tell me I've lost my mind when I've already been in the newspaper three times after living here for less than half a year, okay? You know I'm right to do it this way."

I can't say she's wrong, but hell's bells, it is so damn early.

I groan and scrub my hand down my face again. "But today was my only day to sleep in while Todd opens. Whyyyy?"

"Because this was your only day to sleep in, silly. And I need you to go with me. Plus, this is the absolute earliest I could bribe this doctor into opening for me, and I had to promise a one-of-a-kind Bennett Bishop painting to her in order to do it."

"Norah!" I slam both of my hands down onto my comforter. "And just exactly how are you going to follow through on that one, huh?"

She shrugs. "Easy. I'm still Bennett's assistant. I'm still doing all the legwork for his day-to-day, and Breezy likes me. I'll tell her where the painting is going, and she'll send me the label to ship it."

"Bless it. I need just an ounce of your energy for insane ideas." I swear, my sister has more energy than the Energizer Bunny. And right now, all that energy is being pushed directly at me. My tired body is not a fan.

"Please." She rolls her eyes. "So says the woman who is furthering our grandma's legacy by selling mass-produced candles in a handmade Ponzi scheme."

"Norah…" I pause, and she puts a defiant hand to her hip.

"Josie, get up. I need a support person with me, okay?"

"What?" My sigh is deep and exasperated, leaving my lips on such a hard whoosh of air that it blows strands of hair away from my face. "Handing me the stick with your pee on it four days ago wasn't enough for you?"

Norah slaps her hands to her thighs and stomps her foot on the hardwood floor of my bedroom. "I need official confirmation. I need a reason to get up the courage to tell Bennett. I need…this. Can you just get out of bed…please?"

I shake my head at her dramatics, but I also smile at my crazy, pregnant, over-the-top theatrical sister. "Okay. But seriously, I'm not looking forward to the harebrained ideas you're going to come up with while you're hormonal."

"That's sweet, Josie," she says and rolls her eyes again. "But how about you move your ass, okay?"

"Fine." I huff out a sigh and climb out of bed. "Give me ten minutes."

"Two minutes!" she calls over her shoulder as she walks out of my bedroom. "And I'll be in the car timing you!"

• • •

The last time I was at Burlington Medical Center was almost five years ago for a follow-up appointment after my miscarriage.

That appointment…changed everything.

The bright lights of the exam room pierce my eyes, and my anxious stomach churns from my spot on the black plastic chair in the corner. Norah sits on the crinkly paper of the medical table, worrying her fingers together as we wait for the doctor.

I fight like hell, clawing at the proverbial cliff as my delicate psyche dangles above the painful memory of rock bottom.

A room just like this and news that would change the course of my life forever. News that made me change the course of my life forever.

I've spent so much time compartmentalizing it all, but it buzzes just beneath the surface now. I'm still the only one who knows about that little baby's existence, and a day doesn't go by without me thinking about him or her.

Technically, I never was far enough along in my pregnancy to know if it was a boy or girl, but I always felt like it was a boy. A little boy with Clay's brown eyes and my blond hair.

God, Josie. Stop thinking about it.

I pull my phone out of my purse and pretend to scroll through social media, but I don't actually see any of it.

I feel like a shit sister for being face first in my device while Norah sits nervously on the exam table, but my emotions are hanging on by a thread. A very *thin* thread, at that.

When Dr. Vesper walks into the room, I'm instantly thankful for the distraction, and I sit up straighter in my seat, setting my phone back in my purse.

"Hi, Dr. Vesper," Norah greets her. "Thanks for agreeing to this."

Dr. Vesper's smile is warm and confident as she walks over to my sister. She's a short woman with thick muscles and a wise disposition. Most importantly, though, she's not the doctor I saw all those years ago, thank God. "Yes, well. I'm used to desperate moms-to-be on the phone, but I have to admit your desperation sounded a little different."

Norah cringes, and I bite my lip to fight my laughter. I can only imagine the earful her receptionist got when my sister tried to schedule this appointment. I mean, she woke me up this morning by shaking the shit out of me with two hands that felt stronger than the Hulk. No telling what threats she used against Dr. Vesper's receptionist to get this visit.

"All right, so we ran the urine sample you gave us, and you are definitely pregnant, my dear," Dr. Vesper updates. "HCG levels look good, but since you're only six weeks or so, we're going to hold off on the ultrasound. I don't like to do them until at least eight weeks. That way, we can feel confident we're going to hear a heartbeat."

Norah is pregnant. *I'm going to be an aunt.*

That thin thread inside my body starts to fray even more, but I swallow hard against the onslaught, even covering my mouth with my hand to keep control. Now isn't the time for anything but calm and stoic and supportive. I'm so fucking happy; I am so fucking triggered.

My temples pulse with the effort to fight off the tsunami of ensuing emotion. I've had this news delivered to me before. I've had it ripped away. *God, please don't let that happen to Norah.*

"So, today, all we're really looking to do is get some information about family medical history, for both you and the father," Dr. Vesper announces. "I'll need you to fill out some paperwork, we'll get you started on prenatals, and then we'll get another appointment set up for you in a couple of weeks."

I catch the uncertain look on Norah's face as Dr. Vesper waits expectantly, and I know straightaway what her mind has fixated on—family history. Her throat bobs in a desperate spiral into panic.

"The, uh, father had one other child who was diagnosed with Osteogenesis Imperfecta Type III," I chime in for her, and Dr. Vesper's reaction is a soft nod.

"Okay," she says. "We'll plan to do a full genetic panel then, at around ten weeks, and that'll tell us everything we need to know. Until then, I don't want you to worry. Though osteogenesis imperfecta is a genetic disorder, it's often caused by a mutation in the type 1 collagen genes. If no one else in the father's family has OI, it's likely to have stemmed from the maternal side."

By the time we're in the car, Norah has a folder filled with information, a follow-up appointment already scheduled, and a running river of tears streaming down her cheeks.

She's overwhelmed. She's scared. She's happy. She's terrified. She's all the fucking things right now, and I don't blame her one bit. I try to comfort her as best as I can.

"It's going to be okay," I tell her and try with all my might not to show a hint of emotion, not a hint of weakness in my voice. "Everything is going to be okay. I promise you."

I generally don't like to make promises I can't keep, but I refuse to do anything but make Norah feel okay and attempt to put her fears at ease. It's what she needs right now. It's what her baby needs right now.

Being pregnant is meant to be a joyous occasion. It's something you should celebrate and be excited about. But how can Norah only feel excitement when this pregnancy is coming on the heels of Summer dying?

And more than that, *how will Bennett handle news like this?*

It all feels a little too reminiscent of the past, too much like history repeating itself, and once I feel like Norah is calm, I start the drive back into town.

Forty minutes later, I'm pulling into my driveway when Norah's phone rings.

"Hello?" she answers by the second ring. She nods at whatever is being said on the other line. "Of course. That's what you pay me for."

It doesn't take me long to put together that it's Breezy on the call. Though Norah and Bennett aren't on speaking terms at this juncture, she's still his assistant and an undeniably important part of his life. Calls from Breezy aren't out of the ordinary for Norah or—after our heart-to-heart post-fake-wedding—me.

"Holy shit!" Norah's mouth gapes, and her eyebrows lift to her hairline. "You're kidding me!"

Her reaction is jarring. I listen intently.

"What?" I ask on a whisper. "What is it?"

Norah holds up one hand toward me, still nodding while Breezy continues to say something in her ear. "Jesus. Thanks, Breezy… I will." She hangs up the phone a moment later, audaciously taking the time to put it back in her purse before explaining.

"What? What's going on?" I probe anxiously.

"Thomas and Eleanor…they were running an underage prostitution ring."

My God. "That is so fucked up."

"It's sick," she whispers.

After I read the letter Alexis had given Norah on the day she was supposed to marry Thomas King, I was equal parts shocked and not shocked at all at the allegations pointed toward our mother and Norah's now-ex. Inside that letter, Alexis detailed the evil and manipulative way Eleanor had nearly ruined her life. But she also hinted that she wasn't the only young girl involved. She was just the girl who managed to get out.

And now, it's all coming to a head.

My mind races with thoughts of all the girls' lives our evil mother and Norah's slimy ex have ruined. All the ways I've seen my mother operate in the name of money and greed and power. And all the things Eleanor's gone on to do after ruining her own family's lives.

God, make them pay. Please, make them pay for what they've done.

We sit there in silence for a long moment, but eventually, I break it by admitting my horrifying truth. "But it's almost shocking how a large part of me isn't all that surprised."

Norah's head whips toward me. *"Josie!"*

"I know, Nore. I know." I reach out to grasp her hand. I know she feels shocked. I know something like this is impossibly hard for her to understand. But I don't know if Norah has let herself fully see our mother for who she is. I've known how evil Eleanor Ellis is since the moment I witnessed her neglect kill our baby sister Jezzy and how she never once owned up to her responsibility in her death. I just wish I'd been strong enough to do more about it.

Unfortunately, I know Norah feels responsible too. I squeeze her fingers. "But don't you dare blame yourself for any of it, you hear me? If you hadn't taken off from that wedding and made all the moves you have, they might still be at it, you know?"

She nods, holding my hand back as the two of us come to terms with the weight of where we came from.

I'm so glad both of us got out.

With a final hug, we climb out of the car and slam both of our doors, and I head for the house. I expect Norah to be following me, but she heads straight for the Civic and opens the door, ready to climb in.

"What are you doing?" I call toward her. "You're going somewhere?"

"Yep. To Bennett's house. Wish me luck."

She doesn't even have to tell me why. She's going to tell him that she's pregnant. My chest tightens.

"You don't need luck, babe," I say with an honest shake of my head. "You've got Summer."

Norah doesn't answer, but she doesn't have to. Instead, she pulls Summer's pink sunglasses out of her purse and slides them on her face.

A moment later, she's in my old Civic, driving toward an absolution that, for me, will never come.

By the time she's out of the driveway and on the main road, tears fall in unchecked rivers down my cheeks.

For what is. For what was. For what should've been.

Instead of waiting to find the most perfect moment to tell Bennett she's pregnant, she's going right now. She's doing exactly what I wish I would've done all those years ago.

Maybe we wouldn't have been arguing that night after Thanksgiving dinner. Maybe we would've never gotten in that accident. Maybe our baby would've lived, I would've stayed, and we'd be together with a whole brood of kids by now.

Maybe, just maybe, everything would be different.

Before The Moment: Part 7

The Final Push

49

Josie

Friday, December 2nd

I grab two bottles of water from Clay's fridge and carry them into the living room where he sits on the sofa with his legs propped up on the coffee table. "Make sure you stay hydrated, okay?" I say as I set the water down beside his feet.

I'm exhausted, emotionally spent, and taking my days exactly one minute at a time, but now that Clay's out of the woods, we're at least making do.

He was discharged from the hospital a few days ago and is improving by the day. Dr. Sarens was happy with his progress and even took the conservative route and had him stay an extra three nights just to be sure his body was recovering from the trauma of the accident and the surgery.

I honestly think Dr. Sarens would have kept him another two nights, but Clay was pretty much climbing the walls. Hell, I wouldn't be surprised if he secretly bribed Dr. Sarens with cold hard cash to discharge him.

I'm still bleeding and cramping, but I'm trying like hell to let it all go. I know losing a baby isn't something you just get over, but I'll be damned if I'm going right back to where I was before the accident.

I can't. I won't.

"Okay, you've got your water. You've got some bananas and snacks. You've got your remote and your phone," I rattle off everything I've made sure is within arm's reach of the couch. "Do you need anything else before I head to work?"

"Jose, I'm good," Clay says and makes a show of getting up and holding out both arms. "See?" He smiles and even does a little jig with his feet. But I don't miss the slight grimace that finds its way to his lips or the fact that he stops his impromptu dance. "All good."

"How about you slow your roll, cowboy?" I retort and walk over to him to fluff the pillows on the couch, the spot where he just resided. "Dr. Sarens said you'd need to take it easy over the next week. Your body is still healing. So, sit your ass back down and relax." I place both hands on his shoulders. "Please."

He leans forward and kisses me. He tries to rev up the kiss into a passionate clash of lips and tongues, but I only allow it for a short time before I disengage and eye him with a knowing stare.

"Sit down. Relax. Let your body heal."

"You know," he says, still not sitting down and smiling at me in that mischievous way that only Clay can do. "I forgot to tell you that I have a fear of bandages." He waggles his brows. "So, the next time I gotta change this fucker on my stomach, I think I'm going to need a little help facing that fear."

I roll my eyes. "Clay."

"What?" He holds up both hands. His smile is a perfect replica of the Cheshire Cat. "You've always been so good at helping me face my fears. Remember the water tower?"

I force a smile to my face that I don't quite feel, but I'm trying. I still haven't told Clay about the baby—*don't know how I'll ever tell him*—but for right now, I just want to focus on him and us. I figure if I'm helping him rest and heal, maybe it'll help me too. "If I find out that you left here to drive around town or hear from anyone that you're downstairs tending bar, I *will* make you regret it. So, you better be on your best behavior and stay put."

"But, like, what if I'm a bad boy, Jose?" he teases with a wink. "Will I get spanked?"

I blow out a frustrated breath. "I'm being serious here."

"Fine. I'll promise to stay here under one condition."

"What's the condition?"

"You promise to have a good, easy day at work and not worry about me so much," he says, disarming me completely. "I'll be right here when you get back."

I'm thankful when he sits back down on the couch and starts scrolling through the channels, and a calmness settles over me I haven't felt in a long time.

Maybe we can do this. Maybe we can take it slow, find our way back, and get back on our feet.

Maybe everything is going to be all right.

I tell him goodbye with a kiss, grab my purse and keys, and head out the door with sardonic thoughts about looking to the future.

But no matter how much I wish there were, there's no limit to bad luck.

50

Clay

Friday December 16th

"Looking good, Clay," Tommy Franks says as I slide a beer across the bar. "Glad to see you up and moving. You gave us a scare there, man."

After the accident and the emergency surgery where Dr. Sarens had to sew up my spleen, the bastard kept me in the hospital for what felt like forever. And once he discharged me, Josie rode my ass to take it easy and rest. But two days ago, after I followed up with my doctor and he removed the sutures in my abdomen, I finally convinced her that I was good enough to come back to work.

So, here I am, back to work. Back to living. Back to serving the people of Red Bridge their favorite booze. *Thank fuck.* A guy like me isn't meant to sit on the couch and stare at the walls. Sitting still has never been my forte. I need to be out and about. Socializing. Mingling. Doing shit. And the one and only watering hole in town sure as shit isn't meant to be closed for this long. The people were about ready to take to the fields for some good old-fashioned booze bonfires, zero degrees outside or not.

"Thanks, Tommy," I tell him and clap my hand down on the bar. "Consider this one on the house, and I covered what you already had on your tab. Don't know how I'll ever repay you and Doug for what you did for me that night. Probably owe you my life."

"Actually, I think you owe Josie your life," Tommy says after he takes a sip of his beer. "She's the one who kept you from bleeding out until we got there."

"Next time you see her, mind telling her that for me?" I request. "Because every time I try to tell her, she acts like she didn't do shit."

"Oh, I will," he says and stands up from his barstool with his beer in hand. "And how about the next time you get a shard of glass shoved in your stomach, you leave it in place until we get there?"

I laugh at that. "That was a pea-brained move, huh?"

Tommy grins. "Didn't help you, that's for damn sure."

Note to everyone, if you ever find yourself in a situation where a shard of glass or some other object is hanging out of your body, leave it there and let an actual doctor decide what to do. Per Dr. Sarens, if I would've left the glass be, I wouldn't have lost so much blood, and he wouldn't have been sweating bullets in surgery.

"Cheers, man," Tommy adds and lifts his beer in the air. "Glad to see you here and doing well."

I offer a grateful nod, and he heads toward the pool tables. And for the next hour, I spend my time taking drink orders, chatting with regulars about the accident, and joking around with Marty Higgins and his wife Sheila.

It feels good. Being here, surrounded by some of my favorite people in Red Bridge. And it makes me think about Josie and our wedding and what an awesome time it's going to be. I love this town and the people in it, and I can't even imagine how much I would have missed out on if I'd stayed in fucking New York.

"Well, well, well…" I look up from the register to find Bennett striding toward an open barstool with a smiling Summer on his hip.

I know toddlers aren't traditionally brought into bars, but Summer isn't just any toddler and The Country Club isn't just any bar. It'd be different if Bennett were here to booze himself into oblivion, but that shit's behind him. If he's here, it's solely for the company. "It sure is good to see you. How ya feeling?"

"Like a million bucks."

"Yeah?" Bennett asks, surprise in his voice.

"Honestly? Yeah." I nod and wipe off the bar with a clean rag before swinging it over my shoulder. "It's good to be back in action."

"Reddys! Reddys!" Summer exclaims, and it takes both Bennett and me a hot minute to figure out what she's saying. But when she points a little index finger toward a container of cherries on the bar, Bennett laughs.

"You want a cherry, Summblebee?" he asks her, and she claps her hands excitedly.

"Yes!"

I don't hesitate to cut up a few red cherries and put them in a cup before sliding them over toward Summer. Bennett carefully sets her on a barstool and stands behind her while she grabs one and shoves it into her mouth.

"Good, Summer?" I ask her, and she nods.

"More!"

Bennett chuckles. "Slow your roll, greedy. Finish those first."

"You want anything to drink, sweetie?" I ask her, leaning forward on my elbows to meet her eyes. "Water? Vodka? A beer?"

"Beer?" she questions and Bennett sighs.

"I swear to God, Clay, I'll put you back in the hospital."

I laugh at that and get to work on making Summer a cup of water with a lid and a straw. Once I slide it over to her, she takes a drink. "Beer, Uncie Cay?" she asks, and I laugh.

"No, sweetie, that's water."

"Want beer!" she demands, and even Bennett can't avoid a laugh.

"I can't wait for the day you and Josie have kids," he says tauntingly, but Summer has already forgotten her request entirely and gone back to eating her cherries. Sure, she'll probably bring it up again at a most inconvenient time—like an eventual parent-teacher conference—but that's why kids build character.

I can't wait to have some of my own.

"Oh, get real, Ben. You and I both know you're not capable of the fun uncle role like me," I tell him and add a few more cherries to Summer's cup. "You're too much of a sourpuss, dude."

Bennett flips me the middle finger behind Summer's head. *Poor schmuck knows I'm right.*

I grin. "Love you too, Ben."

His phone rings in his pocket, and he digs it out with a deep sigh, further fitting into his stereotypical role.

"Shit. I gotta take this," he mutters, nodding toward Summer for me to take over. I walk out from behind the bar and take his place behind her on the barstool, ready to make sure she doesn't take a tumble. For any kid, it's dangerous; for her, it could be catastrophic.

Fuck. Now that I'm thinking on it, I've got to figure out some safer seating.

Bennett scoots out the front door to be able to hear his call, and I dig inside her little pink Disney Princess backpack to find a coloring book with crayons.

"You want to color, sweetie?" I ask, setting out the book and crayons on the bar in front of her.

Summer's face turns from focused on cherries to smiling over Disney Princesses in an instant.

"Color!" she demands, but when I start to pick up the pink crayon, she shoves my hand away. "No, Uncie Cay. Mine."

I grin down at her as she picks up the pink crayon, her little toddler fist clenching tightly around it, and starts to scribble lines of pink all over Snow White's face. If Summer had a choice, she'd make everything pink. That's evidenced by the fact that she's currently wearing a pink T-shirt with jeans with sparkly pink shoes and a pink bow in her hair. Pink is Summer's favorite color. Pretty sure it has been since the day she was born.

"Uncie Cay, color!" she requests, and I jump into action, picking up a green crayon and coloring on the opposite page where a mermaid—I think her name is Ariel?—is in the ocean with a few smiling fish surrounding her.

"Pitty!" Summer exclaims when she sees that I've colored the mermaid's tail green. I don't need an r to know she means it's pretty. "Pitty Pi-tty, Uncie Cay!"

"Thank you," I tell her with a smile. "And so is yours. I love her hair."

"Piiiink," Summer says proudly. "Pitty pitty pink."

"What are you two up to?" The question comes from behind me, but the voice is more familiar than my own. I glance over my shoulder to find Josie standing there, her diner apron still around her poodle-skirt waist. She hates that damn uniform, but in my opinion, she's a sight for sore eyes in anything she wears. I feel like it's been weeks since I've spent any real time with her.

Between Camille needing Josie to work a bunch of her shifts at the diner and her sleeping at Rose's house for the past ten days while she tries to go through everything, her surprise visit in my bar is more than welcome. I'm glad she's finally found the strength to make strides in moving on, but I wish she'd let me help her.

"Oh, you know, just coloring Disney Princesses," I say, but I also pull her into my arms and press a smacking kiss to her lips. "God, I've missed you."

"Missed you too."

"Tell me you're sleeping at my place tonight. I can't do another night without you."

Josie's lips turn down in a frown. "I'm still trying to get through more stuff… I don't know…"

"Then I'll come stay at Rose's."

"You don't need to do that, Clay."

"You don't want me to stay there with you?" I question, desperately wanting to break this long-ass streak of us not sleeping in the same bed and barely seeing each other. Ten fucking days without my wife is ten days too many.

"It's not that." She shakes her head and averts her eyes for a long moment. "It's just that… I don't know… I think it's a job I need to do alone."

I'm trying to give Josie the time and space she needs. I know the past few months have dumped a mountain of bad shit on her. But fuck, it's hard. I want my wife, you know? I want her in our bed and in our apartment. Because that's the reality. It's not my place anymore. It's Josie's and my place.

I start to open my mouth, to push her a little more on me staying over at Rose's with her tonight, but Josie pulls her eyes away from mine to press a kiss to Summer's forehead and look down at the pages of her coloring book. It's probably for the best. I know I have a tendency to push too hard.

"Oh, Summer, I love your picture."

"Pitty?" Summer asks and Josie nods.

"Very pretty."

"Piiink."

"I see that."

"Lovvv pink."

"You might love pink as much as my sister Norah does," she says, and I'm shocked at the admission. Josie hardly ever talks about her mom or sister anyway, and since Grandma Rose's funeral, hardly has turned into never.

"Siss-ter?" Summer questions and Josie nods.

"Yep. My sister."

Summer looks around the bar, as if she's trying to find Josie's sister, but Josie is quick to correct her. "Norah doesn't live here. She lives somewhere else."

Summer searches Josie's face, her little mind trying to understand. "Heee?"

"No." Josie shakes her head. "Norah isn't here."

"Sa-sa?" Summer questions. "Saaa-d."

Josie doesn't answer. Instead, she picks up a red crayon and colors in my mermaid's hair.

"Oh, pitty!" Summer exclaims when she sees it. "Red! Pitty red!"

For her age, she's actually pretty advanced with her colors, and my chest puffs up with uncle pride.

Josie taps Summer's nose with an affectionate finger. "Not as pretty as you, sweetie."

Summer grins up at Josie, and it makes my heart grow ten sizes in my chest. Fuck, I love this woman. I love everything about her. Sure, she's complicated and complex and stubborn and sometimes it's hard to get a read on her, but she's my favorite person. Ever.

I want to grow old with her. I want to marry her again in front of all our nearest and dearest. I want it all, and I only want it with her.

"Summer, will you ask Josie when she's going to marry me again?" I say, pretending to whisper into Summer's ear, but saying it loud enough for Josie to hear. "I love her so, so much."

Summer's eyes go wide, and she looks up at Josie. "Many, Uncie Cay?"

"Marry," I correct her.

"Ma-wee," she repeats the word, and I nod. "Ma-wee Uncie Cay?" she asks Josie, and my wife's face would win a poker game.

"Someday, sweetie," is all she says before going back to coloring in the mermaid's crown with a yellow crayon.

"Ma-wee?" Summer asks, her eyes now locked on my face.

"You want to know what that word means?"

"Ma-wee?" she questions again, and I pick up a crayon and draw two figures in a blank area on her Snow White page.

"This one is the girl." I point to the one I drew with long hair, a wedding gown, a veil, and flowers. The name *Josie* is written above it. "This is Josie. She's wearing a pretty wedding dress."

"Flou-ahs?" Summer points at the page, and I nod.

"And she has pretty flowers too."

"Pink?"

"Yes." I smile down at her. "Pretty pink flowers."

"So pitty!" She claps her hands.

"And this one is the boy." I point to the figure with a tuxedo and bow tie and the name Clay written above it. "This is Clay, and he loves Josie very, very much."

"Awwww," Summer says.

"And since Clay loves Josie so, so much, he wants to marry her. When you love someone, you marry them."

"Love? Maw-ee?"

"Yes," I answer and write the words ***Love*** and ***Marry***. "L-o-v-e. Love," I spell it out. "M-a-r-r-y. Marry." And then I write the words ***Clay loves Josie*** above the two figures.

"Awwww." Summer smiles so hard that two dimples form in her cheeks. But it's not long before she's back to coloring with her pink crayon. Though, I don't miss the fact that she carefully avoids the illustrated Josie and Clay on the page.

"So, Josie? You ready to marry me again?" I question, smiling over Summer's head at her. "I mean, Summer seems to think it's pretty cute. Pretty sure she said *Awwww* at least five times. Though, you're probably going to have to consider having pink flowers for your bouquet. Otherwise, I think our girl might be disappointed, you know?"

Josie just stares back at me, her eyes searching mine. I have no idea what she's thinking, and I don't have any time to ask her because Eileen Martin is at the other end of the bar, shouting toward me. "How about a little service?" she calls out, but a smile is on her lips.

I lean forward to press my mouth to Josie's. "April 16th or May 14th," I whisper into her ear after I'm done. "Pick the day so I can marry you again. Personally, I'd choose April 16th because it's sooner, but I can understand if you go with May. Flowers will be in full bloom, and we can probably have an outdoor ceremony in the square."

"Clay, you literally just got discharged from the hospital. We were in an accident where you almost died. Don't you think we should focus on getting over that before we worry about planning parties in the square?" she challenges, her eyes searching mine with a desperation I can't pinpoint.

I can't imagine she'd still be blaming herself for all the shit that's happened, but I take the opportunity to reassure her anyway. "I can't think of anything better than a big-ass party to celebrate our love right now, Jose. You saved my life."

She shakes her head. "I didn't—"

"You *did*." I smile. I don't just mean the accident, though that's the most obvious of it all. Every time Josie Ellis chooses to love me, she saves me. "I love you, Josie. I love you and I'm ready to marry you again and I'm ready to move on, to move past all the crazy shit we've had to deal with over the past few months. I'm ready to focus on our future. On our lives together. I'm ready to build a life for *us* with as many little mixtures of us as this world will allow."

Her lip quivers, but I don't dwell on it, knowing it'll only serve to embarrass her in front of all these people. "Pick the day, Jose," I whisper instead, kissing the crook of her neck. "Pick a day, and make me the happiest man in the world."

Knowing she's had enough, I place a quick kiss to her lips and move down to the end of the bar. I give her space and time.

And with my space and time, I serve customers.

"You want something to drink?" I ask Eileen Martin, and she shrugs.

"That depends."

I quirk a brow. "On what?"

"On whether or not you'll give me the exclusive interview."

"You want to interview me?"

She rolls her eyes. "Clay, I'm the leading journalist in town. And you're the man who almost died in a car accident. Of course I want to interview you."

"You do realize you're the only journalist in town, right?"

"Because I'm the best, and no one wants to compete with the best."

I laugh at that, but I also give in to her demands. I have no problem telling Eileen Martin all about the fateful night that Josie Ellis saved my life. With my renewed lease on life, I have no problem sharing it all.

51

Josie

Sunday, December 18th

Sunday brunch rush at the diner is always jam-packed with just about everyone in town. Basically, most people sit through Sunday service with Reverend Bob and then head straight here. Though, sometimes, depending on how much the sermon makes them feel like they're going to hell for all their transgressions, some people head over to Clay's bar instead.

Evidently, today's sermon focused on the *Jesus loves me* vibe, and the diner is filled with most of the town. It's a lot of work, but I'm thankful for the distraction. My brain hasn't stopped running since my follow-up appointment two weeks ago *and the unexpected surgery that occurred shortly after.*

God, the pain. The pain was so fucking horrible. And yet, I'd swear, even with all the healing I've done, I'm hurting even more now. But that's heartbreak for you.

Once I finish up taking the sheriff's and the mayor's orders, both of them sitting together to shoot the shit and gossip, I head behind the counter.

"Todd, I need a number three and six for table five!" I call toward the window that peeks into the kitchen, and he offers a little nod of understanding in my direction. I shove the ticket on the metal spindle.

I jump over to the register and cash out the Williams family's check, handing the extra change to John Williams while Camille puts their to-go boxes in a plastic bag.

But before I can head over to table ten—where Betty Bagley and her daughter June have just sat down—a hand on my shoulder stops me in my tracks. I turn around to find a smiling Eileen Martin behind me and a newspaper clutched to her chest.

"I've been waiting all morning to show this to you," she says and shoves the paper into my hands. "I even decided to release this morning's paper late just so you could be the first to read the exclusive interview."

My head nags, an ache starting behind my eyes as I try to understand her. I've already overworked myself ten times over from what the doctor advised, and my body is feeling it. All in the name of me trying to pretend everything is okay. *That I'm okay.*

"What are you talking about, Eileen?"

"Read it, dear." She nods toward the paper in my hands. "You'll see."

"I'm a little busy here. But I'll read it when I get a break," I dismiss, hoping she'll forget whatever scheme she's on. I know Eileen well enough to know everything she does comes with an agenda.

"Josie, Betty Bagley and her snarly daughter can wait a few minutes to shove pancakes down their pie holes."

"Eileen, I—"

She grabs me by the shoulders and forces me to sit down on one of the empty diner stools at the counter. "You can take five minutes. And if Harold tries to give you shit, I'll threaten to put a bad foodie review in the paper."

I huff out a sigh, but I also set the paper on the counter. The sooner I read whatever she's wanting me to read, the sooner she'll stop riding my ass.

It doesn't take a high-level investigation to find what she's selling so hard. A photo of Clay sits on the front page under a headline that reads, JOSIE SAVED CLAY'S LIFE. He's standing behind his bar, a kitchen towel strewn across his shoulder, and a relaxed smile highlights his brown eyes.

He's beautiful as always, and I'm sick to my stomach.

Oh God.

Eileen is still hovering over my shoulder, so I sit there and force myself to scan the article, but everything inside me is screaming to get the hell away from here as fast as I can.

The first half is a recap of the accident. The day it happened. The fact that it was snowing and a pickup truck driven by Larry English had swerved into our lane and hit us head on. The reality that I was too busy arguing with Clay to avoid the accident altogether is completely omitted.

> "A LOT OF IT IS STILL A BLUR," CLAY SAID. "THE ROADS WERE SLICK THAT DAY, AND A CAR ON THE OTHER SIDE OF THE ROAD LOST CONTROL AND ENDED UP SLIDING OVER THE YELLOW LINE AND CRASHING INTO US. THE COLLISION WAS SO POWERFUL THAT OUR AIRBAGS DEPLOYED, AND THE FRONT WINDSHIELD SHATTERED. A PIECE OF THE GLASS PIERCED MY STOMACH, AND I DON'T KNOW WHY, BUT OUT OF SHOCK OR JUST BEING A DUMBASS, I PULLED IT OUT WITHOUT EVEN THINKING. I STARTED BLEEDING A LOT. I MEAN, A LOT. AND EVEN THOUGH JOSIE HAD HER OWN INJURIES, SHE REACHED OVER AND APPLIED PRESSURE TO THE WOUND. IF SHE WOULDN'T HAVE DONE THAT, I WOULD'VE DIED. SHE SAVED MY LIFE."
>
> "WHAT A MIRACLE," EILEEN SAID. "YOUR WIFE SAVED YOUR LIFE."

"My wife saved my life," Clay agreed, a smile that only a man in love can showcase etching the corners of his mouth.

"Even though the two of you eloped, I hear you're planning on having a wedding here in town," Eileen stated. "Any news on when the wedding will be?"

Clay's smile grew bigger, the love for Josie Ellis visible in his eyes. "We're planning on a spring wedding."

"Oh, how lovely!" Eileen exclaimed. "And the date?"

Clay grinned. "Soon."

"How soon?" Eileen persisted, always the cunning journalist. "Surely now would be the perfect time to announce the date. That way, everyone in Red Bridge can get excited about such an anticipated celebration. Both you and Josie are so loved by this town, Clay. It goes without saying we're all ready to see the two of you say, 'I do.'"

Clay thought it about for a long moment, but eventually, with the skilled pressure of Red Bridge's favorite journalist, Eileen Martin, he revealed, "May 14th."

My stomach drops into my shoes. Not only did he pick a date, but he let Eileen Martin reveal the date to the entire town. And against my better judgment, I keep scanning the rest of the article.

Get ready, Red Bridge. On May 14th, our favorite couple, Clay Harris and Josie Ellis, will tie the knot in the town square. Clay Harris confirmed that Melba Danser will be making the cake, and he's hoping to have the reception at his bar after the ceremony. And

Anyone in town who would like to help Josie and Clay plan the wedding of their dreams, feel free to give Clay a call. He's still on the lookout for a DJ, caterer, and flowers that he says need to be pink because our little Summer Bishop insisted.

Congratulations, Clay and Josie! Red Bridge loves you and is so happy that you're both okay.

It should also be noted, after the interview was over and Clay was smiling like only a man in love with his wife can do, he also said, "I can't wait to marry that woman again."

Eileen asked him, "You think the two of you will have babies?"

"Babies? With Josie?" Clay's smile got bigger. "I'll take as many as I can get."

Babies. *As many as he can get.*

My heart beats furiously, threatening to rip clear out of my chest.

"Congratulations, dear," Eileen Martin says, squeezing my shoulder affectionately. "And you better get to planning. May 14th isn't that far away."

I'm numb when I start to hand her back the newspaper, but she waves me off, adding, "You keep it. Add it to your scrapbook," before she walks out of the diner.

Nausea rolls through my stomach, and a deafening ring consumes my ears. When the nausea becomes too much, I discreetly sneak down the back hallway and into the employee break room, and I lock myself in the small bathroom. My back hits the door, and my body slides to the floor like a sack of potatoes.

Sobs rack my lungs, and I do my best to keep them stifled, crying quietly into my hands.

I can't do this. I can't live this lie, and I can't bring Clay along for a ride of misery with me.

I know it goes against the saying, but I *don't* want company.

I wouldn't wish this fate on anyone but myself.

I know what I have to do.

Clay *should* move on like he's been talking about for months now. But I understand now. He needs to do it without me.

The Moment I Should've Stayed: Part 2

52

Josie

December 20th

I look up at the clock that sits in my grandmother's kitchen and stare as both hands approach the twelve at the top.

Any minute, Clay should be showing up.

My heart pounds furiously inside my chest, and my hands shake as I lift the sealed envelope out of my purse and set it on the kitchen table. I try to busy myself with washing dishes in the sink even though there's a dishwasher that could make the job go quicker, but the distraction is nothing against the culmination of emotion built in the last forty-eight hours of pure hell.

After Eileen's exclusive interview with Clay hit the streets of Red Bridge, my phone has been ringing nonstop.

Melba wanting me to schedule cake tasting appointments.

Three different men in town who think they'd be great DJs vying for the spot.

Sheriff Peeler wanting to talk about security for the wedding day.

The mayor wanting me to talk logistics of the ceremony in the town square.

And Betsy wanting me to come into her dress shop to go through bridal catalogues for my wedding dress.

Everyone in town is buzzing over the news of the May 14th date that Clay chose for us without my input, and I'm withering inside with the knowledge that it'll never happen.

Not then. Not ever.

I've spent the last two days avoiding Clay entirely, using the same *staying at Grandma Rose's to go through her stuff* excuse I've been using since my surgery two weeks ago and biding my time to get prepared.

It's not easy leaving the man you love behind, and I've talked myself in and out of it at least half a dozen times.

I'm not just grieving over Grandma Rose. I'm not just grieving over the moments when I thought I'd lost Clay for good or the baby I lost. I'm grieving over the future I thought Clay and I would have and figuring out a way to give it to him without me.

Three soft knocks to the door and I pause mid-scrub. My heart jumps back into action, pounding so hard it's consuming my ears, and I turn off the water and set down the coffee cup to head to the front door.

I open it slowly, much like I would Pandora's box. Because I know, of course, that tonight, they're one and the same.

Clay's hair is a mess from running his fingers through it a million times, and his brown eyes look tired from working all day in the bar, but his smile is as beautiful as I've ever seen it. It is wide and genuine, and I swear, he's never let me down when he looks at me.

"Damn, woman, I feel like it's been ages since I've seen you."

He's through the door and pulling me into his arms before I can stop him, and my chest aches like there are a million pounds sitting squarely on top of it.

He puts his lips to mine, and I know I shouldn't let this kiss linger, but I can't stop myself from savoring the feel of it one last time.

The kiss is deep and special, like always, but the occasion makes it seem even more poignant. One day, Clay Harris is going to kiss a woman like that who can give him everything he deserves and then some.

Clay breathes me in, and an urgent sadness makes me push him away. I avoid his eyes, but he's not discouraged.

That's the problem with Clay. He never is.

"So, what did you need help with here?" he asks, following me into the kitchen. "No pressure, Jose, but I'm really hoping it's to help you finally move all your stuff into our place. I miss you so much it's bordering on unhealthy."

God. I knew this would be terrible, but it's so much worse than I imagined. It's debilitating.

Maybe if I were a stronger person, I'd have told Clay the truth from the start. I'd have told him about the baby and that I lost it. I'd have told him I was in pain from the miscarriage and that I was worried it wasn't normal, and he wouldn't have let me wait four days before going to my follow-up appointment. Maybe I wouldn't have been in such bad shape, and maybe, just maybe, Dr. Norrows wouldn't have had to take my ovary.

Maybe I wouldn't have a next-to-zero chance of having the kids Clay so desperately wants, and maybe we'd find a way to move on together.

But none of that is what happened. And now, I have to face it.

I'm not strong enough to be the wife he deserves. And I'm definitely not strong enough to walk down the aisle in the town square with everyone close to us watching on and tell him "I do" again when I know what I've done.

I stand at the kitchen table, staring down at the sealed envelope. I hesitate to pick it up. But when I hear Clay's footsteps stop right behind me, I know it's now or never.

"I need to give you this," I say and lift the envelope into my hands. The paper feels hot against my fingers, like it has the ability to burn my skin, so I shove it into his hands before it can.

Before I can change my mind—before I convince myself to stay.

He looks at me curiously, his eyes flitting between my face and the envelope, and I silently fight the shredding pain of my heart being torn apart.

"Jose, what's going on?" he asks. I blink hard against tears, steeling myself to do what I know is right.

It has to be right.

"Just open it."

He searches my face for a long moment, but eventually, he slides his finger under the seal and opens the envelope. And when he slips his hand inside to pull the papers out, my engagement ring falls into his hand.

His face goes from confused to devastating discomfort in an instant. And it's like I can literally feel his heart sink into his shoes as he stares down at the ring in his hand.

"Why...w-what is this?" he asks, his eyes moving to mine again.

Emotion clogs my throat like a dam. I can barely get the words out, but somehow, I manage. "Just read the papers."

He scans the papers I printed in the library this afternoon, and I lick my lips with anticipation. It's the lowest I've ever felt, and I cling to the freedom I'm desperate for him to have on the other side. It's the only thing holding me together.

"Josie, are these divorce papers?"

"I'm so sorry," I say, my voice jagged and raw, and Clay's eyes jerk up to mine. It's like...until he heard me speak, he still thought it was some kind of joke.

"You want a divorce?"

"I'm so sorry," I repeat.

"What the fuck is going on?" he questions, his voice escalating with a mixture of anger and sadness and a million other painful emotions. He's caught off guard, and that's my fault too. I've willfully fed into his delusions about how we were doing for a long time now. "I don't... I don't...I don't understand. Why?"

"I can't do it, Clay," I tell him, and my voice is so pathetically weak. "I wish I could, but I can't."

"You can't be married to me?" he asks, his posture deflated

and agitated all at once. All I can do is nod. "You want to divorce me? Is this a fucking nightmare?" Tears prick at the corners of his eyes, and my nose burns with the suppression of my own like a raging fire.

"I'm so sorry."

"Yeah." A humorless laugh jumps from his lungs. "You've said that a lot. That you're sorry. But what you haven't said is why you want a *divorce*. This isn't pretend, Josie. This is real fucking life. This isn't a fight we get over and come crawling back from the next day. This is the end of us as we know it. That's what you want?"

"I know better than anyone that life isn't some made-up fairy tale," I spit back. It's unfair in the worst of ways, but I know more than anyone in this world what's at stake here. I know the unbearable, fucked-up pain of knowing I'll never have it. "But you're ready to move on, and I'm not. You want the future, and I think it's high time you looked toward it without me in it."

"Is this because of that stupid fucking article? Because I picked a date for us? If you're not ready, I'll give you time. If you don't want the fucking wedding, we don't have to have it. I just want—"

"It's more than that," I say, knowing the dismissal will feel vicious. I need it to. I need him to hate me. "It's everything. I'm sorry. I can't go back. I can't stay married to you."

"So, that's it?" he asks sardonically, dropping the papers and ring on the kitchen table, poison in his tone. "You've decided you're done, so we're done." He paces the floor in front of me, anger and insecurity making his normally vibrant stature seem two feet tall. "Am I getting this right?"

"I'm sorry, Clay," I whisper, my tears finally bursting through my carefully crafted fortress. He sees my weakness and uses it against me, pulling me into his arms and slamming his mouth down on mine.

"I love you, baby. I love you so much. I love you more than anything," he whispers against my lips, and I push away roughly.

I shove the papers and ring back into the envelope and force it back into his chest, hardening myself out of necessity.

"It's over, Clay. You can't stay. So, go. I want you to go!"

He drops to his knees and pulls my hands into his, but I rip them away and take two steps back. "You need to leave," I say, and when he doesn't budge, I turn hysterical. "You need to leave! It's over!"

I shove him in the shoulder until he sways back on his knees, and I scream over and over again as tears stream down his cheeks. "Leave, Clay! Leave right now!"

"Fine. Fucking fine," he says, stifling a sob and climbing to his feet. "You want a divorce, Josie? I'll fucking give you one." He rips open the pink front door and turns back just once to look over his shoulder. "I'll make sure my lawyer gets these papers filed for you. I'll make sure you never need to see my fucking face again."

The door slams behind him, and I drop to my knees before crumpling all the way to the floor.

It's done.

After The Moment: Part 7

The Months Long Fight

53

Josie

Sunday, October 31st

"Please, Josie," Norah begs, loitering near the counter while I cash out Melba.

I ignore her completely and smile at Melba. "That'll be $6.82."

Melba opens her purse and starts to root around in her wallet, and Norah takes that as the perfect moment to keep hounding me.

"Just come to the Halloween party with me tonight," she says and holds her hands together like she's praying. "It'll be fun."

"Honey, do you mind if I give you two dollars in dimes?" Melba asks, and I want to laugh at how predictable she always is. Melba is notorious for having more change than anyone should have. Grandma Rose used to gift her with coin-wrapping papers in the hopes that she'd cash some of it out at the bank. But no, never. Melba prefers to carry around an extra five pounds of coins in her purse.

And I know I don't even have to answer the question because it's not an option. If Melba wants to give you a hundred dollars in pennies, you best pull up a chair and prepare yourself to watch her count out ten thousand freaking pennies.

"Here, Melba," Norah says, stepping up to the counter. "I'll help you count."

Melba doesn't hesitate to drop a handful of dimes into Norah's hands, and my persistent sister proceeds to count the dimes while she's on my ass about going to Earl's Halloween party tonight.

"It'll be fun, Jose. I mean, how often do we get to enjoy a night on the town together?" she questions, glancing up at me briefly between every few dimes she puts into a stack of ten.

"Nore, like I said the first ten times you asked me when you came in here, I'm not going."

Every year, Earl throws a Halloween party for the whole town, and the location always changes. He used to have it at his actual grocery store, but one year when Lance and Mikey took it upon themselves to raid the chip aisle, Earl had a conniption and never threw the party at his store again. Now, his party flits around to various small businesses that can host a large number of people, and this year, the location is The Country Club.

"Is this because of Clay?" Norah asks, and I roll my eyes.

"No." *Maybe.* Sure, since everything happened with Summer, we've managed to be amicable toward each other. But I still haven't forgotten that the bastard didn't file the divorce papers. I mean, how could you forget you're still married to someone?

"How much was it again?" Melba questions. At this point, she has a dollar bill and five dollars' worth of dimes stacked on the counter.

"$6.82."

She nods and rummages in her wallet again, dumping more change out onto the counter.

"Here, Melba. Let me do that for ya." Norah steps in again and counts out eighty-two cents for her, hoping to speed up the pace.

"Aw, you're such a doll," Melba says. "My arthritis has been bothering me all morning."

Norah rubs a gentle hand on Melba's back, and I quickly cash her out before grabbing her order of hot cinnamon tea and a cinnamon roll and carrying them around the counter. Melba tries to take them from me, but I smile toward the door. "I'll carry them for you."

"You girls are so sweet," she says with a thankful smile. "Rose would be so proud to see how you're both doing."

I don't know if my grandma would be happy with how I've handled quite a few things over the years, but for the first time in a while, I actually believe what Melba says is true. I'm finding my rhythm, if a little wonky, and I'm even communicating with my ex-husband-who's-not-really-my-ex on occasion without killing him. I've got a niece or nephew on the way, my sister is happy and healthy and officially engaged to Bennett, my mom is actually paying for her crimes, and things are looking up. Norah's still waiting on the genetic bloodwork on the baby, but I've got a good feeling that Summer's looking out for us on this one.

Both Norah and I walk Melba out to her car, and we don't leave her side until she's safely inside the driver's seat and backing out of the parking spot. But as we turn to head inside again, Norah is back on my ass.

"So, you're going to go with me, right?" She grabs both of my shoulders with a tight squeeze. "You're going to go with me to the party tonight?"

I shake my head.

"Oh, c'mon, Josie!" she cries out, utterly exasperated. "I need you to go to this party. I have to. And I'd ask Bennett to come with me, but I don't think he's ready for that kind of stuff yet, you know? He'd rather spend his time in his studio painting. And he's been working on a whole series inspired by Summer, and I refuse to pull him away from that. It's bringing him so much peace."

It's been nearly two months since Summer passed away. Some days, it feels like just yesterday, and other days, it feels like a lifetime ago. But every day, her memory is still ever-present in my mind. Probably in everyone's mind.

"I get that, Nore. I really do. And I'm so happy that Bennett has found something that's bringing him peace, but I'm not really understanding why you want to go to this party so bad?" I question. "I mean, you're pregnant, you can't drink, and I know with certainty that your morning sickness times are never in the morning. They're always in the evening…when we'd be at this party. Don't you think you should just skip this year?" I suggest. "Earl throws a Halloween party every year. You can go next year or the year after that or the year after that."

A sheen of tears covers her eyes, and my eyebrows draw together. Is she just pregnant and hormonal, or have I completely missed the boat?

"I have to go, Josie," Norah says, and one lone tear slips down her cheeks. "And it's just a little too hard for me to go by myself… This party was on Summer's list. She wanted to go. She just didn't…"

She doesn't even have to finish the sentence. *Summer didn't make it to Halloween.*

I shut my eyes for a long moment. A small, selfish part of me is pissed off that I'm being dragged into this. I mean, it's not like the fake wedding we created for Summer to attend ended all that well for yours truly. But the biggest part of me, the part that loved that little girl, can't deny this request.

"Fine," I mutter, my voice still frustrated but my heart soaring with grief and solace. "I'll go."

"Thank you!" Norah exclaims and brushes her tears away with a quick hand before diving toward me and wrapping me up in a big hug. "Thank you! Thank you! Thank you! You're the best sister in the whole wide world! I love you! I love you! I love you!"

"Yeah. Yeah. I know. I'm the best." I hug her back, but I also cut the hug short because I'm the only one working at CAFFEINE right now. "Now, if you don't mind, I'm going to get back to work."

"And don't worry. I'll handle getting us some costumes," Norah says over her shoulder as she starts to walk down the sidewalk.

"I'm not wearing a costume!" I shout toward her, but she just raises one hand in the air.

"It's a Halloween party, Jose! You gotta!"

One thing is for certain. She might've convinced me to go to the party, but she can shove the costumes up her ass. Josie Ellis will be going to Earl's party as Josie Ellis, and that's that.

• • •

"I love that we decided to go with a Disney Princess theme," Norah says as we get out of my SUV and walk toward The Country Club.

"I didn't decide shit," I mutter and sling my purse over my shoulder. "I was forced into this costume."

"I didn't force you," she says through a snort, and I glare at her.

"Norah, you brought a bag of fifteen different costumes you got from Darlene's shop, and when I told you I wasn't wearing one, you sobbed…and sobbed…and sobbed." Not even kidding. She *lost* her shit.

"Maybe I was a little dramatic."

"A little?" I laugh. "In a matter of seconds, you went from smiling to the fetal position."

"Must be the hormones." She shrugs and runs one affectionate hand over where her pink Princess Aurora costume covers the small roundness of her belly. Norah is nearing the end of her first trimester, just over eleven weeks, but she is starting to show a little bit.

"Goodness, this is going to be a long pregnancy," I mutter, and she just laughs and locks her arm with mine.

"C'mon, Snow White, how about we go inside and get this party started?"

"Pretty sure I don't have a choice."

"No, you don't." She flashes a grin at me. "But you do have a choice on whether you get some wine to help you survive this night."

Okay. Yeah. If some wine is involved, I *guess* I can handle hanging out at my should-be-my-ex-husband-but-isn't-my-ex-husband's bar. *Fingers crossed he's too busy bartending to even notice.*

54

Clay

Sunday, October 31st

My bar buzzes with noise and chatter and DJ Mikey blaring "Thriller" from his Bluetooth speakers while several townspeople dance. I pour two beers for Sheriff Pete and Mayor Wallace, sliding the pint glasses over to them with a smile. They offer a nod of thanks and proceed to go back to whatever town gossip they're whispering about.

Earl's Halloween party is in full swing, and Marty and I are busy behind the bar making sure everyone's drinks are filled and *re*filled.

I move over to Fran and her husband Derrick, taking their orders and making quick work of their drinks, but once their Long Island iced teas are in hand, the air shifts in the room.

My eyes dart to the door, and that's when I see *her.*

Josie walks inside my bar, arm in arm with her sister Norah.

They're both dressed like Disney Princesses, but it's Josie's costume that catches me off guard the most.

Snow White. She showed up to my bar dressed like Snow White.

Instantly, a visual of Summer's coloring book page that Charlie gave us floats around inside my head, and my heart grows tenfold inside my chest. *Did she wear that on purpose?* She knows what that costume means, and she knows *I* know what that costume means.

That can't be a coincidence, *right?* I shoved that paper in her pocket just two months ago, the night we said goodbye to Summer together.

Both she and Norah walk up to the other end of the bar, but before Marty can take their orders, I all but shove him out of the way with a smile. "I got this."

He just shrugs and goes to the opposite end of the bar to take Harold Metcalf's order, and I flash a big-ass smile in Josie's direction. "Fancy seeing you here. At my bar."

She rolls her eyes. "I've been here before. Quite a few times, in fact."

Oh, I know. I hate like hell that Ben was having the kind of hard time he was, but seeing Josie in my bar those nights was the highlight of my year.

Josie might come across as having a tough shell, but on the inside, she's soft and gooey and warm. That tender heart of hers has always been one of my favorite things about her. And it felt like a fucking honor when I got to be one of the few people she showed it to.

"So...can we get a drink or...?" Josie questions, and I grin.

"What can I get you, ladies?"

"I'll just have a water," Norah says, and it's a brief reminder of the conversation I had with Ben a few weeks ago, when he told me his now-fiancée is pregnant.

"And I'll have a glass of white wine," Josie says, but I don't miss the way she pointedly averts her eyes from mine.

I don't take it personally, though. Again, she's in *my* bar. In a *Snow White* costume.

It's not long before their drinks are in front of them, and Norah practically downs her entire glass of water before Josie can take a sip of her wine.

I smirk, take Norah's empty glass, and refill it. She smiles gratefully at me when I hand it back to her.

"Thank you."

"How are you feeling, Norah?" I ask her without really asking her. I'm not sure who in town knows that she's pregnant, and I refuse to be the one who spills the beans if they're not ready.

"Well, very thirsty," she says with a grin. "But I'm pretty good. Though, Josie might say that I'm a little bossy." She playfully elbows Josie in the side, and Josie snorts.

"Sure, sis. If you want to put it mildly…you're a little bossy," Josie razzes. "Not over-the-top dramatic or anything like that. Just…a teensy bit bossy."

"I like to call it persistent," a deep voice chimes in, and all three of us look up to find Bennett standing there, dressed in a costume I saw him wear one year when he went trick-or-treating with Summer.

"I can't believe you're here!" Norah exclaims, and she doesn't hesitate to wrap her arms around his big shoulders. Bennett smiles down at her, his eyes filled with the kind of love that I know is in my eyes whenever I look at Josie. "And you're Kristoff," she says, and her voice shakes with emotion. "God, Summer would've loved that."

Bennett's smile doesn't falter. "She would've, wouldn't she?"

"Yes." Norah nods, and I don't miss the one single tear that slips from her lids.

He presses a kiss to Norah's lips. "Though, I will say, I do think you look better in it than me."

Norah's head falls back as a peal of giggles leave her lips. Her tears are happy. His smile is bittersweet. "I don't think I'll ever forget the look on her face that day. She couldn't stop laughing."

Bennett's eyes turn wistful, and Norah leans forward to hug him tightly. She whispers something into his ear, and he leans back to meet her eyes again.

"I'm here because I want to be."

And when Bennett pulls Norah in for a deep kiss, my eyes flit to Josie. She's looking at me, directly at me, but when we lock eyes, she quickly looks away.

My mind reels. And my heart soars. And I hardly notice when Norah and Bennett skitter off to go chat with a few people in town. But I do notice when Josie grabs her glass of wine and walks away from the bar without a word.

And I watch her the entire way as she heads over to the pool tables where Tad Hanson is dressed like a cowboy and his brother Randy sports a *Men in Black* costume. Back in the day, Josie and I used to run those fucking pool tables. Whenever a random passerby would stop in The Country Club, she'd play the part of the clueless blonde, and I'd help her bait them into betting money on a few games.

We had a whole routine. And she'd purposely lose the first two games. Just completely bomb them. But by game three, that's when my little pool shark would come out, and a few games later, those bastards would always end up leaving my bar with their wallets empty and their tails tucked between their legs.

One time, we even managed to get Grandma Rose to join in the charade, and that woman being the Scheming Sally that she was, it was our biggest payday of all. We split the cash three ways and laughed about it for hours at Grandma Rose's place over takeout from the diner.

Those were the good old days.

But as I stand here, watching Josie talk Tad's brother Randy into a game, I realize just how much I want those good old days back. How much I want her back.

And when I see how terribly she's playing during the first game, my mind is made up.

She's here. In my bar. *And I refuse to let this opportunity pass.*

55

Josie

Sunday, October 31st

"How much money did you end up taking Randy Hanson for?" Sheila Higgins asks as I walk out of the bathroom stall. She's at the sink washing her hands, and our eyes meet in the mirror.

"One hundred bucks," I say with a grin as I step up to the sink beside hers and put my hand under the automatic soap dispenser.

"Poor Randy." Sheila cackles. "Marty told me you were a bit of a pool shark back in the day, but after seeing you run that table, I realize he was *under*exaggerating. Girl, you're diabolical."

Back in the day. So many memories are tied up in this stupid bar, and every single one of them involves Clay. I hate that my mind wants to reminisce about all of it. I hate that my heart also thinks it's a good idea.

"I'm just a girl who knows how to use men's egos against them,"

I respond, and I have to force an amused smile to my lips. "Grandma Rose taught me well."

"She sure did." Sheila grins as she wipes her hand off with a paper towel. "See you out there?"

"Yep," I respond, but I take my time drying my hands as Sheila swings open the door and walks out. The instant she's out of the room, I toss the paper towel in the trash, but I walk back over to the sink. With two hands gripping the porcelain, I bow my head and force a few deep breaths of air into my lungs.

I'm happy I came here with Norah, happy Bennett ended up showing up and that they've been huddled in a corner of the bar chatting and laughing and kissing and doing all the things a newly engaged couple should do.

But this bar is a trigger for me. A loaded gun pointing at all my hardest memories, ready to blow them right to the surface of my mind. Memories that I've tried so hard to push down deep and forget they even exist. Memories that carry so much pain and guilt and shame and devastation that if I let them all bubble to the surface, I'm not sure I'd be able to survive them.

Luckily, I'm now three glasses of wine deep, and the alcohol has provided enough of a numbing buffer that it doesn't take me long to get myself together. I lift my head, look at my reflection in the mirror, and when I pull the wad of cash I got from Randy out of my bra, a smile makes its way to my face.

Clearly, I've still got it.

Purpose renewed, ready to head back to the pool tables and find out whatever poor soul is waiting to take me on, I swing open the bathroom door and step into the hallway. But I only make it a few steps before I have to skid on my heels to stop myself from running straight into *him*.

Clay stands in the quiet, dark hallway, a knowing smile etched on his mouth. "Having a good time?" he asks, and I shrug one shoulder.

"Sure."

"Saw you over there steamrolling Randy." His eyes flash with pride. I've seen that look before. Loved seeing that look back in the day. His lips join the party, and his smile turns full force. It's a bullet straight to my pathetic heart. "Played the man like a fiddle."

I shrug again. "He's not a difficult mark."

"He's nothing like that guy from Baton Rouge," he says, reminding me of one of the toughest opponents I've ever faced in this bar. And stupid, *stupid* me, I can't stop myself from recollecting right along with him.

I grimace. "I honestly thought you were going to have to fight him."

Clay laughs. "Would've still been worth it."

"Worth it?" I question on a shocked laugh and lean my back up against the wall. "He was twice your size."

"Yeah, but he was slow as shit." He waggles his brows in amusement. "I would've held my own."

I wish I could tell him he's full of shit, but I know Clay well enough to know that he actually would've held his own. He's a big, strong guy with a muscular, fit body and is quick on his feet. Honestly, I swear, he's part cat or something. Hell, he'd always ask me to rub his head, and when I'd do it, he'd practically purr.

"Nice costume, by the way." He steps in front of me, resting his hand on the wall beside my head. He makes a show of taking in my Snow White costume, and I refuse to let him lead me down the path I know he's trying to lead me down.

When Norah showed up at my house with costumes, I could've picked five other options. I could've been a witch or a devil or Cinderella. Hell, I could've been a firefighter or a cop. But when I spotted the Snow White costume, I simply had to choose it.

Though, I didn't tell Norah why I chose it. And I knew the risk I was taking when I elected to wear it to Clay's bar. But I did it anyway. Like a true masochist.

"Not everything is about you," I retort with a roll of my eyes. "Some things are just random without any thought behind them," I outright lie.

"That's ironic."

I furrow my brow. "Why?"

"Because, for me, everything *is* about you." Each word is another bullet, and they go *bang, bang, bang* into my heart, weakening my resolve with each forceful impact.

"Clay," I whisper, and I have to swallow hard against the stupid emotion that's now found its way into my throat.

"Josie," he says my name, and I hate how good it feels hearing it roll off his tongue. My name has never sounded so soft or beautiful than when it's moving past his lips with the kind of affection and reverence every woman dreams a man would show her.

Our eyes are locked, and my heart is thrashing inside my chest like it's trying to escape my body and climb into his. Clay Harris has always been and will always be my biggest weakness. My biggest temptation. My biggest downfall.

No matter how hard I've tried over the years to move on, to become numb to his existence, my body still reacts the same in his presence. My mind still wants to take a million walks down our memory lane. And my heart won't fucking stop loving him.

Between one breath and the next, his lips are on mine and his hand is gently caressing my cheek. I didn't see it coming, but I don't stop it either. My body turns to butter and just melts into his embrace as he slides his hands around my waist and pulls me tight against him.

It's been years since I've kissed him. Years since I've felt him. And yet, it all still feels so familiar, so perfect, so all-consuming.

Clay has always been the best kind of kisser, his lips and tongue knowing exactly how to coax my body and mind into a whirlwind of passion and arousal and want and need and desire.

And I hate it. I hate it so much.

But I love it more.

I don't know how long we're kissing. I don't know if anyone in the bar can see us. I don't know anything but right here, right now. I only know his mouth on mine and his hands touching my body and the way every nerve ending beneath my skin has been set on fire.

I only know that I've missed this.

I only know that I miss him.

"I love you, Josie," he whispers against my lips. "I want to be with you. You're the only woman I want to be with. It's been five years, and I can't move on. Don't want to move on."

His words are a bucket of ice water, shocking me into realization. This can't happen. *We* can't happen.

Like it or not, the important things haven't changed.

56

Clay

Sunday, October 31st

Josie is in my arms, and we're kissing.

She's kissing me and I'm kissing her, and for the first time since she handed me divorce papers, I actually feel alive.

I feel like the world isn't shades of depressing gray without anything to look forward to. *No.* It's bright and vivid and beautiful. It's heaven, plain and simple.

I tell her I love her. I tell her I miss her. I tell her I don't want to be apart anymore. And I kiss her harder after my words, savoring every soft, plush line of her mouth and the silky smoothness of her tongue. She tastes like the white wine she's been drinking all night, but she also tastes like Josie.

My Josie. My *wife.*

And she's right there with me, kissing me right back, sliding her hands into my hair.

Until, she's not.

With two hands pressed to my chest, she shoves me away from her. Both of us are breathing heavily, and her eyes are wide with emotions I can't even discern.

"No," she says, and her mood has shifted from soft and warm to cold. "This can't happen," she adds with a shake of her head. She swipes an angry hand across her mouth, like she's trying to remove my kiss from her skin.

"Why not?" I question and try to step toward her again, but she lifts one hand in the air to keep her distance.

"Stop, Clay," she spats. "Just stop, okay? This… Me and you…" She moves her hand erratically back and forth between us. "It's done. It's over. And it will not happen again."

"I don't fucking get it, Josie," I retort and run an angry hand through my hair. "I've never gotten it, actually. One day, we were happy and married, and then, all of a sudden, you handed me divorce papers. It was out of the fucking blue, you know?" I shake my head as my mind still tries to understand why it all went so wrong. "Why, Josie? Why?"

"Because we do not work," she says, and I don't miss the way emotion makes her lips turn down at the corners. "Because it was too much. Because everything in the entire universe was telling us we're not supposed to be together."

"That's not how I see it. That's not how I see it at all. The universe—"

"Stop, Clay!" she cuts me off on a shout. "Just *stop*." Her hands shake as she pushes herself off the wall, and her eyes are watery with tears as she starts to walk away from me.

"Josie." I reach out to grab her hand, but she yanks it away.

"File the divorce papers, Clay," she says. "You should've done it five years ago when you said you were, but you didn't. You lied to me."

"I'm sorry, Josie," I tell her, but I'm not so sure I actually mean it. I don't like that I lied to her, but at the same time, I didn't file the divorce papers because I can't fathom a life without this woman being my forever.

"Fucking file them, Clay," she says again, and she looks into my eyes. "It's been five years, and we're not together for a reason. We're over. We've been over. It's time to move on."

And then, she brushes past me.

I want to stop her, but I don't. I stand there, watching my wife walk away from me.

She told me to file the divorce papers, but she told me that after she kissed me.

She told me it's over, but she showed up at my bar in a Snow White costume, knowing full well what that means. What that would mean to Summer. What that would mean to me. And she spent two hours being the Josie that I remembered, running the pool tables like we used to do together back in the day.

All of that tells me one thing. It's not over.

The gloves are off now. I'm ready to fight for my wife.

57

Josie

Thursday, November 25th

Fall has officially fallen over Vermont. The trees are beautiful shades of vibrant oranges and reds, and every time a breeze blows through, they flit off the branches, twirling and twisting in the air until they find a landing spot on the ground.

It's chilly outside but tolerable, and I pull my wool coat tighter around my chest as I walk out of Bennett's—and now, Norah's—front door with the rest of the crowd. Today is Thanksgiving, and a few weeks ago, Norah found out the gender of her baby and decided it would be a grand idea to host Thanksgiving dinner combined with a gender reveal at Bennett's and her house.

Now, on the day she found out what she was having, she called me immediately, and we cried like babies over it. We even celebrated the next morning with pancakes at the diner, and I cried all over again when she told me what she and Bennett have decided to name their baby. But I've sworn not to tell a single soul because she wanted to do something special for the rest of the town who have been on pins and needles waiting to find out.

And this whole Thanksgiving dinner plus gender reveal shindig has ended in my sister inviting what feels like half the town and Bennett grumbling all afternoon about there being too many fucking people in his house.

The vibe is a little too reminiscent of the last Thanksgiving I spent at Bennett's house, when Breezy was the one who planned the whole soiree and Summer was just a precocious toddler who giggled her little butt off over the silly faces Sheriff Pete and Reverend Bob were making. The Thanksgiving Clay nearly died.

I try to push the memories down, fearful of where they'll take me if I let myself remember everything. I try to focus on Norah and Bennett as they smile at each other in the middle of his yard as Breezy hands them each a gender reveal smoke bomb.

But when my eyes scan the people standing in front of me and catch sight of the back of Clay's head, it all just comes rushing back to me in guttural, painful waves.

I press on my abdomen, willing the feeling of overwhelming emptiness to subside, but memories stab at me like a jagged knife until my lungs grow so tight that breathing feels impossible. I struggle to regain my composure, fight to focus on anything but the devasting things racing inside my head.

I force my gaze to my sister and take in the way she's smiling at Bennett. I take in how beautiful she looks with a little belly beneath her soft pink sweaterdress and brown leggings and find a way to join the countdown with the rest of the crowd as we count them off to the big reveal, calming myself down.

It's hard, but all the time that's passed does help—even only just a little.

"Three…! Two…!" everyone shouts. *"One!"*

Norah and Bennett try to release their smoke bombs, but nothing happens, and everyone kicks up into a bluster of chatter.

"What the hell?" Bennett grumbles, and Norah shakes her smoke bomb around erratically, trying to get the damn thing to go.

"Hold on!" Earl calls out, striding toward them. "Let me help you."

But the poor man only gets a few feet from Norah before her smoke bomb explodes right into his face.

Gasps move through the crowd as pink smoke puffs out all around him, covering his face and his hair and his entire body, and Norah's eyes go wide in shock. Bennett's smoke bomb decides to join in on the fun and provides a second explosion all over poor Earl.

"Welp. Looks like it's a girl!" Sheriff Pete shouts at the top of his lungs before bursting into a fit of laughter. "Pink looks good on you, Earl!"

Everyone else starts to laugh after that, including my sister and Bennett. Her giggles move her little preggo belly up and down as she cackles so hard she can barely get out her apology to Earl.

I laugh, but it's hollow. Earl is the kind of man who always seems to find himself in these types of situations and it's always funny, but it's especially hard to find humor in anything on a day like today. A day that holds so much history, so much pain, so much tragedy.

A day I wish would've never happened.

A gentle hand squeezes my shoulder, and I glance back to find Clay standing there, right behind me. "Today's always a tough day, isn't it?"

I don't respond, but I also don't break eye contact. No one, and I mean no one, has the ability for empathy more than him.

But ever since Halloween night, when I lost my marbles and kissed him, it feels like Clay keeps managing to insert himself into my life, and I'm suspicious.

The man almost never drank coffee when we were together, but he's shown up at CAFFEINE nearly every single day to order coffee. He's been attending church every Sunday, even though he never used to before.

And while I never used to see him at the Fall Farmers Market, he's been there the last two Saturdays.

I'm half expecting him to try to bait me into a conversation about the past, but I'm surprised when that's not what he does at all. Instead, he just leans forward to press a gentle kiss to my forehead. "You don't have to say anything," he whispers. "I get it. It's always a hard day for me too."

He heads toward Norah and Bennett to offer them hugs of congratulations and I just stand there, trying to understand why I feel equal parts relieved and disappointed.

The last thing I would've wanted him to do was hound me with questions or make me recall memories I've already been fighting against so hard all day, but if there were one person in the whole world I would have wanted to talk about those hard things with, it'd be him.

But it's for the best. The more we talk, the more tempted I am to tell him all the things I never told him.

The more tempted I am to tell him why I couldn't stay.

58

Clay

Friday, December 31st

New Year's Eve in Red Bridge always consists of three very important things—spiced hot chocolate from my bar, cinnamon rolls from Josie's coffee shop, and everyone gathering in the town square at eleven p.m. to ring in the new year together.

And every damn year, it's cold as fuck. Half the time, there's already snow on the ground, and this year is no different.

The night sky is dark with only the glow of the moon and some shimmering stars, and the town square is lit up with the twinkle lights Harold and Earl always install the day after Thanksgiving.

DJ Mikey has moved his set from inside The Country Club to the center of the square, and he is currently blasting music that has several townspeople cutting a rug in the snow. Sheriff Pete is in his uniform, pretending to patrol the square for any funny business, and Mayor Wallace watches on proudly from his perch on one of the benches.

Melba giggles with Fran as they drink their hot chocolate. And Marty Higgins wraps his arm around his wife Sheila's shoulders as he comes to a stop behind her, a towel from the bar still slung over his shoulder. Every year, I shut the bar down from 11:00 p.m. until 12:30 a.m. so that everyone can enjoy the countdown in the square with their family and friends. And clearly, so DJ Mikey can keep the party rocking and rolling.

I'll be honest, the kid is shit at DJ'ing, but what he lacks in skills, he makes up for in personality. It's hard to be mad at him when he's so damn enthusiastic about every song he plays.

I scan the crowd, looking for only one woman, and when I spot her curly blond hair, I slowly head her way. Josie stands beside Norah and Bennett, but they're so damn busy canoodling with each other that she's stuck there as the third wheel.

I'm fully prepared to step in, to save her from her current situation, but before I can reach her, Dale Cowens walks over to her with a smile on his face. He's a handsome, single guy in his midforties and someone I've never had a problem with.

Until now.

I don't like how close he's standing to Josie, and I sure as shit don't like the way she's smiling as he whispers in her ear. I don't like it at all.

"So, yeah, I just figured since I'm single and you're single, maybe we could ring in the new year together." He shrugs and slides his hands into his pockets. "You know, just a hug or handshake or whatever." An outsider would commend him for being so polite, but I think he's crossing the fucking line.

Josie doesn't need someone to ring in the new year with when she has me. She always has me, ready and waiting.

Eileen Martin waves her hand toward DJ Mikey. He cuts the music and plugs in his microphone, handing it to her. She takes it and announces, "It's 11:59!"

The crowd cheers. I stare at Josie.

"Forty-six! Forty-five! Forty-four!" Eileen leads everyone into the countdown, and I watch Josie as she smiles at that idiot Dale.

"Sure," she says, nodding. "That'd be great."

Dale's responding smile is so big, Sheriff Pete should write him a fucking ticket for taking up too much space.

"Nineteen! Eighteen! Seventeen!" The countdown dwindles, and I stare at Josie.

By the time the crowd is reaching ten, I've positioned myself as close to Josie and her little friend Dale as I can without drawing any attention to myself.

Bennett leans forward to kiss Norah when the crowd reaches five, and she laughs, playfully slapping at his chest and telling him he's too early. He doesn't give a shit and just keeps on kissing her.

And when everyone shouts, "One!" Dale turns to Josie.

I don't know what his plan is, I don't give a fuck about his plan, and I all but shove him out of the way as I step directly in front of Josie with a smile.

"Clay," Josie groans when her eyes lock with mine. "What are you doing?"

"Sorry, but I love you too much," I say and pull her into my arms and hug her. "Happy New Year, Josie."

I know she wants to bitch at me, but I don't care. I just hug her and hold her and keep her in my arms until I know I've reached the point where she wants to pull away. I feel fucking victorious when she allows it for a good thirty seconds before I start to feel her body tug away from mine.

I step back, smile intact, and when I see Josie's face is filled with annoyance and she starts to open her mouth to most likely yell at me, I just give her another quick hug and press a soft kiss to her forehead. "I can't wait to see what this year brings."

I meet her eyes one last time before spinning on my heel and heading back to The Country Club with a fucking pep in my step.

Resolutions are for pussies, but I guess that's what I am now. Because I am resolved. Determined. Fucking certain.

This will *be the year that I get my wife back.*

59

Josie

Sunday, April 17th

Easter in Red Bridge is a whole thing.

Almost everyone goes to Sunday service to pray and listen to Reverend Bob's sermon, and then the city council hides a bunch of eggs throughout the square for all the kids to find.

Mayor Wallace dresses up like the Easter Bunny. Harold sets out a table of bagels and fruit and cookies and juice for the kids. Melba used to take on that task—and when Grandma Rose was alive, she'd always be right there helping her—but after Melba's arthritis started to get bad, Harold didn't hesitate to take over.

I open CAFFEINE and serve free coffee and tea for anyone who comes in, and the whole town pitches in to make it special for the kids.

When I step into my shop, I see that both Todd and Camille have worked hard to get several pots of coffee brewed and have already set up a tea station, hot water ready and waiting in my large stainless-steel dispenser.

"You guys did good," I tell them, and Camille gives Todd a side-eye.

"Don't you dare look at me like that," Todd says with a roll of his eyes. "It wasn't my fault. That's the first time I've ever used that stupid dispenser."

Camille looks at me. "He almost burned me alive with that thing!"

"I've said I was sorry like a thousand times!" Todd chimes in.

"Yeah, well, it's hard to accept an apology when my life flashed before my eyes!" Camille claps back. "I'm lucky to be alive!"

Todd rolls his eyes. "Don't be so dramatic."

"Fine," Camille retorts. "I'm lucky I'm not currently being admitted to a burn unit!"

My head bounces back and forth between the two of them like a ping-pong ball, trying to keep up with their bickering.

"Okay." Todd frowns. "Yeah, that's probably valid, but my intentions were not to almost spill two gallons of hot water on you. I swear."

Camille inhales a deep breath through her nose. Todd keeps frowning. And I decide it's high time for me to step into the fray.

"How about the two of you go enjoy Easter with your families, and I'll stay here for the egg hunt?" When neither of them responds and Camille crosses her arms over her chest and huffs out a breath, I decide that gentle parenting is not the way to go right now. "Go home," I demand. "Go home. Cool off. And maybe, you know, remember that Jesus loves you, but he'd be ashamed right now. He's risen today, for Pete's sake."

"You're kicking us out?" Camille questions with a furrowed brow.

"Yep." I nod and point toward the door. "And don't come back until you've both hugged it out and made up."

"Josie, I can't miss my shifts this week. My rent's almost due," Camille says.

"Then, I guess the two of you better work this out before

tomorrow morning," I answer, my shoulder shrug nonchalant.

Camille huffs out another breath, looks back and forth between Todd and me, before finally dropping her arms to her sides and saying, "Fine. You're forgiven."

"Yeah?" Todd asks, his sad puppy dog eyes still intact.

"Yeah." Camille nods, steps toward him, and gives him an awkward hug with a hearty pat on the back. "Just don't try to kill me again, okay?"

"Okay." Todd grins, but when they both start to take off their aprons and grab their shit from behind the counter, it's my turn to frown.

"Hey, you guys don't have to leave now," I say, but Camille is already walking straight for the door.

"Just following the boss's orders!" she calls over her shoulder on a laugh. "See you tomorrow, Josie!"

Is it me, or did I just get manipulated by my own staff to give them the rest of the day off?

"Oh, by the way," Todd exclaims, stopping right at the threshold of the door. "Clay Harris was in here doing something when all the drama went down. He told us to tell you something, but I can't for the life of me remember what. Me and Cam were too busy in the back."

"Huh?"

"Just ask him when you see him, Josie!" Camille chimes in and grabs Todd's arm, dragging him right through the door. The bell chimes, and the door clicks shut before I can question them.

Clay was in here doing something? What does that even mean?

Is it just me, or are my employees not only manipulators but they're kind of clueless assholes, too?

I stand there for a long moment, staring out the window at them as they cross the street. I'm half tempted to call them, text them, pull the boss card and make them come back, but that's never been my style.

And when a very pregnant Norah comes waddling through the front door, I decide to leave the interrogation until tomorrow morning when they're here for their morning shift.

"What are you doing here?" I ask her, my head tilted to the side in confusion. "I thought you were helping with the egg hunt in the square."

"I am helping with it. Clay told me to come in here."

"What?" I question. "What do you mean, he told you to come in here?"

"He told me the—"

Before she can even finish her sentence, the bell chimes above the door, and a mad rush of small kids come barreling through with Easter baskets in their hands. They're screaming and shouting and laughing and zipping around my shop with an intensity I've only seen on the faces of Olympic athletes going for gold.

"Norah! What is going on?" I shout over the noise at my sister, who has now relocated herself to a safe spot behind the counter with me.

But she doesn't even answer because the next thing I hear is, "Found one!"

"Yay! I got a yellow one!"

"I got a pink one!"

And when I start to look around my shop, I quickly realize that these kids are doing an egg hunt *in my coffee shop*. It's not long before my eyes catch sight of all the "hidden" eggs. Beneath chairs, on top of tables, on the windowsills, on the floor—it's a fucking wonder I didn't see them when I walked in.

Hell, it's a true mystery how Camille and Todd didn't notice, but I guess they were too busy arguing over spilled hot water.

"Norah," I say through gritted teeth, my voice still loud enough for her to hear over all the cute kids. Because hell's bells, they are cute. I just wish they'd be cute in the square. Not giving their best impression of tornadoes inside my shop. "Who was in charge of the egg hunt this year?"

Norah looks at me with wide eyes. "I'm not sure I should tell you the answer to that."

"You mean to tell me Clay Harris hid some of the eggs in my shop?"

"He says he hided all the eggs in here, Ms. Josie!" a little red-headed boy named Wally shouts excitedly toward me. His mouth turns up in the most adorable smile, and two dimples pop out of his cheeks.

"Yeah!" a little girl with brown pigtails agrees. "And he tolds us to give you these!" She walks right up toward me and pulls a yellow rose from her basket.

And she's not the only one. Every single kid hands me a yellow rose, and by the end, I have to start handing some of the flowers off to Norah.

"I think Mr. Clay loves you, Ms. Josie!" one of the kids exclaims, and then a fit of child giggles follows.

"Yeah, Ms. Josie! I think Mr. Clay wants to kiss you!"

More giggles ensue, and when I look out the windows of CAFFEINE, there he is, Clay Harris, standing on the sidewalk with a blinding smile on his face.

"He's lucky there're all these kids in here as witnesses," I mutter under my breath, but Norah hears me.

"I'll be honest, Josie, I think it's kind of sweet…" She pauses, and when she sees the glare I'm currently flashing at her, she lets out a sigh and raises both arms in the air. "Fine. I think it's horrible. A man sending all these adorable kids into your shop and making them give you pretty flowers? Gah. What a total jerk."

"Norah, I love you, but you don't even know the half of it when it comes to me and Clay Harris."

"And whose fault is that?" she retorts, rubbing a hand over her round, pregnant belly. "I think it's time you spill the beans, Josie." When I don't respond, she adds, "Are you ever going to tell me what happened between the two of you? Don't you trust me? I'm your sister, Josie. I love you. Let me be there for you."

Instantly, my heart cracks in half. I do trust my sister. I really do. And when she first got to Red Bridge, so much had happened in her life. Between her ex showing up, and her relationship with Bennett, and our mother and Thomas trying to ruin Bennett's life, and losing Summer, my job as her sister was to be there to support her.

Not load her down with all my traumatic baggage.

"I do trust you, Norah. I do," I answer, and my words are true. "And maybe someday I'll tell you, but that time isn't right now."

Norah is pregnant and due at the end of next month. The last thing I want to do to a pregnant woman is make her feel anything but happy. It's what she deserves. It's what my future niece deserves. Nothing but happy, positive, love-filled vibes and hope for the future.

Something Clay Harris and I will never have.

60

Josie

Friday, May 27th

I am officially Aunt Josie.

Norah sits on the bed, happily munching on a burger and fries Breezy grabbed for her from a burger joint up the street, and Bennett sits on the edge of her bed, smiling at my sister like she is his sun and moon and stars.

I cuddle Autumn Josie Bishop—*yes*, I cried when Norah told me her middle name—close to my chest, gently rocking her in the rocking chair in the corner of the room. Her eyes are closed, and I take in every perfect inch of her tiny face. Long, dark eyelashes, so much hair, and the poutiest little mouth I've ever seen, my niece is a beauty. But I'm not the least bit surprised. Norah is gorgeous, and Bennett is crazy handsome. The two of them were bound to make beautiful babies.

Autumn was born at 10:15 this morning weighing seven pounds

and twelve ounces. She has the bluest of eyes—like most newborns do—has a head full of dark hair, and didn't hesitate to let the world know when she arrived. The girl screamed at the top of her lungs, and the instant the doctor put her on Norah's chest, she stopped crying and stared up at my sister in a way only a baby looks at their mother.

Seeing my sister give birth will be one of the most beautiful moments of my life. Norah was so strong, and Bennett was so supportive, and once I knew that both mom and baby were safe and healthy, I stepped out of the delivery room to give them some time alone.

I also had to hide myself in one of the waiting room restrooms so I could sob my eyes out. My heart is so full, so happy for my sister and Bennett, so filled with joy to have this new little person to spoil and love, but I can't deny that a cloud of bittersweet melancholy made my chest ache for reasons no one but I can understand.

It took me a long moment to collect myself, but eventually, I was able to walk out of the bathroom stall, freshen up my face, and head back into Norah's delivery room to celebrate the birth of my niece.

"Congratulations, Mom and Dad!" a voice I know like the back of my hand bellows, and I look up to see a smiling Clay walking through the door. His hands are filled with balloons and a teddy bear and a pink gift bag.

I know that today is a big day, a very special day, and it makes complete sense that he's here to meet his best friend's daughter, but I swear, hardly a day goes by without me having to see him in some fashion.

I'm almost certain he's doing it on purpose, but I refuse to acknowledge it. The last thing you can do with a guy like Clay is give him the time of day. He's like a golden retriever just waiting for any attention you're willing to offer him. And if you do give in and give him attention, it only makes him want more and more and more.

"Congrats, Mama." He walks over to Norah to give her a kiss on the cheek. "How are you feeling?"

"Better now that I have food," my sister says around a mouthful of fries.

Clay grins and proceeds to give Bennett a bro-hug, clapping a hard hand on his back. "Congrats, Dad."

"Thanks, man."

Clay sets the balloons and gifts on the floor beside Norah's bed and heads straight over to where I sit with Autumn in the rocking chair. "Congrats, Aunt Josie."

"Thanks." I offer a friendly smile, and Clay gazes down at the sleeping baby in my arms with nothing but love and affection in his eyes.

"She's beautiful," he whispers, and I nod.

"She certainly is."

He smiles at me, and emotion lodges itself in my throat as I take in how enamored he is with my new niece. I saw how Clay was with Summer, and I've seen the way he always is with all the kids in town, but for some reason, today, it's like I'm seeing it all with a magnifying glass.

It makes it so easy, too painfully easy, to envision what he would be like as a father.

I swallow hard against the tightness in my throat and nod toward Autumn. "Do you want to hold her?"

"Yeah?" Clay asks, surprise in his voice.

"Of course," I say, my words genuine. "Surely this little girl would like to meet her Uncle Clay."

His heart is in his eyes, and I purposely look down at Autumn as I rise to my feet to hand her off to Clay. He carefully takes her into his arms and stares down at her as he gently rocks her within his safe hold.

"Goodness, you're a little sweetheart, aren't you?" Clay whispers toward her. "One day, I'm going to tell you about your big sister Summer, and I'll show pictures of her and tell you all the silly, funny things she used to say." Clay flashes a soft smile to both my sister and Bennett before looking back down at Autumn. "And I'll tell you all the things you need to say to get your grumpy dad to give you whatever you want. Or, you know, you can just ask your mom, because she certainly has your daddy wrapped around her finger."

Bennett chuckles. Norah grins, the lift of her lips knowing and amused.

"It's crazy how you can love a little person so much and you've just met them," he says, and his eyes meet mine.

"I know." *And it's crazy how you can love a little person so much, even though you never got to meet them.*

"Clay, do you think you'll ever want to have kids of your own?" my sister asks, and my back goes stiff. I don't feel angry at Norah for asking him a question like that—a question that threatens to bring so many horrible triggers of mine to the surface. She doesn't know the story.

Though, that doesn't negate the fact that I really wish she'd never asked the question in the first place.

"I don't know." Clay just shrugs one shoulder, still rocking Autumn gently in his arms. "I've never put too much thought into it," he says. "When I think about the future, like five or ten years down the road, I just hope I get to love the kind of woman who makes me a better man, who makes me face my fears of things like climbing water towers. The kind of woman who makes you get down on one knee just to ask her out on a first date." He shrugs again. "Kids aren't really on my radar, you know? I'm not against having kids, but my future doesn't depend on having kids either."

I can feel Norah's eyes on me, but I ignore her and pretend to be busy with rearranging the drawer of Autumn's hospital bassinette, my heart clamoring desperately in my throat. He knows the things he's saying, but I won't give him the satisfaction of reacting. I can't.

The conversation shifts when Breezy steps into the room and she and Clay moon over how cute little Autumn is, but doubt creeps into my mind and starts to fester.

I left Clay because I wanted him to have the opportunity to have kids, and he's saying he might not even use it?

I fight against an evil voice as it niggles at my nerves.

Maybe you should've stayed.

61

Clay

Monday, July 4th

The annual Red Bridge Fourth of July fireworks are about to kick off any minute. The whole town has gathered in the center of downtown, and people have set up chairs on the sidewalk and brought coolers with drinks and snacks. Mayor Wallace is dressed in his infamous American flag suit, and Sheriff Pete has even added a little pizzazz of red, white, and blue to his uniform.

The city council spends all year planning this shindig, and since I'm on the city council, I know all the ins and outs of the celebration. This year, I might've put in a little extra effort to get the fireworks display just right and took it upon myself to switch up the usual routine of where the fireworks shoot off from, making sure they are smack-dab in the center of the square.

A tent that's been approved by the volunteer fire department sits in the middle of it all, and Harold and Marty have already ensured that each set of fireworks, which circle the tent, is the appropriate amount of distance away to prevent a fire hazard.

I check the time on my watch and see the show is due to start in ten minutes flat, and I immediately look around the crowd, specifically toward CAFFEINE, to see if Andy Smith, Chet Smith's son, has managed to make good on our deal.

Another three minutes roll by like the wind. I start to shift on my feet, worried that Andy's fucked up the plan. The fourteen-year-old can be a little dodgy when it comes to follow-throughs, but he's just dodgy enough to take a little cash on the side without saying a damn word to anyone about what I've asked him to do.

The sky is turning dark, and Mayor Wallace encourages the crowd to cheer through the microphone Mikey set up for him this afternoon. Everyone is hooting and hollering, excited to see this year's display, and I'm two seconds away from giving up when I see familiar blond hair walking out of CAFFEINE. Andy is right behind Josie, but when he stops by his parents' current spot on the sidewalk, she keeps walking straight for the tent, straight for me.

With a smile I can hardly fight back, I slip back inside the tent and wait for her. I pretend to be busy with some of the leftover fireworks that won't get used this year when she walks through the white-curtain door of the tent.

She scans the space, clearly coming in for a reason, but when all she finds is me standing there with a box of fireworks in my hands, her brow furrows.

"Where's Marty?" she asks, and I pretend to act clueless.

"Uh...I don't know," I hum. "You need him for something?"

"Andy Smith just came into my coffee shop and told me Marty needed an iPhone charger for his phone because it's being used for the music." She looks around the tent again, but when there's still no Marty, only me, she starts to walk for the curtain door.

"Wait!" I shout and quickly set down the box to look at my watch. *Only one minute to go.*

Josie spins back on her heels, meeting my eyes, and when I don't say anything right away, she scrunches up her nose in the most adorable fucking way. "So…this is the part where you tell me what I'm waiting for…"

But I don't have to respond, don't have to do a fucking thing to keep her, because right on cue, the fireworks start to blast off around us.

"Oh my God!" Josie shouts, her eyes wide with panic. "Clay! I don't think we should be in here!" When she starts to move toward the curtain again, I run over to her and grab her by the elbow.

"Don't do that," I say, pulling her body away from the curtain. "It's far more dangerous out there than it is in here."

"How in the hell is it safer in here?" she spits, worry still in her voice. "There are fireworks exploding all around us, Clay! And we're standing here like two stupid ducks in a flammable tent!"

"It's safe," I try to reassure her. "The fire department ensured it was safe."

"How in the hell would you know that?"

"Because I was the one in charge of getting their approval," I state with a knowing smile. "Remember? I'm fancy-schmancy city council folk. The ones you think are ridiculous."

She rolls her eyes. "I don't think they're all ridiculous."

"Oh, so only me, then?" I question, referring to a day, many years ago, when Josie and I had had a moment of tossing shitty words toward each other.

"Shut up." She snorts. "That was a long time ago."

I smile at her then, snag two chairs that I made sure were in the tent, and pull them over for us to sit.

"You think I'm going to sit here and, what? Hang out with you?"

"Seeing as this fireworks display is thirty minutes long, I just figured you'd want to take a load off." I pointedly sit down in one of the chairs. "But suit yourself."

She huffs out a sigh, but she also sits down.

The silence between us stretches, only highlighted by Marty's playlist blaring through Mikey's speakers and the hiss and pop of the fireworks and the claps of everyone in town as they take it all in.

I let that silence linger for a few minutes, simply enjoying having Josie all to myself. I don't care that she's pretending to ignore me. I don't care that she's not talking. I don't care about anything except the fact that she's here. Right beside me. *The way it should always be.*

"So..." I pause and look over at her, keeping the straightest face I can possibly make. "Is now the time to tell you that I have a serious fear of fireworks? Worse than my fear of heights."

Slowly, she turns her head toward me, and when she meets my eyes, my face cracks into a smile.

I'm prepared to have her tell me I'm an asshole and roll her eyes or some shit, but I'm not prepared to hear the most beautiful wave of laughter roll out of her lungs.

"Oh my God!" she laughs. "You're such a pervert!"

"What?" I'm still smiling like a loon but trying to act confused as I do. "I just thought I'd tell you because I know how good you are making people face their fears."

This time, she rolls her eyes, but she's still laughing. *"Clay."*

"Just sayin', Josie. You have a true knack for it."

She reaches out to slap a playful arm against my shoulder. "Shut up."

I feel like I just won ten gold medals and a Noble Prize and an Oscar at the same time, seeing that smile on her face and hearing that laugh of hers that I've missed so much. I'm high on fucking life, and I'm only emboldened further to spend more time with her. To get more moments where I get to hear happiness vibrate from her lips.

"Come have a drink with me, Josie."

"No." Her answer is instant, but she's still smiling.

"Please, come have a drink with me?" I request, and she looks away for a long moment before meeting my eyes again.

"Why?" she eventually asks, and I decide to go for broke.

"Because I want to spend the rest of the night making you laugh like that."

"Oh, so there's a promise of entertainment?" she questions, and since it's not a "fuck off," I only take it as a good sign.

"You have my word."

She doesn't say no. She doesn't say yes. But she *does* nod and stand up from her chair. "My tab better be on the house."

Hell yes.

62

Josie

Monday, July 4th

I don't know what time it is, and I don't know how many glasses of wine I've had, but I do know that this is probably a big, *big* mistake, agreeing to have a drink with Clay.

The Country Club is closed down for the Fourth of July, but the two of us sit at the bar, fresh off our fourth game of pool, and Clay has the audacity to still be surprised that I can kick his ass.

"What's the secret, Josie?" he asks, taking a sip of his beer. "You spending your free time in pool houses? Are you in some kind of underground pool shark ring?"

"Maybe you just really suck and I'm just really good."

He laughs at that. "Woman, I swear, it's one of the world's biggest mysteries how you can be so fucking good at pool."

"Pool isn't the only thing I'm good at," I say before I can take it back. Before I can stop myself from turning our currently innocent conversation into something that's laced with a little bit of sex. But those words do just that. Not only because of the innuendo but because of the way I deliver them. It's sick and twisted that I would even toy with that line with Clay, but I'm blaming it on the wine. And I'm also hoping he's too filled with beer to notice.

"Oh, I know," he says and flashes a wink at me. "I know you are."

He clearly did notice, and I immediately busy myself with another drink of wine. Which, yeah, not the best plan, I know.

"Will you finally file the divorce papers?" I blurt out in a rush. My mouth is still moving faster than my brain to realize how awful that sounds after we've just spent the last few hours chatting and laughing and having fun.

"Who says I haven't already done it?" Clay tosses back, and I just about fall out of my chair.

"Wait…" I pause, searching his eyes. "Have you filed them?"

"Are you hoping I did?"

My answer to that question should be a direct, *Yes, Clay. I want you to file them.* But instead, I just sit there, staring at him. Our eyes are locked, and I can't seem to find a way out of his depths of brown. It's like I'm stuck here, inside his gaze, without an exit strategy.

"Josie," he whispers my name and reaches out to gently place his hand on my face. His hand is big and his skin is warm, and it's like the only thing my body wants to do is lean into his touch.

And that's exactly what I do. I lean into him, pressing my cheek into his palm, while our gazes stay sealed together in a way I can't bring myself to let go of.

"I've missed you so much," he whispers, and he edges his body closer to mine. "Missed you more than you'll probably ever realize."

I've missed him, too. So much. *So fucking much.*

His mouth is moving closer to mine, and I'm not pulling away. I'm just sitting here, arching into his touch, and leaving myself open for his kiss.

When our lips meet, my whole entire body floods with warmth, and my hands find their way into his hair. On a groan, he lifts me off my barstool, and I wrap my legs around his waist. We're still kissing each other, and he moves me away from the bar.

"Fuck, Josie," he whispers against my mouth. "I want you so bad."

"I want you too," I whisper back even though it's the last thing I should be admitting.

But fuck, I want him. I've never stopped wanting him. Never stopped loving him.

Before I know it, he's carrying me toward the back of the bar, where the stairwell to his apartment is located, and carrying me right up the stairs. We're still kissing and my legs are wrapped around his waist and time feels like it doesn't exist when he shoves open the door and walks us inside.

Somehow, we make it to his bedroom. He lays me down on his bed, and I don't stop him when he starts to remove my shoes and socks and jeans. I don't stop him when he removes my bra and shirt. I only help him, removing his clothes at the same time.

His body hovers over mine, and I reach out to grip his shoulders with both of my hands.

And then he's kissing me again, and I'm moaning against his lips when I feel his hard cock at my entrance.

I shouldn't do this. I know I shouldn't do this. But I've been fighting this for so long that I simply can't fight it anymore. I need this. *I need him.* Even if I know it's just for one last time.

"Yes, Clay." I push my hips up toward him, encouraging him without shame.

"Shit," he mutters. "I don't have a condom."

"It doesn't matter," I say, trying hard not to think about all of the reasons why that statement is true. "Now, Clay. I need you."

And then he's inside me, his hard cock filling me up with one deep, heavy thrust.

I am so full, and I just keep kissing him harder and deeper as he moves his cock in and out of me. My moans are loud and erratic, but I don't care.

All I care about is imprinting every single piece of this night into my mind because I hope it will be enough to last me for the rest of my life.

"I love you," I whisper, my voice so soft, so quiet, I don't know if he can hear me. *I'll love you forever. I just wish it were enough.*

63

Clay

Saturday, July 9th

"What a beautiful day," Sheriff Pete says and lifts the beer in his hand toward me. I smile at him as I take the beer I just ordered from the bartender at Norah and Bennett's reception and clank my glass against his.

"To the happy couple," I say and Pete grins.

"To the happy couple."

We each take a drink, and I watch as the bartender behind the makeshift bar in the corner of the reception tent sets to work on making Marty's rum and Coke.

"Probably feels nice to be on the other side of the bar, huh?" Pete teases and claps a hand to Marty's back.

Marty just laughs and hands his wife Sheila a glass of white wine. Harold Metcalf steps up to join the group, a big smile beneath his handlebar moustache.

Today, July 9th, in a beautiful wedding on Bennett's property, my best friend married the woman of his dreams. And he didn't bitch and moan a single time about half the town of Red Bridge being here.

Two weeks after Autumn was born, Bennett told me that Norah had decided she wanted to get married in a month. I was surprised that a woman could be ready for a wedding after just having a baby, but Norah was determined, the memory of Summer and marrying my best friend her true motivation.

During their ceremony, the sky was bright with the sun and hints of pink fluffy clouds, and the memory of our sweet Summer was in every single detail. Her heavenly presence a shining light, and Norah and Bennett's love for her an intrinsic part of their wedding.

Bennett's smile was a constant. On the altar, he gazed at his bride like she was everything he'd ever wished for, and when Reverend Bob asked him if he took Norah to be his lawfully wedded wife, he didn't hesitate to say, "I do."

And now, they're officially married. Husband and wife. The sun has set, and everyone has gathered inside the large reception tent to continue the celebration. Bennett and Norah are currently on the dance floor, swaying gently together to a soft song that DJ Mikey is playing, while little Autumn sleeps against Bennett's chest.

Before the ceremony got started, I promised Bennett that I'd behave. That I wouldn't stir up any shit with Josie. But now that he's got his wife and baby in his arms and is locked tight in his bubble of happily-ever-after, I start scanning the crowd for the one and only woman who's been on my mind all day.

Four days ago, after Josie and I spent the Fourth of July together, I woke up to an empty bed.

After we had sex, she left at some point in the middle of the night, and ever since, she's been avoiding me. I've tried to call her, text her, even showed up to CAFFEINE and her house a few times, but she's been fucking Houdini, always disappearing before I get to her.

I've tried to play it cool, keep it together, but fuck, I'm hurting. I thought that night I'd finally gotten my wife back. She told me she loved me and I told her I loved her, and I don't think I've ever experienced something as powerful and intense as that moment with her beneath me, her body bared and her eyes gazing into mine while we connected as one.

I had fallen asleep that night with Josie in my arms and happier than I'd ever been in my entire fucking life. And then, she was gone.

Sheriff Peeler moves from the bar to chat with Eileen Martin, and Marty and his wife join Betty and Earl on the dance floor. Lazy Lance is surrounded by a bunch of teenage girls, staring up at him with moony eyes, and Melba is over by the cake table, admiring her half-eaten creation.

I scan all of the tables, noting the names and faces of familiar folks from Red Bridge. And when I spot the back of Breezy's black hair, I dart my eyes to the woman standing beside her, and my heart flips on its fucking side.

Josie.

I've watched her like a hawk all damn day, throughout the ceremony and during the first part of the reception. I've behaved myself. I've held back from confronting her about the other night. But now, it's time.

My strides are steady as I walk across the tent and straight for her. She locks her eyes with mine, and I don't miss the way her cheeks flush pink and she digs her top teeth into her lip. I can't hear what Breezy is saying to her, but it doesn't matter. Josie excuses herself from the conversation and starts walking in the opposite direction of me.

Yeah. No. I don't fucking think so.

I navigate through the crowd, just barely brushing past Breezy, and Josie picks up her pace.

So, I pick up my fucking pace. And I don't stop until I'm reaching out to grab Josie by the wrist and stop her. *"Josie."*

"Now isn't the time, Clay," she says through gritted teeth.

"Oh, but now *is* the time," I retort and gently tug her wrist so that she'll look at me. When our eyes lock, it feels like all the oxygen has been sucked from the air. "I deserve an explanation."

"Don't make a big thing of it, okay?" she says, her facial expression neutral and cool. "It was just one night. It didn't mean anything."

Didn't mean anything? *Bullshit.* I know her well enough to know this is just a mask. It's just a calculated cover for her true emotions. She told me she loved me. She told me she wanted me. She told me she needed me. And when I was inside her, she'd gripped my shoulders, holding my body against hers as tightly as she could.

Her green eyes were bright and vivid and filled with so much fucking love and emotion. They were a distinct reminder of the past. The way she used to look at me, before everything went to shit.

"Stop lying to yourself, Josie," I order and tug her closer to me. Our faces are mere inches apart, and I don't miss the way her breaths come out in heavy pants. "That night meant every-fucking-thing, and you know it. I know it. We both fucking know it. So why did you leave? Why did you run? Why have you spent the last four goddamn days avoiding me?"

"Just leave it be," she says, her voice a whisper, and her green eyes look glassy with emotion. "That night shouldn't have happened, okay? It just shouldn't have happened."

"You're wrong, Josie," I tell her and keep her eyes locked in my gaze. "That night should've happened a long fucking time ago. You and I aren't supposed to be apart. We're supposed to be together, and the way that night felt proves it. You're my wife, and I'm your husband." My voice is harsh and soft at the same time, charged with all the feelings I've been trying to keep under control for the past five fucking years that we've been apart. "I'm your husband. I love you. I've always loved you, and I won't ever fucking stop. Do you hear me? Not ever."

She starts to open her mouth, starts to say something, but I don't want to hear it. Refuse to hear it. So I just kiss her. I press my mouth to hers and *kiss my wife.*

And she kisses me right back, her hands going to my collared shirt and gripping the material tightly between two clenched fists. Our mouths are at war and in love at the same time. Our lips are harsh but soft, and our tongues move against each other in desperation.

But then, Josie is pulling away, and when our eyes lock again, hers are wide with shock and anger. Her red lipstick is smeared across her lips, probably smeared across mine too, and she surprises the hell out of me in one fell swoop.

She slaps her hand against the side of my face in a quick, brisk movement that causes a deep, stinging ache to form beneath my skin.

"Dammit, Clay," Josie whisper-yells, her voice so fucking sad and a lone tear slipping from her eyes. "You can't fix this. You can't will it away. You can't turn back time."

"Jose—"

"No!" she snaps. "After it happened, you kept right on living, but I'll *never* be the same."

I blink, my mind trying to understand what she is saying right now. "Kept right on living? What do you mean?" I question, but she spins on her heel and runs out of the tent, heading straight for Bennett's barn.

And I follow her.

This conversation—this fucked-up shit between us—it isn't done.

64

Josie

Saturday, July 9th

I run, as fast as my feet can take me, and they end up leading me into Bennett's barn. Tears are a river down my cheeks when I reach the still-open doors. The lights are on, and I don't stop until I'm inside, standing beside the large mirror that Norah and I stood in front of just before she walked down the aisle. Our smiles were tearstained, and we'd laughed about how ridiculous we were being, and I'd hugged my sister so tight, telling her how happy I was for her.

My tears were filled with joy and happiness, but they were bittersweet too. Years ago, when Grandma Rose was still alive, I imagined a wedding just like this, in front of family and friends and with Clay standing at the altar.

"Josie!" Clay calls out as he jogs into the barn, hot on my heels. "What do you mean by that? Kept right on living?" he questions, and anger and confusion and sadness, so much sadness, etch every line of his handsome face. This man has been put through the wringer... because of me. I know this to be true, and I hate myself for it. I hate myself for all the things I should've told him but didn't have the strength to.

He's right behind me now, his eyes staring at me in the reflection in the mirror. When I don't say anything, he keeps asking questions, determined to get answers once and for all.

"Are you talking about Rose? The accident? What the fuck do you mean by that?" He's angry, and he has every right to be. I've kept him so far in the dark that he couldn't find his way out of this if he tried.

This battle he thinks he's fighting is a lost cause. It's worthless. Just like me.

"Clay, just stop," I say, my voice a near whisper, and my heart is pounding so erratically inside my chest that I can hardly hear the words when they leave my lips. "Just stop. Just let it go. Just walk away."

"Walk away?" he shouts. "You think I'm going to walk away? I don't think so, Josie. Walking away from you that day you handed me divorce papers is the biggest regret of my life. I should've stayed. I should've fought for you. I should've fought for us."

I don't say anything. I *can't* say anything. He places two hands to turn me around to face him, to lock our eyes together. I hate that tears are still streaming down my cheeks, but I can't help it. I'm powerless against them. All the tragedy and pain and tragic misfortune of our past are hovering over us like a thunderstorm, and I feel lucky that I can even breathe at this point. That I can even stand on my own two feet.

Clay is talking about all of this like it's a straightforward thing, but it is all so loaded that I fear any second the trigger will get pulled.

"Josie, talk to me. Tell me what's going on. Tell me why everything ended up here," he whispers, and I don't miss the way his voice shakes. "Please, tell me the truth. Finally tell me the truth about why you wanted the divorce. Tell me why I've spent the last five years having to live without you. Tell me why every time we kiss, I can still feel how much you love me," he says, and his voice is rising with frustration and desperation. "Fucking tell me why the other night you told me you wanted me and needed me and loved me and why in the fuck having sex without a condom didn't matter to you if you had no plans of getting back together!"

Bang. His words are my official undoing.

"We're not together because the day we got into that accident, I was pregnant! I was pregnant, and I didn't tell you! I was going to tell you, but then everything happened, and I lost the baby, Clay!" I scream at the top of my lungs. The truth flies out into the open and takes up all of the space in the room. "Because I was too busy arguing with you about telling everyone at dinner that we were married and wasn't paying enough attention, we got in an accident that almost killed you, and I lost our baby, Clay!"

"Josie." His breath comes out in a harsh whoosh, as if my words just stole all the oxygen from his lungs.

"The miscarriage..." I whisper. "And complications from the accident. It caused ovarian torsion. I...I can't have kids." I just stand there, tears still running, and let the information soak into his mind.

"Josie," he whispers my name again, and he reaches for my hand, but I can't fathom his touch right now. It feels like it'll shatter me. "I'm so sorry, Josie. I'm so sorry you went through that all by yourself." He is crying now. "I...I can't fucking believe you've been carrying all this for all this time by yourself."

"Stop, Clay. Just stop." I'm breaking down. Fat, thick tears consume my face. "I ruined everything. That's why we got a divorce. Because I ruined everything."

"It's not your fault, Josie," he says. "The accident. It wasn't your fault." I cry harder, and he just keeps saying it over and over. "It wasn't your fault, Josie. It wasn't your fault."

His reaction is the opposite of what I've always expected. And it crumbles any resolve I have left. It forced open the wounds of my past, and I can't keep it all locked up inside me anymore.

"The condom didn't matter because I can't have kids, Clay," I repeat, saying it as much for myself as it is for him. I need something, anything, to put myself back at a distance. It doesn't work. "I should've gone to the doctor sooner, but I didn't. I waited. I waited too long." I have to stop when more sobs bubble up through my throat, and Clay steps forward to place a hand on my back. I let him this time.

My knees buckle, and Clay helps me sit down in one of the chairs by the mirror. Memories of my follow-up appointment with Dr. Norrows race around in my head. I was in a lot of pain that day, but I figured it was because I was still actively miscarrying. Still actively bleeding.

In reality, I was in the middle of a medical emergency. I had to have emergency laparoscopic surgery because cysts on my ovaries had caused them to twist in on themselves. Dr. Norrows had said it was common to get ovarian cysts during pregnancy, but it was usually just one ovary and they usually resolve on their own. But I am one of those very rare few who had cysts on both ovaries that didn't resolve and ended up progressing into a condition called ovarian torsion.

My left ovary was removed, and my right ovary wasn't in great shape. Dr. Norrows said the odds of me having kids after that were highly unlikely.

"The doctor had to remove one of my ovaries, and the other one that's left won't be able to release eggs anymore." I don't sugarcoat it like Dr. Norrows did all those years ago after the surgery. I don't tell him that I could try to do IVF with someone else's egg but there's no guarantee, and also, because it's not something I would ever want to do. I don't tell him any of that because the last thing he needs to hear is that there is this tiny glimmer of hope that it's possible. Because where would that leave us? Him holding on to some minuscule shred of hope that I can have babies? "I can't have kids, Clay," I whisper. "I can't have kids."

"Josie, I'm so sorry. I'm so fucking sorry," he says, sadness in his voice and tears still in his eyes. He lifts me back to my feet and wraps his arms around me, hugging me tightly to his chest. "You should have told me. You shouldn't have carried this by yourself. You shouldn't have carried any of this by yourself."

Hearing him say that hurts. Because if he's not angry and he's not sure he wants kids and he still loves me…it was all for nothing.

I hug him tightly. I love this man. I've always loved this man. That was never the issue.

He leans back to meet my eyes, and when he moves his mouth to mine, I accept his kiss without hesitation. It's masochistic to allow myself to have this moment that I know I'll spend the rest of my life thinking about. But I can't stop it.

I need to kiss him. I need to feel his lips on mine.

Hard and without anything holding me back, I dance my tongue with his and slide my hands into his hair, and I swallow down every single one of his greedy, desperate groans.

"I love you," he whispers against my lips. "I love you so fucking much, Josie."

I love you too, but it's not enough.

When things become too intense, too passionate, and every cell inside my body wants to crawl inside him, I know I have to end this. I have to finally let go.

I pull away from his embrace, tears already in my eyes. Both of our breaths are panting and erratic, and I keep my eyes locked on the ground as I try to pull myself together. My heart never stops pounding furiously in my chest, like the damn thing is angry, so damn angry, for what I'm about to do.

But I do it anyway.

"I love you, Clay. I've always loved you," I say and force myself to meet his gaze. Force myself to stare into his beautiful eyes one last time. "But I'm sorry. I'll always be sorry. This is just how it has to be."

65

Clay

Saturday, July 9th

Josie sobs into my shoulder, and I hold my wife against me, embracing her as tightly as I can. Her body feels weak in my arms, her cries filled with the kind of grief I wouldn't wish on my worst enemy.

My head swims with all of the things she finally told me. She had a miscarriage. She was carrying our baby, and because of the unfortunate accident we were in that one Thanksgiving night, our baby didn't survive.

And if that wasn't awful enough, she had a complication that required surgery and she can't have kids.

All this time, all these years, I've never understood why she wanted a divorce. Never understood why she walked away. I've spent so much time trying to understand it all but never could because she chose to carry the truth on her shoulders. She chose to suffer in silence.

Maybe I should be mad at her for all of this. For not telling me about our baby. For not telling me about her surgery. For not telling me the truth. But I could never be mad at her for this. I know Josie better than I know myself. She might come across as a hard-ass, but her heart is the purest of anyone I've ever known. She will put everyone's needs above her own, and she'll do it even if it means she's sacrificing herself.

And that's what she did. She sacrificed herself for me.

This is how it has to be. Her words roll around inside my mind.

Fuck no. This isn't how it has to be.

"None of it was your fault," I tell her again and lean back to meet her eyes. Her beautiful face is a mess of tears, and it takes a gentle lift of her chin with my fingertips to make her seal her gaze with mine. "Losing Grandma Rose wasn't your fault. The accident wasn't your fault. And the death of our baby wasn't your fault," I whisper and gently press my lips to hers. "None of it was your fault, Josie. None of it."

"I'm so sorry, Clay." More tears flow past her eyes. "I'm so sorry, Clay."

"I'm sorry too," I say and kiss as many of her tears away as I can. "I'm sorry for our wedding night when you wanted to call Grandma Rose and tell her the good news, and I stopped you. It will always be one of my biggest regrets." My voice shakes as I let my own guilt free. "I'm sorry for all the moments I was being a pushy bastard. I'm sorry if I made you feel like I was just wanting to move on from all our tragedy, from all our loss, while you were still hurting. I'm sorry I was too lost in my own shit to see that you were suffering. I'm sorry I was so fucking clueless that I had no idea you had *surgery*. I'm sorry for that night when you handed me divorce papers and I walked away. But most of all, I'm sorry that you've been carrying all of this alone for so much time. I'm sorry that I wasn't there to support you. I'm sorry that I wasn't there to comfort you. I'm sorry that I wasn't there to hold your hand."

"You didn't know," she says through a hiccupping sob. "You didn't know."

"Yeah, but I should've seen it, Josie. I should've seen you in those moments and known that your world was not okay. I shouldn't have been so fucking focused on making our world brighter to not give you the time and space to grieve. Give you the time to find the strength to tell me what you were silently carrying by yourself."

I search her eyes. I don't think anyone has ever loved another person the way I've loved Josie. Even all these years when we haven't been together, she's still the reason I wake up every day.

She's my person. My wife. My forever.

My natural inclinations want to show her I'm still all in in all of the loud and in-your-face and oftentimes lovingly pushy ways I've been before. But I know that's not what she deserves.

Josie doesn't need me standing here and begging her to stay with me. She needs me to respect her and what we have together enough to give her space.

I pull her close again, hugging her against my chest, and silently hold her. I press kisses to her forehead and rub a gentle hand down her back, but I don't say anything at all. And I stand there, with her in my arms, until I feel her sobs turn to soft cries.

Until her soft cries turn to quiet tears.

Until her tears stop flowing down her cheeks.

Only then do I tell her the things she deserves to hear.

"I love you, Josie," I say and lean back to meet her gaze. Her eyes are red-rimmed and puffy, but her face is dry. "I still mean what I said to Norah that day in the hospital. When she asked me if I wanted kids. When I look toward the future, I just want you. Forever. You're all I want. I choose to stay, Josie. I. Choose. To. Stay." I inhale a deep breath, preparing myself to tell her the words I need to say, even if they hurt like hell. "But this time, unlike the past, I'm going to give you the space to choose if you want to stay too. I'm here. I'll always be here." I press a kiss to her lips and give her one last hug. "This isn't me walking away from you. This is me giving you the space to choose. I'm here. I'll always be here. If and when you're ready to stay with me too."

And then, I turn on my heel and walk out of the barn and back toward the reception tent.

Leaving my whole fucking heart behind.

66

Josie

Saturday, July 9th

I don't know how long I stand in the barn, but as I watched Clay walk away, my tears came back tenfold, covering my cheeks and nose and mouth and chin. The taste of salt stings my taste buds, and I swipe a hand across my nose and I just cry.

I cry for Jezzy and Grandma Rose and Summer and Clay's and my baby.

I cry for Clay and the years of pain he's gone through while being left in the dark the entire time.

I cry for myself. For the decisions I've had to make. For the regret and guilt I carry.

I cry until I can't cry anymore. And then, I *run*.

Out of the barn, across Bennett and Norah's land, I run, and I don't stop until I'm back at the reception tent.

The party is still going on. The music is still pounding from

Mikey's speakers. And for the briefest of moments, I spot my sister Norah on the dance floor with Bennett and see that Breezy is sitting at one of the tables with Autumn in her arms.

But I'm only here for one reason. And when I spot him sitting down by himself at one of the empty tables, I head straight for him. His tie is undone, and a half-empty glass of bourbon sits in front of him, and his eyes look forlorn as he stares down at the glass while he runs his index finger over the edge of it.

I don't stop walking until I'm standing right in front of him, until my knees bump right into his legs.

"Josie?" His eyes widen at my presence, a million emotions and feelings flitting across his face.

"I choose you," I say in a rush. "I choose us. I choose to stay."

He doesn't even blink, doesn't even breathe, before he's standing on his feet and pulling me into his arms. "I love you, Josie," he whispers into my hair.

"I love you too, Clay." I stare up into the only eyes I want to stare into for the rest of my life. The eyes I've missed more than anything in this world. "I've never stopped loving you. And I'm sorry it took me so long to get here."

"All that matters is that we're here." He presses his mouth to mine, and it doesn't take long before our kiss gets heated and I find myself wrapping my legs around his waist, not giving a single shit about what my long bridesmaid dress is doing.

I kiss him. I kiss my husband. We may as well be the only two people on earth right now. Everything else ceases to exist.

I'm crying all over again, but this time, my tears are happy. They're relief at me being right where I always want to be.

I don't know how long the kiss lasts, but when the sounds of people clapping and cheering and hooting and hollering start to filter into my ears, Clay pulls away on a laugh.

Only then do I realize that the music is no longer playing, and the entire reception of my sister's wedding is staring right us.

"Hell yeah, Clay and Josie!" Pete shouts with a big-ass smile on his face and his arm wrapped around Eileen Martin.

"It's about time!" Earl calls out and holds up a glass of beer.

And when my gaze meets my sister's, I find her standing on the dance floor, her arms still wrapped around Bennett's waist, but a tear-filled smile on her face. Norah doesn't know everything, and one day soon, I'll tell her.

But right now, I have other things I need to do.

"So…can we leave?" I question, looking right at Clay.

"I thought you'd never fucking ask," he answers through a laugh, but then he pauses for a moment and sets me back to my feet.

"Clay?" I question, confusion highlighting my voice, but he just shakes his head and flashes the kind of smile I feel all the way to my toes as he gets down on one knee.

"Josie," he says, pulling something out of the pocket of his pants. And then, in a matter of seconds, my engagement ring, my ring that's shaped like a water tower that Clay picked out just for me all those years ago, is clutched between his thumb and index finger and being held in front of me. "Will you do me the honor of letting me put this ring back on the pretty little finger that it belongs on?"

"Y-you still have it?" I question, tears in my eyes again. "In your pocket?"

"This ring has stayed in my pocket." He smiles up at me, and his heart is inside his eyes. "Because you've always stayed in my heart."

I hold my hand out toward him, my body vibrating with the kind of love that I could only ever feel for this man. "I love you," I tell him again. "I love you so much."

"I love you always." He slides the ring on my finger and doesn't waste any time after that. Rising to his feet, Clay pulls me back into his arms and maneuvers my body so that he's carrying me in a firefighter's hold.

If I weren't so fixated on my husband, I'd probably notice the additional cheers and hoots and hollers coming from the people around us.

But how can I notice anything else but this man right now? The answer is simple—I can't.

Out of the tent and straight to his truck, Clay doesn't put me down until he ensures I'm buckled in the passenger seat. And when he skids into a parking spot in front of The Country Club, he turns into a madman, cutting the engine and hopping out of the driver's seat before I can even unbuckle my seat belt.

Then he's at my door, swinging it open and pulling me back into his arms and kicking the door shut with his shoe. And he doesn't put me down again until we're upstairs, inside his apartment, and he's laying me down on the bed.

Mere days ago, we were in this exact same spot, ready to do the exact same thing.

But this time is different. This isn't the tragic end. This is the beautiful beginning.

I roll onto my belly, and he unzips my bridesmaid's dress, his hands a gentle caress down my spine. His movements aren't rushed. They're slow and steady because there's no hurry.

We chose to stay.

By the time we're both naked, I'm lying on my back, and Clay is down by my feet. He locks his eyes with mine as he proceeds to kiss my toes and then my feet and then my shins. He moves his mouth up my body, caressing every inch of my skin.

A delicious shiver runs up my spine when he pauses right between the apex of my thighs. And a moan spills from my lips when his mouth is right there, kissing me where I'm already wet and throbbing for him.

I slide my hands into his hair and my hips buck up toward his mouth when he starts to lick and suck, and the pleasure begins to build at the base of my spine. He doesn't stop until stars dance behind my eyes and my body grows slack with pleasure.

And by the time his body is hovering over mine, his hard cock positioned at my entrance, the realization of how much I truly love this man floods my chest. Tears prick my eyes, and when he reverently slides himself inside me, they slip from my lids and down my cheeks.

"I love you so much," I whisper, and he kisses my tears away.

"I love you, Josie. Always. *Forever.*"

Yes. *Forever.*

67

Clay

Sunday, July 10th

The sun is just starting to come into my bedroom window when I blink awake. And when I look down, I find a naked Josie curled up beside me, her head resting on my shoulder. Her hand rests on my stomach and right there, in its rightful place, is her engagement ring nestled on its left ring finger.

I finally got my wife back.

I glance at the clock, and I see it's only a little after nine. I wouldn't be surprised if Josie doesn't wake up for a few more hours. See, when you spend over five years apart from the woman you love, the night that you finally are back together, you end up having a lot of sex.

I'm talking a lot, a lot. I'm not certain what time we fell asleep, but I know it was at least four in the morning.

I grab my phone from the nightstand and quietly scroll through missed texts and calls. Norah, Bennett, Marty, *Eileen Martin*, and several other people who witnessed us kissing at the reception are more than a little curious about what's going on. *Nosy bastards.* For now, I choose to ignore them, and I quietly scroll through some news articles.

I'm tempted to get up and head to Melba's bakery to grab us some donuts, but when Josie starts to stir against me, I glance down and find her green eyes looking right at me.

"Morning," she says, a sleepy smile already on her lips.

My wife stayed.

"Morning." I smile and press a kiss to her forehead. "I was thinking about getting some donuts from Melba's."

"Now, that sounds kind of perfect." She leans up to press a smacking kiss to my lips before hopping out of bed and heading into the bathroom.

"Though, I should probably warn you," I call out toward her. "I've got a shitload of messages from half the town."

"Oh God!" Josie exclaims. "I can only imagine what all those busybodies are saying. Surely Pete and Mayor Wallace are milling about CAFFEINE, trying to see if I'm in there."

"Eileen Martin's message is demanding an interview," I update her, and her laugh echoes in the bathroom.

"That woman is so predictable." The water switches on. "Just so you know, I'm using your toothbrush."

The mere idea of that urges a big-ass smile to my lips.

"Maybe we should skip Melba's and just, like, drive somewhere outside of town?" I suggest, and Josie doesn't hesitate to agree.

"Yes, please!" But her words come out all muffled around the toothpaste because *my wife* is using *my toothbrush* to brush her teeth *in my bathroom* because *she's here.*

Thank fucking everything.

"Quick question," she says and peeks her head out the door. "So, you didn't actually file those divorce papers, right?"

Her silly smile makes me laugh. “Fuck no.”

And my response makes her crack up. “Good.”

Yeah. We’re still married. *But one day soon, I’m going to marry my wife again.*

The Happily Ever After

Josie

2 and half months later
Wednesday, September 22nd

I step out of the bathroom of CAFFEINE and find Norah and Camille putting up blackout curtains on the windows and door so no one can see inside. They already have hair and makeup stations set up on the long counter and a few of the tables, and my white silk mermaid-style wedding dress hangs on the wall.

I walk over to my wedding dress and double-check to make sure that my veil is on the hanger with it. It is. *Thank goodness.*

"You ready?" Norah asks, a smile on her lips as she nods toward one of the empty chairs in front of a hair and makeup station.

"You want to do my makeup?"

"Are you kidding me?" she retorts on a laugh. "I'm honored that I get to do my big sister's makeup on her wedding day."

"Let me get a bottle of water first," I tell her and head over to the snack and drink table Camille set up near the register.

It's hard to believe that today marks my wedding anniversary, the day Clay and I had run off to the courthouse to elope. We were young and in love and happy. Everything had been perfect.

Everything had been so right. Before it had all turned so wrong.

It took us years to find our way back to each other. Took me years to finally tell him all of the things he deserved to know.

I never, in a million years, thought we'd be together again. But here we are, together, happy, and moving forward as a couple.

A few weeks after Clay and I got back together at Norah and Bennett's wedding reception, he told me he wanted to get married. And I had teased him and said that he didn't need to marry me because he was a stubborn mule who never filed the divorce papers.

Eventually, though, he expressed just how much it would mean to him if I'd marry him again, if we'd have an actual wedding. And the stress and fear I had felt all those years ago when he was telling me the same things after Grandma Rose passed didn't exist.

The only thought in my mind was *hell yes. I want to marry you again too.*

I have to give him credit, because when I told him I wanted that too, he didn't push like he always used to do. He just told me to tell him when I was ready and he'd be all hands on deck to help me plan the wedding.

I only needed two days to mull it over. By that point, I'd finally told Norah all the sordid details of Clay's and my past, and I knew she was the one person who would tell me if what I was thinking was crazy or perfect.

Not only did I want to plan a wedding in two months' time, I wanted to marry Clay again on the same day that we got married all those years ago. For the longest time, that date had been fraught with pain and confusion and grief, and I wanted to change that. I wanted to make that date a day to celebrate again. A day to cherish. A day to remember how far we've come and still a day to remember Grandma Rose.

And when Norah's response had been emotional tears highlighted by a smile and a nodding head, I knew it was exactly what I should do.

So, today, on a Wednesday, I'm going to marry Clay Harris again. This time, though, I'm going to make damn sure I take his name.

Even though it's the middle of the week, everyone has town has chipped in to help make our wedding a special day. All the small businesses are closing a few hours early, and no one is mad that CAFFEINE has been shut down all day.

The town square is set up for a ceremony, and the altar faces the small church where Clay got down on one knee to ask me on our first date. The reception is being held at The Country Club, and Marty's wife Sheila has agreed to be an extra bartending hand for the entire night.

"Well, come on!" Norah calls over to me as I finish guzzling down half of the bottle of water I grabbed from the table. "If you make me wait any longer, I'm going to end up bringing the hair and makeup to you. Or, you know, tying you to this chair."

"Hold your horses." I laugh.

Norah has always been a girly-girl who loves hair and makeup and fancy clothes. Her sense of style has always been one of the things I've admired about her.

I sit down in the chair, and she fluffs her fingers through my hair.

"By the way, did you see the latest article about Eleanor and Thomas?"

"What are you talking about?" I meet Norah's eyes in the reflection in the mirror in front of my chair, and she pulls her phone off the counter to hand it to me.

"Breezy sent it to me last night."

My eyes scan her phone, an article about our mother and Norah's ex front and center on the screen.

First Trial Day for Thomas King and Eleanor Ellis-Prescott

NEW YORK, September 21 – King Financial's ex-wonderboy Thomas King and Eleanor Ellis-Prescott, ex-wife of wealthy businessman Carlton Prescott, sat in court for the first day of their trial for sex-trafficking charges. Three of the DA's twenty witnesses took to the stand and provided compelling, emotional testimony in front of the jury.

The defense teams of King and Ellis-Prescott had already tried for a plea bargain several months ago, but the DA denied their request.

Donald Watts, the United States Attorney for the Southern District of New York, is the one leading the trial and made a statement to the press expressing gratitude to King and Ellis-Prescott's victims for their courage in coming forward and testifying on the stand today.

More to come on this trial as it progresses.

"Sometimes, it all feels like a fever dream, you know?" Norah says, and I look up from her phone to meet her eyes in the mirror again. "Our mother and my ex are on trial for sex trafficking. If you would've told me this was going to happen five years ago, I would've never believed it."

I nod. "It's certainly sick and twisted in ways I never dreamed were possible."

But at the same time, it feels like everything I've known about our mother is being exposed.

She is evil. To her core. And I've known that since the day our baby sister Jezzy died.

I hand Norah her phone back, and she doesn't bat an eye as her focus shifts right back to getting me ready for my wedding day.

"So…what are we thinking? Dramatic smoky cat eye with red lips?" she asks, and I jerk my head forward.

"Excuse me?"

"Just kidding!" Norah cracks up and yanks me back toward her with two hands on my shoulders. "I think we need to go natural beauty. Earthy tones to bring out your eyes. A little soft blush to highlight your amazing cheekbones. How's that sound?"

I snort. "Way better than cat eyes."

Norah gets to work on covering my face with a primer, but when my phone starts ringing from the pocket of my white robe that reads "Bride-to-be" on the back, I pull it out of the pocket to find ***Incoming Call Breezy*** on the screen.

"Hey, girl," I greet. "How was your flight?"

"Flight was good," she says, but her voice sounds frazzled. "But there are no rental cars available."

"What? How on earth?"

"I know," she huffs. "I can't get ahold of Bennett. I don't know what else to do."

"Nore, where's Ben?" I ask, leaning my head away from the receiver.

"He has Autumn," she says, and it's all she needs to say. Poor Autumn has been going through a little bit of a colicky phase. It always tends to hit worse in the afternoons.

"I guess I could try to call a taxi?" Breezy questions in my ear, but I quickly calculate a plan in my head.

"Breezy, stay put. I'm going to find you a ride. Call you back in five," I say and end the call, my fingers immediately going to the screen to call Clay.

"Well, hello to my beautiful bride," he greets, and I roll my eyes. I also smile. "Are you ready to marry me again?"

"I am, but I have a little bit of a favor to ask."

"You need me to come over to CAFFEINE and ease your nerves with a little…"

"No, you pervert." I snort. "I need you to go to the airport to pick up Breezy."

"What?" he questions on a half shout. "What do you mean?"

"I mean, I need you to go to the airport to give Breezy a ride into town because she can't get a rental, and I don't want to make her get in the back of some strange man's taxi."

"You do realize that I'm a little busy today, right? You know, trying to get ready to marry you again?"

"Please, Clay?" I ask, forcing my voice to the quiet, needy tone that always ends up with me getting my way.

"Dammit, woman," he mutters, but then it's not long before he says, "Fine."

"You're the best husband-who-never-filed-divorce-papers-that-I'm-going-to-marry-again in the whole wide world."

"Yeah. Yeah." He groans, but he also chuckles. "Love you, Josie."

"Love you too, baby. See you in a few hours. I'll be the one in the white dress."

"And I'll be the stunningly handsome groom, standing at the altar, smiling at you."

We end the call shortly after that, but the smile on my lips is so big that even Norah nudges me with her elbow. "Sis, you are smitten with a capital S. I freaking love it."

So do I. It's about damn time we have our happily-ever-after.

• • •

Clay

"Clay, I know I've thanked you a thousand times, but I feel compelled to thank you again," Breezy says from the passenger seat of my truck as we cross the yellow bridge and head into town.

"Don't worry about it, Breeze," I tell her, even though there's a teeny-tiny part of me that's annoyed I had to make this unexpected trip when I was in the middle of trying to make sure everything is perfect for Josie's and my wedding today.

But again, I love Bennett's sister. I know Josie loves Bennett's sister. The two women have grown so close over the last few months. Clearly, I also wanted to make sure she got into town safely.

"You're in the middle of building your dream home, and you're finally getting your big wedding. I couldn't be happier for you and Josie if I tried, Clay."

I look over to find Breezy smiling at me.

"Thanks, Breezy. Appreciate that."

Everything is coming up fucking roses these days. Josie and I bought the five-acre plot of land behind Rose's old house, so that Josie doesn't feel pressured to sell it *and* we can easily keep it maintained. We're in the middle of building a house on our new land. And today, on the anniversary of our first wedding day, my wife is going to marry me again in front of our nearest and dearest.

It doesn't get any better than that.

Well, technically, only one more thing needs to happen to make it all perfect…

"You excited?" she asks, and I nod, looking up toward the sky for the water tower that's moments away from coming into view.

"Very excited," I mutter, and she asks me another question, but I'm too busy looking at the water tower to hear.

That water tower is a huge part of Josie's and my story, and I enlisted the help of a few boys from town to create something special for my wife. Since we're having our wedding in the town square, Josie will be able to see the water tower from the altar, and there was no way I could let the opportunity pass without capitalizing. I'd planned on staying with them and seeing it through, but I had to leave it in their hands to pick up Breezy.

I guess it should be noted that I didn't get permission from the city council or Mayor Wallace, but I'll deal with their grumbling afterward.

I lean forward over my steering wheel, squinting as I read the words I told Chet's painting crew to write.

Clay loves José

What the fuck? I blink several times and read it again.

Clay loves José

"Are you fucking kidding—" I start to shout, but Breezy's scream stops me mid-sentence.

"Oh my God! Watch out!"

I dart my eyes back to the road, and that's when I see it. One sheep, standing in the middle of the road, the rest of his flock in the grass. Holy fuck! I grip the steering wheel and slam on the brakes, and my truck skids across the gravel, smoke billowing up around us.

The sheep doesn't move a fucking inch, until my truck comes to a stop but just barely bumps the side of it.

It falls over. Just fucking falls over, onto the road, and Breezy jumps out of the car on a scream. "Oh my God! The sheep!"

I hop out of the driver's door and run around the car to find Breezy on her knees, her hands frantically checking the sheep for injuries.

"Clay! He's not really moving!"

Trust me, I am the first person to help injured animals, but I know for a fact that my bumper barely touched this sheep. I can also see that his eyes are open and he's blinking them.

"I think he's just a little shocked, Breeze. Probably just needs a minute or two to get his bearings again."

But a minute or two and then five pass by, and Breezy's panic grows. "I think something's wrong with him. I think we need to get him to a hospital."

"No, no," I refute. No offense to the sheep, but I'm getting married today, not sitting at a vet hospital for hours. Not to mention, I've got a water tower that says I love José. This sheep is going to have to figure his shit out and figure it out fast.

"C'mon, little buddy," I encourage, kneeling down to slide my hands under his side. "Time to get up now and head back to your farm. Probably also time for your owner Tad to figure out how to fucking sheep farm."

I swear, Tad Hanson's sheep spend more time off his land than they do on it. He's the worst sheep farmer who ever lived. Just ask Bennett; his and Norah's property is right beside Tad's. I guess it makes sense, given this wasn't his intended career path by a long shot, but that's a story for a whole different fucking day. Definitely a day other than my wedding day.

"Clay, I'm worried about him," Breezy whispers, as if the sheep can actually understand her. "I think he might be hurt."

I nudge the sheep again. "C'mon, little guy. Let's get moving." When I look to either side of the road, I see that the rest of his flock is just standing there, staring at us. "A little help would be nice," I call toward them. "Mind giving your friend here a little support?"

But they do fuck all, and the sheep doesn't move from his spot on the road.

"Help me pick him up," Breezy says. "We need to at least take him back to his owner."

"Excuse me?" I question, and she glares at me.

"We can't leave him here for dead, Clay! We need to at least take him home!"

Fucking hell.

"Fine," I mutter. "But we gotta hurry because I've got plans today. You know, to get married."

"I know, I know," she says, nodding as she squats down to put her hands under the sheep's side. "Did you say Tad's his owner?"

"Yeah." When I see how awkwardly Breezy is trying to pick up this sheep, I gently nudge her out of the way and lift the heavy fucker into my arms. "Get the door," I grunt out and she runs ahead of me to open the door to the back cab.

The sheep just sits there, in my arms, eyes blinking. He lets out a few mewls, but other than that, he just chills. Either this fucker is playing games with me or he's actually injured. I honestly don't know what.

By the time I get him loaded in, I'm sweaty and panting and silently cursing Tad Hanson's name.

"Where is Tad's place?" Breezy asks as I start the engine.

"You don't know where Tad lives? You invited him to fucking

Thanksgiving six years ago!"

She shakes her head.

"He lives right next to Bennett and Norah."

"Really?" she asks, and I just shrug, my mind solely focused on getting this goddamn sheep to Tad's farm as quick as I can, so I have enough time to climb up that goddamn water tower and strangle every painter on Chet's team before I make them fix my love for José.

And then, you know, get to the altar to marry the woman of my dreams.

It takes me a good ten minutes to get to Tad's farm, and I just lay my hand on the horn as I escort his sheep back to his property. The rest of his sheep are still out there somewhere, but fucking hell, I don't have time to get them home too.

Tad steps out of his front door as I come to a skidding stop in front of his house. And when I look in my rearview mirror, I'm highly suspicious of how goddamn comfortable that sheep looks with the AC blowing on his relaxed face.

Breezy is the first to get out, and she runs up to the house to explain the situation.

I hop out of the driver's seat and open the door to the back cab to get the sheep out. I'm carrying the chill bastard up toward Tad's house when he and Breezy meet me halfway.

"I'm really worried about him," Breezy says in a rush. "I think you should get a doctor here to see him."

"Don't worry." Tad puts a gentle hand to her shoulder. "I'm sure he'll be okay." When he gets a good look at the sheep I'm still fucking holding, sweating like a pig as I do, a small smile forms on Tad's stupid face.

"That's Crosby," Tad updates. "He has a bit of a history of faking injuries to get attention."

I glare at Tad, and he's smart enough to take Crosby from me.

"You mean he's faking?" Breezy questions, a hand going to her lips, a relieved laugh scooting out of her lungs. "He's okay?"

Tad smiles at her the way I see Tad smile at all the women in Red

Bridge, and Breezy gets the same smiley, doe-eyed look on her face when he does it. I don't know what it is about this sheep farmer—who clearly can't sheep farm—but women fucking love him.

Eileen Martin does monthly interviews with him for the newspaper, and it isn't because there's new shit to tell. It's because she likes staring at his handsome face for hours while she gets him to talk about God only knows what.

"Okay, great!" I exclaim and clap my hands. "Crosby's good. And we need to skedaddle." When Breezy doesn't make a move to leave, she and Tad still smiling at each other, I put both hands on her shoulders and gently nudge her in the direction of my truck.

It's time for me to go marry my wife...again. And, you know, make sure everyone knows her name isn't José.

• • •

Josie

It's official. I am Clay Harris's wife...again. And I don't think I've ever been this happy in my entire life.

Actually, I know I haven't.

I spot my husband across the bar. He's standing beside Marty and his wife, smiling and chatting with them both. *God, I love that man.*

I don't know how long I stand there staring at him, but eventually, his eyes meet mine from across the room, and the sexiest kind of smile spreads across his mouth. And it only takes a minute more for him to excuse himself from the conversation with Marty and Sheila and come traipsing over to me.

He pulls me into his arms and presses a slow, deep, delicious kiss to my lips. At one point, he makes a show of dipping me back dramatically. I laugh against his persistent mouth, but I also love every single fucking second of it all.

This is Clay. He's playful and funny and charismatic and loving and adorable and sexy and all the damn things.

He's larger-than-life. And he's the yin to my yang.

The other half of my heart and soul.

It's a wonder I managed to live without him for all those years. It's a wonder I managed to survive, but I did, and now, here we are, wrapped up in each other after saying "I do" again mere hours ago.

This is our happily-ever-after, and I don't expect it to be perfect and I don't expect it to be without hard times. But I do know that we'll be together in all the good times and the bad. And that is something to celebrate. That is something to hold on to tightly with both hands and be thankful for.

When Clay finally sets me back on my feet, he wraps his arm around my shoulders, tucking me close to his side. He offers me a sip of his beer while we both look around the room, at everyone who has shown up for us. Everyone we love and adore.

My eyes catch sight of Breezy, and I furrow my brow a little when I see that she's currently over by the pool tables chatting with Tad Hanson. Clay follows my focus, and a soft chuckle leaves his throat.

"By the way, picking Breezy up from the airport was quite the ordeal."

I look up at him.

"I accidentally ran into one of Tad's sheep."

My eyes nearly bug out of my head. "What?"

"I barely hit the fucker. Crosby. Apparently, he fakes injuries. But Breezy freaked out and made us drive him to Tad's farm. It was a whole debacle."

"Was this before or after you had the water tower painted to show how much you love José?" I question, and Clay lets out a deep sigh.

"I swear to God," Clay mutters, "I might murder Chet. I really might."

"And I think I want to kiss him."

Clay's brow furrows. "Excuse me, woman?"

"That was the funniest thing I've ever seen in my life, Clay," I admit through a fit of giggles when I remember how damn nervous my husband looked when he saw my eyes make contact with the water tower. "It might've been the best part of the ceremony. You know, besides all the lovey-dovey 'I do' shit."

"Lovey-dovey 'I do' shit," he says through an amused chuckle. "Damn, *wife*, stop being so romantic or else I might start crying."

I laugh at that. And he just leans forward to press a kiss to my lips.

"Love you, Josie. Love you so much," he breathes into my hair.

"Love you too."

We go back to people watching, both of us laughing over Pete's dance moves for a good ten minutes, but when I see my sister and Bennett and baby Autumn cuddled together as Bennett sways Autumn back and forth, my heart soars and my eyes move back to my husband.

"Clay?"

"Yeah, baby?" he questions, looking down at me.

"What do you think about adoption?"

A soft expression overcomes his face. "You mean, us adopting a child so we can give them a loving mom and a loving dad?"

I nod.

"Count me in."

"Yeah." I smile then. "Count me in, too."

Some might say this is our happily-ever-after, but I'd call it our happily-ever-forever.

And man, I can't wait to see where our love takes us.

Exclusive Bonus Content

Before The Moment:

A Year After the Arrival of Summer

Clay

Sunday, August 23rd, 1:00am

My muscles tense as I jerk awake to a dry throat and a lightly snoring Josie strewn across my body. It's late, the window still pitched stark black with darkness, and the house is ear-ringingly quiet. I adjust my back on my pillow carefully, looking down at the most beautiful, peaceful version of Josie Ellis as I do. Her face rests on my bare chest, her blonde curls are matted to the side of her face, and her lips are parted as little snores escape her nose.

For the past year, I've spent nearly all my waking moments with this woman. The only time we're not together is when we're both working—me at the bar and her at the diner—and yet, I often find myself longing for just a little bit more.

More kisses, more smiles, more laughs—more of Josie in every imaginable form.

A few more snores escape her cute nose, and I smile to myself as I think about how annoyed she'd be with me if I told her what a racket she makes while she's sleeping.

It's not all the time, but when she's in a deep sleep, her brain must recircuit its idea of breathing. And since she's had two days in a row of pulling double shifts at The Diner to fill in for Todd, I know her exhaustion has sent her into the depths the most intricate caves of Snoozetown.

I don't mind, though.

She may be known to the rest of town as my girlfriend, but that word doesn't come close to describing what she means to me.

Put simply, my whole world revolves around her. She's the sun, and I'm all the planets that are just happy to be in her orbit.

Josie Ellis is a complicated woman with lots of layers, but every one of them is something special—and I hope I get to spend the rest of life understanding them all.

Thank God she's sleeping, though, because in the light of day, these thoughts would scare the living piss out of her. She's not ready for the reality of our happily ever after—the merging of our lives, the marriage, the babies—and you know what? That's okay.

For now, I'm content to be in her bed, in her grandmother's little house, cuddled under the heat of her body until daylight breaks the horizon.

I shut my eyes and tuck Josie closer to my chest, but my throat is still drier than a Brillo pad. I lick my lips and swallow again, but the birds have already started to construct a nest, and beavers locked up their dam. There's no way I'm surviving the rest of the night without a glass of water, no matter how good my woman feels on top of me.

As slowly and gently as I can, I adjust Josie's body, moving her off of my chest and onto her pillow. She barely budges from the movement, and I silently cheer my victory when I slide all the way off the bed and onto my feet without so much as a moan from my sleepy buddy.

I scrub a hand down my face as I head out of her room and down the hallway, the gentle creaking off my feet on the hardwood floor the only sounds within the house.

I flip on the small light above the stove, snag a glass from the cabinet, fill that sucker up to the top with tap water from the sink, and guzzle it down in three hearty gulps.

It's good, but not enough, so I refill my glass and chug another round.

"Josie, honey, is that you?" Grandma Rose asks from the hallway, the sound of her approaching footsteps echoing after her words. Still mid-guzzle, I spring into panic, choking on the liquid and squirting it everywhere in an impressive spray. I dance on tiptoe, jumping for the roll of paper towels hanging to the left of the sink, the bounce of my dick in my boxer briefs only amplifying the point that I'm nearly naked.

Shit.

I have zero time to remedy my precarious situation before sweet Rose shuffles into the kitchen, groggy face atop her own scantily clad figure. A dusty pink floral nightgown skims her well-worn body, upping the ante on this awkward encounter by fifty million or so.

"Hi, Grandma," I greet, a half-smile, half-grimace marring my lips. It'd be real fucking nice if she didn't notice I'm only one pair of underwear away from being in my birthday suit but given that she's still got twenty-twenty eyesight at her age, it's not looking fucking good.

She blinks a few times, the corners of her eyes creasing deep into her wrinkles, her gaze moving up and down my very bare body.

Immediately, she tightens her robe around her small frame, thankfully hiding her previously obvious nipples, and I scramble to cover myself with a wad of paper towels. It doesn't help at all that I'm sporting a half-chub from my body's confusion about the hour or that my little accident with the water spew means I'm covered in a dew of water droplets.

Way to go, Clay. You've turned Grandma Rose's kitchen into the set of Magic Mike Vegas!

"I… uh… got thirsty," I say, my words a half-ass apology for our current situation.

"I see." She furrows her brow. "Is that why you decided to create a trap in my kitchen in the middle of the night?"

"Excuse me?"

"A thirst trap, dear. Isn't that what they call it?"

"*Grandma*."

She laughs. "Melba's gonna love this one. Gonna laugh her perm right off her head."

"You know, I actually wouldn't mind if this story *didn't* make the rounds of Red Bridge." I tilt my head to the side and offer my most charming, please-don't-make-my-life-a-living-side-show smile.

"Oh, Clay. Shoo." She shakes her head. "I'm afraid this is a story that *has* to be shared."

Another soft laugh escapes Rose's lungs as she heads to the fridge to grab a glass bottle of apple juice.

"Right," I agree, the word dissolving into a groan as I shuffle back toward the hall with my tail between my legs.

"Oh, and Clay sweetheart?"

"Yeah, Grandma?"

"I imagine, you in my house, in your underwear, in the middle of the night, drinking my bought and paid for water from this great little town means I can trust your intentions with my Josie are pure and true. Does it not?"

Oh boy. Her eyes are a hawk in a tree, staring down at a small rodent running through a field.

"Well..." I pause and clear my throat. Suddenly, my state of undress isn't the only elephant in the room. This is the moment—*the* interrogation—and the blinding pressure of how I form my response should be criminal at this hour.

Ironically, for the first time in our little meetup tonight, I feel completely at ease. My intentions with Josie are so far above board, they're in the next layer of the atmosphere.

"Yes. It does." I raise my chin and look Grandma in the eye, memories of her nightgown and my dick, a thing of the past. "I love Josie. In fact, I've never loved anyone like I love her, and I wouldn't be standing here in your kitchen in the middle of the night or at any other damn hour of the day if I didn't."

She smirks. "So, you see a future with her? Not just another notch on your bachelor bedpost?"

I smile. *Man, she's a ballbuster.*

"Grandma, Josie is too good to be a notch on anyone's bedpost, let alone mine," I answer the straight-up truth. "Frankly, she's too good for me, too good for any mother—uh, guy—in this town, but I'm hoping she won't notice, and I can eventually convince her to spend forever with me."

"Forever?" Grandma asks, and I nod my head, one hundred percent certain in my motives.

"Forever," I repeat. "Though, if there's a scarecrow's chance in the land of Oz I don't send her running for the hills, that last part needs to stay between us for a while."

A secret smile crests her lips as she pretends to zip her lips shut and throw away the key.

"Thanks, Grandma."

She takes a small sip of her apple juice. "So, I guess I should get used to the two of you living in sin part-time under my roof, huh?"

"That'd be nice," I say and drop my voice to a whisper. "At least until I convince Josie I'm husband material."

"Okay, sweetheart." She takes one final drink of her apple juice before screwing the cap back on and putting it in the fridge. She shuffles toward where I stand, my water glass still clutched in my hand, to point a stern finger in my direction.

"You take good care of my girl." It's a threat and a demand, but it doesn't bother me at all because that's my whole damn plan. My biggest priority. "Don't make me regret liking you, Clay Matthews."

"You have my word, Grandma."

"Good." She nods. "And next time you're in my kitchen, put on some damn pants."

I grimace and smile all at once. "You got it."

"Good boy," she says, patting my arm one last time. "You can atone for your sins at church with us tomorrow."

"I'll be there."

"Be ready at 10:15 sharp, sweetheart. I like to sit in the front and that old goat Betty always steals my spot if I don't get there early enough."

"You got it, Grandma."

She leaves the kitchen and heads back to her room, and I stand there, still in my underwear in the middle of her kitchen, amused and endeared and prouder than a pig in shit.

I may not have pants, but I've got Grandma Rose on my team.

And that means Josie Ellis, one day soon, is going to be officially, legally mine.

I can't wait.

Before The Moment:

The Morning After

Josie

August 23rd, 9:00am

"Morning, Josie sweetheart," Grandma greets as I walk into the kitchen. Both her and Clay stand at the stove, and he flips bacon on one burner while she works on scrambled eggs on another.

They're both dressed for the day—Clay wearing a pair of jeans and a black t-shirt that hug his freaking fantastically muscular frame and Grandma in her best Sunday lilac, ruffled dress.

I'm still in my bedtime attire of pajama shorts and a tank top, on the other hand, but I still have a full hour before we need to leave for church, so the judgement in Grandma Rose's eyes hasn't reached its full potential yet.

"Mornin'," Clay says, looking at me over his shoulder with the kind of handsome smile that I feel all the way to my toes. I don't hesitate to meet him at the stove to press a soft kiss to his lips, garnering a weird squeak from grandma I work hard to ignore as Clay puts a hand to my chin to pull my attention right back to him. "How'd you sleep?"

"Like a log."

He grins. "Liked sawed logs, maybe."

"What?"

"Oh, nothing."

I shove his shoulder and step away toward the refrigerator to grab a glass bottle of apple juice.

"I'd watch being too cute, Clay Matthews, or you'll find yourself sleeping somewhere other than here."

"Oh, Jose, you know you'd miss me."

Grandma is suddenly interested in her eggs in a way Michelin Star chefs only dream of to avoid the tete a tete between the two of us. It's demure and mindful, of course, but it's also completely out of character for the nosey broad and sets my spidey senses tingling. Come to think of it, the two of them cooking together without Grandma bickering about her personal space is weird, too.

"How'd *you* sleep, Grandma?" I ask, wrangling her back into the conversation in attempt to sniff out the source of the smoke.

"Pretty good," she replies, still avoiding my eyes entirely. "Only had to get out of bed once."

When Clay clears his throat and I catch sight of this silent exchange of smiles between the two of them, my investigation grows legs. There's *definitely* something going on here, and I'm going to get to the bottom of it.

"Okay, you two. What am I missing? Spill it."

"What, sweetheart?" Grandma asks.

At the same time, Clay offers only a, "Hmm?"

"Cut the crap. When I went to bed, you guys could hardly get through a conversation about our viewing of *You've Got Mail* without a rapidly intensifying series of questionable remarks, and now, I've woken up to chummed up waters even Steven Spielberg would call over the top. If something happened last night, I want to know what it was."

Grandma's eyebrows raise to her hairline, and Clay looks like he can hardly hold back his laughter. Grandma discreetly nudges him in the side, and he clamps his lips shut, though, the corners of his mouth are still upturned into a smile.

"Okay," I announce, setting my apple juice on the counter and positioning both hands at my hips. "What's going on here? Tell me right now."

"Oh, Josie, don't you think you're being a little paranoid?" Grandma flips off her burner as she lifts the pan of scrambled eggs off and carefully carries them past me. The kitchen table is set with three plates and utensils, but if this carries on for much longer, we're going to have to set out a fourth for the elephant in the room.

"Grandma, are you seriously gaslighting me right now?" I question on a laugh. "The two of you are being straight-up weird and you know it." I look back at Clay who's smiling at me from his spot at the stove. "Clay? What's going on?"

He glances toward my grandma, but I quickly snap my fingers in front of his face. "Ah, ah, don't look at her for confirmation. You tell me. You tell me right now or get out of this house."

A laugh escapes his lungs. "Josie!"

Grandma just tsks her lips. "I'm sorry, Clay, but you've got a life of drama to look forward to."

"Grandma!"

"It's true, dear. If I closed my eyes, I'd swear I was standing on Broadway in Manhattan right now."

I huff, and she laughs.

"Clay and I had a little impromptu powwow in the kitchen last night. He was in his skivvies, and I was in my nightgown and, I guess you could say, we both understand each other a little more now, both mentally *and* physically. That's all."

My eyes go wide for a beat as my brain processes that bomb of information, but when I look at Clay and see the grimace on his face, I burst into laughter.

"Holy shit," I mutter between giggles. "You were in my grandma's kitchen in your underwear? Could she see your penis?"

"Josie!" they both yell in unison, making me laugh even harder.

"Oh my god, Clay!" I cackle. "I can see why you wanted to keep it a secret now. Next thing I know, I'm going to hear you've given the whole town a peep show!"

"Josie, don't make him feel embarrassed," Grandma chastises from where she's scooping the scrambled eggs onto the plates. "He shouldn't feel ashamed of his body. It's very nice."

That only makes me laugh more. I mouth *very nice* to Clay as he shuts off the stove, and he retaliates by reaching out with two strong arms and pulling me against his chest.

"How long are you going to be laughing about this?" he asks, burying his face in my neck and groaning.

"For the rest of my life," I say, giggles still falling from my throat.

"Okay, you two, settle down and get over here," Grandma demands. "We've only got forty-five minutes until we need to leave, and Josie hasn't even brushed her hair."

Ah, yes. There's the judgement.

"Wait..." I pause and look up into Clay's eyes. *"We?"* I question. "You're going to church, too?"

He nods. Smiles. "Grandma invited me last night."

That only starts up my laughter again, but deep down, I know it's for another reason.

If Clay Matthews can survive a midnight, naked rendezvous with my grandmother and still get invited to church, this relationship might just have lasting potential.

It's scary to admit, but quite frankly, I'm starting to hope it goes all the way.

All the way to a happy ending with me and Clay.

Acknowledgments

To all of the most important people in our lives. You know who you are. We couldn't do this without you. We love you.

To our husbands, Craig and Peter. You're all the green flags, and we're both endlessly grateful for your overwhelming love and support. You're exactly the kind of men we write romance books about...go figure. LOL.

To all of our reader friends, THANK YOU FOR READING. You're the best.

To our Entangled Amara Team, thank you for helping us make our dreams come true. Jessica, thank you for believing in us.

To Summer, thank you for changing us forever.

And to Josie and Clay, thank you for reminding us of the power of love.

XOXO,
Max & Monroe

CAFFEINE

COFFEE

Latte

Americano

Black Drip Coffee

Cappuccino
(ask about seasonal specials)

Red Bridge Roar
(Caramel Macchiato with
apple cider drizzle)

Espresso

Mocha

White Mocha

Maple Macchiato

NOT COFFEE

Pink Flamingo
(Strawberry and cherry lemonade
topped with a little lemon
sweet cream cold foam)

Hot Cinnamon Tea

Black Tea

Green Tea

Hot Chocolate

Hot Honey Lavender Tea

Apple Cider

Apple Cider Spritz

Summer Sensational
(Pink Lemonade, Fresh Strawberries,
and Strawberry Cream Cold Foam)

SMALL BITES

Cinnamon Roll

Sausage Balls

Avocado Toast

Chocolate Croissant

Muffins:
- Blueberry
- Cranberry and Orange,
- Cappuccino,
- Cinnamon,
- Double Chocolate

Hot Apple Cider Doughnuts

Chocolate or Cider Cakes